"I date dead people—dead movie stars."

"I always had some talent with this Ouija board . . . my grandmum gave me this when I was a kid. Been toying with it ever since. I just had never used it to get dates before . . . well, before I gave up on breathing men. Sarah . . . breathe, Sarah."

Sarah sucked in a lungful. "You're serious."

"Dead serious."

"Omigod. Look, Anne, thanks for thinking of me and all. But I really do get dates. Once in a while, and—"

"But nothing special, I bet. No one lights your fire." Anne knew she had Sarah there. She suspected the girl hadn't been out in months.

"No, nothing special," Sarah admitted. She dropped her gaze to the Ouija board.

"Then why not double with me? It'll be an otherwordly experience. I guarantee it."

Sarah visibly shuddered.

"I wanted to go . . . *want to go out* . . . with Clark Gable." Anne's expression turned wistful. "I've been trying to channel him for better than a year."

"Clark Gable." Sarah's voice turned dreamy. She looked at the posters again, they were all Gable movies. "I love Clark Gable."

—From "Anne of One Gable" by Jean Rabe

Also Available from DAW Books:

Places to Be, People to Kill, edited by Martin H. Greenberg and Brittiany A. Koren

Assassins—are they born or made? And what does an assassin do when he or she isn't out killing people? These are just some of the questions you'll find answered in this all-original collection of tales. From Vree, the well-known assassin from Tanya Huff's *Quarters* novels . . . to a woman whose father's vengeful spirit forced her down dark magic's bloody path . . . to an assassin seeking to escape his Master's death spell . . . to the origins of the legendary ninsha and the ritual of the hundredth kill . . . here are spellbinding stories of murder and mayhem of shadowy figures who strike from night's concealment or find their way past all safeguards to reach their unsuspecting victims. With stories by Jim C. Hines, S. Andrew Swann, Sarah A. Hoyt, Ed Gorman, and John Marco.

Pandora's Closet, edited by Martin H. Greenberg and Jean Rabe

When Pandora's Box was opened, so the ancient tale goes, all the evils that would beset humanity were released into the world, and when the box was all but empty, the only thing that remained was hope. Now some of fantasy's finest, such as Timothy Zahn, Kevin J. Anderson & Rebecca Moesta, Louise Marley, and Sarah Zettel have taken on the task of opening Pandora's closet, which, naturally, is filled with a whole assortment of items that can be claimed by people, but only at their own peril. From a ring that could bring its wearer infinite wealth but at a terrible cost . . . to a special helmet found in the most unlikely of places . . . to a tale which reveals what happened to the ruby slippers . . . to a mysterious box that held an ancient, legendary piece of cloth . . . to a red hoodie that could transform one young woman's entire world, here are unforgettable stories that will have you looking at the things you find in the back of your own closet in a whole new light. . . .

Army of the Fantastic, edited by John Marco and John Helfers

How might the course of WWII have changed if sentient dragons ran bombing missions for the Germans? This is just one of the stories gathered in this all-original volume that will take you to magical place in our own world and to fantasy realms where the armies of the fantastic are on the march, waging wars both vast and personal. With stories by Rick Hautala, Alan Dean Foster, Tanya Huff, Tim Waggoner, Bill Fawcett, and Fiona Patton.

MYSTERY DATE

EDITED BY
Denise Little

DAW BOOKS, INC.
DONALD A. WOLLHEIM, FOUNDER
375 Hudson Street, New York, NY 10014

ELIZABETH R. WOLLHEIM
SHEILA E. GILBERT
PUBLISHERS
http://www.dawbooks.com

First Printing, February 2008
1 2 3 4 5 6 7 8 9

DAW TRADEMARK REGISTERED
U.S. PAT. AND TM. OFF. AND FOREIGN COUNTRIES
—MARCA REGISTRADA
HECHO EN U.S.A.

PRINTED IN THE U.S.A.

ACKNOWLEDGMENTS

CONTENTS

INTRODUCTION

Denise Little

Most people would agree that dating, especially in the
very early stages of a relationship, is terrifying. First
dates rank up there with public speaking, the dentist, and
death in national polls ranking stressful situations. In
other words, a significant number of people would literally rather die than go on a first date. There's a reason
that dating services have become a high-profile
business—nobody likes suffering through a painful few
hours with an obviously unsuitable person, waiting for
the moment when a speedy exit is politely possible. As
an anecdotal measure of how much people hate the
thought of first dates, I have a friend who refuses to get
a divorce, despite being in a very difficult relationship,
because she'd rather be married to the monster she
knows than have to date again.

There are excellent reasons to fear a first date. First
and foremost, meeting with unknown or barely known
persons carries all kinds of risks. Some of the question
that arise around a first date are fairly straightforward,
even when things are going well: Is he who he says he
is? Is she "normal"? Are we compatible? Is she going
to expect more than a kiss at the end of the evening?
Am I going to want more than a kiss? What if I do?
Should I say so? If I say so, will he think I'm some kind
of sex addict? And so on . . . for hours. It's a mental

1

game that can drive a person insane before and during a first date.

When things aren't going well, then the really bizarre questions start, the ones that replay all the nightmare scenarios from every bad movie ever made, beginning with the banal and ascending to the terrifying: Is it possible to die of boredom? If I try to duck out the back to escape, will this person come after me with a gun? What mental institution did this person escape from? Is this a serial killer? Is this person even human? Am I going to get out of this alive?

Needless to say, most of us have more of the former than the latter kind of dates. But almost every person I've ever met has a bizarre dating story, where danger and fear and a touch of the otherworldly sent chills up our spines despite all the bright lights of the very public meeting place so essential to first dates.

Dating, especially when things go wrong, can skate awfully close to the edge of an emotional and personal meltdown. When things go really wrong, dating can become life-threatening. In fact, it ought, I thought after one of those kinds of dates, to make for interesting fiction. So, after I got home safely and took a few deep breaths, I posed the following question to a bunch of my writer friends:

What happens when the person you're dating REALLY isn't who he/she says he/she is? Feel free to take it as far out as you want, from mystical mismatches to vampire sex to unicorn confrontations and beyond.

You're holding the fruit of those speculations in your hand—the writerly version of "It's just a date. What could go wrong?" Most of these dates end up happily. A few end up horribly. Just as in real life, fictional mystery dates can be risky. But they are all fascinating journeys. I hope you enjoy the ride as much as I did. Happy reading!

WHO'S BEHIND THE DOOR?

Diane A.S. Stuckart

Diane A. S. Stuckart is a member of that proud breed, the native Texan. Born in the West Texas town of Lubbock and raised in Dallas, she crossed the Red River just long enough to obtain her degree in Journalism from the University of Oklahoma before returning home to the Lone Star State. Writing under her own name, Diane is the author of several pieces of short fiction found in various DAW Books anthologies, including *Front Lines* and *Sorcerer's Academy*. Writing as Alexa Smart and Anna Gerard, she has published five critically acclaimed historical romance novels, the first of which was a Romance Writers of America Golden Heart award finalist.

Diane recently moved to the West Palm Beach area of Florida, where she is finding new sources of inspiration among the alligators and palm trees. She has been married to her college boyfriend, Gerry, for more years than she cares to admit. She is thankful that the only dates she has to go on these days are doggie play dates with her pups!

"**H**ey, look what I found!"
Dana's voice sounded muffled, no doubt because

her entire upper body was wedged between an old
steamer trunk and a decaying horsehair sofa. Still, her
words held sufficient enthusiasm that Viv looked up from
the stack of warped record albums she was sorting and
wondered what so-called treasure her older sister had
unearthed this time.

She and Dana were into their first day of clearing decades' worth of accumulated junk from the dusty garret
of the fifties bungalow that they'd recently purchased
together. The attic took up maybe a third of the house's
second story, with two bedrooms and a full bath compris-
ing the remainder of the floor. Thankfully, that storage
space was reached by a door at the end of the hall, rather
than via one of those pull-down ladders that required
acrobatic skills to negotiate while carrying anything
larger than an envelope.

Filling the attic was the typical detritus that the previous owner's heirs—the old woman who had lived there
had recently passed away—hadn't bothered to carry off
for themselves. Boxes of forgotten baby clothes, the
ubiquitous stacks of *National Geographic* magazines, furniture that had long since made the transition from
shabby chic to merely shabby . . . this and more lay
beneath its eaves.

A few items they'd thus far uncovered had some col-
lectible value; those, they would put up for sale on one
of the on-line auction sites. But most of the remaining
clutter was destined for the oversized dumpster parked
on the front lawn, meaning they could look forward to
a goodly number of trips up and down the main stairway
over the next few days. Quite a workout for a couple of
forty-something broads, Viv thought with a small sigh.

Not that the pair would be living there for much more
than a few weeks. They had bought the place as a "flip,"
purchasing it on the cheap, with their goal to remodel
and resell it as quickly as possible, while making a tidy
profit for a couple of months' work. This house would
make their fourth flip in a little more than a year, and
as a result they pretty well had the process down to a
science. If all went well, Viv told herself, they would

have the place papered and painted and back on the market by the middle of next month.

Dana, meanwhile, had freed her lanky frame and narrowly avoided smacking into the bare light bulb that hung from the beam above her. Black dirt streaked her sweaty cheeks, while her auburn curls—the startling color courtesy of Miss Clairol rather than Mother Nature—stuck out in all directions. The effect, Viv thought with an inner grin, was rather like a middle-aged pagan warrior queen returning home from a battle.

And Queen Dana did not return empty-handed. She triumphantly displayed her plunder . . . a flat, dusty box with one corner crushed, and the other three held together with bits of yellowed tape.

"Look, do you believe it?"

"Hurrah, another board game," Viv responded with a roll of her eyes. "What's that, number fifteen or sixteen, so far?"

"It's number seven, smart ass . . . but it's not just any game. It's *the* game."

"The game?"

Viv stared at her, puzzled, until her sister hummed a few notes that stirred a long dormant memory to life. The catchy theme music from a sixties-era TV commercial began to play in her mind, while bits and pieces of long-forgotten lyrics to that song drifted through her head.

Don't tempt fate . . . don't you wait . . . he's your blind date.

Understanding dawned, and she dropped the albums to scramble to her feet, gasping in disbelief. "*The* game?' she repeated. "You mean—"

"Uh, huh." Dana nodded, grinning, and held the rectangular box out to her.

Viv reached for it, embarrassed to realize that her hands were trembling as she took the game. She pulled off the bandana that covered her own silver-streaked dark curls and used the red cloth to clear the thin blanket of dust from the cardboard lid.

A few swipes revealed the familiar illustration of a pert

sixties teen in an ankle-length blue party dress topped by
a gauzy silver wrap, the colors only slightly faded with
the passage of four decades since the game was new. A
gaggle of equally perky girls in various cute outfits clus-
tered behind her, looking as if they'd been caught in
mid-gossip. But the party girl paid them no heed, her
attention instead fixed on red door that had been pulled
aside to reveal the smiling, clean-cut youth in a brown
suit waiting behind it.

"Oh, my God," she breathed in equal parts amusement and longing. "It's *Blind Date*."

She gazed back up at Dana, matching her sister's grin
with one of her own. It had been their favorite diversion
from sixth grade all the way through junior high, a simple
board game where every roll of the bright red die took
the giggling players around the board trying to collect
matching pastel-colored cards. Each move also took
them closer to their goal of opening the red plastic door
in the board's center to reveal their blind date—a pasteboard photo of a dreamboat class-president type, or else
the geeky loser guy with cowlicky hair and mismatched
clothes.

The perfect rehearsal for high school life, they had
wisely assured one another every time they played.

Now, the sight of the well-loved box made her heart
beat a bit faster, just as it had when she was a girl. While
one part of her grown-up, liberated, long-divorced self
obediently sneered now at the game's stereotypical message, the little girl in her still ooh'd and ah'd over the
illustrated teens' sixties-fashionable outfits and their
shiny, all-American beaus.

She hugged the game to herself in a proprietary fashion. Then, striving for a casual tone, she looked back up
at her older sister and asked, "So, you wanna play?"

An hour later, they had both showered and made their
way downstairs to the cozy living room, with its white
brick fireplace flanked by ceiling-high white painted
built-in shelves. To break up the whiteness, they had
furnished the space with some equally cozy consignment

shop finds—a cheerful blue and yellow plaid couch, coordinating blue wing chair, and a serviceable oval-shaped coffee table stained a warm shade of golden oak. The plan was to strip the brick down to its original finish and stain the shelves, budget and time permitting, but for now the bright fabrics helped tone down the hospital look of the room.

The game sat in the middle of the table, along with two glasses of white wine, a bag of corn chips, and big bowl of salsa. Since it was late afternoon, they'd agreed to call it a day and have themselves a little happy hour before taking on the more serious task of deciding on supper. One benefit of living with one's sister instead of a spouse, Viv told herself . . . if neither of them felt like cooking, they could eat cold cereal, and no one would pitch a fit.

Viv kicked off her loafers and sat cross-legged on the floor beside the coffee table. Dana, who rarely wore shoes, simply plopped down on the opposite side of the table and grabbed one of the wine glasses. "Nice outfit," she commented before taking a sip.

Viv felt herself blush. "Big deal," she said, a bit defensively. "So I put on slacks and a blouse instead of a T-shirt and shorts. We've been in that blasted attic all day, and I'm tired of looking like a bum. Unlike some people," she added with a pointed look at her sister's mismatched sweats.

Dana merely grinned as she glanced down at the bright yellow velour top over baggy blue cotton workout pants, and then raised her plucked brows in an exaggerated fashion. "And do my eyes deceive me, or did you put on lipstick, too?"

"Yes . . . I mean, no . . . uh," Viv sputtered, and then finally gave in to good-natured laughter as she reached for her own wine. "OK, I confess. I dressed up to play the game, just like we always used to do when we were kids. Satisfied?"

"Absolutely. And now I will confess that I put on clean underwear *And* deodorant in the hopes that maybe I'll score Mr. Prom King."

She set down her glass and used a chip to scoop up an oversized dollop of salsa, which she managed to get from bowl to mouth without dripping any onto her buttercup colored top. "Well, go ahead," she urged. "Open the box and set up the game."

Viv set down her own glass and wiped her fingers on her slacks to dry the bit of condensation from the chilled wine. Not that dampness would do much further damage to the game box, anyway. Here in the brighter light of the living room, she could see that it was even more battered than she'd thought. Hopefully all the pieces were still there, she told herself as she lifted the lid and peered inside.

"Wow." This came from Dana, who had bent for a closer look. "The box is pretty beat up, but check out the game. It looks brand new."

"It does. Why, no one ever even punched out the pieces from the cardboard."

Viv held up the heavy pasteboard sheet. It bore the shiny figures of four girls that resembled paper dolls, save that they already wore mod sleeveless sundresses with matching pumps. They were identical except for their dress color . . . one in purple, one dressed in hot pink, the third wearing blue, and fourth in green. The matching stands lay neatly in the box, along with the bright red die and the board itself.

She hesitated, her practical side reminding herself that the game would be worth much more if she left the pieces intact and simply sold it online. Her sister had no such scruples.

"Go ahead, punch them out," Dana urged her through another bite of chip and salsa. "For Chrissakes, it's not like you're holding an original copy of the Declaration of Independence or something. You already know you're going to keep the game, so you might as well enjoy it. Just pretend you're ten years old again and do it."

"Are you sure?"

"Positive. Besides," she added with a playful smirk, "this will be the closest you've been to having a date in what, two years? No way I'm going to let you spoil your chances landing Mr. Dreamboat, even if he's a pretend squeeze."

"It's only been eight months," Viv protested, slightly stung. Eight months, three weeks, and a day, not that it mattered. Besides, she'd always been pickier about her men than Dana was. "OK, maybe it's been awhile, but we've been too busy fixing up houses to go out on dates, and you know it."

"Well, maybe you have." The smirk broadened a bit, and Dana added a wink. "Anyhow, forget about that. I've got dibsies on the pink girl."

"No way!"

Forgetting her momentary pique with her sister, Viv quickly separated Miss Pretty-in-Pink from the others, then grabbed the matching stand and triumphantly set the pasteboard figure before her. "You know I always get the pink girl. Here, you can have any of the other three . . . just try not to get any salsa on them!" she finished with a small shriek as Dana snatched the sheet from her and started punching out the girl in purple.

The game cards in four different colors emblazoned with different parts of four various date outfits came next, and then the fat red die . . . and finally, the board. Viv reverently set aside the box and laid the game board in its place, then picked up the cards. They were still so new-feeling that she carefully cut and recut them a number of times to mix them instead of relying on the good old two-handed shuffle that might have creased their pristine edges. With everything organized, she sat back and picked up her wine again, savoring the sight of the shiny new game before her.

"Well, what are you waiting for?" Dana demanded, wiping a drip of salsa from her chin. "Roll the die and let's see who goes first."

Viv won that first roll and dealt a couple of cards to each of them, then set Miss Pink on her path toward the big date.

The game moved swiftly. Each turn consisted of a roll of the die and moving the correct number of spaces, followed by picking or discarding however many cards the spot they landed on instructed them to take. A few minutes into the game, Dana had to call a momentary halt while she brought the wine bottle from the kitchen, since she'd added an impromptu adults-only rule that required taking a sip with every toss of the die.

"Just to make it more interesting," she'd assured Viv. Giggling, Viv realized she was having as much fun playing the game now as she had when she was a kid.

A few rolls and two-thirds of the second glass later, Dana gave a triumphant crow. "Aha, got a full set," she proclaimed as she snagged a card from Viv's hand and gave her one of hers in return. "I'm ready for that beach date . . . just gotta land on the right spot now."

"Not if I do first," Viv countered.

Rolling the die, she moved Miss Pink down the far side of the board. "One, two, three, four, five," she counted, stopping on the bright pink space with a red heart outlined in its center. She set down her cards to show that she had each of the necessary accoutrements required for the bicycle date. "Woohoo, look out! It's time to open the door."

"Well, crap." Dana gave a resigned grin and swallowed down the rest of her wine. Then, humming a few notes again from the long-ago TV commercial, she said, "OK, go for it. But remember, we have to say the words first. Ready?"

At Viv's nod, they chorused, "Who's behind the door?"

Taking a breath, she reached for the red plastic door and pulled it open. The same little stir of excitement she'd always felt as a girl fluttered in her stomach. *Please, please, please let it be one of the cool guys and not the nerd!*

"What the—"

As Viv stared in puzzlement, Dana gave a little shriek of laughter. "Oh my God, this is hysterical! It's a freaking UPS guy!"

And, indeed, the card behind the red door showed a smiling youth dressed in the familiar brown shirt and brown shorts of that well-known delivery company. Viv shook her head and reached for the box lid, with its illustration of teenage boys. She counted the four dates— one each dressed for the beach, a bike ride, the prom, the amusement park—and the loser.

"I don't understand. That's not one of them . . . unless he's supposed to be the nerd?"

"Well, maybe this is an updated version," Dana suggested, still giggling. "They do that, you know—change games to fit the times. Remember *Candy Factory*?" she asked, naming a favorite of theirs from kindergarten. "Heck, they've put out version of that on CD. I gave it to Jenny Floyd's little boy for his birthday last year."

"Yeah, I guess that makes sense. Maybe someone stuck the new game in the old box." Sighing, she tossed her cards into the discard pile and pulled the plastic door closed again, giving the knob a twirl to make sure the door would reveal a different card next time. "Well, he's obviously not the bicycle date. Your turn, Sis."

"Okay, but let me pour some more wine first."

Dana had just set the bottle down, when the harsh buzz of the doorbell made them both jump. Viv frowned and glanced at her watch, then looked back at her sister. "It's almost six. Who can it be, so close to supper time?"

"Probably Cub Scouts selling popcorn. Don't worry, I'll get it."

She headed toward the front door, which was blocked from Viv's view by what was supposed to be a decorative brick half-wall. Eyesore was a better description. *Gotta demo that ugly thing before we paint in here*, Viv told herself. Maybe add some Mexican tile there, to give the entry a bit of visual separation from the living area without eating up a lot of space.

So distracted was she by that bit of mental remodeling that she didn't hear the front door open and close again, nor notice her sister's return until Dana was standing right in front of her. A quizzical look was on her face, and a large cardboard box was in her arms.

"You are not going to believe this, but that was the UPS guy at the door."

"No way." Viv sat back and grinned at sister's expression. "Talk about a coincidence. That's got to be the cabinet hardware I ordered for the kitchen. What, did you think he jumped out of the game or something?"

"Of course not." Dana snorted and shook her head, the puzzled look vanishing. "Like you said, total coincidence. And it's not like we don't get something for the remodel from UPS a couple of times a week."

"Right. Now hurry up and take your turn."

"Looks like the advantage is mine," she said, sitting back down and rolling the die. "And voila . . . a lovely three, just for me."

With exaggerated care, she moved her purple girl three spots, landing on another pink space with a red heart outline. She spread out her cards, showing she had all the beach accessories. "Now, cross your fingers for me, 'cause I'm about to land me a surfer dude. Ready, let's say it."

"Who's behind the door?" Viv cheerfully echoed her sister as Dana pulled the red door open. Behind it lay, not the picture of a cute teenage boy, but that of a middle-aged plumber, complete with upraised plunger and drooping trousers.

This time, it was Viv's turn to burst into gales of laughter, while Dana simply stared. "Now, there's a hot date!" Viv exclaimed when she could speak again. "The beer belly and the nose hair really make him special. I think I'll keep my cute little UPS guy, OK?"

"This isn't funny," her sister complained, setting down her wine to pry at the plastic door. "That's got to be the wrong set of cards in there."

"No, don't tear it up." Her laughter quickly died as she pushed her sister's hand away. "You'll break it doing that, and the door won't ever work right again."

"Oh, okay." Dana huffed and sank back onto the rug, a sulky look on her face as she tossed her cards back into the discard pile, too. Then, an unwilling grin tugged at her lips. "That one *has* to be the nerd. If not, God help us when we finally find him."

"Damn right," Viv agreed as another wave of laughter

shook her. Trying valiantly to subdue her amusement, she reached for the die and rolled again.

The sound of the doorbell's harsh buzz for the second time in less than ten minutes cut her off in mid-snicker.

She heard Dana's quick intake of breath. Slowly, their gazes met before they turned in unison in the direction of the front door. "No freaking way," Dana softly said. "If that's the plumber at the door—"

"It's not," Viv hurried to assure her sister . . . and herself. "I mean, the plumber actually is coming out but not until next week, when the new toilet for the powder room gets here. It's got to be a neighbor dropping by, or something."

"Fine. You get the door, then. I'm sure as hell not going to."

Projecting more confidence than she felt, Viv got to her feet and headed toward the door as the buzzer sounded a second time. "Hold your horses," she muttered, pausing with her hand on the knob. That was another thing they needed to install, one of those peephole thingees in the door . . . that, and a chain to go with the deadbolt. Taking a deep breath, she twisted the knob and opened it, then gasped out, "Holy shit."

"Yeah, lady, we hear that one a lot in our business."

A grinning bald guy in his late thirties stood before her on the step. He was dressed in a workman's short-sleeved blue shirt and navy pants, carrying an oversized metal toolbox in one hand and a clipboard in the other. The embroidered name on his shirt proclaimed him to be Jason, while the ballcap-style hat he wore proclaimed him a member of the Roto-Rooter team.

Well, at least he was better looking than the guy on the game card, she faintly told herself. Just to be certain, she asked, "Y-You're a plumber?"

"Yes, ma'am." Jason's grin faded a little, and he looked down at his clipboard. "This is 4108 Stanhope, isn't it? You need a toilet installed?"

"Yes, it is . . . and we do. But you weren't supposed to be here for another week," she explained, certain of the date she'd agreed upon with the young woman on the phone yesterday.

Jason squinted at his paperwork again and then gave his head a disgusted shake. "Never mind. Looks like someone stuck your ticket in tonight's emergency call stack by mistake. According to what's written here, we're not scheduled until next week, like you said. Sorry for the inconvenience."

"Not a problem," Viv assured him. *Just a coincidence*, she reassured herself. "I guess we'll see you in a few days."

"Me or my partner will be back and take care of things then. Have a good night."

She closed the door behind him and turned back to Dana, who was anxiously watching her from where she sat crouched behind the coffee table. "It was a plumber, wasn't it?"

Viv nodded, telling herself that the sudden light-headed feeling that gripped her was the wine kicking in. She forced a small laugh as she rejoined her sister on the floor.

"Yes, it was a plumber, and no, there wasn't anything magical about it. They got the dates mixed up and sent someone out tonight instead of next week, like they were supposed to."

"Uh, huh." Dana sounded unconvinced . . . or maybe she sounded a bit tipsy. She picked up her purple girl and idly danced her atop the rim of the now empty salsa bowl. "You know, if you ask me, there's something strange about this particular version of *Blind Date*."

"And if you ask me, you're being overly dramatic, as usual. Why don't we put up the game and fix something to eat, and then we can watch a video or something?"

"Let's play one more round. No, just humor me," she pressed on as Viv opened her mouth to protest. "One more, and if we don't get another strange guy at our door who looks like the guy behind the game door, I'll believe that everything that's happened was a coincidence."

"OK, one more . . . but that's it."

This time, rather than giggling, they silently took turns rolling the die and drawing cards while moving their pasteboard figures about the board's perimeter. Finally, Viv landed on the pink heart square and displayed her hand, showing all the prom date cards. "Satisfied? Let's see what happens now."

"OK. Who's behind the door?" Dana asked, her tone holding a note of uncertainty. Despite her scoffing, Viv couldn't help her own small, superstitious shiver as she reached for the red plastic door. *Coincidence, coincidence, coincidence,* she inwardly repeated in some lame sort of mantra as she pulled the door open to reveal the date behind it.

"Biker dude," her sister proclaimed in a wary tone.

The gray-bearded older guy in the picture was covered head-to-toe in tattoos and black leather, a helmet tucked beneath one arm. Not exactly a dream date, Viv decided, unless you were the type of girl who hung out in rough bars and drank lots of whiskey. "Biker dude," she agreed and braced herself for the doorbell to buzz a third time.

It didn't.

Even so, she and Dana remained at the table, aimlessly chatting about the remodeling while pretending not to glance toward the front door every minute or so. When a half hour had passed, however, and no Hell's Angel had appeared on their doorstep, Viv allowed herself a relieved smile. Briskly, she began packing up the game again.

"See, the spell's broken," she proclaimed in a cheery tone as she put the battered lid back on the box. Ignoring the pins and needles in her feet, she managed to stand again, then reached a helping hand toward her sister.

Dana grabbed the proffered hand and, groaning, got to her own feet.

"OK, I believe you" she conceded with an answering smile. "It was all coincidence. So let's whip up a couple of omelets and watch a sappy video before we crash for the night."

*   *   *

Thud, thud . . . buzz . . . thud, thud . . . buzz . . . thud, thud . . . buzz.

Viv was dreaming she was at a basketball game, with the players pounding along the wooden court, and the buzzer going off after each play. Except that the players were all cardboard girls in bright cardboard dresses wearing matching high top sneakers, and the ball was a giant red die. She and Dana were sitting frontcourt cheering them on, along with the plumber and the UPS guy. Somebody kept passing them wine . . . probably the plumber. Finally, the game ended. And yet the thumping and buzzing didn't.

"What the—" she muttered groggily. She leaned over and flipped on the bedside lamp as Dana, wearing only a long T-shirt, came rushing into the room. She had her cell phone in one hand and a fireplace poker in the other.

"Someone's at the door," she hissed, as the buzzer sounded again. "I'm going to check it out. Grab a weapon, you're coming with me."

Viv glanced at the alarm clock next to the bed. One-seventeen a.m. Chances were, it wasn't the Cub Scouts. She shoved aside the covers and grabbed the broom she'd left in the corner, and then swiftly padded down the stairs after her sister.

Barely had they made it down to the darkened living room when the doorbell buzzed again, the sound followed by another knock. This time, however, they could hear a faint voice beyond the door. "Anybody home?"

"What do you think?" Dana murmured in her ear. "Answer, or pretend we're not here?"

"Answer," Viv whispered back, much to her own surprise. *Stupid, stupid, stupid*, her inner voice warned. Ignoring the voice, she went on in a low tone, "I'll flip on the porch light and open the door at the same time. You wait behind the wall with the poker in case it's a mad killer or something. Hurry!"

Setting aside the broom, she gave Dana a few seconds to get into place, then gripped the doorknob with one hand and the light switch with the other. "Ready?" she whispered, "Now."

She jerked open the door as the porch light illuminated the startled face of a man with a salt-and-pepper beard wearing a black leather jacket and fingerless black leather gloves. He dangled a motorcycle helmet by its strap from one hand, while with his other he pressed a bloodied red bandana to his brow. One knee of his blue jeans was torn, revealing raw flesh.

"Oh, my God," Viv gasped. "Are you OK?"

"Just a little banged up," he rasped out, though his pallor made her wonder if he wasn't downplaying his injuries. "Some lunatic without any headlights pulled out from the curb, and I ran right into his bumper. Son of a bitch never stopped." He shook his head in anger, then winced at the movement. "Anyhow, my cell phone went flying out of my jacket when I went down, and it's too dark to find it. Can I get you to call the cops for me?"

She glanced over at Dana, who had leaned her poker against the half wall and was staring at the man, opened mouth. Snapping to attention, her sister flipped open her own mobile phone and said, "Sure, I'll call 'em. And, Viv, don't leave the poor guy standing on the porch."

"Of course," Viv replied and switched on the living room light. Then, abruptly, she realized her silver-brown curls were sticking out at funny angles and that all she was wearing was an old blue flannel shirt that had belonged to her ex.

The man must have noticed the same thing, for he backed away from the door, embarrassment putting a bit of color back into his face. "Hey, it's the middle of the night. I don't want to put you out anymore than I already have. I'll wait on the porch for the cops, if that's OK."

"They'll be here in a few minutes," Dana spoke up as she closed her phone. "You want a glass of water, or a Band-Aid while you're waiting?"

"I'm fine," he insisted, sliding onto the old wicker chair they'd left on the porch. "And thanks for answering your door. I tried the place across the street first, because they had a light still on. Guess they thought I was a mad killer, or something."

He gave them a faint smile, and Dana realized that,

despite the beard and the blood, he was rather good
looking. And he wasn't much older than she was, she
judged. Too bad she wasn't into bikers.

Bikers!

She managed not to gasp as she shot Dana a look.
Her sister met her gaze with a lifted brow and a slight
nod, and Viv could all but read her mind. *Coincidence?
Riiiight.*

"Look, we've got to go," she blurted. "But if you need
anything else, ring the bell."

She shut the door and turned the deadbolt, then swung
about to face her sister. Dana was looking at the *Blind
Date* game still sitting neatly on the table, arms extended
and forefingers crossed in the universal sign that meant
"Back off—Evil." From the unsettled expression on her
face, Viv decided the gesture was not entirely mocking.
Hell, she was tempted to do the same thing, herself. Instead, she marched over to the coffee table and grabbed
up the game, then purposely strode over to the built-in
bookcase. Rising up on her toes, she shoved the box up
onto the topmost shelf.

"There, no more game. And tomorrow it goes into the
dumpster. And not a word about the biker guy at our
front door . . . deal?"

"I'm pretending none of this ever happened," Dana
agreed. "But while we're waiting on him to clear out"—
neither of them had said anything, but Viv knew they'd
not go back to bed until he was gone— "I'm thinking I
might have some of that chocolate mocha caramel su-
preme that's in the freezer. You want me to fix you a
bowl?"

While Dana padded off to the kitchen to scoop ice
cream, Viv eased over to the front window and cautiously pulled aside the curtain. At least the police response in this part of town was prompt, she told herself.
The red and blue lights of the patrol car now parked at
the curb sent flashes of color spinning across their front
lawn, while the car's headlights illuminated the battered
motorcycle that sprawled halfway onto the sidewalk. She

could see the biker talking to the officer, who was using his headlights for a writing lamp as he took notes.

Viv shivered. Thank God the poor guy wasn't hurt any worse than he was. And who in the heck was the hit-and-run driver that apparently had been lurking out there in the middle of the night? None of the neighbors parked in the street at night unless they had guests, and she hadn't noticed any strange cars at the curb when she'd made her last trip to toss junk into the Dumpster. Unless the lunatic had been considerate enough to leave his wallet behind, chances were that the police would never find him.

She let the curtain drop again and went to join Dana in the pocket-sized dining nook for her share of ice cream. Neither spoke in the several minutes it took to finish their respective bowls. Viv had just licked the final bit of caramel off her spoon, when the doorbell buzzed.

"Must be your date again," Dana said, absently frowning at the half scoop of ice cream still left in the container. "Do you want me to go with you to the door?"

"No, I can handle it."

And she meant it. While the entire situation with the game had become more than a bit unnerving, the biker himself didn't set off her internal creep-o-meter. He seemed like a nice enough man despite the beard and leather. Besides, she wryly told herself, the police had all his personal information now, so that if Dana found her lifeless body on the lawn, at least they'd know who the guy was who was responsible for killing her.

She opened the door wide enough for him to see her face and asked, "Did you get everything taken care of with the police?"

"Report's filed, though chances are they'll never find the guy," he said, echoing her earlier thought. "Best I can do is turn a claim into my insurance agency and see what they will do." He sighed. "Hell, I just put a new set of pipes on her, too. They're pretty well shot now."

"That's too bad," Viv commiserated. She'd seen enough bits and piece of those bike building shows on satellite TV to know some motorcycles cost as much as cars . . . or even more. "Can you ride it home again?"

"Not a chance. The cop let me use his cell phone, and a buddy of mine will be by in a minute to pick me up." He hesitated, and then went on, "I've already put you out enough tonight, but I need to ask one more favor. It's gonna take a trailer to get my bike to the shop, and tomorrow afternoon would be the soonest I could make it back here with one. Any chance I could leave my bike there in the gap between your house and your garage, in the meantime?"

She considered the request for a moment before nodding. "I suppose it's OK. I don't think Dana would mind, and I can't see that the bike would be in the way if it's only for a day."

"You're the best." He gave her a lopsided grin, looking suddenly younger than she'd first judged him. "I don't know which hurt more, my head, or seeing her all beat up like that."

"Her? Your bike is female?"

His grin broadened. "She sure as hell better be. You won't catch me straddling no fellow like that."

"Oh." Viv felt her face redden, but she couldn't help a small smile in return. "I see what you mean. I've always thought of my cars as guys. By the way, my name is Viv . . . Vivica Martin. And that was my sister, Dana, who called the police for you."

"I'm J.D. Turner," he replied and stuck out a beefy hand.

The soft leather of his glove was warm against her hand, his fingers strong and calloused. She tried to ignore the tingle that raced up her spine at that brief handshake, but she couldn't help recalling that he'd said he had called a friend to pick him up. A buddy . . . not a girlfriend or spouse. Still, to be certain, she casually asked, "Won't your wife be worried that you're not home yet?"

"Honey, the only time she worries about me is when the alimony check is late." He glanced back at the street, where a late model sedan was pulling up. "That's my ride," he said. "We'll move the bike real quick, and then we'll be out of your hair."

She remained at the door, leaving the porch light on until the two men had righted the motorcycle and pushed it alongside the detached garage, far enough back that it was hidden from a casual looker. Then, with a final wave, she closed the door and firmly locked it behind her, listening until the soft rumble of the departing car faded. Sighing, she glanced at the clock on the bookshelf. *Two-thirty.* Morning was going to come awful darn early.

"He's gone, but the bike's still here until tomorrow," she told Dana as she padded into the kitchen again. "I hope you don't mind, I told J.D. it would be OK."

"J.D., is it?" Dana gave her a weary smirk and spooned out the final bit of ice cream from the carton. "Looks like your date might work out, after all. As for me, I'm going back to bed, and no plumber or delivery guy or biker is going to tempt me out of it before noon, at least!"

It was a little after eight a.m. when Viv dragged herself out of bed and into the shower. Much as she would have liked to sleep in, as Dana had said she was going to do, she couldn't bring herself to waste the entire morning. Feeling slightly better after a good quarter hour under the steamy water, she dressed in jeans and a bright red sweatshirt; then, tiptoeing so as not to wake up her sister, she hurried downstairs to the kitchen.

"You're next," she muttered to the room as she took in its worn linoleum, plain white cabinets, and outdated flowered wallpaper. Keep it cozy, but bring it into this century. She and Dana had agreed already to ditch the solid cabinet fronts in favor of paned glass ones and to replace the scratched laminate countertops with faux granite. The only open issue was the flooring. She favored a bright patterned linoleum, while Dana wanted cool white tile.

Still lots to be done, Viv thought with a sigh. She poured a bowl of cornflakes which she carried to the living room, planning to eat while watching her favorite morning news program. She nearly dropped the bowl, however, when she walked through the living room door to find Dana sitting cross-legged beside the coffee table, the *Blind Date* game before her.

The board was set for two players. A fan of playing cards lay face-up at either end, while both the pink and the purple girls had been resurrected from the box and stood upon their respective squares. As for Dana, she still wore last night's mismatched sweats, hair askew and dark rings beneath her eyes as she shook the die and then moved the pink girl five squares. She didn't look up until Viv was standing right in front of her.

"What in the hell are you doing?" Viv gasped out, setting her cereal bowl next to the board. "I thought I put this thing up last night."

"I couldn't sleep, so I took it out again," Dana coolly replied, swapping cards between the two hands as the instructions on the square indicated. "I'm playing both sides, but you can have the pink girl back if you want."

Not waiting for an answer, she rolled the die again, this time moving the purple cutout along the board. Viv watched, stunned into unaccustomed silence. She'd seen this same sort of dull-yet-focused expression that was on her sister's face somewhere else before. It reminded her of Las Vegas, and the glazed look worn by the ubiquitous chain-smoking old women who perched on metal stools and single-mindedly fed quarters into slot machines.

"How long have you been playing?" she finally managed.

Dana shrugged and tossed the die. "Awhile."

"But why? I thought we agreed to get rid of the game, after last night?"

"You agreed," she countered, drawing a couple of cards from the main pile and discarding the same number from one hand. "I think we should figure out the game's little secret before we toss it out."

Viv sank down onto the couch and ran a hand through her silver-brown curls. "There is no secret," she stated flatly. "Last night was a coincidence. I'll even prove it.

Go ahead and pull apart the plastic door like you wanted to last night. Let's see what cards are in there."

"Can't do it. I tried." Dana glanced up at her again, her bruised looking eyes narrowed now in suspicion. "Unless you land on the right spot with the right cards in your hand, the door won't open. It's like the entire thing is melted together into a solid piece. I tried a nail file and everything, but it didn't work."

"OK, so supposing something *is* strange about the board. What good does knowing who is going to be at the door before they actually show up do for you?"

"Hell, I don't know. But there's got to be some way to make it work for us. After all, it can predict the future . . . at least, part of it."

She moved the pink girl three more spaces, once again missing the square with the heart outline. Muttering a few choice curses, she drew another card, then glared up at Viv. "Damn game thinks it's being funny. It doesn't want to play right with only one person. I don't know how many times I've rolled the die, but I have yet to land on the pink spot. Come on, sit down and play with me, and maybe it will work."

Viv hesitated, studying her sister's face. She'd never seen the carefree Dana like this before, obsessed with something to the point that she wasn't sleeping or bathing. First chance she got, she was going to run that game right to the trash container out front. Hell, no . . . she'd drive it down the street to the shopping center and toss it in one of their garbage bins, to make sure her sister wouldn't do a bit of Dumpster diving and try to recover it.

"All right, I'll play . . . but only if you promise you'll quit once one of us wins. Agreed?"

"Yeah, sure." Dana gathered all the cards and shuffled them, then dealt out a pair of cards to each. "Go ahead, I'll let you take the first turn."

The game progressed swiftly. Indeed, the frenzied pace with which they moved the pieces about the board would have been comical to watch, Viv thought, had she not known the reason for their haste. In a few minutes, Dana managed the right combination of plays and marched the purple figure onto the square with the heart.

"Got it," she clipped out, though Viv could hear the excitement beneath the matter-of-fact tone. "Now let's see what the future holds for us. C'mon, you S.O.B., who's behind the door?"

She reached out with the same care she would use to pet a rattlesnake and pulled the plastic door open. They both stared silently at the card for a moment, Dana's expression echoing Viv's own puzzlement. Finally, her sister spoke.

"Looks like a doctor to me. What do you think?"

"White coat, stethoscope." Viv nodded. "But what would a doctor be doing here?"

"Maybe he's not supposed to be a real doctor," Dana said, sounding pensive. "It could be symbolic. What about the name of that landscape company that you called? It was kind of a strange name that sounded medical."

Viv thought a moment, then brightened. "They're called the Plant Doctors. One of their estimators was supposed to stop by in the next couple of days to check out the yard. Maybe that's what the game is trying to tell us, that they'll be here today."

"So big whoop. We knew about the plumber already.... the UPS guy was iffy but no big surprise . . . and now the landscaper." Dana snorted in disgust. "The only surprise so far was the biker guy. Talk about a lame fortune-telling game. We'd have been better off finding one of those Magic 8 balls."

So saying, she pushed back from the coffee table, seemingly not caring that the movement made her purple girl tumble onto her pasteboard face. "You win. Throw the game out if you want. I'm going upstairs to take a shower and then catch a quick nap."

While Dana headed toward the hall, Viv reached for her forgotten cereal bowl. The cornflakes had long since settled into a soggy lump at the bottom of the bowl. She shrugged. Oh well, she could always pour another serving. At least Dana was now over her obsession with the blasted game, and life could get back to normal again.

And then a scream sounded from the hallway, followed by a series of loud thuds, and abrupt silence.

Viv leaped to her feet. "Dana!" she shrieked, rushing toward the hall. She screamed again, seeing her sister lying at the foot of the stairs, eyes closed and moaning softly. She dropped to her knees beside her, frantically trying to recall the first aid class she'd taken several years before. *Don't move her, just see if she's conscious, if she's breathing!*

"Dana," she called, trying to keep the panic from her voice. "Can you hear me? Where are you hurt?"

"Grabbed me," her sister whispered, eyes shut even while she made as if to sit up. Then, with another moan, she sank back to the floor.

"Phone, where's the damn phone?" Viv half-whispered, half-wailed as she scrambled to her feet again. She found the cell in her purse and made the quick call to 911, then rushed to unlock the door for the paramedics before hurrying back to where Dana lay.

"You're pretty damn lucky," Viv scolded a few hours later. "Only a fractured collarbone and a bump on the head. You could have broken your neck, you know."

"Yeah, thanks for reminding me." Dana whispered with a crooked grin. She lay propped on half a dozen pillows in her hospital bed, her left arm splinted and wrapped to her body. "I guess I was so tired, I didn't see that last step when I got to the top of the stairs."

"Well, anyhow, the doctor said you could go home tomorrow. They want to keep you overnight for observation since you hit your head."

"Hell, I can use the rest." Then her expression grew serious, and she reached her good hand toward Viv. "I'm sorry, Sis, I really screwed up. With my collarbone broken, I'm not going to be able to do much of anything for a few weeks. I've really messed up our timetable."

"That's OK," she replied, smiling as she gave her sis-

ter's hand a warm squeeze in return. "Truly, I mean it.
It will be nice to stay somewhere for a while without
spending every minute of the day doing projects. Take
all the time you need to get well."

She hesitated then, wondering if she should bring up
the question that had nagged at her from the moment
she found Dana lying injured at the foot of the stairs. It
was probably nothing. Probably. Taking a deep breath,
she casually asked, "Do you remember what you told
me after you fell? You said something about someone
grabbing you?"

Dana gave her a look of groggy puzzlement. "I did? I
don't remember that. But I did have the weirdest dream
while I was lying there on the floor."

At Viv's encouraging nod, she woozily went on, "I was
playing the game, when the old lady who owned the
house before us sat down and started playing with me.
She was holding a pillow, and she kept looking over her
shoulder, like she was scared. She tried to tell me something, but I couldn't quite make it out, as if something
were muffling her words. And that's all I remember."

"Weird," Viv agreed, frowning slightly. "How did you
know the old woman playing with you was the same one
who owned the house?"

"Beats me . . . I just knew. She seemed like a nice old
lady. I wonder if she was the one who grabbed me?"

With those cryptic words, Dana dozed off. Viv stared
down at her sister, feeling even more uneasy. She never
had been the type to go in for ghosts or the supernatural,
but things had long since passed the point of coincidence.
Was the previous owner maybe haunting her old
house . . . maybe trying to tell them that she didn't want
them redecorating the place?

Then Viv shook head and gave a scoffing little laugh.
If the old lady really were haunting the place, she'd have
to do a better job of getting her point across. Otherwise,
the redecorating was going to continue, no matter that
Dana was relegated to the sidelines.

Odd, though, she thought with a reflexive shiver, that

a doctor had appeared behind the game's plastic red door right before Dana had her accident and was rushed off to the hospital.

After assurances from the nurses that Dana would sleep for the next several hours, Viv decided to come back later in the afternoon and check on her sister. In the meantime, she would head to the house to tidy up a bit and review their remodeling timetable. Even if Dana came home tomorrow, she'd likely need a couple of days in bed. They'd best reschedule some of the subcontractors for the following week, when Dana would be feeling better.

Traffic heading home was light. Once there, she pulled her shiny new VW inside the garage and parked next to Dana's SUV, then took a walk about the front yard. In the excitement over her sister's accident, she had all but forgotten the other drama, the biker, J.D., and the mysterious car that had left him and his bike sprawled across her curb last night. In the daylight, she could see the single line of skid marks and a sprinkling of broken glass in the street, both of which must have come from the motorcycle. A section of lawn next to the curb was gouged out, though it was nothing that couldn't be fixed. But what was that?

A fist-sized black object lay near the hedge beneath the front window. She bent and saw that it was a cell phone . . . no doubt the one J.D. had said he'd lost in the accident. Wrapped in a leather case, it appeared to have withstood the wreck better than its owner. She'd hang onto it for him until he came back later in the day with the trailer to pick up the bike.

Once inside, she set the cell phone on the half wall by the door so she wouldn't forget it and then headed toward her room, suddenly exhausted by the day's events. If J.D. stopped by, he'd better knock awfully loud, she wryly told herself, because he'd probably have to wake her from a nap. She took the stairs a bit more cautiously than usual, however, Dana's murmured comments still echoing in her head.

Grabbed me. She couldn't help a small shiver. Hell, if some ghost lady grabbed *her*, she'd probably drop dead of a heart attack and end up a ghost herself!

With those less-than-cheery thoughts, she made her way to her bedroom, only to stop short in the doorway. Before showering that morning, she had made her bed. To be sure, the crisp white quilt was still neatly pulled up, but the pillows in their flowered shams were no longer propped against the headboard. Instead, they lay precisely in the center of her bed, one piled atop the other.

Viv frowned. Maybe she was mistaken. Maybe she'd been so tired when she got up that she had forgotten to put the pillows in their usual spot. She plumped the first one and set it in place, then picked up the second pillow, and let out small cry.

The pink girl from the *Blind Date* game lay beneath it.

Viv backed away from the bed, gooseflesh crawling about her body like an army of ants on the march. Why in the hell had someone piled pillows on top of a cardboard cut-out of a girl?

She was holding a pillow. She tried to tell me something, but I couldn't quite make it out, as if something were muffling her words.

"Oh, crap," Viv muttered as she recalled Dana's description of her dream.

She rushed downstairs to get her purse, dumping its contents onto the living room floor as she searched for a certain business card. Finding it, she grabbed her cell phone and punched in the number, pacing impatiently until she heard a familiar hello.

"Becky," she breathlessly said into the phone, "this is Viv Martin."

"Hey, I was wondering how you and Dana were getting along," the real estate agent's husky voice replied in her ear. "What can I do for you? You ready to sell the place already?"

"Not yet. I have a question for you . . . kind of a strange one. Remember the disclosure from the sellers, the one that said someone had died here?"

"Sure, honey," Becky said, sounding puzzled. "If someone dies in a house, the sellers are obliged by law to disclose that fact, but I told you before I even took you out to see the place."

"Yeah." Viv hesitated. "Becky, are you certain that she died of natural causes?"

"Well, honey, she was in her eighties and had been under a doctor's care," the agent soothingly replied. "What makes you think she died of something else?"

"Nothing in particular." Just a really, really bad feeling and a couple of pillows on top of a cardboard girl. "She didn't have any enemies or anything, did she?"

The real estate agent's laugh was loud enough so that Viv had to pull the phone from her ear. "Mrs. Biggerstaff was the nicest old lady you could find. She went to my church, and up until a year or so ago she was still helping out in the nursery. Everyone loved her. Her daughter's a sweet lady, too . . . but I can't say as much for the grandson."

Becky's tone of amusement faded into faint censure. "From what I hear, he's pretty much a loser . . . does drugs, gets into fights. Heck, he even missed his grandmother's funeral because he was in jail for a DUI. But what's that have to do with how Mrs. Biggerstaff died?"

"Oh, nothing. I just wanted to make sure nothing bad had happened to her."

"Believe me, if there had been something suspicious about her death, I would have heard about it. Now, you give me a call when you and Dana are ready to sell, you hear?"

Viv said her good-byes and snapped her phone shut, her unsettled feeling growing. Despite Becky's assurances, what if Mrs. Biggerstaff hadn't died of natural causes? What if she had been murdered . . . smothered in her bed with her own pillow? Old as she'd been, no one would have found her death suspicious, and pillows wouldn't have left a bruise. Maybe the old woman was trying to communicate with her and Dana to let them know what had really happened to her.

But then, what did the game have to do with it?

"This is crazy," she said aloud as she shoved her scattered belongings back into her purse. "No old lady is trying to communicate with us from beyond the grave about a murder. Dana's accident was an accident. And I'm going to toss that silly game into the dumpster."

So saying, Viv marched over to the table where the game still sat. The red plastic door was closed again—had she or Dana done that?—and the cards were neatly stacked. The purple girl still lay facedown atop the board, her head pointing in the direction of the door like a cardboard arrow.

As though she were saying, "open here."

Slowly, Viv reached for the door. It won't open, she told herself. Dana had tried and failed to open it by herself, so why should it work for her? Even so, she inwardly whispered, *Who's behind the door?*

To her surprise, the door easily pulled back. This time, it revealed a smiling, dark-haired man dressed in a sports coat and slacks. In one hand, he held a briefcase, and in the other . . .

Viv bent closer, squinting at the picture. His other hand was half hidden behind his back, but she could make out something in clutched in it. *A pen?*

"Oh my God, it's a knife!"

She weakly sank onto her knees, staring more closely at the picture. It was definitely a knife that he held. As for the young man's smile, now that she looked again, she could see the cruel twist to his lips and the flat expression in his eyes. Was this the person who had killed Mrs. Biggerstaff? Was she trying to reveal her murderer's identity to Viv?

Or, far more frightening, was she trying to warn Viv that he was coming back for her?

Maybe that had been the point of the game, she reasoned, while another chill raced through her. The first date that the game produced was a UPS guy, and a UPS guy showed up at the door. Same thing for the plumber, and the biker . . . and even the doctor, if a paramedic or three rushing in to help Dana counted. It made sense in a strange sort of way. In order for her warning about the guy with the knife to be taken seriously, the old lady would have had to first prove to them that the game really did predict who would be at the door.

The doorbell buzzed abruptly. Viv let out a small scream that she tried to suppress by clamping her hand over her mouth. *Get a grip,* she silently told herself. *For all you know, it's J.D. come back to get his motorcycle, or the police here to get more information on last night's hit-and-run.* Besides, she was certain she'd locked the door when she came inside.

Then she heard the knob slowly turn, and saw the door swing open.

"Hello," called a male voice. "Anyone home?"

A handsome, dark-haired young man stuck his face around the jamb, his eyes opening wide in surprise when he caught sight of her. Swiftly, he held up a hand in a gesture of dismay, displaying a key. "Begging your pardon, ma'am, I thought the place was still on the market. Another real estate agent gave me a key. I guess no one changed the locks yet."

"And you are—?" Viv demanded, finally finding her voice as she scrambled to her feet.

He stepped past the threshold and set down his briefcase "I'm Bill Langsford, First Choice Realty. Our office is down on 54th Street in the old plaza." He slapped at his jacket pockets with either hand. "Sorry, I think I left my business cards in the car. But Becky Malloy had told me about this place a few weeks back, and I have a client who might be interested in buying the place. So, has it already sold, or is it still available?"

"My sister and I own it now . . . but it will be for sale again in a few weeks," she replied, her wariness easing slightly at the man's mention of her real estate agent's name. Slightly.

He grinned and grabbed up his case again. "Great. Mind if I take a look around the place? I've only seen the house from the outside, and I'd like to be able to tell them something about it. It's two stories, right?" he asked and headed for the hallway.

Viv rushed to block his way, indignation overriding

any fear. "Sorry, this isn't a good time. Maybe you can come back another day. Now I'm going to have to ask you to leave, okay?"

"Sure, I'll just take your number. Let me get something to write with," he said and reached into his briefcase.

Barely did she glimpse a flash of steel when she felt the point of a knife abruptly pressed to her throat. She froze, not daring to scream, feeling as if she might faint on the spot.

"You shoulda let me take a look around," he said, the earlier grin replaced by a sneer. He dropped the briefcase and grabbed her arm. "So, have you been poking around Grandma's attic yet? I'm looking for something I left behind in that steamer trunk near the back."

"Th-The trunk's still up there," she choked out, realizing this must be Mrs. Biggerstaff's grandson . . . the one who had been in jail. "We didn't even open it yet."

"Lucky for you. If I find it, then I'll just grab it and be on my way. No harm, no foul." Then he paused, and his voice took on a suspicious tone as he gripped her arm even harder. "You said 'we'. Who else is in the house?"

"No one," she managed, trying not to flinch from the pain. "My sister had an accident, and she's in the hospital."

"Yeah, well, accidents happen. Just ask Grandma." He let loose a nasty little chuckle and then gave her a shove. "Come on, let's get this over with."

He stayed close on her heel as she started up the steps, trying not to stumble on shaky legs. *Please, Mrs. Biggerstaff, give your bastard grandson a shove down the stairs,* she frantically thought, though without much hope. The old woman might have been able to startle Dana into a tumble, but Bill—or whatever his name was—likely was a hell of a lot tougher.

She halted uncertainly at the attic door. "What are you waiting for, lady?" came Bill's sneering voice behind her. "Open up."

She flipped on the light switch outside the door and obediently pulled the door open, then she felt the prick of the knife below her ear. "After you," he said with mock courtesy.

The steamer trunk remained untouched in the far corner, barely visible in the circle of light that the bare bulb emitted. "So far, so good," he proclaimed. Gesturing with his knife in the direction of the horsehair sofa, he said, "Sit down, and don't move a muscle. You try anything, and I'll slit your damn throat for you, understand?"

She nodded and sat. Becky had said that the grandson had missed his grandmother's funeral because he'd been in jail on a DUI. It must have happened the same night he killed his grandmother, she reasoned, or surely he would have long since recovered whatever it was that he had hidden in the attic. There could be no other reasonable explanation for his waiting so long after his relative's death to reclaim it. And what he must have cursed as bad luck for him had actually been the first step for her toward some truly horrific fate.

For Viv was suddenly certain that, even if she followed his every instruction to the letter, she was still going to die. If the son of bitch could murder his own grandmother, why would he hesitate to kill her, especially now that she had heard him all but admit to that crime? But she damn sure wasn't going to go without a struggle. All she needed was a moment's distraction.

Bill, meanwhile, had heaved open the trunk's heavy lid and was rooting through its contents. A moment later, he triumphantly pulled out a shoebox, which he opened. Smiling, he held up a large zip lock bag filled with white powder. "Here it is, the mother lode," he said in an admiring tone. "I bet you have no idea, lady, what this stuff is worth on the street."

Balancing the knife on the trunk lid, he carefully rolled the baggie into a smaller bundle and tucked it into his inner jacket pocket . . . and Viv took off at dead run toward the open door.

"Motherf—"

His curse was cut off as she slammed the attic door behind her and flipped off the light and then raced down

the short hallway to the stairs. Behind her, she could
hear a series of loud shouts and thuds as her captor
stumbled about in the dark before reaching the attic door
and flinging it open.

"You're gonna die!" he screamed as he pounded down
the hall after her. By then, she was halfway down the
stairs, but she knew he would catch up with her before
she could get out the front door. And even if she did
make it, what was to stop him from stabbing her before
he took off in his car?

Later, she'd marvel at what adrenaline and a healthy
dose of terror could do for one's athletic ability, but for now
she was barely aware of her feet touching the ground as she
raced though the living room toward the door. No, not the
door, not yet! In less than a heartbeat, her gaze sharpened
and focused on the object that she sought. She snatched it
up, then turned and rushed back toward her assailant.

Her unexpected counterattack caused him to stumble
and lower the knife for an instant . . . and that was
when Viv swung the fireplace poker. She caught the man
squarely in the temple, heard a sickening crack of bone.
He dropped like a sack of rocks at her feet, the knife
skittering across the carpet and the bag in his jacket
bursting open as he hit the floor, sending up a small
cloud of white dust.

She'd killed him . . . maybe. Gasping for breath, she
backed away, remembering all the movies where the bad
guy revives after the heroine turns around after suppos-
edly taking him out. No damn way was she going to
blithely look away. If he moved, she'd be right there to
see it, and he'd get another taste of the fireplace poker.

And that was when the doorbell buzzed.

At the all-too-familiar sound, the burst of adrenaline
drained from her. She stumbled to her knees, would have
fallen had she not had the poker to lean against. "Help,"
she croaked, so softly that she barely heard herself. Taking a breath, she tried again. "Help! Help me! Help!"

The door behind her burst open, and a raspy voice
shouted, "What in holy hell is going on here?"

J.D. dragged her up from the floor and half-carried

her to the couch. He plopped her onto its cushions and grabbed the poker from her now-limp fingers, then purposefully strode back to the limp body on the floor. He gave the man a nudge with one booted foot, getting a moan in return. His face darkened at the sight of the knife gleaming on the carpet, and he kicked it out of the fallen man's reach . . . not that Bill would be attempting to murder anyone else anytime soon.

J.D. turned to her. "Did you take out this slimeball all by yourself?" At her numb nod, he gave a low whistle of appreciation. "Hell, remind me never to rile you up." He spotted his lost cell phone on the ledge of the brick wall and snatched it up. Flipping it open, he punched in 911 and gave the dispatcher Viv's address.

It was while he was talking that she saw it behind him . . . a shimmer in the air, like a summer heat wave over a hot asphalt road. The wavering image of a tiny, elderly woman formed, looking like an out-of-focus photo that had been kept strictly for sentimental reasons. Her gaze was on the fallen man, and Viv could see a phantom tear trickle down her wrinkled cheek. Then the woman met Viv's gaze, smiled sadly at her for the space of a heartbeat, and was gone.

J.D., meanwhile, had snapped the phone closed again. He tucked it into his black leather jacket and headed toward the sofa. "I'm guessing you have a real interesting story to tell the cops," he said with a shake of his head. "Hope you don't mind if I hang around to hear it."

It was dark before the dust—both literally and figuratively—finally settled. The ambulance had taken Bill away, but not before the paramedic had opined that he probably would survive to go to trial. Viv wasn't sure if she should be relieved or disappointed by the news. The police assured her that she'd acted in self-defense and promised they would pursue the possible matter of Mrs. Biggerstaff's murder. This would be in addition to charging Bill with assault, attempted murder, possession with intent to sell, and anything else they could come up with.

They'd been almost as pleased when J.D had pointed out some new-looking dents in the rear quarter panel of Bill's late model sedan, the burgundy paint of which matched some paint flakes on his bike fender. No doubt Bill had been casing the place the night before, a possibility that made Viv shiver. What if he'd tried to break in last night, while Dana had been up all alone? Would the game have tried to warn her, too?

Afterward, when the police had left and Viv suddenly recalled that Dana would be wondering where she was, J.D. had volunteered to drive her to the hospital to visit her sister.

"Take as long as you like," he'd insisted once they got there. He pulled a copy of *Zen and the Art of Motorcycle Maintenance* from his leather jacket and settled into one of the waiting room's plastic orange chairs. "And if you feel up to it when you're done," he added, "I'll take you out for supper."

Dana had been awake. Thanks to her pain pills, she felt quite well enough to insist upon an instant-by-instant retelling of the afternoon's events once Viv had broken the news of her own close call. Viv complied, adding those details that she had refrained from telling the police lest they think she was some sort of crackpot. Things like the mysteriously moving game pieces, and the odd vision Viv had experienced after she had laid Bill out with the same fireplace poker that Dana had left by the door the previous night.

"And you actually saw Mrs. Biggerstaff's ghost?" Dana asked in amazement, sinking back into her pillows with a shiver.

Viv shrugged. "I thought I did . . . though maybe it was my imagination. I was a bit wrought up at the time, you know."

"It had to be her," Dana insisted. "And to think he killed his own grandmother, probably because she found out he was hiding drugs in her attic. That is amazing how she used the game to warn us about him, and even solve her own murder that no one even knew happened."

"Pretty amazing," Viv agreed, and then yawned.

Dana patted her arm with her good hand. "You'd better get back to the house and get some rest," she insisted, "that is, unless you're scared to stay there alone now?"

"I'll be fine. After all, I think I've got myself some heavy duty protection now."

"You mean the ghost of Mrs. Biggerstaff?"

Viv shook her head wearily. "No, I'm pretty sure she did what she needed to do, and that she's moved on. The protection I'm thinking about comes wrapped in a black leather jacket and rides a motorcycle."

"I knew it," Dana exclaimed in satisfaction and started to hum the familiar tune. "Looks like your blind date worked out, after all." Then, with a conspiratorial wink, she leaned forward and whispered, "So, do you think he has a friend?"

VENUS IN BLUE JEANS

Jody Lynn Nye

Jody Lynn Nye lists her main career activity as "spoiling cats." She lives northwest of Chicago with two of the above and her husband, author and packager Bill Fawcett. She has published over thirty books, including six contemporary fantasies, four SF novels, four novels in collaboration with Anne McCaffrey, including *The Ship Who Won*; edited a humorous anthology about mothers, *Don't Forget Your Spacesuit, Dear!*; and written more than a hundred short stories. Her latest books are *An Unexpected Apprentice*, *Strong Arm Tactics*, first in the Wolfe Pack series and *Class Dis-Mythed*, co-written with Robert Asprin.

"**W**elcome to FindingLove.info," the site banner said. Steven Chan leaned in nervously, his fingers on the keyboard. He could see himself reflected faintly in the screen. His narrow oval of a face, with large, brown eyes, short straight nose and thin-lipped mouth, and topped off with gelled, black hair combed up into a shock, peered back suspiciously at him. He was dressed reasonably well, in a polo shirt and baggy pants. He didn't look so bad. He was a smart guy. His friends liked being with him. Was it just too sad that he felt forced to look for a date this way?

A musical chime brought his attention back to the website. Beside the words "WHAT ARE YOU LOOKING FOR?" a cursor was blinking busily.

Steven had to think for a moment. What *was* he looking for?

The site looked interesting. The home page had a lot of lively animations, none of them the sickening throbbing hearts or happy faces moving into a kiss that he had seen on a lot of similar sites. The graphics weren't too kinky or too conservative. He had found Finding-Love listed in the San Francisco Free Paper, which was distributed on his university campus. It promised absolute confidentiality for all "clients." He fervently hoped his parents would never find out about this, at least until he had had a chance to find a few decent date prospects.

His parents were not happy with him, especially not since he had started college. Mother and Father felt that American culture was pulling him too far from the ways of their ancestors. Both of them had emigrated to the United States from Shanghai, China. They thought he should be looking for a Chinese girl to marry. He thought that bordered on hypocrisy. They were very modern people, Internet aware, with plenty of technical know-how, as well as expertise. Both of them worked in the computer field, in engineering jobs. They ate out a lot, text-messaged him and one another, watched the newest movies and played the most up-to-date computer games; but when they socialized, it was largely with the expat Chinese community. Mother dressed well, and chicly. She had never worn casual clothes on a Friday in her life. Father wore a tie to work, something that not even the president of his Silicon Valley company ever did. They wanted him to follow their lead and keep China alive in his life.

It wasn't as though he was ashamed of his heritage. Steven tried to comply with their wishes. In high school he had not been allowed to date alone. Now that he was in college—majoring in computer design—he had joined the Asian-American Society on campus and was on the e-mail lists for the cultural outings. He'd taken a few girls from the club out for a burger, but no one clicked with him. Besides, all the girls in the club had black hair. He really liked blondes. His mother always disapproved of his choices anyhow.

Since he had reached the ripe old age of twenty, his parents offered to meet with a matchmaker, but Steven protested. He was an American. It was far too soon to marry. He wanted to find girls on his own, without their help, date for a while, and think about marriage after he had left college and become established in his career. Still, he felt stymied. All his efforts to meet nice girls fell apart. It was embarrassing to think that Internet dating might be his answer. Internet dating was for losers.

If that was true, then why were his fingers poised to fill in the blanks? The cursor blinked invitingly.

"A girlfriend," he typed at last.

The screen changed.

It filled up with short paragraphs decorated with icons and pictures, like a blog. He started to read them and realized they were personal advertisements. This site was far weirder than the others he had tried before. The ads were written in a fantastic vein.

"ISO a lady who likes wild rides through the clouds, poetry, fine food, and is interested in mature gentleman. Travel, no problem. Write to Zeus."

"Wanted to find: a real man who is smart enough to look more than skin-deep. One date with me, and you will forget about any other girl you've ever met. —Medusa."

"Do you love the beach? Keen swimmer seeks a similarly minded male, to frolic in the waves, loll on the beach, and enjoy fantastic seafood suppers at sunset. —Selkie."

"I want to meet the girl who knows how to wait until she finds what she truly wants. I promise you a good time, and I will never hurry you. I am waiting for you. —Unicorn."

Steven shook his head. The local Dungeons and Dragons crew must have launched this business. The avatars

used pretty good graphics, much more suited to a game
site than to a dating service. "Medusa's" face was really
scary. Each waving snake had its own flicking little
tongue, meaning someone had actually spent a lot of
time on it. Was this the kind of service that he really
wanted to use? Why not? He was a role-play gamer, and
he belonged to a few massive multiplayer games that
sometimes kept him online all night. He hesitated for a
moment before entering his details on the registration
form. *What harm could it do?* He wondered. He could
always delete the answers again.

It wanted to know what he did for a living. "College
student," he typed. He could have put in something fake,
but he would be exposed on the first date. Maybe he
was stupid to trust the confidentiality claim, but he admitted he was desperate.

Someone smart was running the AI in this program.
"MAJOR?" It asked him next.

"Computer design."

"HOBBIES?"

"I guess no one ever told you that typing in all caps
is considered shouting," Steven said, austerely. He put
in all of the things he enjoyed: computer games, going
to concerts, listening to music, texting and hanging out
with his friends, watching television, reading books. He
was dismayed how nerdy the list sounded. He added running, since he did put in seven miles every morning.

He hit ENTER, and waited. He kept expecting a
graphic to come up instructing him how to send payment,
but when the screen changed, it merely set him back on
the page full of personal ads. Free. Cool. He scanned the
list. Now there was a new entry:

"Quickly, looking for someone who is more than the
girl next door. I'm smart enough to love you for who
you are, not just what you look like. —Hermes."

Steven frowned and hit the BACK button to return to
his entry form. That wasn't true, exactly. If he was being
honest, he wanted to date a pretty girl. It would not be
fair if the service sent him some plain jane. She would

see the dismay in his eyes. Okay, he knew it sounded shallow, but wasn't he allowed to have personal tastes taken into account?

He tried changing the entries in his form, but nothing happened. He scanned down to see if there was a "Contact the webmaster" link. There was none. He slammed a hand on his mouse pad.

"I take back everything I said about the AI author. He's an idiot."

His Blackberry buzzed. He snatched it off his belt. Three messages. The first was from his mother.

"DNR 6?" Would he be home for dinner at six?

He texted back, "Y TKU." Yes, thank you. It took a little longer, but his mother was a stickler for manners.

The other two messages were from a couple of his buddies who were also in the computer department. Hugh had uploaded a site link to him that was full of hot babe pictures. Not porn, just hot. He saved it for later perusal. Aliki wanted to know if he had finished coding his share of the assignment they had for the upcoming project in Graphics. Steven glanced at the ragged calendar hanging from the file cabinet next to his desk and sighed. Another Friday night without a date. Unsatisfied, he logged off his desktop and shut down. He answered the other messages as he headed for the dorm elevator.

"What did you do today?" Mother asked, as she passed the platter of steaming scallion pancakes to him. Father had already been served, and Steven was next in the proper Chinese order of precedence. In an American family, Mother would have been next, but it was her duty to feed her menfolk before herself. Next to the eight thousand dollar Viking stove, in a red enameled shrine to the Kitchen God, a stick of incense fumed, flavoring the air as much as the spices in the food. Steven counted the pancakes. Five left. He could have eaten all of them himself, but that wouldn't be polite. Mother would never say anything, but she would *look* it at him. Meekly, he drew two onto his plate and passed it back to her. She smiled her approval. "What classes did you have?"

"Computer-assisted design," Steven said. "I only have one today, but I studied with my friends."

"Ah," Father said. "When many eyes look, little is missed."

Steven cringed. The fortune-cookie patter meant Dad had spent at least part of the day with his grandparents. Normally, his dad was full of technical talk about the latest computer equipment Westchip was working on.

"Did you see any nice girls this week?"

As if he believed the home page from FindingLove was imprinted on his forehead, Steven felt his cheeks grow hot. "No."

"Angela Li said her cousin has just moved here from Beijing. She has a daughter about your age," Mother said, with a suggestive lift to her eyebrow.

"Mom, no. Please," he implored her. "I can do it myself!"

Mother threw her hands in the air. "All right! I am just trying to help you, you know. Don't you agree, Gui-La?"

"What?" Father asked, glancing up from his meal. "Of course, I do."

"Good. Remember, Steven, we are very supportive of you, whatever you do."

As long as it goes along with your views, Steven thought sourly as he rode back to the dorm on the bus with a bag of food he hadn't the guts to refuse taking, even though his housing package included full board.

His roommate, Ricky, was still out when he got back. Quickly, he logged onto his computer and took a look at his mailbox on the site. No messages. He felt like a total loser. How bogus was this, desperately checking in after just a few hours? It was a good thing that his potential dates didn't know. He would have dropped through the ground in shame. He rolled over to the latest online game site to see if anyone he knew was on the Player Killer server.

Demure tapping on the door interrupted his first battle. Ricky never knocked. Must be someone looking for one of the guys who lived on the floor.

Steven opened up to find the most gorgeous girl he

had ever seen, leaning with her arms folded against the door jamb.

"Hi, Hermes," she said. "It's not how I expected to see you look, but not bad."

She smiled. Her teeth were perfect, straight and white, like so many American girls'. Her cheeks were slightly pink, like her lips. Her eyes were a deep, sparkling blue, like the glass in church windows. Steven swept a casual glance downward, hoping he wasn't being too obvious about it. The waistband of her yellow sweater clung to a very narrow middle. The garment bloused out above to skim a pair of generous breasts, the top curves of which were visible in the deep v-neck. She had been poured into a pair of skinny, worn, black jeans with one torn knee. Pink-painted toenails peeked out of open-toed high-heeled sandals covered with golden rhinestones.

Steven couldn't believe that anyone who looked like that was standing there, breathing. She made the sterile dorm corridor look as decrepit as an alley. She was absolutely perfect, except her hair was shining dark brown. Almost perfect. He glanced down her gorgeous form again.

"Oh, that's right," she said, as if remembering something. "You like blondes."

He looked up at her, meeting the surprisingly dark blue eyes. Had it been a trick of the light in the hallway? Her hair *was* blonde, a thick cascade the color of oak wood.

"Can . . . can I help you?" he gasped.

"Aren't you Hermes?" she asked.

"No . . . I mean, yes," he exclaimed. "You mean, my ad?"

"Yes. I read it." Her long eyelashes closed halfway over her lovely eyes. "I liked the sound of it. I don't believe it, of course. Men don't mean it when they say looks don't matter, but it was sweet. You have always been good at communicating."

"I have?"

"After such a long time, I want this to be the perfect

date, of course," she said. "Let's see, what is it that you really like to see in a girl? Are my breasts too big?" She took a hand mirror out of the dainty purse on her wrist and surveyed them. "No, I think they're about right. Hmm. Are my hips too wide? Perhaps just a little narrower."

It wasn't the way she was standing, because they actually did narrow. The pelvic bones peeking out above the waistband of her tight jeans became just a trifle more prominent. Steven goggled.

"How . . . ?" he asked.

"Wait a moment," she said. "It'll just take a little time until I have everything *just* right. Oh, I know—the final touch!" And her slender neck seemed to lengthen just a little bit.

Steven found himself staring at her open-mouthed, almost salivating. Now she was *absolutely* perfect. He just couldn't control the bulge growing against the front of his baggy pants. Instead of being embarrassed, she surveyed the effect with pleasure.

"Yes," she said, "I can see you like it."

"How?" Steven asked. "How could you . . . how could you possibly do that?"

"Because I'm a goddess, of course," she said, simply.

Steven thought about her statement for a moment, and delight dawned. A goddess? Like in mythology? Like in the online games?

"Hey, *cool!*" he said.

"Just like you're a god," she added, with a strange look. "Hermes."

"But that's just on the website," he said. "I mean, that was the name the sysop assigned me."

She peered at him, the blue eyes becoming anxious. "You're not Hermes?"

"Well, I am," Steven stammered. "I mean, that's my screen name the site gave me. I'm really . . ." Abruptly, he thrust out his hand. "My name is Steven Chan. Hi."

"Aphrodite. You're *not* Hermes," she said with finality. "So, what is the deal here? Did the big coward put you up to this? I am going to lock him in a room without even a magazine to keep him busy. I am going to cut all his connections off! The nerve!"

Steven looked forlorn. "Does that mean our date is off?"

Aphrodite tapped her foot impatiently. "It would be just like him to duck out on a date with me. I remember a hundred and forty years ago when we were supposed to have a really wonderful night out, and the next thing you know—no, he has to run off and do an errand for Zeus! Absolutely, right then. Wouldn't it figure that I was all dolled up, in the latest fashions. I had gotten Demeter to grow me some very special orchids. They were in my hair. I smelled like a dream—like a dream! I had everything waiting—and nothing. Do you know what it's like for the goddess of love to be stood up?"

"Er, no," Steven said, but she charged on as if she hadn't heard him.

"I thought after all this time he was trying to make it up to me!"

"I don't know how you can find out," Steven said. "I tried every which way to get a reply from the sysop of that dating website I signed up on, and there is no link at all."

"Oh, there are ways," Aphrodite said. "Let me see your computer. Is this it? Oh, my, a Delton 480. Very nice." She sat down.

She's gorgeous and *she's a programmer?* Steven thought, his eyes widening as he watched her slender fingers fly over the keyboard. *This girl IS my ideal.*

Somehow she got access to screens that he couldn't have accessed. She typed in code after code, but the cursor just blinked stupidly back at them.

"Typical!" she said, turning away from the keyboard. "Hermes absolutely is the webmaster on that site—I don't know why he decided to go into the matchmaking business—but he is not taking my calls. Oh, never mind. Perhaps he really is trying to make up for his bad behavior by fixing me up with you. I don't mind hanging around with mortals, especially cute ones like you." She looked him up and down. "I thought from your ad you at least had things in common with him."

"Like what?" Steven asked, willing to live up to anything.

"Well, you run, don't you? Or did *he* make that up?"

"No, I do run."

"And you're really smart. You think a lot. I like that. I like smart guys. I think that's what attracted me to him. I only hope you don't share one of his traits. I mean, fast-moving isn't an attractive characteristic in *everything*."

"What's that?" he asked, then suddenly regretted it when she grinned wickedly and looked down. "Oh."

She fluttered her eyelashes up at him. "Don't worry," she said. "I won't push you any faster than I think you can go."

"Uh, thanks. I think."

Aphrodite cocked her head prettily, angling that gorgeous neck. "Do I make you nervous?"

"Uh . . . yes. I can get my head around the goddess part—intellectually. It's the reality that I'm finding a little difficult to manage."

"That's all right," she said. He melted at her smile. "You already love me. And I love you."

Practicality warred with hope. "How would you know I love you? I just met you."

"Because we all have our attributes," she said. "And I am the goddess of love. I can feel love when it's present. Not just lust." An impish grin made him want to touch the dimple in her cheek. Before he thought about it, his hand had risen to stroke her face. She leaned into the caress. "That's better. Treat me like any other girl."

Steven let his hand drop. "I couldn't. Besides," he added, ashamed of his own inexperience, "I haven't had a chance to date any other girls. Not alone. My parents were pretty strict."

"Ah!" Aphrodite's perfect oval-shaped face lit up. "Then you don't have any bad habits to unlearn. So, what do you do for fun around here?"

Once again, Steven found himself tongue-tied.

"Well," she said, rising from the computer chair and

attaching herself to his arm, "why don't you show me around? I've never been to Stanford before. I don't usually have a lot to do on the technical campuses. People are very driven. And even if I do match up couples, with the help of my son, Eros—oh, don't I look as if I am old enough to have a son?" she asked, coyly, as he gawked. "That's so sweet of you!"

Steven blushed again, glad he hadn't said what he was thinking.

"You would be surprised how I can look," she said, cuddling closer. "And how I can act."

"My roommate, Ricky, uh, he's . . . I . . . I don't know how to explain you to him. I mean, a normal girl . . ."

Aphrodite shook her head, and her hair fell fetchingly around her shoulders.

"Don't worry. If he is anything near as resilient as you are, I shouldn't have any trouble getting to know him, too."

Steven couldn't help himself from looking indignant.

Aphrodite laughed. "Oh, no, no, no! Serial monogamy is much more my style."

Steven had to admit he felt like a king as he escorted this incredibly beautiful young-*looking* woman around campus. People turned to stare at her, women as well as men. He thought he had enjoyed it when he had won the Sammler Prize for Advanced Program Application in his sophomore year, the way everyone stopped to whisper behind his back in admiration. This was completely different. Every time they passed underneath one of the street lights, she collected another set of sighs.

Unfortunately, she seemed to attract other, not so appealing, elements. The pair of them found themselves being followed across the campus by a group of men from the Stanford football team, who just didn't seem to want to go away.

Aphrodite didn't notice, or didn't care, that she was attracting that kind of attention, but Steven knew that he would be totally outmatched if they decided to start pushing him around—and in front of her, no less. It was what Dad called "the demon time." After dark, everyone's worst nature seemed to come out. The goddess seemed to carry a golden glow around with her.

"Hey, skinny, that's a real woman! She wants real men!"

Steven turned. Conflict was unavoidable. "Listen, guys," he began.

They pushed in close until they towered over him. Steven braced himself but tried to remain calm. Suddenly, Aphrodite was in their midst. She gave the group one of the most mindblowing smiles he had ever seen. It was like getting chocolate cream pie, a full scholarship, a new car, and all the way to third base all at the same time, without any physical contact at all. Bright blue sparks danced in a circle around their heads.

"Guys," she said, "you're sweet, but we two would really like to be alone now. Do you mind?"

Instead of looking embarrassed that his date was defending him, Steven concentrated on looking macho possessive and tough, which was pretty difficult, since any one of their thighs was wider than his shoulders.

"Sure," the biggest one said, sounding dazed. "Have a nice night."

"Thank you!" Aphrodite said, pulling Steven away with her. The football players simply stood and watched them go. "How's the pizza here?" she asked. "The last time I was in California, it wasn't that good. You would think that mortals who were trying to solve all the problems of the universe would certainly have explored the correct culinary proportions of cheese, sauce and crust wouldn't you?"

Steven had had a more than adequate dinner at home with Mother and Father, but he felt all kinds of hunger gnawing at his insides. In the campus pizza café, the two of them polished off a large pizza with everything. He also seemed to be carrying around a fairly permanent erection. They went from the café to the campus game room. She loved the old pinball machines. He enjoyed watching her hips thrusting from side to side as she tried to give some body English to the ball in play more than taking his own turn at the paddles. She laughed whether she won or lost. When they ran out of quarters, she pulled him out of the game room.

The next thing he remembered clearly, they were sitting up on top of the Astronomy Building, holding hands in the moonlight. Then, she leaned over to kiss him. He didn't have a clear recollection later of all the things that they did together, though she took care of the erection in a perfectly ladylike manner that somehow didn't embarrass either one of them. He would never have been able to explain to anyone in a million years what happened or how, especially not his parents.

His parents!

How was he going to explain taking an immortal goddess out for pizza, video games and necking to his parents?

So he didn't explain himself. For a couple of weeks, he didn't say a word about FindingLove.info, or Aphrodite, or any of the places that they found to make out on campus. He was monosyllabic at dinners at home, almost as terse as Dad and his ancient Chinese adages. If Mother was troubled by his silence, she didn't say so.

When he wasn't in class, he spent almost every moment of every day with Aphrodite. She turned up whenever he was free, enjoyed doing anything that he wanted. Her idea of great makeout spots included the top of the carillon tower on campus, behind the waterfall in the rock grotto outside the Botany building, and just plain up in the clouds. He accepted the idea that she could fly with the same dazed acknowledgement that she could change her shape to suit what she was wearing. She always kept her hair blond, for him. He just barely got his homework in, and his friends began to complain they weren't seeing anything of him. More importantly, his parents were upset that he wasn't coming home more often. But how did you explain a Greek goddess to your parents?

Steven hated to share any time with anyone else that he could otherwise have with her. He had never been so happy. Just being able to look at her made him feel complete.

Finally, Mother texted and insisted that he come home or they would disown him. Over her special sizzling rice, she asked, "You're in love, aren't you?"

Steven dropped his chopsticks with a clatter. "Wha . . . how would you ask such a thing?"

Mother smiled. "I know all the signs. I was young once myself, and not all that long ago, I might add. Who is she? What is her name? Tell us about her?"

"She is *beautiful*, Mom," Steven said.

"Is she from the club?" Mother asked, with a warning note in her voice.

Steven hung his head. "No. She's not."

"How did you meet this young lady?"

Steven's voice dropped lower still. "Through a website."

"A *website*? Where anyone can read your private details? You have no idea what she is, or what she could be!"

Steven felt indignant, since she worked in the IT field herself, but he found himself grinning at the memory of just a few of the transformations Aphrodite had gone through for him. "Oh, Mom, she could be *anything*."

"What does that mean? Oh, never mind. Bring her to dinner next Friday. I would like to meet this paragon for myself. If she is so special as to bewitch you so much you forget to tell your parents about her, then she must be amazing indeed."

"Are you sure you want to meet them?" Steven asked her that evening.

"We'll get along," Aphrodite assured him. "Let's go. I can't wait to meet them. I am sure they are wonderful."

Steven surveyed her, admiring the baggy, lowcut blue T-shirt that she had on. "I wonder, could you dress up a little for dinner when we go? Maybe appear more . . . well, goddesslike?"

"Why? I *am* a goddess. It doesn't matter what I wear

or what I look like. It doesn't change the inner me. I am still the absolute aspect of Love. You read Aristotle, didn't you?"

Steven was impatient. "Yeah, yeah, I read Aristotle. Look, my parents are a little old-fashioned."

"They couldn't be more old-fashioned than I am," Aphrodite drawled, with a slow smile.

Steven groaned. She would see. He doubted that even Zeus could live up to his mother's standards.

At the door, Mother met them. "Well, at last!" she exclaimed, opening the door and ushering them inside with the wooden cooking paddle she held in one hand. She was dressed in a handsome summer weight linen suit with an apron tied over it to protect it. She hustled back into the kitchen to the huge wok that sizzled over the stove. "Gui-La! Your son and heir is here, and his guest!"

"Mom, this is Aphrodite," Steven said.

"Of course she is," Mother said, stirring furiously. She shoveled cooked meat onto a plate and plopped a platterful of vegetables into the hot oil. She looked up, and her face went slack with shock. "I am pleased . . . O, Honored One, forgive me!" She yanked the pan off the heat and ran to drop into a deep bow before the visitor. "How you bless our poor house with your presence! *Gui-La!*"

"What is all the shouting about?" Father asked. He came out of the bedroom, buttoning his collar. He saw Aphrodite, and ran to join his wife, bowing like a barometer bird. "To what do we owe the privilege, Holy One?"

"Mom, Dad, what are you doing?"

Mother looked up at him with reproachful eyes. "You did not tell us who was your special friend. You lead us all this time to think you have an ordinary girl!"

"Well, Mom, she answered a singles ad."

"She what?"

He tried to explain. Mother waved away his sputtered explanation.

"Never mind. Keep her well propitiated." She turned to Aphrodite and bowed again. This wasn't his thoroughly modern mother! "I hope our son is treating you as a holy presence deserves."

Steven thought about some of the things they had done together, and blushed. Still, Aprodite didn't turn a hair.

"He treats me as I would expect a worshiper to," she said. Steven's cheeks burned more fiercely. She smiled at him with loving indulgence. His parents couldn't miss the inference, but ignored it. After all, they had accepted her as divine.

Mother hastily took a handful of incense sticks and lit them at the Kitchen God's shrine.

"I must thank the household protector for such a favor as you show our humble family," Mother said.

"It's nothing," Aphrodite said, giving Mother a warm hug. Mother stiffened in the embrace, but she couldn't help but relax. Steven saw her face change as the lovely girl's charm enveloped her.

Mother threw herself into cooking with enthusiasm, and rustled up the meal on their holiday porcelain dishes. She served the guest first from each dish. Aprhodite was given the best of everything, the most succulent meat, the crispest vegetables, the largest and plumpest pancakes. Mother kept asking her if she was pleased with her humble offerings.

Steven was still astonished that they had been able to see something in her that he had not. Maybe he hadn't been paying attention to the old ways that his parents had brought with them from China. They clearly saw a divine aura about Aphrodite, where he just saw a really pretty girl—who could change shape and fly, admittedly, but he had no inkling looking at her that she could do something like that.

"Have you chosen my son as your consort for any divinity you see in him, Honored One?" Mother asked, passing the bowl of rice to her.

"Not really," Aphrodite laughed. "I thought he was someone else! But it turned out all right. Your son is very lovable."

Mother beamed at Steven as though she had invented him, which in fact she had. "I am glad you think so, Honored One."

Steven relaxed. His parents didn't mind after all that he was dating a blond non-Chinese girl. He was just beginning to get used to the idea, and he liked it a lot.

So did his parents. From that day on they encouraged him. When Mother called him at school, she would always ask after Aphrodite's well-being.

"And how is the honored one?" Mother asked, one Wednesday, about a month after they had started dating.

"She's fine, Mom," Steven said, trying not to react as the "honored one" nibbled on his other ear. They were curled up together on the shabby couch in the corner of his dorm room.

"Please bring her for supper again at the weekend, if she so pleases to honor our poor, humble house." Mother never talked like that. It was usually Father who invoked the spirits of China in his speech patterns. He turned his face toward Aphrodite, who captured his mouth with her own. He moved his head back enough to speak. "Mom says would you like to come to dinner on Friday again?"

"Oh, yes! She's a terrific cook."

"Aphrodite says yes, Mom," Steven said. The kisses tickled down the side of his neck below his ear. The sensation overwhelmed his brain so much he just barely heard his Mother's next words.

"Tell her we are most honored."

"They're most honored," Steven relayed to Aphrodite.

"That is so sweet of her to say so. I am honored by her invitation."

Steven passed it along and just barely got the phone back on the cradle before she thought of a new position to kiss in.

On Friday afternoon, Aphrodite met him with a passionate embrace at the door of his dorm room.

"Shall we go?" she asked.

She was dressed in tattered khaki chinos and a thin pink shirt that was more or less barely clinging to her sumptuous torso.

"You're not going like that, are you?" Steven asked, aghast.

"Why not? It's what I am wearing today." She pirouetted. "Don't you like the way I look?"

He thought his heart would sink through the floor. "I love the way you look. I'm blown away by the way you look. I can't believe that someone as amazing as you wants to go out with me, the way you look. It's just that my mother . . . Oh, never mind. She thinks everything you do is right."

"So, what is the problem?"

Steven sighed.

Once again, Mother had gone all out on dinner. With understandable pride, she served the first course, golden lucky cakes made with salmon. Aphrodite was lavish in her praise. Both Father and Mother looked proud.

"I want to introduce you to the rest of the family," Mother said, as she offered a platter of dumplings to Aphrodite. "Have you . . . I am curious . . . have you ever met our ancestors?"

"Sorry, no. I've never been much for family reunions with other people's relatives, since I'm still dealing with my own, who are very much alive and kicking. My father, for example . . ."

She told them stories of her immortal relations that fascinated them through the pickled fish, the stir-fried meat and vegetables, all the way to the rich, almond-scented cake Mother had made from her great-grandmother's best recipe. To Steven, it sounded like mythology class brought to life, a way of looking at the world that was so different from his own experience.

"It feels like I'm always fighting with my brothers and sisters," she said, airily. "That is, if I'm not fixing them up with one another, or dating them myself. I'm shocking you, aren't I?" she said, putting a hand on Father's arm. "But when your life is infinite, all the taboos that you live with just don't matter after the first ten or twelve thousand years. Differences don't matter. In the end, we love one another."

Father cleared his throat. "We Chinese have come to the same point in our philosophy over history. In the 1920's, there were studies . . ."

But time and again, Mother's eyes darted to the torn

T-shirt that just barely kept decency under wraps. She kept glancing at Steven to see if he saw what she did. There was no doubt about it: she disapproved.

She was endlessly nice to the guest throughout the evening, but the next day she called Steven on his cell phone.

"Steven," she said, "you are letting down the honor of the house."

He looked around the cafeteria to see if anyone could hear him. "Mom, I'm dating a goddess! How could I possibly be letting down the honor of the house?"

"The ancestors are surely mortified. That girl dresses in rags! It makes me uncomfortable that a god doesn't behave or look like a god. In my opinion, of course. It means a great deal how people present themselves to one that they choose to honor. How would your grandfather have felt if you went to his home wearing torn clothes? He would have been disgraced. You may feel differently because you were brought up in the American culture. I feel that we have let you down."

"Mom, there are plenty of gods who don't even look human. What would you say if *they* dressed in jeans? She said appearances don't matter. It was the infinite that mattered. Last night you agreed with her."

"You know what I mean," Mother said. Steven did know what she meant. "Perhaps you can persuade her to dress more to her station. She is so beautiful. Anything that she wears . . . well, not *anything* . . . would show her off to such advantage. Try. She says she loves you. Do it for me."

He hung up with a sigh.

It was no use. Steven had taken enough physics classes to know that when the irresistible force meets the immovable object, there is no movement. He tried telling Aphrodite his mother's feelings, but she continued to wear the sexy clothes she enjoyed to the Friday night dinners, and Mother continued to disapprove of them to the point where Steven felt critical mass approaching.

One day it happened. Mother called him early in the morning, her voice sounding as shrill as the telephone's ring.

"H'lo?" he murmured.

"Steven, I don't want you to see that woman any more."

He was wide awake in a moment. He signed apology to his roommate, whose head rose turtle-like from the midst of his bedcovers. "Aphrodite? But, we're in love! We're happy!"

"She will never marry you, Steven. Do you expect her to stay forever? To take vows with a mortal? Have your babies?"

"But, Mom!" he groaned. "You seemed to think it was such a great idea!"

"I've changed my mind," Mother said. "She is only toying with you, son. I love you so much that you must understand that my interest is in your well being! Your *welfare*."

Steven thought that it was more for appearance's sake than it was for his benefit. He could not imagine Mother introducing Aphrodite to the rest of the family, even if they accepted that she was divine. For his goddess, every day was casual Friday.

In the infinite it didn't matter, but on Earth it was enough to begin to spoil even a perfect relationship.

That afternoon after Chemistry class, Aphrodite took him up to make love in a cloud. He felt himself melded with her, every nerve ending tingling with anticipation, delight and fulfillment. The culmination of their physical relationship should have been the most sublime moment of his life. Yet, he found himself sighing.

"What's the matter?" she asked, rolling up onto an elbow to look at him. Steven stared straight up at the clear blue sky.

He sighed again. "Mother has decided she doesn't approve of you."

She studied him. "She has a little too much of my sister Athena in her. She's thinking far more than she needs to. It would do her good to *feel* a little more."

"Oh, I agree," Steven said, unhappily. "But she has this pride thing going, and I just don't know how to get around it. She's just driving me crazy, harping on what you wear, how you act, how you look . . ."

One perfect eyebrow rose. "What's wrong with how I look?"

"Oh, there's nothing wrong with you. I think you're perfect."

She smiled. "See? That's why I love you. But I love your mother, too."

Steven frowned. "You do? That's weird."

"No, it isn't. I love everyone." She regarded him sadly. "I can see how unhappy all of this is making you. I have been thinking. It might be best if we broke up."

"No! No!" Steven said, sitting upright. The cloudstuff rolled under him like an armload of cushions. "That's not a good idea."

Aphrodite shook her head.

"Your mother was right, you know. This wasn't meant to be forever. In fact, it was an accident that we got together at all. I've enjoyed it very much."

He gathered her in his arms and held her tightly. "Well, I have, too! Please don't break up with me just because of what my mother said."

"But you love your mother," Aphrodite said, her voice muffled in his shoulder. "She is going to be in your life a lot longer than I am. Let me tell you, mixed marriages, mortals and immortals, don't really do very well for too long. Look at my father and all of his girlfriends! If the relationship lasts up to the birth of the baby, believe me, that's it. Perhaps now would be a good time to part, while you're not too attached to me yet." She looked up at him, and tears stood in her glowing blue eyes. "It could have been fun, Steven. I know you will have a good future. You certainly have the capacity to love. I hope that I have helped you build your confidence. You can find someone who is more your type."

"No, I don't want someone who is more my type," Steven said. He knew he sounded petulant as a small child. "I want . . . I mean . . . I am saying it all wrong! I want *you*!"

She shook her head. "Everyone always strives for the absolutes, Steven. That's one thing I have discovered over the years. I will always be here. I'll be part of the girl that you fall in love with. I'll be part of the children that she bears for you. I'm part of your parents, and I'm

part of you, forever. It's not just ancestor worship that
your parents have taught you: it's the worship of the
infinite, that which is greater than all of us."

"I know," he said grumpily, realizing how silly he must
look, naked on a cloud, arguing with a dream. "But I liked
it when it was in a package I could put my arms around."

"You're a programmer," she said, with a twinkle. "Figure out how to do it, and you'll make countless people
happy. After all, isn't everything a microcosm of the
macrocosm?"

"That's not how it works," he said, peevishly.

She shrugged. "I'm not the goddess of wisdom. I'm
the goddess of love. Anyway, tell your mother she wins.
That will make her feel good. And I promise, pretty soon
I'll send you someone who's right for you. Have I ever
lied to you?"

"No," Steven said, feeling despondent. "You never
have. You've been everything to me, and I love you
for that."

"There, you see? I've been a good influence on you.
But I'd keep that from your mother."

She put her hands on his cheeks and kissed him
deeply. Before he knew it, he was fully clad, standing in
the middle of the quad, and she was gone.

Steven felt sorry for himself. He stayed in bed for the
next day and a half, playing video games and refusing to
answer the phone.

Friday rolled around again. He went home to dinner.
All he could do was pick at his food, even when his
mother nudged the nicest of the dumplings onto his
plate. Father tried to talk computer games with him, but
he just couldn't muster any interest at all. He kept thinking about the most beautiful girl in the world—in any
world.

His aunt called during dessert. Mother took the call in
the kitchen, but he could still hear her.

"Oh, yes, he was dating that goddess, but he broke up
with her. Even the divine ones are not good enough for
my son!"

"She is right, you know," Father said, busy with his

food. He seemed sad that Aphrodite was not there, too. She had managed to liven up the family dinners so much. The room seemed colorless without her, in spite of the red walls and the kitchen god's shrine.

Steven moped back to the dorm and settled down on the rumpled couch to go over his assigned history text. Occasionally, he checked on line to see if there were any more hits on FindingLove.com. He wondered whether he was going to have to give in and go out with one of the girls Mother kept wanting to fix him up with. But who could possibly measure up to the Goddess of Love?

A knock sounded at the door. Steven couldn't be bothered to get up from the couch.

"It's open!" he shouted.

The door swung wide. A girl lounged there, holding up the door frame with an elbow. Her hair was the color of wheatfields, and her eyes were sky blue in a pink-cheeked heart-shaped face. Her figure, though not spectacular by Aphrodite's standards, was pretty good. She wore a diaphanous blouse striped like a rainbow, swirling down over a blue skirt the color of her eyes. It had an intact hem. In all the time he had dated Aphrodite, he had never seen a whole hem. Her gold sandals were tiny, containing carefully manicured little feet. Steven jumped out of his couch and held the door for her.

She smiled up at him. The top of her head was only as high as his chin. "Hi."

"Uh, hi," he said.

"My cousin Aphrodite sent me. She said you really know how to treat a girl." She smiled and looked up at him through thick golden lashes. "My name's Iris. May I come in?"

SUBTLE INTERPRETATIONS

Kristine Kathryn Rusch

Kristine Kathryn Rusch is a best-selling, award-winning writer. She writes brilliantly in multiple genres, and under more than one name, as well. Her work has won awards in a variety of languages. Most recently, her novella, "Diving into the Wreck" (*Asimov's*, December 2005) won the prestigious UPC award given in Spain.

Lieutenant Richard Cooper found her in the Paris International Telephone Exchange. She sat in the large hot room, her black hair pulled into a bun, legs crossed at the ankle and off to the side like the photographic models he'd met. She leaned forward as she spoke into the microphone, plugging metal edged prongs into lit areas of the electronic board.

The room was a cacophony of women's voices, something he hadn't heard for years, that high-pitched, warm sound of dozens of women speaking all at once. It didn't matter that they spoke mostly in French; what mattered was the musicality and softness of their voices, the way that they all put a hand to the headphones as if adjusting an earring.

He had come to interview the best among them, the ones who could handle most international calls as they came in, switching from French to Russian to English without a breath, helping the unseen caller on the other end get connected with the correct exchange or the right person.

He watched from the supervisor's booth, just above the main doors. Even the window looking down was hot. Fans worked the back and on the ceiling. The rooms below had no ventilation, but they were where the equipment still was, in a basement, protecting everything from bombs that had never come.

Most of the women below were matronly, and those that weren't looked hard, as if nothing could surprise them. Their clothing, which ten years before would have been fashionable, was worn and thin, their shoes so old that they looked scuffed even from a distance.

"Let's see how good they are," he said to Yves LeRoi, the man who ran this part of the exchange. "All except that one."

He pointed at the woman he'd been staring at. She sat in the exact center, and unlike the other women, she did not look tired. Her touch on the headset was light, her movements economical. She might have been a bit too thin, but her face hadn't hardened into a mask of suppressed hate.

"Mademoiselle Renard?" he asked. "But she is the best. I believed you would want her. She is fluent in six languages that I know of, and perhaps more."

Cooper sighed. His boss, Lieutenant Command Alfred Steer, had told him repeatedly that finding the best translator was imperative. All other considerations had to be set aside, even if he felt the woman was too beautiful to live among GIs for several months.

"All right then," he said. "I'll listen to her as well."

Cooper, Steer, and a handful of deputies had only a few weeks to find the best translators in Europe. And not just translators who worked well on paper, but translators who could handle simultaneous translation from one language into another.

They were conducting an experiment on the world's largest stage, the International Military Tribunal at Nuremberg. The man in charge of setting up the tribunal,

Judge Robert Jackson, had somehow gotten IBM to speed up production on its experimental simultaneous-translation equipment. The equipment would be tested—in action—at the trial of high level Germans for war crimes.

Although many were disappointed that Hitler wasn't in the dock—the coward had killed himself as Allied troops entered Berlin—many of his henchmen were. From Hermann Göring, Hitler's number two man, to Field Marshall Wilhelm Keitel, the chief of staff of the German Armed Forces, every surviving Nazi leader would sit in that courtroom and answer for his crimes.

And in order for this trial to work, the judges, from all the Allied countries, would have to hear translations in their own language, while the defendants would have to hear the same words in German. Cooper was told to be prepared for every possible European language, just in case the witnesses spoke something other than French, German, English, Russian or Italian.

The task, when Steer explained it, seemed impossible. Particularly with only a few weeks to find the right candidates. Especially after the debacle at the League of Nations in Geneva. Steer and Cooper had gone there themselves, expecting to find the best translators in all of Europe.

Instead, they found dusty old men who hadn't lifted their heads out of texts in decades. One of the reasons the League failed, in Cooper's opinion, was that everyone had to present a position paper, wait until it was translated, and then conduct questions and answers on the page so that the translators would have time to find the exact right word.

As Jackson had told them before they left, Steer and Cooper didn't have time to find the right word. But they had to find the best verbal translators. Because if the translations were even slightly incorrect, the trial would fail. The defendants could claim that they had not heard the same evidence as everyone else.

Before he sent them to Nuremberg, he would see if they had the basic skills to translate on the fly. Once in

the city, they'd be tested for accuracy and speed. He just
had to find the most able linguists in all of Europe.

He had been given this assignment because his German was good, but his French was excellent. He understood a small amount of Italian and had gained enough
Russian to make casual conversation. He knew a smattering of other languages.

But he had failed one of the early translation tests.
His mind froze—literally froze—when he had to speak
in one language while listening to another.

He knew how hard this task would be. He also knew
that a war crimes trial would include testimony he did
not want his mother or his sister to hear. And then there
was the problem of Nuremberg itself, a ruined city filled
with starving people, too many lonely GIs, and not
enough women.

That was why he didn't want the young beauty to join
the team. He would discourage her if he could.

His early interviews went well. LeRoi had shown him
to a small room, several floors above the international
exchange. Someone had brought a carafe of American
coffee and a single cup for him. A nearby table held an
assortment of cheeses and baked goods.

He made use of all the refreshments during the interviews.

The interviews happened individually. So he had time
to ask each woman to sit, make herself comfortable, tell
him about herself. After three interviews, he also started
with a speech, telling the women he didn't care how they
spent the war. He was tired of hearing made-up tales of
being in the Resistance. If every French woman had been
in the Resistance, France would not have surrendered.
The country would have been able to fight no matter
what the politicians did.

A lot of the women had lost their husbands or sons
and wanted to get out of Paris. Most hadn't been able
to leave before the city surrendered because they lacked
the money. They had some now, but they had no idea
where to go. The entire world was different, and they no
longer knew where they belonged.

Some of the best candidates turned him down instantly when they heard that they had to go to Germany. (*I have had enough of the Boche*, they'd say. *I do not care what kind of wages you pay.*)

But others lit up when they heard they'd make double, sometimes triple what they were making now. Their food would be provided and so would their accommodations. For many of these women, the job he offered seemed like the answer to their prayers.

He had a hard time explaining that they'd be tested in Nuremberg and sent home if they couldn't perform the task to Leon Dostert's specifications. Dostert was the man in charge of this program. He was an Army colonel who had been one of Eisenhower's chief interpreters during the war. That was the unusual part of this program. People from all branches of the military had come together, brought for their talents instead of following some personnel quota.

Colonel Dostert was trying to convince Cooper to reup, just to have him on hand in case the translation program failed. Cooper couldn't imagine himself whispering in the ear of some French journalist and had delayed making a decision until this task was done.

Part of his brain played with the notion as he listened to the women's enthusiasm. He understood the ones who said no. But the ones who said yes suddenly looked younger, as if he had given them hope.

He had just gotten up to get a brioche and pour himself more coffee when she came in. LeRoi had called her Mademoiselle Renard.

Cooper set the brioche back on the tray and went to his notes. Her first name was Nathalie, which did not suit her. He would have given her a more exotic name, something that sounded a lot more foreign.

She did not smile when she saw him. Instead, she nodded just once and waited for him to offer her a seat. Then she slipped into the chair, folding her legs to one side as she had done in the exchange.

"I'm Robert Cooper," he said, deciding to leave off his rank. His uniform made his position clear. He was an American, and he was in the military. She didn't need to know more. "I am with the International Military Court in Nuremberg. Have you heard of it?"

"I have been following the news," she said stiffly. He wondered for a moment if French was her native language. But her name suggested that it was.

He did not have complete dossiers on any of the women. They would provide as much information as they could, but on some levels, he would just have to trust.

"We are in need of translators," he said, settling into his speech. He picked up his pen, pulled the paper with her name on it aside, and made a line, as he had done with all the others. "What languages do you speak fluently?"

"I do not know," she said. "Many."

He had never had that answer before. He frowned at her. She had folded her hands across her shabby dress. She was smaller than she had looked from above, her features delicate. Her eyebrows, plucked to a thin line, swept upward, and she had clearly replenished her make-up before coming into the room.

"How many?" he asked.

"I do not know," she said again. "I have a gift."

He wanted to roll his eyes. All interpreters had a gift for language or they would not be able to do their job. "Give me a guess."

She shrugged one shoulder. "Ten? Twenty? I am not sure."

Either she didn't understand him or he was asking the wrong question. He switched to German. "Tell me which languages you speak fluently."

"I do not know," she said in that language.

"The key word," he said in English, "is 'fluently.' I need translators who know all sorts of idioms, and have large vocabularies."

"I love words," she said in American English, the accent Midwestern and strong. "I remember every one I have heard."

"Then why is your speech so formal?" he asked in French.

"Because," she said in the same language, "this is an interview. Would you like me to be less formal?"

"Yes," he said in Russian. "Tell me your name."

"Technically," she said in that language, "you just told me to 'give' you my name. It is an American construction, not a Russian one."

"Your name," he said in Polish.

"Nathalie," she said in Polish, after a slight pause. Her pronunciation of her own name did not have the soft "th" that the French version had. It had a harder "t," just like it should. "It is on that paper before you."

He didn't have any more languages to test her with. But he wasn't supposed to test. He was supposed to get simple answers to simple questions.

He decided to move on. He asked in English, "Where were you born?"

"Paris," she said.

"Here, then," he said in French.

"I've never been to Paris, Texas," she said in American English. The accent was Texan this time. "I believe it's the only other Paris on the map, but I could be wrong."

The hair rose on the back of his neck. Her accents—at least for American English—were uncanny. He had never heard anything like it.

"You can mimic," he said in English. "What other accents can you do?"

"In English?" she asked.

"Sure," he said.

"I do prefer the British upper class," she said with a posh accent. "Bu' coc'ney suits me just fine, guv'nor."

His breath caught. "And in French?"

"Well, everyone knows there is Parisian French," she said in French, using a refined Paris accent. "But most nonnatives do not realize that French has many different accents as well. And variations. Would you like to hear Canadian, which many of my people say is not French? Or Cajun, which is old bastardized French or perhaps—"

"Enough." He was unnerved.

She leaned back in her chair, subdued. As she spoke

of the languages and accents, she had seemed animated
for the first time. Her eyes had sparkled, and what he
had initially thought was rouge was actually a natural red
that wisped across her high cheekbones.

"I did not mean to frighten you," she said, in that
same formal French she had started with. "For this reason, I do not tell people of my gift."

"Monsieur LeRoi says you are his most talented
operator."

"He believes I have learned phrases in various languages. I have not disabused him."

Cooper set down his pen and templed his fingers,
banging the tips against his chin. "Why are you telling
me, then?"

"Because I am tired of saying *Buena Sierra! Guten Tag!
Es posible a ayudarle?* I would like important work."

"Helping people place calls is not important?" Cooper asked.

"Not like during the war. Then I thought each call might
be, as you say in English, life or death." She switched from
French to English with the word "English."

"Have you family here?" he asked.

"Not any more." Her voice was soft. One woman before her had burst into tears when he asked that
question.

"What other jobs have you had?" he asked.

"This," she said. "I started for Monsieur LeRoi when
I was eighteen. I told him I had a gift. He did not care.
He needed women to risk their lives in a place that might
become a target if the Allies had decided to bomb
France."

He had heard this before as well—communications were
always vulnerable to the bombings—but he also knew
that no one had targeted Paris, nor did anyone want to.
Venice had been the same way, a pristine island in a sea
of rubble.

"How old are you now?" he asked.

"I will be twenty-five in December," she said.

He had the odd sense that she was lying. But she had
at least told him her age. So many of the other French

women hadn't, slipping instead into that coy flirta-
tiousness that was a little too sexual for his hick American tastes.

"They tell us the trial will end in December," he said.
"But I don't believe it. I think it could take a long time.
My boss says that translators must prepare to be gone
for six months, minimum. Would that be hard for you?"

She shook her head.

"On the other hand," he said, "we might send you
back after two weeks. We have to test your skills, you
see. We—"

"Is that not what you just did?" she asked.

"No," he said. "You'll be tested in your ability to
speak one language while . . ."

He went through the speech again. It was as if he were
a record stuck in a groove. He could probably say that
speech in his sleep, in both English and French. Maybe
he should try it in German once or twice, just to mix
things up.

When he finished, he said, "Does that sound like
something you want to try?"

She nodded.

"Then you have to tell me which languages you would
like to be tested in."

"Whichever ones you need," she said.

He sighed. "I have to write something down. Prefera-
bly the names of the languages. We'll start with French."

She smiled and watched as he wrote *French* and
English.

"If you want to try other languages, tell Colonel Dostert in Nuremberg when you show up for the test, okay?"

"Okay," she said, and this time, he heard his own Midwestern roots in her voice.

"Let me tell you the pay schedule, and then ask a few
more questions." He tapped the pen against the page.
"And I have to say, if I feel like you're toying with me,
I won't send you to Nuremberg."

"I am not a cat," she said. "I do not toy with anything."

* * *

Yet by the end of the interview, he wondered. He still had that odd sense that she was lying to him. After she left, he sent for LeRoi.

"Do you have any papers for her?" Cooper asked. "Some kind of file?"

"I have her work records. Hours, pay records, that sort of thing." LeRoi sat in the chair the women had sat in. He looked smaller than they had, and older, as if the war had diminished him.

"What about a resume? Some kind of application? Any personal history?"

LeRoi smiled. The smile was slow and knowing. "You are interested in her."

Cooper was, much as he didn't want to be. He took nonfraternization rules seriously. Or he had, until he saw her.

"For our project, yes. But she's not being forthcoming. I need to know how many languages she speaks, how old she really is, and where she comes from."

"I do not have such papers," LeRoi said. "I have not found a language she cannot speak. I send for her if someone is having trouble, and within a moment, she can resolve the problem. She is truly gifted."

"That's what she said." Cooper tapped his pen on the page. "If you don't have any background on her, how did you come to hire her?"

"I had a sign, asking for multilingual employees. She came in and dazzled me."

"By talking in half a dozen languages," Cooper said dryly.

"I could not find one she did not know. I even sent for one of our older employees. He had been a missionary in China and spoke some of that language."

The Chinese spoke many languages, but Cooper did not correct LeRoi.

"She was able to answer him. Then they had a discussion, until his Chinese wore out, not hers. I hired her on the spot."

Interesting. Cooper kept tapping his pen. He was so used to the Navy. All the regulations and approvals had become part of his life. And he was becoming more and more paranoid. He wanted everyone checked out. After being in Germany for two months, he found himself believing that everyone could be a spy. Even though the German government—Hitler's government—was gone, there were the Russians. Even though they were allies, he hated them, every one he'd met, with a passion that surprised him.

"What do you know about her then?" Cooper asked. "The personal things."

LeRoi smiled that odd smile again. "She lives near the Sorbonne. She lives alone, so far as I can tell, and never speaks of family. Nor do young men come for her, and she does not participate in those discussions about husbands lost at the front. For all her languages, she says little to the other women here. She keeps to herself."

"What happened to her family?" Cooper asked.

LeRoi shrugged. "What has happened to most, I suppose. Even for France, it has been a difficult few years."

Cooper didn't reply to that. Paris stood. The French countryside was lovely. Families escaped or they survived under the Vichy regime. A few got caught resisting. Some became sport for the Nazis.

And, he supposed, hundreds—maybe thousands—of French Jews were sent to the camps. He did not know and he did not ask.

He tried not to talk about the camps. He had been to Bergen Belsen just before going to Nuremberg, trying to get statements from the survivors.

He doubted he would ever speak of the camps again.

"*Monsieur*?" LeRoi leaned forward.

Apparently Cooper had been silent longer than he thought. "I am supposed to take the best candidates with me. Do you know any reason why she shouldn't go into Germany?"

"No one should go to Germany," LeRoi said. "It should rot. But beside that? She is my best employee. If you do not want her, I shall gladly keep her. She is a gem."

"She is, isn't she?" Cooper said. "She truly is."

*   *   *

The gem stood outside the Telephone Exchange as he left. She was smoking a cigarette and looking down the street for the bus. He looked too. It was only a few blocks away.

"Have you had dinner?" he asked.

She whirled, as if she hadn't realized he was there. Then she blinked, and he thought for a moment that she didn't understand him.

That would be impossible, though, right? Maybe she hadn't heard him.

"Dinner?" she repeated, just as he was about to ask again.

"Yes." He regretted the invitation now. He hadn't asked any of the other women.

It was just another sign that he was tired, tired of the rules, tired of not having a normal life.

She smiled. Her entire face transformed. She was, without a doubt, the most beautiful woman he had ever seen.

"I would love to," she said. She pinched out her cigarette, then carefully set it in a small metal cigarette case that she kept in her purse.

Suddenly he wasn't sure if she was coming to dinner because she wanted to be with him or because she hadn't had a decent meal in months.

It probably didn't matter. He shouldn't have asked in the first place.

He took her arm and together they walked down the street to a small restaurant that had somehow survived all the deprivations. He had loved this restaurant before the war and had been pleased that it was still here.

She stopped at the door.

"It's all right," he said. "I know it's expensive, but the meal is courtesy of the American government."

She shook her head. "That's not it. This was a Boche favorite. I . . . I cannot get past the sense that it is somehow tainted."

"Is there someplace else?" he asked. "I'd be happy to learn of a new restaurant."

She straightened her shoulders as if that made her stronger. "All of the good ones, they are Boche favorites. I must get past this."

Then she pushed open the door and stepped inside.

After the remains of daylight on the street, the interior seemed dark. As he followed her down the stairs that led to the dining room, he too felt a bit of unease.

He blamed it on his actions—his request for this date—because he didn't want to believe the Germans could have tainted everything as she had said. If that were the case, nothing that survived had any value at all.

A maitre d', stiffly formal in his tuxedo, led them to a table in the back. The table was around a corner and, like most in this place, was very private.

He handed them the menus, advised Cooper on wines as if he were the most ignorant man on the planet, and Cooper smiled because he couldn't help himself. Before the war, the French had treated Americans like bumpkins, but after the liberation, Americans had become gods. He was happy to return to bumpkin status. It meant, in some places at least, things were returning to normal.

Nathalie stroked the linen tablecloth as if it were made of gold. Then she fingered the crystal water glass.

"We can still go somewhere else," Cooper said.

"No." She picked up the glass and took a sip. "It is nice to know such things survived. So much did not."

"Your family?" He hadn't meant to ask the question so crudely, and yet he had, proving that he was an American bumpkin.

She nodded her head once. "My family."

"Were they in Paris?"

She raised her chin. "Until the trains took them."

"You're Jewish?" He couldn't quite rid his voice of the surprise he felt. She didn't look Jewish. And then he cursed that thought. It was the kind of thought that led to the walking skeletons that he had seen—the very idea that someone's religion could be seen just by the shape of their face. Sometimes, he felt, he was no better than the men he had defeated.

"Would it matter?" she asked, apparently catching his tone.

"Not to me," he said. "But the Tribunal might be hard for you. The war crimes these men are accused of include what happened to people who boarded those trains."

All the beauty leached from her face. What remained was a hatred so deep he nearly slid his chair backwards.

"I am aware of that," she said.

"Can you faithfully translate what's said? No embellishments, no changes?"

"Of course." Her tone was flat as well. He wondered if he was hearing her real accent for the first time.

"What about testimony about the camps? I've been there. I've taken some. It's—"

He stopped, and waved a hand in lieu of finishing, as his stomach turned.

"I am not delicate," she said.

"I know," he said. "I'm not either. But this . . ."

She shrugged. "Humans have always been brutal, no?"

A waiter arrived with their wine. The rituals—opening the bottle, sniffing the cork, taking a sip—prevented Cooper from answering. He wasn't sure he had an answer anyway.

"I can do your job," she said as the waiter left. "In fact, you want me."

He did want her. He touched her hand lightly. Her skin was smooth and warm. She glanced at him as if his fingertips had given her a small shock.

He certainly felt that way.

"This job will be hard," he said. "I don't want it to harm you."

Her smile was bitter. "I have already been harmed. At worst, I shall be reminded on a daily basis. As you Americans say, so what? So many others no longer have days. It is better to live and to be aware of the living, is it not, than to hide as if the past has never happened?"

He wasn't sure. But for this moment, he was willing to go with the thought, to believe what she said.

As the waiter returned, this time with menus, Cooper steered the conversation away from the job and the war, finding, to his surprise, that she loved music as much as he did—all kinds ("particularly," she said, "your American jazz"), and that she was wider read than he could ever imagine being.

He had never met a woman with such breadth of knowledge, particularly on the things that interested him, and it fascinated him.

She fascinated him.

They talked for hours, and then he walked her home. The student district, once the site of protests and unusual political attitudes, seemed subdued and quiet. The narrow cobblestone streets still had smoke stains from the fighting that occurred here between the Resistance and the Germans as news of the Allied approach reached Paris.

She lived on a charming side street, the walls of the buildings laced with flowering vines. Elaborate ironwork covered the doors. She stopped in front of one, whose ironwork imitated the creeping vines nearby.

He started to take her hand, about to give her a friendly American handshake, when she raised her head to his. Her mouth was small and perfect, her cheeks still flushed, her eyes so dark they seemed infinite. Before he could stop himself, he dipped his head.

She lifted her chin ever so slightly, and their lips brushed. Then he pulled her to him and kissed her. She slipped her arms around his back, holding him against her, and deepened the kiss. He felt dizzy and aroused at the same time, barely able to contain himself.

"Upstairs?" she whispered, but he wasn't sure which language she used.

"Yes," he answered in English, and they could barely stop kissing long enough for her to fumble with the lock. He half-carried her up a flight of stairs, and then another. She giggled against his mouth when he tripped, catching himself on the plaster walls.

"One more," she whispered, and he hoped she was referring to the flights of stairs, not to the kisses.

She pulled him up the last flight, then pushed open an old door and led him inside an attic room, decorated with more flowering plants than he'd ever seen inside. They crowded the two windows, spilled over the tables and chairs, and nearly covered the floor.

She unfolded the couch into a bed, then grabbed him by his belt and yanked him onto the lumpy mattress.

And there, surrounded by the scent of her and flowers he couldn't name, he fell in love.

He barely made it to the seven a.m. check-in breakfast. He didn't have time to go back to his hotel room. His uniform was wrinkled, his hair still wet.

She hadn't had a shower, just one of those silly hand-held things he'd seen all over Europe. She'd had to help him turn it on, and her presence in the tiny bathroom had delayed him even more.

He had promised to find her for lunch. He would meet her just outside the Telephone Exchange. He already knew where he would take her.

The meeting went longer than he planned. It took place in the hotel's breakfast nook. When Cooper arrived, he got a knowing look from Steer. Cooper's own assistant, Andrew Gabler, raised his eyebrows in surprise. Gabler had gotten the fraternization lecture from Cooper. He felt his cheeks redden.

Cooper ate a soft-boiled egg and too many pastries as he told the other men about the women at the exchange. Then he handed his notes to Steer, who would give them to the head of the Paris unit to compare to known troublemakers.

Cooper's assignment this morning was, of all things, at the main Catholic diocese. Some of the priests, Gabler had learned, had linguistic abilities that extended beyond French, Latin, and ancient Greek. Cooper was to check that out.

The assignment embarrassed him almost as much as his appearance. Even though he wasn't Catholic, the last place he wanted to go to was a religious setting. He felt distinctly profane at the moment.

When breakfast finished, he hurried to his room,

changed, and came back down. Gabler was waiting for him, that smile still on his face.

"Do I know her?" he asked.

Cooper shook his head.

"Do I want to?" Gabler's tone was suggestive.

Cooper felt a surge of anger, but pushed it back. He understood why Gabler had made that assumption. So many women all over Europe were poor, and many of them used the only thing they had left to make money.

"She's not like that," Cooper said.

"My," Gabler said. "*C'est l'amour?* So soon?"

"Shut up," Cooper said, and headed off to church.

One of the priests spoke excellent Greek. At least, Cooper thought it was excellent, but his own Greek was terrible, so he needed help making the determination.

An hour before lunch, he stopped at headquarters to request his afternoon assignment and to get someone else to return to the diocese.

Cooper stepped inside military headquarters to the clatter of typewriters. Secretaries hurried back and forth, carrying messages and looking important. Men sat outside doors, hat in hand, waiting for meetings.

It almost seemed as if the war were still going on.

Matt Accordino, one of the general staff headquartered here, beckoned him forward. "I vetted your list."

Cooper took a seat beside Accordino's desk, almost in the aisle. A secretary, her skirt slit on the side against regulation, brushed against him as she passed.

"And?" Cooper asked.

"You have one questionable on here." Accordino pushed a file forward. "You have her as Nathalie Renard."

Cooper felt cold. "What's her real name?"

"Wish I could tell you. She went by half a dozen names. Renard is just one of them. It's actually one of the early ones. She must have gone back to it."

"What's the problem? Was she a collaborator?"

"Just the opposite," Accordino said. "She was with the Resistance."

Cooper let out a breath he hadn't realized he was holding. "Then what's the problem?"

"Her specialty." Accordino opened the file and tapped the top page. "High-level assassination."

Cooper was reeling as he headed to the Telephone Exchange. He'd glanced through the file. He really hadn't had time to read it all, even though it was one of the most complete dossiers he'd seen outside the German high command.

Of course, he realized halfway through looking at it, it was complete because much of it had been compiled by the Germans stationed in Paris. Nathalie Renard, aka Marie Laurent aka Béatrice Brel, had murdered every single important German she had gotten close to. Calculated murders, all with different weapons, most usually done up close.

The Germans had no pictures of her, but the Americans found one when they arrived because she had dated an intelligence officer briefly in Brussels. Apparently she traveled all over the French-speaking world, trying to cozy up to Nazis and assassinate them.

She succeeded more than she failed. She had moved up to high-value targets by the end. The one she missed, the one she claimed to regret the most, was Göring. Her attempt on his life was the only failure she would admit to.

Göring. Who was now on trial in Nuremberg for crimes against humanity.

His death would not be a great loss. His death in custody of the Allies as he was about to go to trial would be an international scandal.

She was waiting outside the exchange, smoking the second half of that cigarette. When she saw him, she tossed the butt onto the sidewalk and ground it under her heel.

She did not smile. She seemed to sense immediately that something was wrong.

"Did it not go well?" she asked in very formal English.

"Well enough," he said.

"Are you in trouble for me?" It was the first linguistic mistake he'd heard from her. It surprised him, and it made him wonder if she had sensed his nervousness.

"You mean for being with you?" he asked.

"Yes."

He leaned against a lamppost, his back to traffic coming up the road. Passersby would think he was flirting with her and most likely avoid him. The post put him in an oddly vulnerable position, but he kept it, partly because he wanted to see her face and partly because he didn't want to talk about this anywhere that they could be overhead.

"If I took you to Nuremberg," he said, his voice deliberately low. She had to lean in to hear him, "how long would it take you to murder Hermann Göring?"

She blanched, then turned her head. She fumbled in her purse for a moment, her hands shaking.

"What makes you think I would?"

The sentence didn't cover her, but it bought her time. He knew that and was surprised that she uttered it, that she stayed rather than taking off down the sidewalk.

"Heinrich Jessler, Joachim Mauser, and Otto van Kleghaurn."

She closed her eyes, then let out a small sigh.

"Or had you turned your attention to the Allies? Was I supposed to give you entry? Has someone hired you to disrupt the proceedings?"

Her eyes opened as color rose on her cheeks. "You came to me. You solicited me. I have done nothing. I did not know who you were or what you wanted. I would never kill anyone who was not a Nazi. You know that. You have to know that."

Midway through that speech, she had switched to colloquial French, and her accent became strongly Parisian. He was hearing her own accent for the first time. Her true voice.

And she was worried about what he thought. She was angry at him.

Could she be that good an actress? Or did she care about him too?

"But you weren't going to say no to the opportunity," he said. "If you could have murdered Göring, you would have."

"Your Tribunal will hang them, won't they?" She snapped her purse shut and pushed it up her arm to her elbow. "You wouldn't need me."

"We hang only the guilty ones."

"They're Boche," she said. "They're all guilty."

His heart was pounding hard. A few people passing on the street glanced at them, but no one stopped for long. If someone came to the bus stop, Cooper waved them on.

"So, in an international tribunal, with well-respected judges and jurists from all over the civilized world, you would act as judge, jury, and executioner."

"I see the papers. You have your own executioner."

"Only if the prisoners are found guilty," Cooper said again.

"They will all be found guilty."

He shook his head. "This is not a show trial. They might not be. We're stressing fairness. You know this."

"I do not believe it." She raised her chin. "I would have done you a good job."

"Killing the prisoners."

"Translating their words," she hissed.

"Tell me," he said. "How did you do it? Jessler and von Kleghaurn had guards standing only a few feet away from you. They saw no weapons."

Her skin was mottled. Tears lined her eyes. "Last night, you said we had something special. Last night, you said I was different from anyone else."

He nodded.

"How can you ask me?"

"I've asked you many things you haven't answered," he said. "Answer me this one."

She crossed her arms. "The Germans, they have killed my people since they found us. And then they made our stories theirs, so that the entire world would find us."

He shook his head. "What?"

"You asked if I was a Jew. I am not. Nor am I a

Gypsy or any other race that is somehow unpure to those Nordic bastards. My people are older."

He didn't know of any people older than the Jews, but his knowledge of history was limited.

"I'm still not following."

"You've heard of us," she said. "You read the stories. The Grimm Brothers, no? You've read them in translation."

"You're a wicked stepmother?" he asked.

"*Merde*," she said. "You call it Faerie. You have heard of Faerie, have you not? My people are nearly gone. A few have hidden, many have been deported and murdered, never fighting back, because we were raised that we would lose our magic if we fought."

She was now leaning so close to him that he could feel her breath on his cheek.

"But that is a lie, a lie to keep us from becoming the creatures that frightened your people in the first place. When we use our magic for harm, we become stronger. I have more magic now than I did at the beginning of the war. At first, I could only use magic for languages. Now I can do many things. Many unusual things."

He was pressed against the pole. Part of him wanted to stay and hear her out, while another part wanted to flee those dark eyes.

"How would I kill the Nazi butcher Hermann Göring? Like I killed the others. I would take his life from him with a slight touch, pull it out and extinguish it, so that no one would ever find its like again."

Cooper's mouth was dry. "You have to be close."

"I have to touch him," she said. "I had to touch all of them."

And then she shuddered.

"Like you touched me?" he asked.

Her head tilted slightly. The hair fell away from her ears. They rose into slight points. He hadn't noticed that before.

"What do you mean?"

"If you can take, were you then giving so I felt strongly about you? So I'd take you to Nuremberg?"

She closed her eyes and backed away. Then she took a deep breath, opened her eyes and faced him.

"What was between us was real," she said. "I did not make it up."

"Not even to finish your assignment."

"It was not an assignment," she snapped. "It was revenge. I wanted them all dead. I wanted them all to die as horribly as my family did. As my friends. Can't you understand that?"

The pole was gouging into his back. He had seen what remained, what passed for life in those places. He could understand it, perhaps better than anyone else.

"If they had magic," he said, "why couldn't they get out?"

"I don't know," she said. "I expect some of them tried."

"And succeeded?"

She shrugged. "I will never know. Even if they lived, if they did not use violence, then they will not seek me out. I'm tainted now. I will be alone from now on."

He reached out. She watched as if she wasn't sure what he would do.

He wasn't sure until he took her hand in his shaking fingers.

"It's war," he said. "We do what we must in war. Surely they understand that."

"We are forbidden to fight for any reason," she said. "There are other ways to avoid capture, we're told. Other ways to avoid the violence."

'You don't believe it."

"Do you?" she asked. "Do you think this trial of yours will stop other criminals from trying to take over the world? Do you think this is anything but civilized revenge?"

He'd been trying not to think about it, but it nagged at him. It had been nagging at him from the start, getting worse at the camps, and made him wonder why someone didn't just shoot all the German leaders and have done with it.

"I've been trying to decide whether or not to stay," he said.

"In Paris?" she asked, with just a bit of hope in her voice. Just a bit, so small he wouldn't have heard it if he hadn't train himself to listen to every inflection in every speech.

"In the military," he said. "I can re-up for two more years."

"Why would you?"

"Civilized revenge."

Her hand slipped from his. He caught it again.

"But I'm tired," he said. "Finding translators could be my last assignment."

"Then you would go home."

He shook his head. "I don't really have one. I haven't lived anywhere longer than three months for the past ten years."

"But your family?"

"My parents," he said. "They don't need me. They have other children. They would be content to hear every now and then."

"So there is no place for you either," she said.

"I used to think maybe a university. I could teach languages and linguistic theory."

"It would be a good life."

"But why would they want a man who has done the things I have?"

"What have you done?" she asked.

"I have a gift for languages," he said, mimicking her phrase. "What do men with that gift do?"

"Listen," she said.

"And occasionally make people shut up."

She frowned, as if she didn't understand him. Then she laughed. The laugh surprised him. He had just confessed something to her he had told no one else, and she laughed at him.

"We are the same then," she said.

"No," he said. "I wish I could use touch. You have more finesse."

She stopped laughing, her smile fading. "You will not take me to Nuremberg."

"The war is over," he said. "I could stay here. With you."

"And what would we do?"

"Besides what we did last night?" he asked.

She nodded.

"We would listen," he said.

"And sometimes make people shut up?"

"I hope not," he said. "I hope it never comes to that again."

He kissed her. She kissed him back. Then she pulled away. "But humans have always been brutal, no?"

"Even when they fight for the right things," he said. "Are you human?"

"In all ways that matter," she said.

He nodded, not entirely understanding her. But, he just realized, he was going to take the time to find out what she meant. He was going back to headquarters and submit his resignation papers.

Finding the translators had been his last official job.

He would stay in Paris, with her, until he knew what was going to happen next.

But he knew whatever happened next, it would be touched by a very subtle magic.

They would interpret it together.

CHOOP

Nancy Springer

Nancy Springer is closing in on: (1) time to receive Social Security, and (2) the fifty-book milestone, having written just about that many novels for adults, young adults and children, in genres including mythological fantasy, magical realism, contemporary fiction, suspense and mystery. Among other honors, Springer has won two Edgar Allan Poe awards from the Mystery Writers of America, encouraging her most recent project: a children's series, *The Enola Holmes Mysteries*, featuring Sherlock Holmes's neglected but resourceful much younger sister, whose first name backward spells "alone." Springer is happy to report that "alone" is *not* a description of her own circumstances as she continues to enjoy the daily weirdness of life and writing, and to add that, despite her mysterious activities, the creation of fantasy stories remains her first love.

No weirder than any of the other men she had met at singles dances, Mandy reminded herself, facing him across the restaurant table. So far there had been the Harley-obsessed motorcyclist with half a head, the seminary professor who wouldn't kiss but phoned at two a.m. to discuss the Kama Sutra, the ex-cop impotent since he'd given back his gun, the guy with a big butt who had turned out to be a transsexual. What the heck—to a woman starting all over again at age fifty the whole world was surreal anyway, so what difference did it make that this date was almost certain to be another doozey? An ectomorphic thirty-something with hairless taupe skin and a pronounced underbite, tucking his napkin into his collar beneath his receding chin as he ordered "tender calves' liver in burgundy sauce" for dinner?

"I forgot you're a vegetarian," he apologized to Mandy as the server departed. "Do you mind?" He spoke with a rather charming accent she could not identify.

"Not at all," Mandy said almost truthfully. "It's mostly because of my job." She worked at A is for Animals, a small nonprofit rife with crusading vegans. "I still eat fish and, occasionally, chicken. I figure it's a free country."

"Yes, and that is what I like best about it."

"Are you from somewhere else, Choop?" Mandy knew the slender young man only by that rather peculiar moniker she had seen on his "Disco, Discover" name tag—of course he didn't know her surname either, not yet—and she couldn't place his nationality. All she knew was that he liked to dance, was very good at it, and was therefore almost certainly not from Pennsylvania.

"Oh, yes, quite." He smiled toothily, deliberately teasing her curiosity. "Many places."

"Such as?"

"Bolivia, El Salvador, Michigan, Mexico, Washington, D.C, Chile, Brazil, Dominican Republic, Texas, Panama, Puerto Rico, California, Argentina—"

Divorce had bled most nice-girl manners out of Mandy; she interrupted. "Are you an American?" She did not want to get mixed up with an illegal alien.

Choop said, "America, you know, it extends from the southernmost tip of Tierra del Fuego to far north of Hudson Bay." His heavy-lidded coal-dark eyes laughed at her.

Mandy tried again. "I mean, are you a United States citizen?"

"Better. I am an autochthon."

Undoubtedly he was playing mind games, and while she did not particularly resent his making a fool out of her—her ex-husband had already done that to death—she did wonder why this relatively young man was bothering to date her. Mandy had a realistic view of herself; what did this thirty-something want with an overweight, graying woman whose round face, all abloom with menopausal pimples, resembled a pot of geraniums?

But what the hell. It was nice to get dressed up, drape her favorite silk scarf (fuchsia, to complement the zits) around her neck and go out to dinner. As long as the guy didn't treat her like bed meat.

"All right," she said, smiling, "I'll bite: what's an autochthon?"

"An aborigine."

"Oh, that's *so* much better."

However, Mandy was able to translate "aborigine" and felt annoyed at herself for not having guessed sooner; she should have known by the almondine fold of his eyelids, by his beardless cheeks, his hawk nose and especially by his hair, so intensely black that it seemed to suck color out of his tawny skin, tingeing it gray. "You're Native American?"

"Very native indeed."

Even so, she thought, he still did not look like any other human being she had seen. Definitely not Cherokee. Maybe some exotic vanishing native from, what had he said, Bolivia?

But before she could ask what tribe, or maybe "nation" was the P.C. word, he changed the subject. "Tell me now about yourself and the animals."

"What's to tell? It's just another job, really."

"No, no." He shook his head. "To me a job is just a job—"

Chatting in the car on the way to dinner, she'd found out he'd been a wholesale mutton products salesman, an Español-Ingles translator, an inspector of ornamental trees for plum pox, a timeshare "body snatcher," a roadie for a third-rate rock band, altogether a *pateperro*—"dog foot"—one who wanders.

"—but not to you, not this job. You wear it like a crown wherever you go. Always the creature jewelry looking back at me. The golden collie brooch the first time I saw you. Tonight, the tiger cats most beautiful on your ears."

"Just ordinary tabbies." But she felt herself fingering her expensive intaglio earrings and trying not to blush, much affected by the poetry of his insight. "Thank you."

"I suspect that you wear every day the tee shirt with the picture of the dog or cat on it."

"You suspect right."

"Which do you love better, cats or dogs?"

The word "love," so effortless, impressed her even more than his accent and his exotic lineage. "I—I couldn't say; I think I love just about all animals except maybe garden slugs."

"You have many pets?"

"No, none actually, because I had to move into an apartment after—" She stopped herself; she was able to do that now, keep herself from spilling her guts about the divorce, even though it had torn her wide open. "But then I started to work at the animal shelter, and they're all my pets, my babies." Sixty homeless cats, forty stray or throwaway dogs, most of them as sweet as puppy love. A is for Animals had been her family and her sanity for the past couple of years. "The most adorable Rottweiler came in yesterday, half starved and so—so—" Trying to think of the right word, Mandy envisioned the drop-off dog's yearning yet stoical dark eyes. "So *noble*. She's been neglected, dumped, but she doesn't hold a grudge at all." Unlike certain people; Mandy hoped she would never be one of those. "It always amazes me how forgiving dogs are, and how—willing, how devoted . . ." Mandy found herself sidestepping the l-word, love. "But no matter how much Lamb has to offer—"

"The Rottweiler?"

"Yes, that's what we named her, Lamb, to show how gentle she is." All of the dogs and cats had names, photos, casebooks. A is for Animals had been founded by and was operated by an elderly woman, Betty Calhoun, a.k.a. Loony Calhooney and proud of it. Her eccentric ideas included: no cages or concrete runs; the cats lived communally in rooms with cushions, climbing apparatus, and screened-in outdoor patios; the dogs were in packs according to size, with sofas, blankets, toys, and fenced yards, free from being penned in metal crates as long as they stayed "nice." Lamb was as nice as they came. "She's a total sweetie. But she's going to be very difficult to place."

"Place?"

"Find a home for. Not many people are able to adopt big dogs. Plus, she has hip dysplasia."

"She is crippled? So what will happen to her?"

"We will keep her for as long as she needs us. We're not like those other so-called rescues. Only as a last resort, if an animal doesn't have any quality of life left at all, then we put it down."

"You mean kill it?" At her sad nod, Choop raised his heavy black eyebrows. "But only when it is sick, or old?"

Nodding again, Mandy sighed. Choop leaned toward her over the restaurant table. "It troubles you? But why? It is nature's way, is it not, that the strong shall live and the weak shall die?"

"Um, maybe, but me, I want to save them all, diabetic cats, dogs with parvo, even with distemper. It's a hard decision to let an animal go, and when we do, it's because we love them and don't want them to suffer."

"Do you love wild animals too?"

"Of course."

"That is to say you, individually?"

"Except garden slugs, like I said before."

"When the panther leaps on the deer, which one do you love, the panther or the deer?"

"I, um—"

"The panther is hungry, she has cubs to feed. But the deer cries out as the fangs break her neck."

"Um—" Something about his steady obsidian gaze shook Mandy, mixed her up like a whiskey sour, so that she felt simultaneously zing and tingle and revulsion. The question, the way he asked it, was not nearly abstract

enough, far too intense; she almost felt claws and
smelled blood.

The approach of the server saved her from response.
"Here comes our dinner."

A few moments earlier she had considered herself hungry, like the mother panther with cubs to feed, but now
she found herself picking uncertainly at her "tangy
broiled salmon cerise." Taking a bite of liver, Choop said
with zest, "I can never get enough organ meat."

Mandy murmured absently, "I must admit I sometimes
have a yen for bacon."

"It is hard to find a restaurant that serves good organ
meat."

Mandy glanced up to notice in surprise that her dinner
date had already devoured most of his large portion of
liver. He certainly ate fast, hunched over his plate, but
otherwise not lacking in table manners: no slurping or
noisy chewing. Indeed, he hardly seemed to masticate at
all. The "tender calves' liver in burgundy sauce" must
have been tender indeed, for seemingly, like a vacuum
cleaner, he sucked it down.

"What do you want to do now?" he asked her as they
left the restaurant. "See what's playing at the Cinema-
Plex?"

Usually Mandy liked to go to the movies, so her own
answer surprised her. "Nah. I don't feel like sitting
around." Something, maybe the cool yet tender night air,
maybe some courteous yet feral quality of the "autochthon" by her side, was making her restless.

"Bungee jumping?" Choop suggested.

"I don't think so!" Yet Mandy laughed easily, nothing
tight in her chest or her thoughts. She had not yet decided how to feel about this weird guy, but joking around
with him was definitely better than sitting home by
herself.

"Roller skating?"

"If I were twenty years younger."

"Tell you what." Before they reached the car, Choop

stopped and turned to face her. "Would you like to take me to meet Lamb?"

The Rottweiler? He remembered what she was called? Mandy focused on his face, although in the benighted parking lot she could not see him very well. "Do you really care about dogs all that much?" she demanded.

He replied whimsically, "My name backwards, you know, it spells Pooch."

Mandy laughed again, figured it out and said, "Not quite."

"Almost."

"What does your name mean, really?" Aborigines were supposed to have names with meanings.

"Choop Akkabra?" There, he'd told her his last name. "Why should it mean anything? What does 'Mandy' mean?"

"I've often wondered."

"It means, maybe, woman with a big heart for animals. Come on, you take me to see your babies, yes?" He handed her the car keys. That impressed her; in her experience of men it was a rare one who would voluntarily occupy the passenger seat.

"Okay," she murmured almost shyly, as if he had given her flowers.

Driving made her feel good. She actually hummed happy tunes to herself as she steered his car along dark country roads to the animal rescue where she worked. Choop was right, she did wear her employment like a crown, would willingly have spent all her time with her babies; there was no place she would rather go on a starry night than the cinder-block building isolated amid farmland so as not to disturb neighbors with stench or noise.

As Mandy pulled up to the gate, a familiar brown fetor greeted her nostrils, and all of the dogs started barking. The shelter was closed, of course, and there was no one around at this time of night, but it didn't matter; she knew the combination to the padlock.

After they had driven in and parked, she led Choop

to a back door with a machine that swallowed her employee ID card, spat it out again, and clicked the latch, admitting her and her guest to a utility room.

"Um, listen," she told him, realizing suddenly that she should brief him, "you don't mind walking into a whole bunch of dogs at once?" She had to stand close to him, almost shouting, to be heard over a bedlam of barking from just beyond the utility room's several doors. "Let them sniff you, but the more you ignore them at first, the less they'll bother you. If you don't want them to jump on you, just shove them away, and otherwise don't respond. Don't yell or sweet talk. Just stand there like nothing's happening. Don't stare any of them in the eyes; that's a challenge. After a few minutes they'll settle down, and then you can make friends with them."

His toothy, overshot grin flashed in the shadows. "Not to worry. I like dogs."

"Okay." Briefly she considered whether she should take him into the small-dog area first, but she dismissed the thought; there was no danger, really—none of her babies had ever bitten anybody that she knew of—and moreover, all of a sudden Choop sounded a bit cocky. Something in his tone repelled her, making her hope he might step in dog doo or otherwise embarrass himself. She found herself turning away from him and telling herself that, after all, it was the Rottweiler, Lamb, they had come to see, and Lamb was of course in the room with the large-dog pack. Might as well take him on in.

The dogs' excited clamor crescendoed as she turned the doorknob. Reaching in to switch on the overhead light, Mandy called cheerfully, "Shut up, guys!" as she stepped into the canine maelstrom.

Her greeting was automatic and rhetorical; the dogs would not shut up. German shepherds, Labs, Dobermans, Goldies and mutts indefinable would leap in ecstatic greeting while continuing to bark, bark, bark—

Not so.

They gave all at once a canine cry, yelp, yip, as if hit by cars—or clubs—that yowl wrenched Mandy's heart. "What's the matter?" she exclaimed, standing open-mouthed inside the doorway, as Great Danes, Pit Bulls, and all her other big babies scattered with their tails between their legs to hide behind the furniture, cowering against the farthest walls of the large, open room. Sixteen sizable dogs crouched against white enamel paint, shivering and mute. So profound was the silence that it sucked down surrounding noise, quieting the yapping of the beagles and terriers next door. "Lamb, sweetie, what's the problem?" Not yet comprehending the weird hush, not yet afraid, Mandy stepped toward the trembling Rottweiler.

Lamb whimpered.

The chupacabra leaped past Mandy on four long-fingered paws, flipped Lamb as if the big dog were a stuffed toy, and with its fangs sliced into her belly; all in the same swift and preternaturally strong motion it sucked, emptying its prey of life and innards simultaneously. There was not much blood. Lamb only screamed once, at the same time as Mandy did. The—she did not yet know the name of it—the gray-skinned, nakedly hairless creature—never before had she seen anything like it—slender like a small deer, bony of ribs and ridgy of spine, with long hind legs like a rabbit, the invader looked far too frail to be so fearsome. To be a predator, a killer.

But as Lamb's shrunken body lapsed to the floor, as the creature looked up and scanned for its next prey, Mandy saw how its delicate, pointed head culminated in white razor fangs and the undershot jaw of a shark. And against all reason she realized what she had done.

I come from many places.

I am an autochthon.

I can never seem to get enough organ meat.

"No!" she shrieked as it leaped again. "Choop, no!"

I like dogs.

Raw and slippery, the way some people liked oysters, evidently.

The chupacabra's prey seemed immobilized by the force of its stare or its strangeness. Fifteen big dogs made no sound, no attempt to flee. With its front paws, their claws as long as its fangs, the creature grabbed for its next victim.

Mandy did not wait to see which dog her date was going to disembowel now. She got moving. She was the mom, she was the pack leader. The past few years had broken her so badly that crazy-glued together again she was strong enough to face anything, and she was running—not as fast as she would have liked, overweight, too damn old, short of breath—grabbing for the emergency equipment in the corner, a device she had never used, the rabies pole. Five feet of hollow steel rod with a handle at one end connected to a sturdy noose at the other.

Deploying the loop, Mandy turned and puffed toward Choop. Engrossed in gourmandizing the guts of a pit bull/wolfhound cross, the predator remained blissfully unaware of her as she positioned herself behind him.

The instant he lifted his head, she dropped the loop over his muzzle, pulled it past his pointed ears, and, with the handle at her end of the pole, yanked it tight around his neck, turning a clamp to keep it that way.

That, she thought, should take care of the brute. He— the weird liver-sucking thing that had been Choop— couldn't hurt her as long as she kept the "control pole" between the two of them, and with her weight advantage, certainly she could keep him from hurting the dogs. God, what he had already done broke her heart, but there would be no more of it, no more—

With a banshee screech he leaped to stand on his hind legs, tall, twisting in the noose, turning on her.

—no more dogs killed—

The force of the chupacabra's black-eyed glare hit her like a physical blow or an illness. Stricken, nauseated, she felt her knees weakening—and he lunged, leaped, attacked, clawed at her, hurling himself against the scant sixty inches of steel that kept him from sinking his fangs into her. He might not weigh much, but he was strong, preternaturally strong, and he was Choop, long arms and human hands groping—no, humanoid; he was a gray man with a sickle-spined back and an elongated face stretching into a sucking beak, a mosquito man . . . with scales. Reptile now, an upright lizard with a black forked tongue, hissing, dripping yellow drool, striking, and giving off such a stench that Mandy felt as if she must faint—but she must *not* faint or the dogs would all die.

She fumbled at the control pole's handle, trying to turn the knob, tighten the noose, to strangle the invader, the nameless, sucking—but he saw what she was doing. Humanoid again, he grasped his end of the rod in clawed long-fingered paws and tried to wrench it away from her. Strong. Far too strong.

Weight advantage, ha. Take care of the brute with the control pole? Choop was the one in control, swinging her in a circle around him while all she could do was cling, cling, and not let go, dizzy, faint, sick, must not pass out. Must save the dogs. Must save the dogs. Must save the—

Savagely he banged her against the wall. With a cry, losing hold of the pole, Mandy fell to the unforgiving tile floor, and the impact knocked the scant breath out of her lungs. Sprawling on her back, she couldn't move.

She could only lie there with her eyes wide open.

She saw Choop morph once more into a weird sort of hairless, feral gray canid. She saw him tower on his hind legs, oblivious to the noose still on his neck and the pole dangling. Sick with the knowledge that another dog would die, Mandy struggled for breath, and managed to beg in a ragged whisper, "No—Choop—don't do it . . ."

He didn't.

Instead, turning his gargoyle head toward the sound of her voice, fixing her with the stony power of his coal-black glare, he lunged straight at her.

Laughably, almost, it had not occurred to Mandy that Choop, with whom she had enjoyed a rather nice dinner, might now wish to suck out *her* liver. *Freaking cannibal*! she thought crazily as her date hurtled toward her with its shark mouth wide open, its gaping maw as big as the world, filling her vision, fangs aimed for her belly. Stark staring doomed and unable to move, she could not even scream—

Choop screamed.

Mandy saw his horrible white grin writhe, then skew toward the ceiling. As if she were watching a storm-dark sky and had seen lightning, a heartbeat afterward she heard thunder growl, snarl, roar. But it took her shocked eyes a moment more to focus, her stunned mind a moment more to comprehend: a pack of wolves, attacking Choop from behind, tearing his flanks, dragging him away from her. Although they might look like German Shepherds and Doberman Pinschers, Goldies and New-fies and Labs and big nameless mutts, they were all wolves at heart, and every one of them had sunk teeth into the chupacabra's back or haunches or hamstrings. When it tried to turn on them, the pole dangling from its neck wedged against the floor, preventing it. The power of its paranormal eyes could not reach its attackers.

They hauled the thing back from Mandy, mauling it, tearing at its flesh.

It screamed again. Agony.

Mandy closed her eyes. She rescued dogs, and now the dogs were rescuing her. She had wanted to save them, and they were saving her. The old, old, feral way. But she could not bear to watch.

Just as it was all over, just as she sat up, shakily, the door to the dog room burst open and Loony Calhooney, all featherweight five-foot-three of her, strode in, barking, "What the devil?"

"Betty," Mandy panted. She had forgotten that an alarm rang in the main office whenever anyone grabbed a rabies pole. She had also forgotten, if she had ever known, that any alarms that went off in the animal rescue also sounded in Betty Calhoun's home.

Looking around at Mandy struggling to her feet, at dogs licking their red-stained flews, blood everywhere, at two distorted, obviously dead canine bodies against the wall, and—and most of all at the thing lying on the floor with the noose around its neck—Loony Calhooney said again in a softer, starker tone, "What the devil?"

A bit unsteadily, Mandy limped over to stand beside

the old woman, both of them staring down at a scrawny gray-skinned hairless animal lying flat on its side, bleeding red runnels onto the tile, very still, looking no more dangerous than road kill.

"That's one of them things they shot in Texas," the old woman said almost in a whisper. "Saw it on the news. Killed sixty head of sheep in no time at all. How'd it get in here?"

"My fault. We were on a date, we needed something to do, and—" Mandy's hand flew to her mouth, partly to stop the insane things she was saying, but also because she had seen a slight movement of gray skin stretched over gaunt ribs.

Choop had breathed.

Within a heartbeat, instinctively, Mandy kneeled on the floor beside him, feeling the hollow of his neck. Yes, he had a pulse.

"He's alive!" she blurted. "We need to get him to emergency—"

"Whoa. Get *what* to emergency? Just because that thing can turn human, we should save it?"

Mandy felt her jaw drop, partly because she had never known Betty to say "whoa" in regard to saving any "thing," but mostly because Betty—what Betty understood—or knew . . . Speechless, Mandy gawked up at the old woman.

"Saw his clothes," Betty answered the look, jerking a thumb over her shoulder toward the mud room.

Vehemently Mandy shook her head. "He's just a— some kind of dog now."

"They tried to say in Texas that it was a coyote with a deformed jaw and with mange all over it. Bullshit."

"He's an animal," Mandy appealed. "Even if he's human he's still just an animal. We save animals, don't we?"

Loony Calhooney stared down at her with eyes that age had bleached nearly white, like flat full moons. "Am I mistaken," she asked, expressionless, "or didn't that so-called animal try to kill you? And didn't it kill those two?" She jerked her cleft chin toward the dead dogs.

"And wouldn't it have killed every single living creature in the place if it wasn't for you tackling it with the rabies pole?"

"Even so," Mandy said, still kneeling by the monster that had tried to suck her guts out, pulling the pink silk scarf off her neck and folding it, applying pressure to a gushing wound in the creature's side. "Hurry, please, call somebody before he bleeds to death."

Betty Calhoun did not move, just continued to look at her with moon-gray eyes. "It's the divorce, isn't it," she said, not as a question but as a statement. "Some women have the kind of heart that just won't quit. Can never get enough. Any sort of soul-eating heart-sucking bastard could do anything to you, anything, and you'd still want to bring him back."

Mandy jerked her head up, and if she had seen pity, or condescension, or scorn—but she saw none of those in Loony Calhooney's bleak gaze.

She saw an intimation of some larger understanding.

"You're crazy," Mandy mumbled, but she dropped the scarf.

"As if life isn't?"

Wordless, Mandy got up and placed herself by the old woman's side. There she stood over the grotesque bleeding thing and watched it die.

THE PERFECT MAN

Pauline J. Alama

Pauline J. Alama's first fantasy novel, *The Eye of Night*, was a finalist for the Compton Crook/ Stephen Tall Memorial Award and the *Romantic Times* Reviewer's Choice Award for Best Fantasy. She is hard at work on a second fantasy novel, *The Ghost-Bearers*. Her short stories have appeared in an earlier Denise Little DAW anthology, *Rotten Relations*, and Marion Zimmer Bradley's *Sword and Sorceress XVIII*. A freelance grant writer and former medieval scholar, she lives in New Jersey with the perfect writer's husband, the perfect kid, and two perfectly neurotic cats.

From: "Zoe DiGiovanni" <zoed@digitekgroup.com>
Date: February 15, 2006 8:10 AM
To: "Allie Herman" <hermana@nuwave
           communications.net>
Subject: You won't believe this, but . . .

. . . I've just met the perfect man.

Valentine's Day started out a disaster. Marla said the recently dumped have to stick together, so she dragged me to a bar so we could console each other—and then, of course, fifteen minutes into Happy Hour, my darling sister disap-

peared with some biker dude and left me alone to cry
into my Chianti. Happy Valentine's Day to me. :-(

Then Ross came along. He sat down next to me and gave
me this irresistible slow smile, and the next thing I knew,
I was pouring out my heart to him. And he *listened.* When
was the last time you met a guy who could listen?

Then he said, "Dear lady, have you completely given up
on love, or will you allow me to give you the Valentine's Day you deserve?" Well, what do you think? He
swept me away, out of that beery dive, to go ball-
room dancing till 4 a.m. By the time he walked me
home, I was so tired I was almost relieved when all
he did was kiss me goodnight at the door.

I got his phone number. The only question is, when is
it safe to use it? I mean, he already knows I'm
dumped. I don't want him to think I'm desperate.

I haven't slept at all, I'm so excited.
Belated Happy V-Day!
Zoe

From: "Allie Herman" <hermana@nuwave
            communications.net>
Date: February 15, 2006 8:58 AM
To: "Zoe DiGiovanni" <zoed@digitekgroup.com>
Subject: Re: You won't believe this, but . . .

Hey, Zoe. Glad your Valentine's Day didn't suck, in spite
of Jack just having won the World's Biggest Asshole
award.

That said, I'm going to risk winning the World's Biggest
Wet Blanket award by saying, as your friend, I don't want
to see you get your hopes up over this Ross.

To steal your own words, when was the last time you
met a *straight* guy who could listen?

I hope I'm wrong. You deserve your perfect man after putting up with Jack. Just don't set yourself up for disappointment. After all, even if you've just made a friend, that's still better than an evening wasted with Jack. Better than my V-Day, too. Scott made sure to take me to a restaurant attached to a sports bar, so he could sneak off and check the basketball scores now and then. How romantic.

Allie

From: "Zoe DiGiovanni" <zoed@digitekgroup.com>
Date: February 15, 2006 9:25 AM
To: "Allie Herman" <hermana@nuwave
           communications.net>
Subject: Re: You won't believe this, but . . .

No, you got it wrong. That kiss goodnight was a *real* kiss. At least, I think it was.

I'm calling him tonight.

Wish me luck!
Zoe

From: "Allie Herman" <hermana@nuwave
           communications.net>
Date: February 15, 2006 9:41 AM
To: "Zoe DiGiovanni" <zoed@digitekgroup.com>
Subject: Re: You won't believe this, but . . .

No, you're not!!! Repeat after me: NOT desperate. NOT desperate. NOT desperate.

From: "Allie Herman" <hermana@nuwave
           communications.net>
Date: March 6, 2006 8:50 AM
To: "Zoe DiGiovanni" <zoed@digitekgroup.com>
Subject: Earth to Zoe!!!

Zoe,
Where've you been, girlfriend? Look, I'm sorry I said

your perfect man was gay. I could be wrong, all right? I just wanted to protect you. Will you please pick up the next time I call, or at least call me back?

love and worry-lines,
Allie

From:	"Zoe DiGiovanni" <zoed@digitekgroup.com>
Date:	March 6, 2006 9:17 AM
To:	"Allie Herman" <hermana@nuwave communications.net>
Subject:	Re: Earth to Zoe!!!

Oh, yes indeed, you *could* be wrong about Ross. :–) Don't worry, I'm not mad at you. Just very, very busy.

And not with work. :–) :–) :–)love, peace, and little rose-colored hearts all over everything,
Zoe

From:	"Allie Herman" <hermana@nuwave communications.net>
Date:	March 6, 2006 12:01 PM
To:	"Zoe DiGiovanni" <zoed@digitekgroup.com>
Subject:	Re: Earth to Zoe!!!

Hey, wait!!! After all these days of talking to your voice-mail, you can't leave me like that. I don't even know his last name. I want DETAILS, girl. Didn't I tell you EVERYTHING about Scott—right down to the freckles around his Prince Albert?

love, outrage, and little spycams all over everything,
Allie

From:	"Zoe DiGiovanni" <zoed@digitekgroup.com>
Date:	March 6, 2006 12:47 PM
To:	"Allie Herman" <hermana@nuwave communications.net>
Subject:	Re: Earth to Zoe!!!

OK, OK. His name is Ross Archer. He has gorgeous

wavy black hair and really roguish eyes. He's one of those baby-faced men who always look young, but I think he must be older than me because he's a widower. I have to guess because Mr. Baby-Face is too vain to tell! But I can't complain. He's the most understanding man I ever met. It's sort of his business to be understanding because he's a couples' counsellor. I guess that's why he's such a good listener. Though he says a lot of what he does is more like sex therapy. All I can say is he certainly knows his field. :—)

Zoe

From: "Allie Herman" <hermana@nuwave
          communications.net>
Date: March 6, 2006 4:56 PM
To: "Zoe DiGiovanni" <zoed@digitekgroup.com>
Subject: Re: Earth to Zoe!!!

Hey, blissed-out one! Come on, give me some more! Where's he from? What kind of dysfunctional family does he come from? (Of course it was dysfunctional. Happy families don't spawn therapists.) What's he do when he's not fixing people's love lives? And what do you mean, he really knows his field, you little vixen?

Widower, huh? Probably divorced, but widowed sounds more romantic. Look his first wife up on the web and you'll find out more about your beau than he's let on.

Insatiably yours,
Allie

From: "Zoe DiGiovanni" <zoed@digitekgroup.com>
Date: March 6, 2006 6:17 PM
To: "Allie Herman" <hermana@nuwave
          communications.net>
Subject: Re: Earth to Zoe!!!

Ross doesn't talk much about his family or his past. I think he doesn't like to talk about it. When I asked whether it freaks out his parents that he's a sex thera-

pist, he said his father was an engineer and was
disappointed he didn't take after him. It must be a sore
point, because he changed the subject as fast as
he could. Besides, unlike some other guys I could name,
he's such a good listener that I end up talking about
myself a lot more than he ever talks about himself.

He hasn't even mentioned his first wife's name. I think
he doesn't want me to think he's still hung up on
her, which may mean he is, if you know what I mean.

And as for bed, well, that's another place where he's not
like other guys. He really seems to focus on me, like my
pleasure's the most important thing. He knows all the
right moves, where to touch, when to let go, and he
takes his time till I'm begging for him to take me. And
then he does, and I keep coming and coming till I'm
in another world, and I don't even notice when he comes.

Now you can think about that and blush lobster-red when
you finally meet him in the flesh. Which I hope you'll do the
next time you're in town. When can I see you?

Zoe

P.S. Look, but don't touch—he's mine!

From:	"Allie Herman" <hermana@nuwave communications.net>
Date:	March 6, 2006 8:30 PM
To:	"Zoe DiGiovanni" <zoed@digitekgroup.com>
Subject:	Getting together

I'll be traveling in on the 20th for a conference. How
about lunch on the 21st?

Allie

P.S. I never blush.

From: "Zoe DiGiovanni" <zoed@digitekgroup.com>
Date: March 22, 2006 8:17 AM
To: "Allie Herman" <hermana@nuwave
           communications.net>
Subject: What do you think?

Well, now that you've met him, what do you think?

I really want to know. I think he's working up to the M-
word. I want to say yes. I find myself staring at bridal
magazines. I want to know if you think I'm crazy.

Zoe

From: "Allie Herman" <hermana@nuwave
           communications.net>
Date: March 22, 2006 12:30 PM
To: "Zoe DiGiovanni" <zoed@digitekgroup.com>
Subject: Re: What do you think?

Wow. Wedding bells coming between you and me?
And no prospect of Scott uttering the dreaded M-
word to me. Has Ross got a brother? No, I don't mean
that. I really don't.

I don't think you're crazy—he's nice, really nice, just as
sweet and considerate as you said—but something about
him set me on edge. I always think that if something
seems too good to be real, it's not real. And Ross
seemed like that. Unreal. Too perfect. Almost like a
state-of-the-art romance dispenser, programmed
with all the right moves.

Do you remember that weird old story by that guy Hoff-
mann that the German prof had us read, about some
sensitive poetic type who thinks he's found the perfect
girlfriend, because she never gets tired of listening
to his poetry? It turns out she's some kind of android.
After that, all the other guys are glad their girlfriends
don't hang on their every word, because at least it

means they're real. Ross sort of reminds me of
that story.

I know you'll hate me for saying this, but be careful, all
right? It may be that I'm just paranoid, and he sincerely is as sweet as he seems. But is he for real? How
much do you know about him, even now?

But I'm with you on one thing—he's absolute eye candy.
Have I ever seen a more delicious man? No, not
even Scott. (I'll kill you if you tell him I said so. I mean
Scott, of course. What you tell *your* boyfriend is
up to you.) Does he look just as good in the altogether?

love,
Allie

From: "Zoe DiGiovanni" <zoed@digitekgroup.com>
Date: March 24, 2006 12:20 PM
To: "Allie Herman" <hermana@nuwave
           communications.net>
Subject: Re: What do you think?

You're not *seriously* suggesting that my boyfriend is a
robot??? Honestly, Allie, you've been watching too
much science fiction.

I don't think I'd like to tell you what he looks like in the
altogether, thank you very much.

From: "Allie Herman" <hermana@nuwave
           communications.net>
Date: March 24, 2006 1:12 PM
To: "Zoe DiGiovanni" <zoed@digitekgroup.com>
Subject: Re: What do you think?

Relax, girlfriend. Of course I wasn't serious. I just
thought any guy who seemed that smooth might be hiding
something. My mistrustful nature, I guess.

Though, come to think of it—no pun intended—it could explain a lot. Like why you never notice when he climaxes. Maybe he's not programmed for it. ONLY KIDDING!

This must be serious. You're getting all defensive over him, like a mother bear with her cub. Or is that a lioness? I forget. Anyway, I guess it's true love, and what can I say to that?

From: "Zoe DiGiovanni" <zoed@digitekgroup.com>
Date: March 27, 2006 9:00 AM
To: "Allie Herman" <hermana@nuwave
           communications.net>
Subject: Re: What do you think?

OK, I'm sorry. I asked for your opinion, and I shouldn't get all squiffy about it just because you don't see Ross the way I do. (I should be glad you don't see him the way I do, or I'd have to kill you.)

But it's funny you should ask how he looks nude, because he has this kink: He won't have any light at all in the bedroom. There are no light fixtures, the windows are shuttered, and he won't even let me bring in a candle. He says it's more romantic in the dark. The first time I was cool with that, but lately I've been asking him, just for a change, can't we do it in the light? It seemed to upset him, so I let it go. Maybe he has a scar or something that he's self-conscious about. It can't be anything major, because I can't feel anything abnormal. All right, maybe his back feels a little hairy, but as I told him, I find that kind of erotic, so what's the big deal? Oh, well. One kink's a small price to pay for the best lover on the planet.

Zoe

From: "Allie Herman" <hermana@nuwave
communications.net>
Date: March 28, 2006 9:02 AM
To: "Zoe DiGiovanni" <zoed@digitekgroup.com>
Subject: Re: What do you think?

Maybe he just doesn't want you to find his off switch.
ONLY KIDDING!!! More likely he's got an embarrassing tattoo on his butt. "Lulu Forever" or something
like that.

From: "Zoe DiGiovanni" <zoed@digitekgroup.com>
Date: March 28, 2006 5:20 PM
To: "Allie Herman" <hermana@nuwave
communications.net>
Subject: Re: What do you think?

Heh, heh. Yeah, you're right. That's probably the whole
dark secret. Except it would be "Kiki Forever." That
was his first wife's name. Or something like Kiki. I
couldn't quite catch what he was saying, and I've
never seen it written down.

From: "Allie Herman" <hermana@nuwave
communications.net>
Date: March 29, 2006 8:52 AM
To: "Zoe DiGiovanni" <zoed@digitekgroup.com>
Subject: Re: What do you think?

Was that Kiki or Kinky? :-)
I did a search for Kiki Archer. No hits.
Of course, you probably tried that already.

From: "Zoe DiGiovanni" <zoed@digitekgroup.com>
Date: April 11, 2006 10:23 PM
To: "Allie Herman" <hermana@nuwave
communications.net>
Subject: Weird Encounter

Went out to lunch with Ross today, and while we were
waiting for our order, I saw him sort of hunch down

in the booth. Then a woman came over to us, all clicking
heels and flashing diamonds, smiling a honey-sweet
smile, too sweet, like a candy apple with a razor blade
in it. And I had the distinct feeling the candy was
for him and the razor blade for me. She looked like Ross
in drag, except that makes her sound masculine, and
she definitely wasn't. She seemed as perfect a female
specimen as Ross is a male.

"Hey, kiddo," she said to him, "who's the date, and why
haven't I heard of her?"

And I waited for him to introduce me to his sister. But
instead, he goes, "Hi, Momma," in this sheepish,
little-boy tone.

My jaw dropped. She didn't look a day older than Ross.
She must have spent a *fortune* on plastic surgery.
I just gaped at her and waited to be introduced. But
Ross shifted his gaze like a little boy caught with his
hand in the cookie jar and said nothing.

Finally, I stuck out my hand toward Momma and introduced myself. She shook my hand, and I was relieved when she let go. Her fingernails must have been
four inches long, and her smile looked so predatory
I was surprised not to see fangs. "How long have you
been dating my son?" she asked—as if it was her
business!

I had the feeling anything I said would be used against
me. I did my best to match her ferocious smile, but
I knew I couldn't. "Oh, for a while," I said as breezily
as I could.

She turned her eyes back on Ross. "You never call
anymore, sweetie. We'll talk tonight." And then she
swept away in a cloud of expensive perfume.

When she was out of earshot, I said to Ross, "Why
didn't you introduce me?"

He hunched down further in his seat. "I was hoping I
could keep you away from her a little longer. Momma

just can't help interfering in my love life, and when she gets involved, she has a way of wrecking my relationships. She did her best to break up my marriage."

"I thought you were widowed," I said.

"Yes," he said, "but we were separated for a while near the beginning, and Momma provoked the whole thing. I don't want her to get started on you. She's the reason I decided to be a couples' therapist. She thinks she knows everything about love, but she's a disaster. Sure, she's great at getting lovers, a real free spirit. But a lasting relationship? Forget about it. I don't even know if Dad's my real father."

"That must have been rough for you," I said. "But you know, you're not her little boy anymore. She can't do anything to our relationship unless we let her."

That seemed to cheer him up a little. But I can't help thinking, he's the couples' therapist. I shouldn't have to tell him this. Why does he still think his mother could break us up? Sure, he looks like a kid, but doesn't he realize he's a big boy now?

Granted, she looked like a real piece of work. I might be scared of her, too. But who wants to marry a guy who's still putty in Momma's hands? I don't know about this.

From:	"Allie Herman" <hermana@nuwave communications.net>
Date:	April 12, 2006 9:02 AM
To:	"Zoe DiGiovanni" <zoed@digitekgroup.com>
Subject:	Re: Weird Encounter

Do men *ever* get over being Momma's Little Boy? This is the most normal thing I've heard about Ross so far.

Except for the mother looking his age. That is so creepy.

I know it must be Dr. Lift and Tuck, but part of my brain says that's one more piece of evidence. "Momma" is one of the engineers who made him. And she made him look just like her—except as a guy. Maybe Kiki is just some sort of back-story they programmed in so he could pass as an adult with a past. Maybe he was brand new when you got him. Your first virgin.

From: "Zoe DiGiovanni" <zoed@digitekgroup.com>
Date: April 12, 2006 11:23 PM
To: "Allie Herman" <hermana@nuwave
           communications.net>
Subject: Re: Weird Encounter

Stop! You're starting to make me believe it. This is crazy. He's *not* an android. Granted, they're doing some pretty remarkable things with artificial intelligence these days. But why would anyone create an android sex therapist? If there's some advantage in that—like giving clients a sense of privacy—wouldn't they advertise him as a robot instead of passing him off as human? And if someone programmed all his actions, why would he seduce *me*? It doesn't make sense. Except for the parts you explained. Those make too much sense. Arggh! Why did you put this in my head?

From: "Allie Herman" <hermana@nuwave
           communications.net>
Date: April 13, 2006 8:51 AM
To: "Zoe DiGiovanni" <zoed@digitekgroup.com>
Subject: Re: Weird Encounter

Sorry. Overactive imagination, I guess. Look, if you want to set your mind at ease, you know what you have to do. Next time you go to his place for an overnight, sneak in a little flashlight and take a peek at him in bed. If you see circuitry, then you know. If you see "Kiki For-

ever," well, then, pinch his tattooed cheek for me.
:-)

Either way, I'm *still* dying to know what he looks like
in the altogether.

Allie

From: "Zoe DiGiovanni" <zoed@digitekgroup.com>
Date: April 18, 2006 1:23 PM
To: "Allie Herman" <hermana@nuwave
           communications.net>
Subject: Re: Weird Encounter

I've been thinking it over rationally, and you know, I've
decided, it doesn't matter.

So what if Ross is an android? I love him. Doesn't love
conquer all? Why should I discriminate against a
silicon-American? This is the 21st century, after all. I
can be open-minded.

And, frankly, where could I find a more perfect lover?
Maybe his machine nature makes him a better man
than all those jerks I've put up with, all just out for their
own gratification. Ross puts my feelings first. What
more could I ask for?

Zoe

From: "Allie Herman" <hermana@nuwave
           communications.net>
Date: April 18, 2006 5:31 PM
To: "Zoe DiGiovanni" <zoed@digitekgroup.com>
Subject: Re: Weird Encounter

You may be right. The way Scott's been acting lately,
I'd prefer a nice reliable machine, who'd remember our date
anniversary and what time he promised to meet me and

so on. Does Ross have a brother? Sorry, wrong
term. Is there another unit for sale, or is he a prototype?

I guess this means you're not going to report back on
how he looks barenaked. :−(

Allie

From: "Zoe DiGiovanni" <zoed@digitekgroup.com>
Date: April 19, 2006 8:45 AM
To: "Allie Herman" <hermana@nuwave
           communications.net>
Subject: Re: Weird Encounter

Allie, I say this in all love and affection, as your sincere
and devoted long-time friend: You are the most in-
corrigible dirty old broad I know!

And, you know, I can't get that flashlight idea out of my
head. At least, once I've seen, I'll know one way or
the other. After all, either way it's OK with me. Why not?

From: "Allie Herman" <hermana@nuwave
           communications.net>
Date: April 19, 2006 4:59 PM
To: "Zoe DiGiovanni" <zoed@digitekgroup.com>
Subject: Re: Weird Encounter

You go, girl!

love and wicked thoughts,
Allie

From: "Zoe DiGiovanni" <zoed@digitekgroup.com>
Date: April 21, 2006 9:01 AM
To: "Allie Herman" <hermana@nuwave
           communications.net>
Subject: You are REALLY not going to believe this

Well, I used the flashlight. He was lying on his side completely out of the covers, so I got a good look at him, front and back. What I saw wasn't normal, but it sure wasn't circuitry.

For the most part, Ross looked just like I expected. Better, even. If he's sexy dressed, he's devastating undressed. Smooth olive skin, compact but shapely muscles, soft dark hair on the chest, descending in a narrow line to a thicker tuft of curls below. And, yes, something in the midst of the curls that makes Jack seem an even smaller man by comparison.

But on his back—that wasn't hair. Folded across his back were neat, graceful wings, finely covered with downy white feathers. Propped up next to the bed were an ancient bow and a quiver of very phallic-looking arrows.

I gasped, "Omigod!"

He woke up and saw me looking at him. And for a moment, he forgot who I was. "Kiki!" he yelled, except it wasn't really Kiki. More like Siki, or even Psiki. Then he corrected himself, "Zoe! Why didn't you listen to me?"

In an instant the room was full of light. The shuttered window burst open, and a flock of doves pulled a gold chariot into the room. At the reins was Ross' mother.

She was smiling her Venus Flytrap smile. "Well, Eros," she said, "you've lost your bet. Again. Amazing how they all take, take, take from you, and will never give that one thing you ask of them in return." She looked me up and down. "Dear me, how your taste has declined over the ages. You know I never liked Psiki

much, but this little tart will never measure up to her,
I'm sure. Well, you've had your chance to test your
wings, my fledgling. Time for me to gather you up again.
Go on home." With that, she waved her hand, and
he vanished, just like that!

"Where's he gone?" I sputtered. "What did you do
to him?"

She just showed me her teeth and gloated, "He's safe
from climbers like you, mortal. I can't believe you
thought yourself good enough for the young God of Love."

"The what?"

"Oh, of course you didn't know what he was. You mortals today are so ignorant. What did you think he
was—a space alien?" She made a genteel noise of dis-
taste. "He's better off without you."

"You can't do this!" I shouted. "He can choose for
himself. He's his own man."

She laughed. "Oh, he *thinks* he is. The little archer
even set up shop for himself! But he doesn't realize
that even now, he works for me. He belongs to me. *I*
wrote the book of love, darling. And you're in for
some remedial reading. You need to learn proper spiritual values. The REALLY old time religion. Come to
my spirituality seminars."

She shoved a card into my hand. It read, "APHRODITE,
COUNSELOR/GODDESS, SENSUAL MYSTERIES
INC. DISCOVER THE SEXUAL PATH TO THE
HIGHER SELF. All major credit cards accepted."

I stared up at her, dumbfounded. She smiled back. "You
have a lot to learn. But if you can pass my few little
tests, maybe I'll let you see your boyfriend again."

"TESTS?" I was furious. "What gives you the right to test me?"

"The Fates, of course," she said. "You DO have a lot to learn, don't you? But don't worry. The tests can be passed. They have been passed. Once, a couple thousand years ago." She chuckled. "Not just any woman is good enough for my special boy."

"You are sick, lady. Sick." I meant to stay and argue with her, but I found myself halfway home without knowing how I got there.

I keep trying to get through to Ross—Eros, I mean—but his line's disconnected. His e-mail bounces back. His apartment—well, the whole building doesn't seem to be where it was. The only contact I have is his mother's card, with her business address, phone number, and website.

If I go to those bogus seminars, is she really going to let me see him? Or is this just her sadistic game? Could it be some kind of money-making scam that he was in on all along? All major credit cards, indeed!

Even if I have a chance, do I really want to find him? He deceived me. He didn't tell me who he was. I was ready to accept him as an android. But as Cupid—I don't know how to handle that. It's so old-fashioned. And a love god—especially one with a mother fixation—might be, you know, kind of emotionally needy? I don't know about this. It's not what I thought I was getting into.

From:	"Eros Archer" <lovegod@truelove.org>
Date:	April 24, 2006 12:03 AM
To:	"Phoebus Apollo" <hot1@greekgod tanning.com>
Subject:	Here I go again

Another relationship shot to Tartarus. She's not even
going to try to get past Momma's obstacle course
and find True Love. None of them do any more. Romance is dead. I'm not sure why I'm still around.

I miss Psyche. I hate the 21st century.

When I get out of Momma's clutches, let's look up Dion-
ysus and get plastered like a fake Venus de Milo.

Eros Archer
Counselor/Clinical Director
True Love Unlimited

From: "Phoebus Apollo" <hot1@greekgod
          tanning.com>
Date: April 24, 2006, 5:45 AM
To: "Eros Archer" <lovegod@truelove.org>
Subject: Re: Here I go again

I feel your pain.
Try being a sun god in the age of SPF 60 sunblock.

Phoebus Apollo, Owner/Manager
Greek God Tanning: Look Great and Live Forever!

From: "Allie Herman" <hermana@nuwave
          communications.net>
Date: April 24, 2006 9:01 AM
To: "Zoe DiGiovanni" <zoed@digitekgroup.com>
Subject: Re: You are REALLY not going to believe this

Sorry I didn't reply sooner. Scott dumped me, and I've
been too depressed to even login.

And I'm so sorry about the mess with Ross. I feel responsible, you know, for suggesting the whole flashlight thing. But, like you said, maybe you don't really
want this, anyway. After all, who'd want that control-
ling harpy for a mother-in-law?

But, well, if you're not interested any more, could I have that card with the contact information? Just, you know, for curiosity's sake.

love and commiseration,
Allie

UNDER MY SKIN

Diane Duane

Diane Duane was a psychiatric nurse before turning to writing full time in 1980. Since then she has published more than forty novels, including several collaborations with her husband, Peter Morwood. She also writes screenplays, served as senior writer for the BBC-TV education series "Science Challenge," and writes scripts for CD-ROM computer games. Duane lives with her husband in rural Ireland.

Now this time, Caroline thought, *it* has *to be right.*
The screen in front of her filled up with about eighty lines of code, and she peered at the section in the middle that had been causing her all the trouble for the last six hours of her workday. *I mean*, she thought, *I've fixed this about twenty times. It* has *to be right now.* But with code, a single semicolon out of place in a line, or a line that ended without a carriage return, could screw up hours and hours of work unless you caught it—

It all looked just fine. But she was not deceived into any excess of pleasure with herself—she knew better. "Okay," she muttered. "Let's see."

She pulled down the menu at the top of the screen, selected the option that said *View in browser*, and held her breath.

The browser window popped open, showing her noth-

ing but white for a few moments . . . then filled with the
green baize background of PokerPlayerzz.com. The table
structure that overlay the background started to sketch
itself out, filling with pictures and words. Then the animated hand of cards, a restatement of the PokerPlayerzz
logo, started to deal itself down onto the table structure.
Royal flush: ace, king, queen, jack, ten.

And every card was backwards.

Caroline shrieked out loud, and pushed the keyboard
away from her, furious. "I can't believe this!" she
moaned. "I can*not* believe this!"

From a few cubicles down came the sound of rueful
and sympathetic laughter. "Two hundred and *eight* . . ."

"Shut up, Michelle!"

"I'm betting you'll hit your three hundredth scream by
next Wednesday."

From anyone else Caroline would have refused to take
this kind of thing, but Michelle was working on a different part of the same project—"grooming" code files that
had been generated by some of the company's less talented coders in eastern Europe. *Grooming, hell,* Caroline
thought. *It's a total rewrite. Not that we're being* paid *for
original work* . . . And Michelle's sufferings had been as
extreme as Caroline's, if not worse.

"The hell with this," Caroline said. "I'm done. Come
on, we'll go get a beer and plan the invasion of Bulgaria.
When we rule the place, the first ones up against the
wall are going to be all their coders."

"I'd really like to go, but I can't," said the long-
suffering voice. "This module's got to be turned in before
start of business in New Delhi. They're rolling it out
tomorrow at local midnight."

"What time is it there?"

A pause. "Two-thirty in the morning." A sigh. "I'll
make it . . . just."

Caroline sighed too, looking at her own monitor. Even
though she knew she could leave now, she could just
hear what Walter, the Boss from Hell, would say when
he dropped by the cubicle ever so casually around Monday lunchtime and found that the graphics routines on

the new splash page were still misbehaving. *Can I get this thing to behave by lunch on Monday? Can I really?*

She reached out to her trackball, killed the browser window, and stared at the screen full of code one more time. *That routine right there. If I move that—*

"You screamed," said a masculine voice, slightly European-sounding around the edges, and concerned. "Are you all right?"

Caroline glanced up at her cubicle door. Standing there, with his head cocked just slightly to one side and a curious expression on his face, was a tall, slim, broad-shouldered guy in Friday casuals, a fawn shirt and mahogany sweater, and fawn chinos and brogues. *Now where have I seen him before? Oh, I know, he's one of the implementation-and-logistics people up by the north windows.* Caroline had seen him up there a few times when all the networked printers down her way were busy, and she'd had to go farther afield than usual for a printout.

"I'm fine, uh—" She made the trying-to-think-of-your-name-help-me-out-here gesture with one hand while she hit the scroll key with the other, but she wasn't looking at the screen; she was looking at him. *I really should get up that way more often.* Dark hair, late twenties, high cheekbones, big dark eyes . . . . *Oh, what's the point? Odds are he's gay.*

"Matiyas. Matiyas Ferenj," he said. "Or Matt—whatever. And you are, uh—" He made the help-me-out-here gesture back at her, with a slight wry smile.

"Caroline Desantis," she said. She nodded at him, glanced back at the screen. "You can't have been here all that long or you'd know that hearing me scream is no big thing . . ."

"It is if you're just down the hall from it," Michelle said.

"Shut *up,* Michelle," Caroline said. From two cubicles down came the sound of poorly stifled laughter.

Matiyas looked at her a little oddly. "Marcus Donnelly said you were from Ireland," he said.

Caroline just glanced at him sideways, her eyebrows

up. *Okay, here we go. 'You don't have an Irish accent. . . .'*

"But you don't sound Irish," Matiyas said. "Are you really from Belfast?"

Caroline smiled, though as smiles went it was probably a pretty weary one. "Heard that, did you? Think I might start planting bombs under people's desks?"

He gave her a slightly embarrassed look. Caroline laughed, shook her head. "I was born here, though," she said. "Accidentally."

Matiyas's look got more embarrassed still. Caroline grinned a little, as that was the expected result. "Not that way," she said. "My dad was a correspondent with Reuters; he met my mum when they assigned him to their Belfast bureau. After they were married, they wanted to start a family. But he got reassigned over here right away, and my mum wanted to wait till they got back to the North. Except it didn't turn out that way."

Matiyas blinked. "Your mother," he said, "thought Northern Ireland was a better place to be born than *here*?"

"Less dangerous," Caroline said, "yeah." Now his look of complete astonishment was really amusing her. "Are you surprised? You have no idea what New York looks like to people over there when they see it on the news. Lots more gun crime than we ever had in Belfast, even before the cease-fire. Five, ten people gunned down every day: Murder Central! When I finished school and decided to come here to work, you should have heard all my friends." She purposely turned on the harsh Belfast accent. " 'Oh no, don't go to New York, you'll get shot!' "

He laughed. It was a particularly nice laugh; for some reason, the hair stood right up on the back of Caroline's neck when she heard it. Maybe it was the sudden warmth of his eyes as hers met them—the sudden sense of connection, as if a stranger were somehow seeing that another stranger had the same problems, and wasn't so strange any more . . .

"Anyway, work kept my dad here a while longer than

planned, so I wound up being born here," Caroline said.
"Then, when I was six, we moved back to the wee North.
Too late for my accent, though—it was well stuck in
Manhattan by then. I took a lot of stick for that at school.
But eventually they learned to let me be." She smiled.
"Finished my leaving cert, went to university,
graduated . . . and saw where the good jobs were, back
then. Moved back here five years ago." She shrugged.
"What about you?"

"It's a long story," he said.

"Ten million of them in the Naked City, I hear," Caroline said. She sighed, leaned back from the computer.
"And I'm done with this one for today."

"I'll see you later, then," Matiyas said. And suddenly
he was turning to go.

There was something about the suddenness that surprised her. What surprised her even more was her voice
saying, "Matiyas?"

He paused, looked over his shoulder.

"I didn't mean you should sod off or anything!" Caroline said. "Gonna clock out in a few minutes, sure. But
if you're not busy, and you're done for the day, some of
us go out on Fridays about now. Come on out with us!
Mich, you *sure* you can't wriggle free?"

"Not a chance. Thanks, though . . ."

"But there's still Tessa and Tad—they're always up for
a drink on the way home. Come on out with us."

Matiyas looked surprised. "Uh," he said. "Okay."

He wandered off across the wilderness of cubicles
toward where his was. Caroline didn't know him all that
well; she didn't normally visit the north-side people, the
rollout crowd. Mostly she socialized with the other de-
buggers and the software implementation jockeys. *But
listen to me! We get as insular in here as we do in our
neighborhoods. God forbid someone from the Upper East
Side should shop west of Fifth Avenue; the heavens would
fall if someone who lived in SoHo went north of Twelfth
for their groceries! And obviously the world will end if a
code wrangler has a beer with some rollout guy . . .*

But it didn't quite wind up that way, for Tessa had

gone home early, and when Caroline went looking for Tad, it turned out that Tad hadn't come in today at all but had called in sick. And there was Matiyas, standing there by the door to the elevator lobby with his coat over his arm, looking like someone who suspected he was about to be ditched after all.

Oh, jeez, just look at the poor guy, Caroline thought, as she headed in that direction. *One beer with him won't hurt, no matter how much of a bore he turns out to be.*

"So where are we going exactly?" he asked, as they went through the glass buzzer-door. He actually held it for her: *old-fashioned manners, how nice . . .*

"There's a place down at the corner of Central Park West," she said. "Their happy hour just started, and the prices aren't too bad . . ."

"Sounds excellent," Matiyas said.

They made idle elevator chatter on the way down, headed across the sterile polished black stone downstairs lobby, and came out into the wet dullness of a Manhattan autumn afternoon. All the traffic in 65th Street was at a cacophonous standstill, stuck behind some huge delivery truck further up the way. The two of them dodged across the wet street between cars, heading up toward the corner of 65th and Central Park West. There yet another plan came undone as they discovered that the front and sides of the bar were covered with scaffolding and the windows boarded over with CLOSED FOR RENOVATION signs.

"Well, that is annoying," Matiyas said. Briefly, that accent Caroline couldn't quite pin down came out fairly strongly. *European, yeah, but not German or anything like that . . .* She was tempted to ask about it but decided to let it be; she'd had more than enough of that kind of thing from various of her coworkers when she first took this job. And after they'd made up their minds that she wasn't a terrorist or a bigot or someone who might go postal on them, it seemed as if everybody wanted to know everything about her—which wasn't something she was used to. *So many people just don't seem to have any sense of privacy any more. Just leave him his . . .*

"Yeah," Caroline said, "it is." She looked at the crammed blue and white M72 bus that was presently turning past them into Central Park West, its windows almost opaque with condensation from people's damp clothes and damp selves. "Look," she said, "there's not much in the way of decent bars on this side of the avenue till you get right down to Lincoln Center. But I know a good one almost straight across the Park. We can cut through there, if you don't mind getting rained on a little."

"Sure, why not?" Matiyas looked around him equably. "After being cooped up all day, a little fresh air is good. Even when it's a little wet as well."

They paused at the corner of 66th and Central Park West, waiting for the light to change. Across the street from them, to the left, the ever-present white holiday lights of Tavern on the Green were already turned on, outlining the building and twined through and around the trees, an unsubtle glow against the sullen overcast of the surrounding trees' uplifted limbs. "You ever eat in there?" Caroline said as the light changed and they crossed the street.

Mike nodded as they bore right toward the underpass that avoided the inflowing traffic onto the transverse road. "Once," he said. "Never again. The place is full of posers. Especially the ones who insist on sitting out there." As they came up out of the underpass, he jerked his head leftward in the direction of the restaurant's glass-walled conservatory wing, blazing with light across the undercut transverse road and through all the intervening trees. "So everyone can see them, and know how much money they've got to blow on mediocre food . . ."

Caroline grinned as they hung a left onto the first of the paths inside the Park's low outer wall, heading east. To her, even the least-native New Yorkers seemed to turn into restaurant critics within days of their arrival. Matiyas was no different. "I guess you have a better class of posers where you come from?"

It was as nosy as she planned to get, but even so, he

gave her a look of slight amusement, almost as if he'd
known what she was thinking before. "Well, class is always something of an issue," he said, "in the older parts
of the world, no matter how we pretend otherwise. You
see those who flaunt old titles and have nothing else to
recommend them, and others who work hard and wear
the titles only as ornaments, for public functions—like
tiaras. The princess who runs MTV Europe . . . the prince
who brews the best beer in Bavaria . . ."

"You know those people?"

Matiyas shrugged. "You run into them at parties. Or
their kids, at school."

"Very high-end," Caroline said, as they came around
the rightward curve of the path and headed toward the
center of the park. "So what's a guy who rubs shoulders
with royalty doing laboring in the concrete canyons?"

He flashed a grin at her. "Well, you can rub shoulders
all you like, but rubbing money off, that's another story!
I did some web development work in Munich and
Frankfurt . . . but the pay wasn't great, the advancement
was slow, I was bored. Then—" He grinned a little more
broadly. "Well, they call Frankfurt 'Manhattan-am-
Rhein', you know: the skyscrapers, the busy lifestyle. I
thought, why not try the real Manhattan? And so here
I am. It took a while to get the work visa, but it was
worth it. The pay's better, and besides, it's useful being
foreign here—the company wants people with 'the international outlook.' Whatever that is."

"Maybe just that they actually believe in other countries," Caroline said, amused. "At least insofar as they
can make money off them."

He laughed again, a soft appreciative sound, and once
again Caroline got goosebumps. *Or maybe it's just the
weather,* she thought; the coat she'd brought this morning
was soaking up the rain a bit, chilling her down.

Fortunately the rain was already letting up a little as
they passed south of the Sheep Meadow and into the
center of the park. Despite the dull gray weather, the
place was pretty enough, here at the tail end of the glory
of the autumn leaves. It had been an unusually brilliant

fall, early frosts setting the leaves ablaze more emphatically than usual; but that same seasonal precocity meant that there was little left of the splendor now, only a few trees in sheltered spots having managed to hang onto their leaves this long. As they headed downhill, some of the stubbornest trees were flanking their path—beeches and oaks that seemed to be practically clutching the leaves to keep from letting them go, as if to spite the nearby maples, which had by and large given up and now stood dark and bare against the slowly falling dusk.

Matiyas had fallen silent for the last couple of minutes, looking up and around him as they walked. "Do you get color like this back home?" she said.

"Not so much. It was mostly conifers, Douglas fir and so on. Some of them go gold at the end of the year, but otherwise, everything just stays green."

"That's a shame," Caroline said. "I love this time of year: everything suddenly looks so different. Sometimes I wish it could last a lot longer."

"I don't know," said Matiyas. "I kind of like it when everything comes off the trees, at last. You can see all the shapes: what the trees are really like underneath."

"Aha. A winter fan."

"Spring is best," Matiyas said. There was something surprisingly wistful and sad about the voice. "But until it comes, you handle winter the best you can . . ."

He smiled at her again; once again, Caroline had to suppress a shiver. And then that smile went off, suddenly, as if a switch had been thrown.

It was odd; but who knew what workaday thought might have interrupted the moment. "Yeah," Caroline said as the path bottomed out and they paused in front of the cream and russet-striped brick of the carousel building, now closed on weekdays. It looked abandoned and sad—shut iron gates grim under the building's arches, dimly seen carousel horses barred inside, wet brown blown-in leaves scattered across the floor. She remembered the last time she had ridden that carousel, when she'd been going out with Colin before he dumped her. She hadn't been on it since—or out with anyone. *A year and a half? Two? And I hardly care* . . . . Caroline huddled into her coat a little, shivered again. "Snow would be nice, too. Anything's better than this damp gray."

They walked on through the tunnel on the east side of the carousel plaza, out again into the cloudy afternoon, and up the slight hill toward the tree-occluded vista of the apartment buildings east of the park, on the other side of Fifth. The way out led past the old steep-roofed Dairy. As they passed it, Mike stopped for a moment to look at the old wooden sign with the park's bylaws carved into it. " 'No one shall be permitted to drive *swine* into the park?' " He looked at her with a peculiar expression. "There were pigs here?"

"Whole herds of them, apparently," Caroline said as they headed toward Fifth. "And cows, but they were here on purpose. Seems that there was a shortage of commercially available milk that hadn't been watered down to make a profit."

Mike gave her a look. "How very New York."

Caroline snickered. "Yeah," she said. "So the City started doing their own. You could come down here and have a cow milked for your kids, my dad told me."

"You have any of those?" Mike said.

Caroline put her eyebrows up. "Kids? Why?"

He shrugged inside his coat, a chilly gesture, as they came around the corner of the old Armory building and headed up the path toward the eastern wall and Fifth Avenue. "Everybody at work seems to be either about to get married and have kids, or getting over being married and having had them," Mike said. "Just curious to see if you fell into either category."

Caroline shook her head. "No plans that way," she said. "Other people may have some kind of clock ticking, but I can't hear it."

They came up onto Fifth Avenue and headed for the corner of 65th Street. She hefted her briefcase and groaned. "Mind if I stop off and dump this thing?" she said. "It's on our way."

"Sure, why not?"

They crossed Fifth and walked almost the length of the short block down 65th. There Harry the doorman saw Caroline coming, swung the door open for them. "Be back down in a sec, Harry," Caroline said, giving him the quick look she normally gave him when going up to her place with someone for the first time. Harry nodded, saying nothing, merely touched his hat to Mike. The message was plain: If Caroline didn't come back down "in a sec," Harry would quickly be checking to find out what was the matter.

"Nice building," Mike said. "It's really good for the bus from work."

"Yeah," Caroline said. "Usually I take it when I think I'm not going to get steamed to death." The elevator door opened; she hung a left, with Mike in tow, and got her keys out. Several locks later, Caroline pushed the door open. "Come on in."

Mike stood in the hallway, looking around, as Caroline disabled the alarm system, then headed into the living room and chucked her briefcase on the couch. She slipped out of her work coat and pulled a waxed Burberry jacket off the back of a chair. "Nice place," Mike said, glancing around.

She could just hear him thinking: *And how can you possibly afford it on what the company pays you?* "A co-op," said Caroline, slinging her purse back over the Burberry. "My mom left it to me in her will after my dad left it to her."

"Oh, I'm sorry."

"Don't be. They both loved it. I love it too. They're always with me, kind of . . ." *But more Mum, really,* Caroline thought. Out of habit she glanced across the living room at the window with the couch where her mom had loved to sit, looking down over the city where she had never really felt at home though she'd done her best. *I have too much of the old country in me,* she remembered her mother saying. *I just wonder if you have enough . . .*

"Does the fireplace work?"

He sounded wistful now. "Yeah," Caroline said, head-

ing for the door, and Mike went out into the corridor to
wait for her as she locked up. "That was the main reason
my dad bought it for my mum. Most Irish houses had
fireplaces when she was growing up; she refused to live
in any house that didn't have one." And she smiled again
all the way to the elevator, and all the way downstairs,
hearing her mother's voice: *Only a heathen would live in
a house without a hearthstone. What protection's there
against the night, and the things of the night, without fire?*

Out on the street, Caroline turned to the right again.
"Down this way," she said. "You ever been to La
Finezza?"

"No," Matiyas said. "Italian?"

"You got it. And a nice bar." They headed around
the corner, past the cleaner's and the newsstand and the
pet shop. And there Caroline had to pause for a moment,
peering in the store's bay window, which was filled with
wood shavings, and pet food dishes, and fluffy striped
kittens. "Awww!"

"I didn't think they were allowed to have pet stores
like this any more," Matiyas said, smiling down at the
kittens; then he peered past them into the dimness—the
store was closed now—at the softly lit aquariums full of
bright fish, or in some cases lizards or tarantula, and
nearest the window, the still, black, coiled silken rope of
a single dark rat snake.

Caroline followed his glance, shivered one last time.
"I could do without those," she said, "but the kittens
are great. I always want to buy them all. It's a good thing
my building's no-pets."

They walked on down to the door of La Finezza, went
in. The whole front of the bar and restaurant was glass,
a set of wide folding shutters. "In the summer they fold
all this right back," Caroline said, and had no time to
say more because Peppino, the broad, dark, rotund boss
of the restaurant, had spotted her coming in the door
and was already advancing. "Carolina, *bella,* finally you
come with a friend!"

She slipped out of her coat and exchanged a couple

of uptown-Italian cheek-kisses with him. "I come with friends all the time, Peppino, don't give me that!"

"Ah, but not one special one. Sir, may I take your coat?"

Caroline was blushing—and astonished that she was blushing. Matiyas slipped out of his coat and handed it to Peppino with a slight bow. "The bar tonight?" Peppino said before he turned away to deal with the coats. "Or the restaurant?"

"Just the bar," Caroline said. But she smiled at Peppino as they went past him and sat themselves up on the big comfortable seats in front of the dark marble bar.

" 'Carolina?' " Matiyas said.

She chuckled. "I know. On the street, I'm a woman: I walk in here and become a state. North or South, I don't know."

Carlo, the barman, came over and smiled at them. "Caroline," he said. "The usual?"

"Americano," she said, "absolutely."

"You, sir?"

"I've never had an Americano," Matiyas said. "What's it like?"

"Strong," Caroline said.

"Sounds perfect," said Matiyas.

The drinks came, tall, cool and deceptively pink-looking. Caroline took a long hit of hers, felt that here-comes-the-alcohol shiver that she saved herself for every Friday evening. Matiyas drank cautiously at first, and his eyes widened. "Well!" he said.

"You like?" Caroline said.

"Very much. They do something like this at Raffles in Singapore."

She laughed at him. "You're just showing off, now. Frankfurt, Munich, Singapore—Where *haven't* you been?"

"Here," he said, raising the glass. *"Zum wohl."*

"Slainte," she said, and they banged the glasses together.

They talked casino games, a little, to start with, because considering where they worked, that was common ground—the inherent folly of the concept of a successful roulette system; card-counting and how no one really needs it that much because most blackjack players play so very badly; whether the House really always rakes off ten percent; game theory, lottery odds, where probability prediction software fails and how it can be made to fail. By then they were both laughing harder than could be blamed on the booze alone. *Tension?* Caroline thought. *Who cares?* For by the end of the second round, he was "Matt" and she was "Caro," and they had moved on to the decline of pinball machine art since Photoshop came in, and the intolerable noisiness of gaming machines in English pubs, and whether British humor was really humor at all (a thesis Matt defended with a truly horrific joke about wounded soldiers, wire brushes and chlorine bleach), and how much British food had improved in the last twenty years, and how insane restaurant prices had become on the West Side lately, and comfort food, and where to get the best pasta, and how spaghetti and meatballs didn't really exist except in takeaway pizzerias, and how no one really did a decent Bolognese sauce outside of Bologna—

"They do here!" Caroline said.

"*I'll* be the judge of that," said Matiyas.

"Well, so you shall. Peppino?" Caroline called over her shoulder.

"Right over here," Peppino said, pulling back a chair from one of the better tables, the one in the corner by the front window.

And then when menus had been perused and the orders given, including for a bottle of wine, the conversation quickly slid away into computer games in general, and why the single-person shooter was or wasn't dead, and how to sabotage pinball machines without getting caught. And when the first bottle of wine arrived, and the appetizers, the really serious laughter began.

It wasn't nonstop laughter, of course. Every now and then there had appeared a sort of secret smile on Matiyas's face, a surprisingly reposeful expression for someone whose expressions were usually so mobile. And Caroline had been charmed to see it there. But then, as in the park, it would abruptly fall off. And then it would come back and fall off again. *Something bothering him, maybe. Maybe it's been a while since he had a date. Who knows?* Though it seemed unbelievable. *Such an attractive man. So personable.* But maybe there was some other problem. *Maybe somebody hurt him, too, once—*

Oh, stop projecting your own stuff all over him!

Nonetheless, she kept waiting and watching for that smile. And when she realized she was doing that, Caroline started to become very suspicious of herself, for she never talked like this to people she hadn't known for a long, long time. *What is it about this guy? What gives here?*

Am I possibly—

Naah.

But the idea came back to haunt her like a screenful of buggy code.

Am I—falling in—

Naaaaah!

Yet the screen inside her mind filled up with code again. What *was* it about him? It wasn't just that Matt was charming. He was. Or that he was cute. *He is!* Boy, *is he.* There just seemed to be something else going on. *It's not like he's desperate. Why would he be desperate, the way he looks, the way he acts? He's witty. He's urbane. He even cooks, it sounds like. He's so . . . accessible.*

That might have been it. As he poured her one more glass of wine when the main course plates went away—*see that, he doesn't even wait for the waiter to do it*—Caroline looked across the table, and Matt was smiling at her, and it wasn't just one of those facial smiles: The eyes were deeply involved.

And inside them, something happened.

This time it was the eyes that changed. Nothing about the expression about them, not a muscle shifted. But suddenly Caroline started to see something hard about them, something strangely chilly that didn't sort well with the warmth in the face. He started saying something about dessert, and Caroline nodded and kept her smile exactly where it was, while thinking two things.

Is there something funny about the lighting in here all of a sudden? His eyes were brown. Why do they look lighter now? Almost gold.

And when did he last blink?

The dessert menu came along, and Caroline opened it, and made "hmm" noises, and kept on thinking, and smiling. And the thought occurred to her:

How many drinks have I had? There was the Americano, twice. And, what, two glasses of wine? No, this is the third one—

She looked up from the dessert menu, looked across the table.

The eyes were still there, and they still had not blinked. And they were indeed golden. But they were set on either side of the foot-and-a-half wide head of a gigantic snake.

She blinked, as casually as she could. The snake was still there. It was actually rather pretty, as snakes went: scaled in handsome patterns of green and gold, sort of a more attractive version of a rattlesnake's patterning. But as it opened its jaws to say something about tiramisu, she could see the poison fangs angle forward, each as long as her index finger; and a long, pale forked tongue flickered out, tasting the air for her breath.

Oh, no, Caroline thought. *Not this. Not now.*

For quite a long time, when Caroline was younger, she'd wondered why her mother never drank. It was one of those things they'd never discussed until the day she turned twenty and her mother sat her down "to have a little talk." Even in this bizarre moment, Caroline still had a momentary flashback of that long-ago moment's amusement—her idea that she knew what her mom was about to lecture her on. Afterward she'd wished it was something so mundane as a discussion about the birds and bees, because it had explained things that she'd started noticing while she was in college and had just begun, rather belatedly according to all her friends, to experiment with booze. She had started to "see things"—

images that made no sense, odd changes in people. They never lasted. At first she'd been able to dismiss the strange shifts in perception as something to do with the alcohol itself, possibly an allergy. Yet drinking had never made her sick, and soon enough she'd learned that she could simply prevent the effect by limiting her intake.

But it had all fallen apart when her mother asked, both kindly and rather sternly, "Do you see things?"

"What?"

"Things that are only there for a few moments and then vanish. Or things that seem to last a while before they fade. Visions. Creatures that can't be there, but are. Do you See things?"

Now Caroline was feeling again the shock she'd felt then. *It's been so long, now.* But then she'd been so careful for such a long time, especially right after that conversation—or rather, after the one experimental bender she went on after the conversation, that had confirmed it all: the beautiful historic city pub that had suddenly revealed itself to be full of peculiar animals, fabulous beasts, and people who were revealed as not quite human, or rather more than. The next day, when her blood alcohol was down to zero and she'd looked into the pub, everything had been normal again . . . except her. Her mother had been telling the truth: The women of her family could view the invisible, See spells and curses, peer a little way into the Other Side . . . or into some of the truths of this side, normally hidden.

And now here she was, looking at a dessert menu while having dinner with a giant snake. *And how the hell is he holding his dessert menu?* Still carefully keeping her smile in place, Caroline glanced at Matt's menu and saw the small delicate forelegs that ended in clawed talons. Not exactly a snake, then. *Sort of a—what did they call it? Mum told me a story when I was little about some kind of long skinny dragon that didn't have wings but did have legs. And they weren't the romantic kind of dragon. They ate people. Young women, mostly.* She shivered again. *What did they call that thing? Damned if I can remember—*

"Tiramisu," Caroline said aloud, in a musing kind of way. *And I can't believe I did this to myself. Five units of alcohol, it must have been! I talked myself right into it. He's so cute, I'm so nervous, I'll just have a glass or two to take the edge off*—

But instead it had put an edge on her ability to See. Now all that remained to Caroline was to figure out what she was Seeing. Was this vision just a sort of analysis of Matt's personality, a warning that he was a snake in the relationship sense? Or was he actually this weird dragony-wormy-snaky thing, pretending to be Matt?

There's a reason you've been given this gift, her mother had said. *You have a responsibility to help people! Sometimes a seeming will be a warning to someone: You must deliver it. Sometimes the seeming will be a hidden reality, a spell, a curse: You must act to help.*

Which was one of the reasons Caroline had been so careful not to get into any situation where she'd have to use the gift, if she could at all avoid it. Now she looked up at Peppino as he came to take their orders, and she ordered tiramisu and a double espresso, which she really needed to steady herself a little. Then, when he was gone, she glanced across at Matt again and did her best to stay as calm as if nothing were happening. *Oh yeah, like* every *Friday night you have dinner with a giant snake! And a smart one.* There was entirely too much going on behind those golden eyes, a sense of intelligent calculation.

But something else, too. *Who's doing the calculating?* Caroline thought. *Or what?* For as she looked at him now, she thought she could see something else behind the mica-like sheen of the eyes—something that was struggling, like a just-eaten mouse inside some snake in a pet-shop aquarium. Not just something: some*one*. Trying to get loose, trying to warn her; but as helpless as the mouse inside the snake . . .

You could be imagining it, some freaked-out part of her mind insisted. But somehow Caroline doubted it. *Even before he started looking like this to me, there was something about him that was changing. On and off, like flipping a switch. What's doing the flipping? Is it Matt? Or something inside him—or something done to him?* For her mother had said, *You will see spells, curses . . .* At the time, she hadn't believed it. But now—

And that was when the hair started to stand up on the back of Caroline's neck again. *How many other women have flipped this switch?* she thought. *How many others have been charmed by him, and done the My Place Or Yours thing . . . and never seen 'their place' again?*

The switch. *Could it be that the moment* he *starts to feel something for somebody, then something done to him, the curse laid on him, wakes up, takes over*—

Her heart leaped at the thought; but her heart was cold, too. She had been eating the tiramisu more or less on automatic pilot; now she picked up the wine glass for one final sip, waiting for the espresso to arrive.

Across the table, golden eyes, unblinking, were fixed on her. "You're quiet all of a sudden," the snake said. "Are you okay?"

She kept her smile in place. *Absolutely not! But this is something I have to deal with. There's something else under the surface here. If I don't do something about it, he'll do something about somebody else.* And whatever her friends in Belfast might have thought, there was enough death in this city as it was. *What kind of person would just turn her back and walk away and let more of it happen?*

Caroline swallowed. Then she took one more sip of the wine, staring down into the glass, catching there the dark reflection of her own eyes, in which no one would have needed the Sight to see her fear. Caroline blinked, drank, put the glass down, and very, very slowly— because it took some work—she raised her eyes again, and smiled at Matt.

"Do you want to come back to my place for coffee?" she said.

They went back slowly, at a stroll—or what was a stroll for Caroline. Next to her, the upper third of his body upright like a cobra's, the giant serpent glided along, seemingly as leisurely as she. *It's going to drive me nuts,* she thought, *if I can't remember what mum said these things were called.*

She was thinking hard, paying no attention to the rain, which had started up again, or to the yellow glow of the streetlights, or the white and red glare of headlights and taillights pouring past. In Caroline's mind, another light suffused everything—firelight. Underlying it, she could hear the murmur of the stories her mum would tell her while she lay on her stomach, as close to the grate as she could get without singeing herself; watching the shapes take form in the flames, springing from the wood, in New York, or on the peat, back in the little country townland of Aghalee.

When she was younger, the action in those stories had seemed random, unpredictable: a spell cast here, an evil fairy cutting up cranky there, people turned into beasts or monsters, people turned back. But later in life, when she'd done some study of folktales as part of her college education, Caroline had started to realize that the randomness was an illusion, mostly born of uneven storytelling. Inevitably, when you took them apart, spells had breakers built into them. It was just a matter of finding them, figuring out what they were. *And it's not like we're exactly prepared for this kind of thing, anymore. You can't walk into a bookstore and buy* Spellbreaking for Dummies. *Or download the user's manual from the manufacturer's website.*

But if the stories *were* the user's manual . . . . *Or what's left of the stories.* For so many of them had been dumbed down over time, Disneyfied—rendered more politically or environmentally correct, less potentially offensive. *And who knows whether the active ingredient, the real information about the 'unreal' world, is still there? Have we removed the reason the stories were told in the first place? If we have, the de-Grimmifiers and the Hans Christian Andersens of the world have a lot to answer for.*

But those answers were going to have to come later. Right now she and Matt, or the serpent-thing that was pretending to be Matt, came to her building's lobby door, and Harry the doorman opened it for the two of them. She saw his glance at Matt: veiled curiosity, nothing more. *Plainly, everybody else sees the disguise, no matter what I see. Interesting.*

And will it stay that way after he eats me? asked some cold thought in the back of Caroline's brain as they went up in the elevator. *And what exactly am I planning to do about him? Lecture him on the error of his ways? What if, to keep him from eating me, or anybody else, I have to kill him? Whose body winds up on my kitchen floor? A giant snake's, or Matt's?*

The elevator door opened, and they headed down toward her door, where Caroline paused, fumbling around in her bag for her keys. She paused in front of her door,

So . . . coffee. *Take your time making it. Think. Think.* "Regular coffee," Caroline asked, slipping out of her coat and tossing it over one of the dining room chairs, "or more espresso?"

"Regular's fine," the snake said.

"Milk? Sugar?"

"A lot of milk."

Yeah, she thought, *milk. Snakes were supposed to like milk. It's in Kipling.* But Kipling was the wrong place to be looking for answers right now. *He had that story about the sea serpent, but that thing was the size of a steamer. No hints for me there . . . .* Caroline looked into the little living room, saw the snake gliding gently along the wall and looking at her artwork, or pretending to.

"Some nice watercolors," the snake said.

It was almost Matt's voice: almost. There was a strained quality to it. The mouse, inside, struggling—

"Got them in Scotland," Caroline said, turning away for a moment, trying to get a grip on herself. She glanced at the knife block on the counter. They were all extremely sharp. There was also the gun in the gun safe, but probably no time to get it out or do anything useful with it. *And do guns work on curses? Cold iron is the usual thing, in the fairy tales . . .*

The coffee machine gurgled quietly to itself. Caroline

wandered into the living room, knelt down by the fire-place, where the fire was laid ready as usual, got down a box of matches from the mantelpiece, and reached in to open the damper. The wood caught quickly: It was dry. She looked up, saw the snake looking down at her, gleaming a little already in the light of the flames that were coming up.

She stood up hurriedly. "Sorry," she said. "I was distracted." *Smile, smile like it's him that's distracting you. Or like it's Matt! Hang in there, Matt!* "You take sugar?"

"No, milk's fine." With those big cold golden eyes he looked up at the watercolor over the mantelpiece, a landscape, all Scottish heather and clouded hillsides, and a stream running through the heart of it.

Caroline swallowed, turned away again; then she paused, surprised. Matt's coat was on top of her own, over the dining room chair. *Now how'd he manage that?* she thought, picking it up—anything to buy herself a few more moments of time. *His clothes, then, aren't just part of an illusion. They're real, they're just hidden somehow.* "I'll hang this up for you," she said and headed back to the hall closet.

"Thanks," he said. Caroline was uneasy about turning her back on him, but at the same time, he didn't seem likely to do anything sudden. *Why should he? He thinks he has me where he wants me . . . .*

Which he does! yelled one of the more panic-stricken parts of her mind. But Caroline took a long breath, opened the closet, felt around for an empty hanger, didn't find one right away. She pushed her coats and jackets aside, one after another. *All these coats, who needs all this stuff, they're all out of style, I should take some of them to the Goodwill. If I live that long!*

She found an empty hanger and put Matt's coat on it. Without warning, in the back of her mind, something surfaced—a strange image. Something to do with snakes, and clothes. *Now what on earth—?*

Caroline paused. A woman taking off some item of clothing. A snake shedding its skin. And a sudden memory of her mother's voice: just a phrase or two. *And she told them to light a fire in the bridal chamber, and hang*

*a pot of lye over it, and leave on the hearth three strong
scrub brushes—*

Caroline's mouth dropped open.

Lindworm! That *was the name!*

Her eyes narrowed, and she smiled; and this time the
smile was real. She remembered the whole story, now.
And now she knew how this story could end—if she was
smart about it.

In the kitchen, the coffeemaker chimed. Caroline
closed the closet door, and as she went back through the
living room, she looked over at the fire, which was burning brighter every minute. *You really* are *with me here
all the time,* she said silently to her mother. *Now we'll
find out if you're here enough.*

"You want a mug or a cup?" Caroline said.

"A mug'll be fine," said the lindworm, slithering down
so it lay against the couch, in front of the fire.

Yeah, Caroline thought. *You get yourself real comfy
there while I think this through.* She got two mugs down,
filled one of them two-thirds full, one nearly full;
dropped three sugars in that one, poured the other one
nearly full of milk. She brought them both over by the
sofa and handed the milky one to the lindworm, which
took it with some difficulty in those delicate little claws.
Then she put the other one down on the hearth.

"Would you excuse me for a moment?" Caroline said.
"I want to go slip into something . . . different."

The lindworm smiled.

So did she as she vanished into the bedroom and shut
the door.

It took about ten minutes to do what she had in mind.
At the end of that time she came out into the living
room again and sat down on the floor in front of the
sofa, next to the lindworm. And instantly Caroline broke
out into a sweat because she was now wearing, over her
Friday casuals of oxford shirt and jeans, a total of six
more pairs of pants, five shirts, two sweaters, and a
hoodie.

"How's the coffee?" she asked, picking up her mug
and sipping at her own.

The lindworm stared at her with those great chilly golden eyes. It was impossible to make out expressions in them; but the voice, when it spoke, was a little rough around the edges: the sound of a surprise that the speaker was trying to conceal.

"I think," the lindworm said, stretching some more of the length of its body out toward the fire, "that you should really take all those clothes off."

She gave him as level a stare as she could manage. "*I* think," she said, "that *you* should really take all yours off first."

He smiled, slowly, and the front fangs glinted in the firelight. "Mmmm . . . kinky."

"Not half as kinky," she said, working to keep her voice steady, "as a one-night stand with a giant snake."

He held absolutely still.

"Oh, yeah," Caroline said. "You think I didn't notice?"

"Uh," he said, sounding very much as though he was trying to find a way to respond that wouldn't give anything away. "Maybe you've had a little too much to drink . . ."

"Oh no," Caroline said. "Just about enough. And as for you— You think I couldn't just about hear you thinking, anyway? Asking all the right questions, finding the right answers. Your dream date, huh? No parents. No kids. Perfect. She vanishes, and it's just another missing person. And when you're hungry again—a couple of weeks from now, a month, I don't know or care—you find yourself another date. And then before too long, you change companies, because it's smart to get out before anyone who might start investigating these murders starts seeing a pattern."

The cold, brassy, blank eyes rested on her, just watching her with that dry, unmoved gleam. *That's what freaks people out about snakes,* she thought suddenly. *The eyes aren't wet. At least that's what's freaking* me *out . . .* At the same time, she was watching the way the rest of the lindworm's body was coiling away from the fire, getting a little closer to her . . .

"Oh no you don't," Caroline said, standing up. "That's not how it's going to go down."

"And what makes you think you get to say how it's going to go?" the lindworm said.

"Because I 'read the F-ing manual,' " Caroline said, "and I know how this curse works. If we'd gone to your place, this might have been a whole different story. There's still a game to be played, sure. There are some moves that have to be gone through. You've got your chance to win. You've just got to get the clothes off me first . . . because only a nonmagic snake would be stupid enough to eat someone with their clothes on: It'd come down with a case of gastroenteritis that'd kill it stone dead." She grinned—a far more savage look than the one she'd been holding in place for the last half hour. "Problem is, those little claws aren't strong enough to do much more than hold a menu. And type, I guess. Any clothes that come off me, I'm going to have to remove."

"And why would I go along with you on this?"

"I'm betting," Caroline said, "because having gotten this far, you just can't resist the challenge. How many other poor women just fell into your arms, pulled their clothes off, never had the wherewithal to resist? Easy meat. But this time—this time you get a crack at someone who knows what's going on. You get to see how good a curse you are. Can I wear you down before you do the same to me? Let's find out."

"And suppose I decide to . . . force the issue?"

Those golden eyes were somehow looking bigger than they had any right to as they bent close to her. The mouth opened, slowly . . .

Caroline reached under the hoodie and whipped out the vintage eighteen-inch carbon steel Henkel kitchen knife, the one that her father told her Julia Child had used to refer to as "the fright knife," holding it right in front of the lindworm's nose. It shied back sharply. "This isn't stainless, Slinky-boy," Caroline said. "Cold iron. You betting you can try something cute with me before I do you some serious damage? Let's find out."

The lindworm closed its mouth, saying nothing. But the eyes started to look angry.

"So," Caroline said. "When I take off a piece of clothing, you take off something too."

"Like what? I have no—"

"Snakes," Caroline said, "shed their skins. That's 'like what.' "

The glare became more furious still—but this time Caroline saw what she'd been waiting for: a tiny glint of fear.

"And just to make sure that everything goes ahead in a nice organized kind of way—"

She turned to the sideboard up against the wall, pulled a drawer open, rummaged, then shut the drawer, turned, and she dropped a pack of cards onto the shining mahogany table.

"I'll deal the first hand," she said. "Five card stud?"

The lindworm's eyes narrowed. Again it said nothing . . . and then it glided around to the far side of the table.

Sweating, sweltering, Caroline sat down. To her left, the fire burned bright. It glinted on the snake's scales, burned in those golden eyes. Caroline tapped the deck of cards out of the pack, tapped them even on the table, started to shuffle, dealt.

They played. Caroline studied her cards, watched her adversary do the same. It was not the best hand she'd ever had, not the worst. *Thirteen hands to play,* she thought. *The law of averages may be my best friend tonight. At least half the deals are mine.*

It proved so on the first hand, at least: her ace-high flush against the lindworm's three of a kind. It stared at its cards as if it couldn't quite believe what was happening.

"Well?" Caroline said.

The lindworm glared at her again. Then it put the cards down, lowered its head . . .

The skin split all down one side of it with a weird, wettish sound like a nylon zipper. The lindworm scrabbled at itself with its little claws, and scratched and scraped against the edge of the mahogany table as the translucent old skin started to peel away.

"Hey, watch the finish," Caroline muttered. But the lindworm paid her no mind. Finally the skin was off, and the much shinier, damper-looking lindworm seized the cast-off skin in its little claws, crumpled it into a ball, and tossed it onto the table.

"Your turn," it said.

Caroline stood up, pulled off the hoodie and the old ski pants that made up the outermost layer, rolled them up and chucked them onto the table too. Then she pushed the cards across the table to the lindworm.

It shuffled, though not terribly well: The claws seemed to interfere. Then it dealt.

She picked up her cards, shook her head. Straight: nine, ten, jack, queen. "Hit me," she said. But the draw didn't improve matters. The best she could come up with was two pair to the lindworm's full house. It laid down the cards with a nasty look of triumph, and said, "Your turn . . ."

Caroline let out an annoyed breath and pulled off a sweater and another pair of pants, three years-ago's superannuated baggies. She took the cards and started to shuffle . . .

. . . and had to stop, for she found herself feeling an increasing sense of pressure, and not anything to do with those tight clothes, either. She glanced up quickly and then glanced down again, realizing that that had been a mistake. Those golden eyes were fixed on her, huge, insistent, and it was from them that the sense of pressure came.

"I gave up staring games in grade school," Caroline said, resuming her shuffle. "Let's go." She dealt.

The cards were much better this time. But somehow she had trouble feeling good about it. She already felt very hot, and suddenly she started to feel very tired as well. *And why not? It's been a long day. It'd be great to just lean back in the chair and close my eyes for a moment . . .*

Caroline shook her head. *Not right now.* She studied her cards, glanced across the table, looked no higher than the delicate little claws. They were rock-steady; She supposed it was too much to ask to see her opponent trembling with any kind of emotion. She hung on, keeping herself still. When the cards went down on the table, she had four of a kind against the lindworm's straight. *Not bad. Stay with it . . .*

The lindworm hissed, straightened a little at the table. Then it hissed again, and the skin split again down its other side, a louder sound this time, as if the split was deeper. The lindworm shuddered, as if this time the splitting bothered it more. This time, when the skin came away, it wasn't dry: The tissue under it wept, and a faint strange metallic smell started to fill the room.

The skin went into the middle of the table, and Caroline stood up, her eye on the knife, and pulled off another layer of clothes. She was getting cooler, which was a relief, but she was also wondering whether the story was going to be right about how many skins this thing had. *Oh, mum . . . it had better be!* She sat down again, pushed the deck across to the lindworm.

It shuffled, gazing at her. Once again Caroline started feeling that strange drowsy pressure, and along with it a feeling, not of tiredness this time, but of hopelessness. She won that hand, and the next; and, hissing more loudly each time, the lindworm split its skin away. But somehow it didn't seem to matter. Twice more she got up and pulled off a layer of clothes; and once more she dealt, and once more the lindworm did. And somehow none of it seemed to matter.

The cards hit the table before her, face down, and each one seemed to say in a whisper as it hit, *What possible difference will this make? As if, even if you did win, as if whatever was left over, whoever was left over, would want* you. *Just give it up, just let it go. You're going to lose anyway. Why prolong the inevitable?*

But Caroline concentrated on those cards, and particularly on their backs, the designs on them, graceful and precise. She picked them up and studied them for meaning. It seemed to take longer than usual, a lot longer.

"You're stalling," the lindworm said. "It's not going to help."

Caroline wavered in her seat, staring at the cards. *How many hands now?* she thought. But this one, anyway, this one was good.

"Just give it up," said the lindworm. "What's the point? Let it happen. You know it's going to . . ." It sounded almost kindly. The voice reminded her of Matt's . . .

Caroline swallowed, sat up straighter. She dared a glance at the lindworm, not so much at its eyes as at the rest of it. It looked bigger, somehow: taller, wider. But somehow it also looked more bloated, less substantial, less scaly. There was something less solid about it. Caroline stared at her cards one last time, laid them down. "Four of a kind," she said. "Show."

The lindworm hissed, laid its own cards down. Two pair.

Caroline grinned, but the grin felt weak. She stood up to slip out of one more layer of clothes. She started to feel chilly as she sat down again, despite the fire burning right beside her.

Across from her, the lindworm squirmed, coiled, uncoiled. It made a thin, high, whining noise for a few moments, like a power saw, and then its skin split again, with more force, as if something was pressing it more forcefully from inside, almost pushing to get out. The creature that came out of that skin was even less scaly, more like a slug or worm; only a few scales seemed to cling about the plates of the head, and only the eyes kept that brilliant gold. Everything else about the thing was going wet and leaden, like the sky outside.

Caroline took the cards to deal again, but her concentration was starting to fail her. *All that wine, all this stress . . .* The fire burned brightly behind her; she tried to keep that firelight in her mind as well, but it kept fading. She glanced up at the bloated, pallid thing coiling and pulsing across the table from her. The eyes . . .

Caroline looked away, and kept nearly looking back

again, and had to stop herself and concentrate as best as she could on the shuffling.

Snake and bird . . . snake and mouse. The images kept occurring to her. Those "fascination" stories were, well, just stories. But at the same time, what if they had some basis in truth? What if they had the same kind of basis that the lindworm story itself had? If there were actually serpents who were the expression of some kind of curse, why couldn't they have unusual powers over the minds of their victims, why couldn't their eyes swallow you up like, like—

She shook her head brutally. The lindworm was glaring at her. "Deal," it said.

The pile of shed skins and shed clothes in the middle of the table was getting higher, getting in the way of the playing space. Caroline shoved it over to one side, looked at her opponent, shook her head again. It was hard not to look at those eyes. In poker, you looked at the other player's eyes if you could. And with the lindworm there was no other way to judge expression.

Matt, she thought. *Matt. Poor Matt.*

She dealt, put the deck down, and stared at her cards. A feeling of horror crept over her. *Oh, no. I can't do anything with these.* She started to say, "Dealer draws—," feeling those eyes resting on her, overwhelming her, making her hand reach out—

Then Caroline took control of her hand back, reached sideways instead, and gripped the blade of the Fright Knife, hard.

The pain shocked straight through her as if she'd grabbed a live wire. The lindworm hissed in fury. Caroline looked at her cards again. She looked up, met those eyes full on.

They froze her in place, descended on her, devoured her. *You are fit to be nothing but meat,* they said, and she knew it in her soul to be true. *There is no single soul on this planet who will ever waste his or her time loving you. Your last bedmate should have taught you that. You will live alone. You will die alone. No victory is worth enduring years and years of such a life. Take death now, in company, while you can, because no one will ever care about your death as much as I will.*

Caroline felt the tears running down her face and slowly stood up to do what was the only thing left to her, to take off the last layer of clothes, to stand bare before her doom. She felt the blood running down and didn't care about it, saw the taut, shining, swollen head come toward her—

—and caught a flicker of firelight out of the corner of her eye, and on the cards she held.

"No," she whispered.

Those impossibly huge eyes seemed to recede. The wavering, shivering, pallid shape across from her began to tremble.

"Nice try," Caroline said, in a voice that barely worked. "But not quite nice enough."

She put down her cards on the table. Ten, jack, queen, king, ace of hearts.

Royal flush.

Slowly, slowly, shivering like jelly, the lindworm started to slowly rise from where it coiled behind the table. *"You cheated!"*

"Oh?" Caroline said. "How?"

"You—they—"

With the greatest effort, Caroline managed a smile.

"They were marked! The cards were marked!"

Her grin didn't change. "Prove it."

The lindworm started scrabbling with its claws among the undealt cards. The look of balked fury on the snake's face, the spell's face, was hilarious. But Caroline wasn't going to waste precious time enjoying the show. "Cut the crap!" she said, picking up the Fright Knife. "Show your hand right now, or I'll save you the trouble and pin you to the table!"

The lindworm screamed. The drying tears sticky on her face, Caroline took a hasty step backward, ready to use the knife.

And, still screaming, the lindworm burst, the last skin shredding away from it like something caught in a hailstorm of razorblades.

Caroline stood there in the sudden wet silence, panting with exertion and terror and the sudden removal of that awful pressure on her mind. There was slime everywhere, and a truly revolting smell. For a moment, she didn't move. Then she reached out to the wet, messy cards, and turned them over.

All spades: ace, King, eight, seven, three. Busted flush. *How appropriate,* she thought, looking around. *I just wish it didn't mean I was going to have to replace my carpet. There goes that long weekend in Paris* . . . . She stepped around the table to look at what was left. It was gross in the extreme: a nasty slimy translucent mess of . . . *what?*

And—was there something still buried in it?

The phone from the lobby rang.

Gasping, Caroline staggered down the hallway, gulped a little air, and picked up the phone. "Yes?"

"Is everything all right up there, Miss Desantis?"

She gulped again and tried to get her voice to sound at least slightly normal. "Uh, fine, Harry. Why?"

"Your nextdoor neighbor called. Said that someone was getting very . . . *loud* in there." His voice suggested that he very much didn't want to say loud *how*.

"Uh, sorry, Harry, it was the, uh, the entertainment system. We were watching a monster movie, and the volume got out of hand."

"Oh," her doorman said. It was not precisely a tone of voice that suggested he believed her. It sounded more like Harry wanted her to know that the excuse was just *barely* acceptable . . . just this once.

"It's okay, though," Caroline said, turning to look back toward the dining room table. "We're, uh—" That shape underneath the slime was moving slightly, weakly. And abruptly something stuck *out* of the slime.

A hand.

"We're done with the horror movies for the evening, I think," she said. "Sorry about that."

"I'll let the neighbors know," Harry said. "Good night."

He hung up, and Caroline could have sworn she just

barely heard him chuckle. She hurried back to the table,
knelt down beside it, paused for a moment, and then
thrust her hands into the awful heap of slime, pulling out
with great difficulty what lay inside it.

At least the slime made it somewhat easier to manhan-
dle him down into the bathroom, though he was likely
to have some carpet burns later. With considerable difficulty, Caroline shoved the slimy naked form into the
shower stall, turned the shower on, and then stood back
as the gasping noises started and the naked shape started
flailing around.

"Sorry," she said, turning to grab a towel for him, "it's
always pretty cold when it starts up—"

The spluttering and gasping got louder. "What happened?" asked that slightly European voice after a moment. "Oh, this is *disgusting,* what is this stuff, it won't
come off—"

"The story calls for lye at this point," Caroline said,
kneeling down . "But that's not something I'd have in
the house. I guess we can use Clorox if we have to."

From the floor of the shower stall, Matt began to laugh
weakly. "Please, no," he said. And then he started laughing again.

"What?" Caroline said, kneeling down by the shower
stall and looking into those wonderful eyes.

"Clorox, yes, all right. But not the wire brushes!"
Matt said.

She stared at him—then held out the towel for him,
and a moment later she pulled him close.

It was quite some time before he pulled back, and
even then, he only pulled back slightly. "Thank you."

"You're welcome," she said.

"I am . . . more than grateful."

"You should be," Caroline said. "It's not every day I
bring home a magic giant snake for coffee."

"Magic giant snake *prince*," Matt said.

She gave him a look. "Oh, really? Prince of what?"

"One of those little European countries you probably
never heard of."

"Oh? Try me."

"Cariola."

"What?"

He looked suddenly abashed—at least, as abashed as a half-naked guy sitting on the floor of a shower stall might normally have time to. "Okay," he said, "so I lied. *Not* prince." Caroline gave him a look. "Duke."

Her look got more incredulous. "Well, you don't hear a lot about enchanted dukes!" he said, sounding annoyed. "You have to admit, 'Prince' sounds better—"

"Give me a break. And 'Cariola?' You're making it up."

"I am not!"

"Then why have I never heard of it?"

"Because you have no grasp of history. Or possibly geography. But it's not your fault. Democracies often have lousy school systems."

"I beg your pardon!" she said, outraged. "Ireland is a democracy!"

"Only for the last century. Your people had kings. *High* Kings."

She laughed. "You can just leave out what they were smoking," she said. "So. An enchanted duke, huh?"

"Disenchanted," Matt said. "Cursed. But now the curse is broken."

"Don't tell me. Bad-tempered fairy left out of the christening invitations?"

Now it was his turn to give her a look. "Evil chief minister with a pet sorcerer and a preferred heir. Comes to the same thing."

"If you say so."

He laughed for sheer joy. "Oh, Caroline, you have no idea how impossible I thought this was ever going to be, how long I was trapped that way." And if his eyes had not been wet before, they were now. "Caroline—"

She put a finger on his lips. "Ssh," she said. "I've got an idea."

"What?"

"Let's go get us some happy ending."

*   *   *

Much, much later, Caroline said, "So where *is* Cari-ola exactly?"

"Oh, so you believe in it now?"

She punched him in one arm. He grimaced, then grinned.

"No, really, where is it?"

"Slovenia. For the moment."

"Oh? You have plans?"

"Right now? Only dental. Unless you say otherwise."

She shook her head, entirely happy for things to be just the way they were—and, it seemed from the way their conversation had been going earlier in the evening, the way they would likely be for the rest of their lives.

"But can I ask a question?"

"Sure."

"Were those cards marked?"

Caroline just grinned. "Your curse was cheating," she said. "Let's just say I leveled the playing field."

He smiled back, and once again Caroline got goose-bumps. "Now," he said, "my princess. About that happy ending—"

"Yes?"

"Seconds?"

BY ANY OTHER NAME

Laura Resnick

Laura Resnick is the author of such fantasy novels as *Disappearing Nightly, In Legend Born, The Destroyer Goddess,* and *The White Dragon,* which made the "Year's Best" lists of *Publishers Weekly* and *Voya.* Winner of the 1993 Campbell Award for best new science fiction/fantasy writer, she has published more than fifty short stories. You can find her on the Web at www.LauraResnick.com.

At first, I thought Will Arden seemed to be your traditional, standard-issue, yuppie, gay blind date.

He had been conscientiously screened and chosen for me by two friends of mine who were almost pathologically eager to see me get back into the fray after my disastrous relationship and painful break-up with Jai de Joi, a Chelsea-based performance artist. (I have a theory that happy couples feel so compelled to force their single friends to date because, being happy couples, they've selectively deleted all memory of how much they hated dating back when *they* were single.)

Despite what the words "performance artist" inescapably imply, Jai was, in fact, fairly successful and able to pick up the dinner tab now and then. Unfortunately, he was also prone to extreme mood swings that corresponded to his artistic highs and lows, he was obsessed with his work to a degree that (I assert) any lover would find demoralizing before long, and he was a kind of psychic vampire, sucking the life out of his boyfriend (briefly *me*) to sustain the tremendous emotional drain of his creative endeavors.

I never knew Jai's real name. He'd had it changed legally to Jai de Joi when he was twenty-two. By the time I met him, a decade later, he claimed that even his parents called him "Jai" now. (Since we broke up before I ever met them, I can't say for sure.) After the break-up, I wondered what attracted me in the first place to someone who'd deliberately *chosen* a name like "Jai de Joi." And I realized that I was, of course, drawn to the exact same qualities that had ultimately convinced me that I faced a choice between ending the relationship or losing my mind: the color, energy, and originality of a genuinely creative personality.

I'm a software consultant. Mostly, I help companies choose, install, and train their employees to use the data processing software that best suits their needs. Hey, not all gay men are colorful punsters running around on hit TV shows teaching straight men how to choose clothes, decorate their homes, and groom themselves. Some of us lead ordinary lives, doing ordinary work.

It was only after breaking up with Jai, shortly before my thirty-fifth birthday, that I faced the truth about myself: I was an ordinary person with a fatal attraction to the extraordinary. Besides Jai de Joi the performance artist, my relationships since college had included a drummer, an actor, a set designer, an aspiring screenwriter, a sculptor, and a guy who created interactive computer games. These relationships all had one thing in common: None of them had lasted.

I was drawn to creative men, but this tendency clearly wasn't healthy for me. If I didn't break my pattern, I'd spend *another* fifteen years in a series of passionate but short and doomed relationships, and when I was fifty, I'd still be single, alone and—God save me!—*dating*.

So I made a solemn, sincere resolution to change my ways. I canceled my season tickets to Lincoln Center. I took my name off every art gallery mailing list I'd been on for years. I stopped attending readings at the 92nd Street YMCA. I started spending my spare time at the gym and attending financial planning seminars.

And I instructed all of my friends to stop introducing me to guys who were my type.

"No more actors and playwrights," I said emphatically. "No more musicians. I don't want to meet any mural artists, novelists, or furniture designers. I only want to meet the men you've never before considered introducing me to because you knew it would be a waste of time."

The brand new list of "types" I wanted to meet for a change included doctors, lawyers, accountants, sales reps, bankers, and pilots. My friend Doreen asked if I'd like to meet her neighbor, a single thirty-something pastry chef with a nice dog, but I declined. I'd watched enough of the Food Channel to suspect I would fall hopelessly for him, only to find his side of the bed cold one night because he suddenly felt compelled to experiment with an idea for white chocolate, marzipan-trimmed petit-fours in a gooseberry reduction sauce at three o'clock in the morning. And I just couldn't take any more nights like that.

So when my friends Janet and Steve (did I mention they're straight?) told me about Will Arden, someone who had never before been my type, he sounded *exactly* like my type now.

"He teaches Latin at Fordham," Steve said. "In his spare time, he volunteers at the Botanical Society."

A dead-language teacher who gardened?

"When can I meet him?" I said.

I chose a quiet, traditional French restaurant for our first date. I wanted the food and the ambience to make my intentions very clear: I was looking for a stable, conventional guy. Which ruled out spending our first date at my favorite restaurant, where the meals were served in color-coordinated towers of organically grown native Peruvian produce cooked by purple-haired metrosexuals who sang old showtunes by request.

I found the name "Will" very reassuring. I'd never

before dated anyone whose name I could spell on my
first try. I found his white shirt, tweed jacket, boring tie,
and brown pants even more reassuring when we met at
the restaurant. He looked like exactly what I had hoped
for: a pleasant, ordinary guy. A guy like *me*.

He was a little older than I'd expected, a little bald,
and slightly overweight, but still an attractive man. Also
very charming and articulate. As soon as he opened his
mouth to speak, a quiet wit and complex personality
seemed to pour gently from him, and his ordinary looks
became somehow alluring, his brown eyes holding a
warm glow as his hands gestured with enthusiasm.

He had a British accent and a very unusual way of
speaking. Old-fashioned? Lyrical? I wasn't sure how to
describe it, but I found it delightful.

"So, I gather you're originally from England, Will?"
I asked.

"A hit, a very palpable hit!" he said—which I took as
an affirmative.

"What part of England?"

"Oh, a prosperous town in the Midlands."

"Do you ever miss it?"

"By and by, through the vale of years, I have had
occasion to miss it," he admitted. "After all, it was the
place of my salad days."

"Speaking of salad . . ." I said, as ours were put before
us by our discreet waiter.

"A feast for the eyes," Will said of the elegant pre-
sentation.

I was glad he liked the restaurant I'd chosen, since I
certainly liked the blind date my friends had chosen. "So
how did you wind up moving to America?"

He smiled in a friendly way but replied, "Oh, that's an
improbable fiction, so we had best let sleeping dogs lie."

A love affair gone wrong, perhaps? I decided not to
pry on the first date. Instead, I asked, "Do you like living
over here?"

"Indeed, I do!" he said with enthusiasm. "There are
more things in America than were ever dreamt of in
my philosophy."

"So you're here long-term, then?" I didn't want to get too interested in a guy who might moving back to Europe soon.

"My position here is as constant as the stars," he declared. "After all, what is needed that is not here? Though bound by mortal flesh, when in this country, I count myself king of infinite space."

"It is a big country compared to England," I agreed. "So New York's your home now?"

"I could call nowhere *else* home," Will said with enthusiasm. "Never again."

"Ah, so you've become a real New Yorker, then?"

"I cannot hide it," he beamed. "For this city, I am proud to wear my heart on my sleeve."

"There is no place like the Big Apple," I agreed. "There's always something new here, something happening."

"Precisely! Age cannot wither New York, nor custom stale her infinite variety."

I frowned. "That sounds familiar. Is that a quote?"

He sighed and looked suddenly weary. "Oh, probably."

"Hmm. Where have I heard it before?" It was on the tip of my tongue.

"Cudgel thy brains no more about it," he advised. "You have a lean and hungry look, so eat, eat."

To be honest, I had really come out tonight just to try the water and get my feet wet, so to speak. To ease back into dating, and to start meeting a different type of man than I was used to. So it was a hugely unexpected pleasure to find myself so swept off my feet by my Latin-teaching blind date. I'd hoped that the evening wouldn't be torture, but I had not expected to be smitten with Will by the time the evening ended—which was all too soon.

He seemed to feel the same way. I hailed a cab after we left the restaurant, and when I turned to him to say goodnight, he looked at me with those melting brown eyes and said, "Parting is such sweet sorrow."

It took me only a split second to decide to ask him to come home with me. He accepted just as fast.

We barely made it inside the door of my apartment before we tore off each other's clothes. The rest of the night was spent in hot sex and sleepy conversation. By morning, when Will had to leave for his volunteer shift at the Botanical Society, I was already off the dating market again, hopelessly in love with this tweed-wearing, Latin-teaching Englishman.

All those years of dating creative types. I'd had no *idea* what I was missing.

We'd been dating for several weeks, spending almost every night together, when Will finally decided to come clean about his past.

I'd realized by now that it was a troubling subject for him, and I hadn't wanted to push. When he was ready, he'd tell me.

Apparently something about my favorite restaurant, with its singing purple-haired cooks and organic Peruvian food, stirred up his demons. After I took him there for the first time, he was tense and morose as we entered my apartment together that night.

He sat down on the couch with me, holding my hands, and said, "Nathan, I feel that between us, what's past is merely prologue."

Accustomed by now to his way of phrasing things, I said, "Me, too, Will. This is barely the beginning. This is the real deal for me." I'd felt this way before, but never with an ordinary, stable guy. A guy like me.

"You feel as I do, that we will be together tomorrow, and tomorrow, and tomorrow?"

"Yes," I said firmly.

He squeezed my hands, then sat back and said, "Then I must tell you the meat of the matter."

"Good. I'm glad. We should have this talk."

"In one fell swoop," he warned, "I may end our happiness."

"No," I said. "Whatever is in your past, Will, I'm ready to accept it."

"I am fortune's fool," he said sadly.

"Go on."

"I must begin by telling you that I have not been truthful about my name."

"It's not Will?" I said in disappointment. Such a sturdy, solid, simple name.

"Er, no, it's not Arden."

"No?"

"No, that is a convenient guise. Arden was my mother's family name."

"Oh. All right. What's your real name, then?"

"Screw your courage to the sticking place."

"Just tell me, Will."

"Shakespeare."

"Like the playwright? Oh, no wonder you don't use it. The jokes and comments must get old *real* fast."

"Not *like* the playwright, Nathan. I *am* the playwright."

"You're a *playwright*?" I said in horror, rising to my feet.

"I am William Shakespeare." He pulled me back down to the couch. "I can see I should have prepared you better for this shock."

"You're a *writer*?" I said angrily. "You lied to me? You're not really a Latin teacher?"

"No, I *am* a Latin teacher. Well, these days. I excelled in the study of Latin as a youngster, so it seemed a fitting profession to assume when I came to America. But I used to be a playwright."

"I *cannot* date a playwright, Will. I can't cope with that kind of relationship anymore!"

"Never fear," he said morosely. "I have not penned a piece for the stage in nearly four hundred years. Nor a poem. Nor any other work of writing."

"You haven't?"

"No."

"So that's all behind you now?"

"Alas, yes."

"Oh. Okay," I said in relief. Then I realized what else he had said. "Wait a minute . . . *The* William Shakespeare?"

*   *   *

If you ever happen to visit Shakespeare's grave at Stratford-upon-Avon (which was already a prosperous town when the Bard was born), you'll see a grim message written on his tombstone: "Good friend, for Jesus' sake, forbear to dig the dust enclosed here. Blessed be the man who spares these stones, and cursed be he who moves my bones." (Except that it's written with rather creative spelling and punctuation.)

Will explained to me, "I had to write something that would prevent them from opening my grave to lay Anne's bones with mine."

"Anne?"

"My wife."

"Your wife?" I shot to my feet again. "You were *married*?"

"It was not a marriage of true minds," he assured me.

"You're bisexual?" I demanded.

"Er, perhaps the time is out of joint for that particular discussion."

"Answer me!"

"Well, let us say that I am no stranger to the way of a man with a maid."

"Oh, good God." The nasty shocks just kept coming.

Will continued, "Anne died years after I shuffled off the merely mortal coil. There would have been cries of havoc and foul play if my grave had been opened and the discovery made that I lay not within it. Ergo, my epitaph. Anne was instead laid beside my grave. Beside where they merely *believed* I lay."

"And why exactly *don't* you lie there?"

"You need not sound as though you wished me there now," Will said a little snappishly.

"I'm sorry. I'm feeling a little overwrought."

"Have patience with me," Will pleaded. "For in love, the quality of mercy is not strained, it droppeth as the gentle rain—"

"Will, tell me how your wound up living for four hundred years after your funeral, or I swear I will box your ears," I said tersely.

"It is a round unvarnished tale."

"Somehow, I doubt that."

It all happened during a drunken tavern brawl that, after four hundred years, he still couldn't recall quite clearly. The upshot was that he got bitten by what he thought at the time was a rabid actor and only much later realized was really a vampire.

"You can't be serious," I said.

"Chance may crown me a cuckold or a fool, but not a liar," said Will. "I swear to you that my tale is the truth."

"So you became a vampire?"

"Yes. And when people call me the Immortal Bard," he said wearily, "their words are truer than they know."

"So why haven't you tried to bite me?" I challenged.

"Because I am not a rabid actor."

"Don't you get a craving for blood?"

"Sometimes. Especially around the holidays."

"But . . . it's not a daily hunger? An insatiable need?"

"No," Will said. "The instances of vampires attacking people to drink their blood are hugely exaggerated."

"But you can't be a vampire! I've seen you out in the daylight! You enjoy *gardening*, for God's sake!"

"Of course I enjoy gardening. I'm English."

"But how can you—"

"Sun block. Extra strength. Especially around my eyes."

"If you're really William Shakespeare . . ." I thought about it. "I suppose that explains why everything you say sounds so good to me. Also why so much of it sounds so familiar."

"I have a habit of quoting myself. I assure you it is not intentional. I was so *prolific*, it's simply hard to avoid."

"But if you're *the* Shakespeare, then why hasn't there been a new Shakespeare play in four hundred years?"

"There was one not long after I was bitten. I made my deadline despite the trauma of becoming one of the Undead," Will said defensively. "Fittingly, I called it *The Tempest*."

"And Shakespeare died a couple of years later," I pointed out.

"I didn't *die*, I was found dead drunk and asleep. Since vampires have no pulse—"

"Oh, my *God* . . ." I said slowly, realizing I had indeed never heard my lover's heartbeat. I had just assumed he had low blood pressure or something.

"—they declared me dead and laid out my body. When I awoke and discovered what had happened, I realized it was my chance to depart my mortal life without facing awkward questions. Or being executed in a most unpleasant manner once someone finally noticed that I was no longer mortal."

"So you . . ."

"*Fled*, of course. But first I made certain that my epitaph discouraged anyone from opening my grave."

"Where did you flee?"

"Italy. I had always wanted to go there." He rubbed his jaw. "Though it was an embarrassment to discover how inaccurately I had written about it in my plays."

"Which brings me back to my question: If you're *that* William Shakespeare, then what have you written lately?"

He sank back into the couch cushions with a sigh and covered his eyes. "Nothing."

"Nothing?"

"Nothing."

"Oh, come on. How can I believe that William Shakespeare—"

"I went to Italy to rest. God's teeth, Nathan, I had written thirty-seven plays! As well as more than one hundred poems! I was *tired!*"

"So you rested?"

"Yes! I rested! And by the time I returned to England years later, believing it safe because there was no one left alive who could recognize me, and feeling ready to resume my profession . . ."

"Well?"

He shuddered and buried his face in his hands. "I had been *immortalized*. People spoke my name with *reverence*, they extolled my virtues as a writer, they treated my plays as great works of genius. Even *Titus Androni-cus*! Have you ever *seen* that play?"

"Yes. I guess everyone has their bad days, Will," I said consolingly.

"Oh, no," he said, "not everyone. Not 'the greatest writer in the history of the English language!' Not Will Shakespeare the Immortal Bard. Not the greatest play-wright who ever lived! Not *he*. Pure genius flows from his quill, as effortlessly as water flows down to the sea!"

"You felt the pressure of high expectations?" I guessed.

"I felt that no work of mine—or any other writer—could ever meet the expectations that had somehow been created during my absence. So the result was inevitable." Will sighed and looked at me with sad brown eyes. "Writer's block."

"You haven't written a play since *The Tempest* because . . . you've have *writer's block?*"

"For four hundred years," he said miserably.

"William Shakespeare has writer's block?"

He leaped to his feet. "There! You see? *You're* doing it, too!"

"Now, Will—

"I can't *possibly* have writer's block like every other writer on the planet gets from time to time because *I'm* Will Shakespeare, and he's not *a* writer, he's *the* writer!" he raged. "Who can live with that kind of pressure? Who can *create* under the weight of that yoke?"

"So you don't . . . don't . . ." My heart flooded with relief and joy as I suddenly realized what this meant. "Will! You don't *write* anymore?"

"Have I not been saying so quite clearly?" he snapped.

"Will!" I threw my arms around him. "You're *not a writer!* Not anymore!"

"Nathan, please, how can you abuse me so?"

"You really are a Latin teacher!"

"Must you torment—"

"I love you!" I shouted.

He blinked. "You do?"

"Yes!"

"Even without my talent? Bereft, as I am, of my great gift?"

"Oh, Will!" I hugged him. "We're going to be so happy together!"

It was not long after Will and I moved in together that I found something that made me sick with dread. When Will came home that afternoon from the Botanical Society's monthly meeting, I clutched the evidence of his perfidy and waved it under his nose.

"What's *this?*" I demanded.

"Oh, no! You have spoiled my surprise." He beamed at me, not particularly distressed by this.

"*What* surprise?"

He gently removed the sheaf of papers from my rigidly grasping hands. "Your love and unconditional acceptance have changed me, Nathan. After four hundred years . . . I've finally started writing again!"

"*What?*"

"Yes! Isn't it wonderful? I am so excited, I have wanted to tell you one hundred times. But I decided to wait until I had completed the first draft."

"The first draft?" I repeated dully.

"Of my new play. My first play since *The Tempest!* I wanted it to be a special surprise for you."

"Oh, it's a surprise, all right."

He waved the papers in his hand at me. "So what did you think?"

"Huh?"

"When you read it?"

"I haven't read it."

"No?" He looked disappointed for a moment, then his expression brightened "Ah! Of course. You want to wait until the whole draft is finished. I shall get right to work on it."

"*Now?*"

"Yes."

"But we're supposed to go to dinner in thirty minutes. We have reservations!"

"Hmm? Oh, you can call and cancel, can you not? I really want to write this evening."

It wasn't long before I awoke one night at three o'clock in the morning to find Will's side of the bed was cold and empty. I found him in the living room, writing away madly, muttering to himself and littering the room with coffee cups and junk-food wrappers.

I asked him three times to come back to bed before I gave up and returned to our bedroom alone. I don't think he even knew I'd been in the room or spoken to him.

For the next two weeks, he only spoke to me occasionally, we didn't have sex even once, and he spent his meals staring off into space, his lips moving faintly as he worked mentally on the next scene, the next revision, the next hurdle in his writing.

Then one night, the dam broke. He woke me at 4:00 A.M. by flinging himself across the bed, moaning and sighing and cursing.

"I have ruined everything," he said piteously, when I asked him what was wrong. "I have made such a mess of things! Was there ever such an ass as I?"

I was deeply touched. "Oh, Will, no, no, of course not."

"How can I make it right?"

"Shh . . ."

"Is there any way to repair the wreckage?" he pleaded.

"I love you," I said.

"What can I do? Oh, Nathan, what can I *do*?"

"Why don't we go away for a few days together? Maybe to Martha's Vineyard? Just spend some time—"

"Of course!" He suddenly sat bolt upright. "That is what I need to do. *That* is how I can fix it! Why didn't I see it before? I'll move the love scene to the island, so that the murder must occur *there! Of course!*"

He leaped out of bed and raced out of the room.

I moved out the next day.

I'm not sure Will even noticed.

About a year later, his play, *By Any Other Name*, opened to rave reviews on Broadway, and the movie rights were quickly optioned by Miramax. When Will won the Tony Award for it, he dedicated the award to me, his "dear friend, Nathan, without whose love and belief in me, I never would have written this play."

I watched the ceremony on TV with the guy I had recently started dating and whom I live with now. He's an accountant at IBM, and it's the longest, sanest, most stable relationship of my life.

YOU'VE GOT MALE

Janet Deaver-Pack

A Missouri expatriate, Janet Deaver-Pack lives in southern Wisconsin with cats Tabirika Onyx, Syrannis Moonstone, and Baron Figaro de Shannivere. She also writes as Janet Pack. Her time revolves around creating stories, novels, interviews, newspaper articles, and editing anthologies. Her background in amateur acting and comic opera lets Janet give entertaining speeches about writing; she also leads writing seminars for teens and adults throughout southern Wisconsin and northern Illinois. She's been an Author Guest and panelist at many conventions. An avid reader, Janet studies mythology, history, books about writing, and occasionally delves into novels and mysteries. She adores traveling, cooking, walking, watching movies, playing with her furry trio, and hatching new plots with her co-author from Illinois. Investigate her website at www.janetpack.com.

M edusa's long restless fingers twisted the stem of her wine glass. *Where is he?* The crystal goblet glimmered in the subdued light of the Plaza III Restaurant in Kansas City as she turned it; its foot made the snowy tablecloth bunch.

He said he might be a little late, but it's been twenty

168

minutes. The rat! She didn't wear a watch; she didn't need to. No matter what zone, Medusa always knew the time. She let her eyes rove over the brick interior trimmed with brass and mirrors to the wooden doorway of her dining area. No one.

Snakes stirred at her irritation beneath her red-gold wig. *Careful,* she counseled herself, glancing in the mirror at three businessmen laughing several tables away and at two couples on the opposite side of the room. Even with thick contact lenses covering them, Medusa didn't want her eyes to cause a stony accident. That would reveal her intent and make her intended prey flee.

If he ever gets here. Maybe the lowlife got nervous and won't show. Delicious scents wafted from the kitchen. Her stomach complained. She hadn't eaten or drunk anything except bland coffee hours ago during her preflight check.

Where are you, Man o' War? she thought. That was his email name. She didn't like most of the men she investigated who habitually preyed on women. *I deal mostly with the dirtbags because other women can't or won't.* The snakes stirred again, this time in anticipation. Medusa allowed her poisonous associates to take the worst offenders out of the gene pool. Hundreds of years' experience had taught her to make victims disappear so no one ever found the bodies or traced her. Built over centuries, her wealth allowed her to keep a private jet; she traveled anywhere in the world at any time, barring natural disasters and full-scale wars.

Her current cover name was Millicent. She'd finally agreed to meet Man o' War in Kansas City, about half way for both. Medusa lived in upper New York state, and he'd sent her a message from the San Diego airport after finishing an assignment.

Medusa had been surprised when he'd suggested this rendezvous. *We only exchanged a couple dozen emails,* she thought, sipping wine again. It had a velvety texture, with a hint of satisfying spice. *Most romance-seekers trade hundreds of messages. He works fast, and that makes me suspicious. But he's probably suspicious, too. He's got some ulterior motive for suggesting this meeting.* She allowed herself half a smile. *As I have.*

More disturbing thoughts surfaced, and her smile vanished. *He's different from anyone else I've met online. And, even though I don't want to admit it, he's . . . interesting. Perhaps too interesting. But he's a rat.*

She huffed out a sigh. *Thirty minutes. Where is he? You'd think he'd send a message; I know he's got a fancy PDA.* She twisted the stem of her goblet again.

The hostess entered, followed by a man in a dark blue silk shirt and charcoal slacks carrying flowers. It took only a heartbeat for him to notice Medusa, as if her presence called to him. After thanking the hostess, he approached.

Those roses aren't from Wal-Mart, she thought, eyeing the green tissue. *Where did he find a florist open after 6 P.M. on Wednesday?*

"Millicent?" His accented baritone tugged at her ears.

"Yes."

He handed her fragrant burgundy and cream roses. "I'm Man o' War, also Scott Starker. I apologize for making you wait. Commercial flights are so unpredictable these days." He reached for her hand, brushing the back of it with his breath, then straightened and cocked his head. "May I join you?"

"Of course. They're beautiful, thank you," she said in her husky soprano, settling the flowers on an empty chair as he sat down across from her.

He's certainly a gentleman in public. But many men she'd met over the course of her vocation had a charming public persona and a very different private one.

"I'm happy you made it. I'd almost given up."

His smile flashed boyish enthusiasm. "I always get to where I'm going. Eventually." He glanced around. "Looks like a good place. Have you been here before?"

"Once, a long time ago. I've always wanted to come back."

"I hope the food is as good as it smells." He sucked in a breath and looked for their server. "I haven't eaten all day."

"I haven't either. This is one of the best steak restaurants in the Midwest. Nothing compares to a well-prepared Kansas City steak." She tapped her glass. "And if you like merlot, this one's particularly good."

"I do, but I'm in the mood for something stronger tonight. It's been a very long day. Actually, a long week. I want to celebrate finally meeting you." He turned to the hovering server. "Missouri Norton if you have it, please. And bring another glass of merlot for the lady, if she so desires."

He knows wine, and how to push my buttons, Medusa thought. *I'll have to watch it—he's charming as well as thoughtful. He might try to use both to flatter me into getting what he wants.*

They ordered appetizers of Steak Soup and Seafood Bisque, and Prime Porterhouse and Tenderloin Oscar, accompanied by Spinach Salad. Medusa and Scott made ridiculous conversation about the weather and airport delays until the server returned with two bottles. She uncorked the first and poured a taste. Scott sipped, and nodded. The server presented a full glass with a flourish, then waited for Medusa's indication to replenish her glass.

"Leave the Norton, please," Scott requested.

"Very good, sir. Is there anything else, sir, ma'am?"

"Not at the moment, thank you," Medusa replied.

She studied him, just as Scott was studying her. Both were trying not to show their attraction. Their energies met midway above the table and sizzled.

He was of medium height, just a little taller than she, with a compact body. His dark hair mirrored the color of his deepset brown-black eyes. Those showed calculation and sureness. High cheekbones ended in a chiseled jaw which balanced the rectangular shape of his face. A small Van Dyke beard framed a severe mouth, but his smile eclipsed any harshness. Fluid motions suggested fencing and martial arts training, both of which he'd mentioned in his emails.

Craggy, but handsome enough. Capable. And . . . somehow dangerous. Medusa twisted her goblet again. *Oh, I think I like this man. I really like him, despite his being a lowlife. But his name doesn't fit. Odd.*

"The portrait you emailed doesn't do you justice," Scott said softly. "I didn't expect a classic beauty. You look very Greek, like a statue."

Is that a hint that he knows more about me than I think? Medusa made her way in life mostly by her wits. Her face was pretty enough to lure nasty men into her trap, and that's all she cared about.

"Thank you," she said. "Tell me, what do you do for a living?"

"All sorts of research. I also trace lost things and lost people. Here, on the continent, in the Middle East and Africa. And I'm a professional troubleshooter." He smiled as their soups arrived. "Ahhh, that smells great."

Disturbed by Scott more than she cared to admit, Medusa spooned up bisque. *He knows how to find hidden information, and therefore he is dangerous to me. Is he good enough to discover what I do? How far back?* The rich mixture of seafood and cream bloomed in her mouth. *Let's see what the next stage in this game brings. I'll have to be extra careful.*

"You know," she said between bites, "we've traded fewer emails than most people who meet via internet."

Scott nodded. Looking at the candle flame trembling in the air currents, spoon in midair, he hesitated. Conflict clouded his eyes.

"There's something different about you that I like very much," he said slowly. "And I needed to see you before . . . well, before going on with us."

That was a leading statement if I ever heard one! Medusa sensed the import of what he was going to say and braced herself. Both held silence while the server removed their bowls and presented the salads.

"Are you doing research on me?" she teased.

"Listen." Scott suddenly leaned forward, looking into her eyes and keeping his voice low. "You've been in touch recently with a young man named Robert Gordon Shurman."

"Who?" She kept her face a pleasant mask despite a jolt of nerves. *How does he know about that?*

"I studied his records as part of a recent assignment. He emailed someone named Alissa on Yahoo for awhile, then met her. Much like we're doing tonight. And then Robert disappeared. Vanished." He flicked his fingers. "Poof."

I'm really good at "poof," Medusa thought, remembering.

"The father, Wilfred Tucker Shurman, has no idea what happened. He's very upset. Robert was his only son and heir. No one has yet found the body."

And they won't. Warning jangled in her mind. *Tread carefully with this man. He's a big rat!*

She said aloud, "What does this mean to me?"

Scott glanced around without moving his head, making certain no one was listening. She was impressed by his technique. He was definitely a pro.

"Wilfred Shurman hired me to find whoever killed his son," he whispered in tones meant only for her ears. Sitting back, he stabbed his spinach. The sigh that ripped from his chest betrayed more conflict. "Even though you seem the least likely person to be a predator, I discovered several links to you. Emails in particular." He stared at her. "But perhaps that's what makes you a good predator."

You have no idea. Medusa smiled. "This game is fun. I think I'm going to enjoy dinner with you tonight much more than I'd thought. Perhaps we could write this up as a fantasy book; you're very creative."

"I haven't finished. Robert Shurman preyed on women," Scott said softly, punctuating his words with his fork. "He lured them into email encounters, then to dinner, and afterwards to private places. His habit was to beat, rape, and kill them. His father's rich—he's had the cases confused or ignored each time it happened. Robert never struck twice in the same place; because he traveled for his father's business, that was easy. Daddy Shurman covered up for his bad little boy.

"One day, Alissa appeared in Robert's emails. After

a lot of messages dodging his pleas to meet, she finally agreed. Apparently, they did have dinner."

"And then?" Medusa toyed with her salad.

"No one knows. Robert Shurman was never heard from again."

"What a dreadful story. Why are you telling me this?" Medusa sipped her second glass of wine, looking at Scott over the rim.

For the first time during their encounter, he seemed at a loss. "I'm really not sure. I just had to meet you, find out what kind of person you are."

"There's got to be a better reason." Medusa suddenly needed to know his motivation. His honesty beat against her mistrust. "You don't fly halfway across the country just to tell a near-stranger such a peculiar story. Even if I am Alissa, that doesn't make sense."

Their beautifully presented steaks arrived, giving them time to recover a little before delving farther into the odd situation.

Scott sliced into his meat like a surgeon, then glanced again around the room. The businessmen and one of the other couples had gone. "Okay," he said softly. "I believe you're in danger. If I can ferret out the information I found about Robert Shurman and Alissa, so can someone else, given time."

"How intriguing," Medusa said, cutting into her fork-tender meat. "But if I'm Alissa, I'm also in danger from you. You may scout for Shurman's thugs."

He shook his head. "Look, I *know* you're Alissa. But I'm not working for him any more." His voice was contemptuous. "I'm not one of his goons."

"Why should I trust you?" They were finally getting to the point.

"This sounds very odd, especially since we've traded only a handful of emails." Scott laid down his knife and fork as if he'd suddenly lost his appetite. "I don't want to work with anyone like Shurman ever again. He's worse than his son was, in different ways. Add blackmail and extortion to Robert's repertoire, and you get the picture. The other reason is because I'm—well, I'm attracted to you." It cost him a lot to admit that aloud. "All right. More than attracted." He gulped wine to hide his unease, then took a deep breath. "I think I'm in love with you."

One of Medusa's eyebrows raised. She laughed softly. "This depth of emotion happens through a few emails and a picture?"

"Most of what I do is driven by hunches. I don't question them," Scott said. "I have a feeling about you, a strong one. I've met predators, and you're very different from the rest.

"By the way, I'm not Scott Starker. My name is Paul Guerrero. Guerrero means 'warrior' in Portuguese. I took care of Starker for you. Otherwise, you never would have met me."

What? Is he lying, or telling the truth? Medusa wondered. *Is it possible he might NOT be scum?* She considered that for a dozen heartbeats. *I hope not. Let's take this a little further.*

"You've admitted to what you say is your real identity—who do you think I really am?" she baited.

"I don't know." That statement came from his heart. He was obviously intrigued by her mystery. "I couldn't trace your background. You just disappear. Except . . ."

Paul made a decision and reached for the PDA on his belt. He punched in a code, then slid it across the table. Botticelli's portrait of Simonetta Vespucci glowed onscreen.

"It's a remarkable likeness, don't you agree? That blouse you're wearing even resembles hers. After seeing this, I *had* to meet you."

"What a compliment." Medusa peered at the familiar portrait. "Do you collect Renaissance art?"

"No. I appreciate old masterpieces." He tucked the machine back on his belt. "Either you had an exact twin five hundred years ago, or you're much older than you admit. Want to explain this mystery, and your unusual hobby?"

"One question at a time." She plunged on. "Far too many men victimize women. I am, and have been for a long time, an advocate for the abused."

When did I decide to trust him? The line was an invisible one, lying somewhere between the salad and the steaks. Medusa wasn't aware she'd wanted to cross it until her words betrayed her emotions.

Have I gotten in too deep too fast?

"What would you do if I am Robert Shurman's assassin?" she asked.

"When I took the job to find him, I intended to discover Robert's killer and do to her what she does to her victims," Paul said slowly, pouring himself more wine. "But for the first time in my life, I couldn't. I severed my connection with Shurman before I left. I told him that I couldn't find y . . . his son's murderer. The links were too weak, there was no proof. That's it. End of story. He won't quit, though. He'll hire someone who'll find you eventually."

The flavor of her food soured. "You quit him and came straight to me, leaving a trail a child could follow." Her words were cold.

"No. My path will take an expert to unravel." He stared at Medusa, eyes begging her to believe him. "I'm here because, first, I wanted to warn you, and second, I think we might make a great team. Why limit yourself to predators who prey on women? All sorts of trash needs to be taken out."

"What if I don't want a partner?"

"Then I'll go back to what I was doing solo, only I'll do it better by being more particular about my targets, thanks to you."

Medusa surprised herself by thinking hard about his proposal. *It might be fun working with someone else for awhile, even though I'll have to watch him age. And I'll also have to be careful how I look at him.* One casual glance from her unprotected eyes, and Paul would become a statue. Her snakes might also be a problem if their relationship got physical. And she suspected it would.

I've conquered such difficulties before. I can again. He's really not a rat.

"What if Shurman sends someone after you?" Medusa asked. "He's not the type to appreciate you quitting."

Paul nodded, and began eating again. "I'll deal with it," he growled. "If they come after me, they're taking on more than they can handle. I'd enjoy that."

"You know," she said slowly, finishing her steak, "it might be fun to let them try. And it would give us practice working together."

Medusa enjoyed watching Paul's amazement. It was a long moment before he could control his voice.

"So you believe me," he said.

"For now," she answered.

I'll have to win his complete trust before telling him my history and showing him my snakes. I hope he likes snakes.

"We've got planning to do!" He pushed back from the table, his enthusiasm overflowing.

"Wait. Hold on. We've got time for dessert." Medusa used her Cheshire cat expression. "I have a little jet."

"Let me guess—that sleek Maverick Leader III on the private side of the airport is yours? The one with the snake on its tail?" His grin flashed as he settled back in his chair. "I knew there was more than one reason to like you."

She lifted a shoulder. "I might let you fly it if you behave."

Paul leaned forward. "You little snake!"

The server took their plates. They ordered creme bruleé and Kona coffee. It was after 10 P.M. when they finished.

Paul claimed the bill, waited until Medusa had picked up her roses, and offered his arm as she stood. "I haven't had such an enjoyable meal in years," he said as they exited the bronze medallioned door and turned toward the footbridge spanning Brush Creek. "Mostly because of the exceptional company."

"It's surprising who you can meet on the internet if

you look hard enough," Medusa replied. "Gives a whole new meaning to 'You've got mail'."

They laughed at her joke, crossing Ward Parkway into the park.

Author's Note: Profound thanks to Bruce A. Heard for his suggestions, readings, and editing assistance. I love our idea-generating Sunday morning walks!

THE MANSION OF
GHOULISH DELIGHT

Alice Henderson

Alice Henderson has been writing since her father gave her his old Underwood manual typewriter when she was six. She is the author of two Buffy the Vampire Slayer novels, *Night Terrors* and *Portal Through Time*. She earned her B.A. in Writing and her M.A. in Folklore. For her master's thesis, she interviewed people who have seen Bigfoot, lake monsters, and other strange folkloric creatures lurking in the woods and outskirts of American cities. She loves to travel and has journeyed extensively through the American and Canadian Rockies, the great deserts of California, and the cities of Europe. Most recently, she visited the national parks of the western U.S., and canyoneered through slot canyons in Zion National Park, took in fiery sunsets over the strange rock formations of Bryce Canyon, thrilled to fossils in the Badlands, and witnessed wolf packs and grizzly bears roaming free through the wilderness of Yellowstone. She lives in San Francisco, where she is at work on her next novel.

From the parking lot, Meg could hear the screaming. As she climbed out of her car, she looked up at the old, rickety warehouse of Pier 34. Paint peeled down its sides, missing completely in some parts.

Light gleamed from a crack in one wall. Another scream filtered through the thin walls, and Meg looked over at her boyfriend Max. "Are you sure about this place?" she asked dubiously.

"It's the best!" he cried, taking her hand and pulling her forward. A tattered banner strung haphazardly across the front of the warehouse read, "Dr. Krypto's House of Fear." It fluttered in the wind whipping off the bay. Meg moved a little closer to Max.

He'd worked at this haunted house last Halloween and had raved about it at the time. But she was still in grad school then, living in Northern California. When the same outfit had returned this year, Max had opted not to work for it again. The hours had been too insane, he said, and he'd come home at night with bruises from worked up-patrons who occasionally shoved and even punched, depending on their level of panic or bravado.

They entered the House of Fear together, arm in and arm, and paid their $24.95 to be terrified.

Gloom hung inside the warehouse, the air filled with fog from hidden smoke machines. A few laser lights cut and danced through the thick haze. The dull thumping of bass met her ears, and as they ventured farther into the warehouse, she made out house music pounding out a monotonous, hypnotic rhythm.

"There are three different sections," Max told her. "A prison infested with zombie prisoners on the loose, a haunted forest with werewolves, vampires, and shapes-hifters, and then the longest one—the Mansion of Ghoul-ish Delight."

An old feeling of fear began to creep up on her. It must be over twenty years now since her dad took her to the Parlor of the Haunted Dead, an annual haunted house in her hometown in Ohio. The town was small, only about three hundred and forty people, and they never held back on Halloween. She remembered jack-o-lantern carving contests, pumpkin pie bake-offs, costume raffles, and always the Parlor of the Dead. She was only six when he last took her there. Each year the town transformed the old abandoned Thayton mansion on Route 4 into the greatly anticipated haunted house. No one had lived in it for thirty-five years, but every Halloween it was decorated and readied for squealing children. Most kids her age just imagined they had a creepy house on their block. She really had one. The Thayton mansion stood just down the street from their white clapboard farmhouse. She could see it mornings when she waited for the school bus, standing against the gray sky, almost leaning in toward her. She often sensed it listening for her.

The last year she went, the last year anybody went, the basement had flooded during unusually heavy rains, bringing a torrent of rats up from the cellar. She and her dad, passing through the kitchen redecorated as Lizzy Borden's infamous murder scene, had heard a strange eruption of scrabbling in the walls. Then suddenly the cellar door burst open and thousands of rats poured forth, streaming over the floors in their rush to get out of the water below. They crawled over her shoes, tore by them, ripping her stockings in their mad rush for escape. Finally her dad picked her up, placing her on his shoulders.

And then someone had run by the kitchen door, screaming, and slammed it shut, locking it. With the rats scrabbling over them, desperate to escape, yet finding no outlet, Meg and her dad had to spend the night in that old house. The next morning, neighbors realized they hadn't come home and returned to the Thayton place and unlocked the kitchen door. They found Meg and her father sleeping on the kitchen counter, Meg shivering in the unheated house, her lips and fingernails blue, her feet numb with cold and soaked from the wet rats.

She never wanted to visit another haunted house again.

Then Max started working at this one last year, kept

asking her to come down and visit it. She'd always managed to find some excuse or another, feeling too silly to admit her real reason.

But now she was here, and the screams reverberating through the warehouse reminded her of screams long ago.

Max steered her through the haze, and she could just make out a series of makeshift plywood walls that had been erected to partition off the different attractions.

Up ahead she saw a hulking guy in a San Francisco State University sweatshirt. Clinging to his arm was a petite woman with short, attractively styled brown hair. On his other arm clung a stocky man who, despite his manly tattoo of a bulldog on one forearm, shrieked with excitement. He squealed as a huge monster on stilts came lumbering out of one of the attractions and passed by them, snarling and whipping its claws shockingly close to their faces. Another woman clung to the tattooed man. She wore jeans and a sweatshirt. They looked like college friends, out for a good scare on Halloween.

"Which one should we do first?" Meg asked. "You're the expert!"

Max glanced around. He was distracted now, barely paying attention to her. He stared over at the entrance to the Mansion of Ghoulish Delight, peering intently at the darkness beyond the opening.

"Max?"

"Huh?" He looked back at her.

"What is it?"

"Nothing," he said dismissively. "I guess I'm a little distracted. So much noise and smoke."

"Well, which one should we try first?"

"Definitely the Mansion," he answered, propelling her forward again. At the entrance, a curtained opening between two plywood walls painted black, a man in ghoulish makeup examined their ticket with a small flashlight. Then he switched it off, looked at them somberly, and pulled the black curtain aside.

At first she couldn't see, blinded by a throbbing strobe

light illuminating the fog. Then she passed through a patch of intense light and entered a world of madness.

The first room, open and cavernous, lay strewn with hacked and decapitated bodies. Horrific ghouls leaped and cavorted around the bodies, feeding on them. As soon as Max and Meg entered, they snapped their heads up to face them.

Now this was what Meg really didn't like about these haunted houses. The things chased you. And inevitably there were secret passageways and shortcuts known only to the actors, so that they could always cut you off, scaring you again and again. She could remember the feeling vividly, tearing through the Parlor of the Haunted Dead with her dad close behind, squeezing his hand, unwilling to let go.

The three ghouls rose up, blood smearing their white faces. The makeup was incredible. Max had described it to her last year. Cold foam latex prosthetics, fully made up, fake bones sticking out of rips in shirts and pants, blood streaming down teeth that came to a point.

The ghouls, with yellow contacts that reflected the lights from the strobe, leaped up, moving eerily fast.

Meg let out a squeal and darted around the strewn body parts on the floor. Max caught up quickly as Meg passed through a small tunnel into the next room. Behind them the three ghouls trailed hungrily, banging on the plywood walls with hacked off bone props.

This was a classic haunted house trick to make up for the fact that the actors couldn't physically touch the patrons. Instead, they slammed objects into walls and floors, crashing furniture about. Each crack and thump made Meg's heart speed up, and she rushed into the next room.

This vignette featured a kitchen gone wrong. Meg pushed away memories of another kitchen, long ago. An old woman stood behind a stove, stirring a huge pot full of something thick and red. Meg felt the giddiness of fear creep into her. She knew the old woman wouldn't let her make it across the room without jumping out at

her. But the wrinkled crone didn't move, just watched
them intently as they walked by.

Meg did not see the man crouching under the stove.
He leaped up, lumbering toward her, a flap of half-eaten
flesh hanging from his mouth.

She gasped and ran around him and he staggered behind her, moaning.

"You freak!" she heard Max yell at him. "Stay back!"

She entered the next room alone. Max still hung back
a few feet. Just as she turned to peer through the fog
for him, he appeared, the ghoul still trailing behind him.
"These guys are fucked up!" he said, and his tone
wasn't amused.

"Did he touch you?" Meg asked.

"No, but something's not right. It's just like last year."

"What do you mean?"

Before they could finish talking, a boom brought her
attention to the scene before her. A man sat in an electric chair, firing an air cannon as patrons walked by. She
caught a glimpse of the guy in the San Francisco State
sweatshirt, far ahead, disappearing around a dark corner.

As she strained to see where to walk, the fog grew
thicker, lit up by dozens of flickering blue lights. The
guy leered from the electric chair, stomping his feet and
cackling. Two dark hollows marked his eyes, and
crooked, yellow teeth filled his mouth. "Come closer!"
he urged her. "Come closer, Missy!"

"No thanks!" she said, feeling her heart beat faster.
She resisted the urge to run. She knew it was just a fake
haunted house, that all these people were merely actors.
Yet ever since she was a little kid, when she'd spent the
night in that looming, almost breathing house, she'd had
the horrible thought that a real insane killer could break
into one of these places and come after you with a chain-
saw, and you wouldn't know to run until your torso was
cut in two.

"Don't come near me!" Max screamed at the actor as
they passed near the chair. The man grinned with yellow
teeth, then fired the air cannon again.

"That's it!" Max yelled.

He turned to Meg, grabbing her arms harshly, forcing her to face him. "These guys, they're not actors. These aren't props!" he shouted, pointing at a severed arm lying in a corner. "They're real! Don't you see that?"

"Max—" She would have thought he was kidding, but she knew him too well. His eyes filled with rage. "I thought something was up last year. The way they looked. I never saw them put on their make up, Meg! Not once. And they seemed to be living in the warehouse! They never came to work. Every night when I showed up, they were already there. I tried to play it off. But it kept bothering me. I thought if I came here tonight, I'd see that I was just imagining things." His eyes narrowed, and he lowered his voice. "But I wasn't."

"Max," she said, "I don't really see what's so strange about all of this. It's just an ordinary haunted house—" They'd stood still for too long. Now ghouls gathered on all sides of them, emerging from hidden passageways and shortcuts, at least six of them, mouths dripping with gore, tense and hungry, grinning with sharpened teeth.

He grasped her hand tightly and tried to hurry her through to the next room. But the actors closed together, blocking the path. Meg stepped back. "Get out of our way!" Max screamed. They stepped forward, nearing him, arms outstretched. "Get the hell away from us!" He backed up, still gripping Meg's hand so tightly she felt the bones move together. "I'm warning you!" he went on. "I know about you people!" He gestured to a severed torso lying a few feet away. "I know that's not a prop!"

They closed in, and Max let go of her and ran, barreling into the nearest ghoul. The actor fell to one side, knocking Meg over, too. She landed next to the torso. While Max grabbed the grinning ghoul again, she reached over, tentatively, and felt the flesh of the torso. Rubber. Completely fake, though well done. She grabbed another body part and another, all rubber, all well-crafted, but completely fake.

"Max!" she shouted. "It's not real! Stop it!"

He continued to fight with the actor, ripping at his

face, his clothes. The other actors moved forward, pulling Max off. He slashed at them with his nails, ripping off the latex on their faces, tearing the sleeves off their shredded clothing to reveal normal, human flesh beneath.

But still he didn't stop. He screamed, cried out, tore into them. They tried to restrain him, all six actors pulling him to the ground. Meg leaped up, unsure of what to do. The muscles and tendons strained in Max's neck as he fought them. "I know what you are!" he shouted. "You can't silence me!"

Then the crowd suddenly parted, stepping quickly away. In his hand, Max held a long, unfolded knife. He rose slowly to his feet.

"He took my damn shop knife!" one of the actors cursed.

Max regarded them all coolly, sniffing and breathing heavily, gasping for air. Then he spun and plunged the knife deeply into the actor directly behind him.

The man cried out, sank to his knees, grabbing his stomach.

"Someone call Security!" one woman yelled. The ghouls scattered, disappearing through the same short-cuts they'd appeared from.

Meg stood alone in the room with Max and the wounded man. She moved toward the actor, but Max screamed at her. "Don't get near him!" he shouted, hysterical. Spittle rained out of his mouth. "He'll bite you! You'll be like one of them!"

Meg stopped. "Max," she said soothingly, watching the wounded man out of the corner of her eyes. He doubled over, groaning. She wondered how long it would take security to get there. Not long, she imagined. They must have to break up fights in these kinds of places all the time.

She would just wait for the guards to get here. They'd know what to do.

But they didn't come.

And Max still glared down at the man. "Oh, stop it!" he shouted at the actor, who looked up at him with pleading eyes. "I know you're not really dying! You don't die! You just feed and feed. So stop pretending! You make me sick!" he shouted, kicking the actor over. Then he thrust the knife suddenly under the man's chin.

"No, please!" whimpered the man. "I don't know what you're talking about. Please just let me go."

But Max's eyes fixed cruelly on the man's face, and he bent in to drag the blade across his throat.

"Max, don't!" Meg yelled, lunging forward to stop him. She grabbed his knife hand, jerking it away from the man's throat, and for several long moments they struggled.

"Max," she pleaded.

Slowly, inexorably, he twisted free and shoved her to the side. She stumbled over the prop of a chewed leg and almost fell over. When she righted her balance and spun back around, Max had already placed the knife against the man's throat. The man she had loved for three years began to drag it across the actor's throat.

Meg surged forward, slamming into him with all her weight. He stumbled to the side and she bit the hand that held the knife. He yelped, but held fast, trying to shove her out of the way. They staggered over a rusted pot, then a severed arm.

The knife came up unexpectedly as Max went off balance, and Meg jumped out of the way just in time.

Where the hell was Security?

And then she stumbled forward as well, and the knife slipped down, temporarily out of his grasp. He grabbed it again. She fell hard on top of him and the knife jammed between them. As the handle drove up hard into her solar plexus, Meg saw stars and lost her breath.

Hands grabbed her back. Voices erupted around her. She blinked, felt herself being lifted off Max. She still couldn't breathe.

And then she saw Max below her as the hands set her on her feet—his wide, open staring eyes, the knife buried deep in his chest. Perfectly aimed at the heart.

She had killed him.

Her mind froze. For a second she could only imagine it as another tableaux from the House of Fear. The Murdered Lover. And she the Grieving Widow, ready to jump out and scare passersby.

In a daze she looked down at her hands, her purple shirt now dark with Max's blood.

"You saved Bill's life," said someone next to her. "That guy would have killed him."

She heard the voice as if it were very far away, barely audible over the sound of her pounding heart. Finally her aching lungs managed a breath. An arm came around her shoulder, turning her away from Max's body.

"Miss, let's get you out of here. The police are on the way."

She had killed him.

She walked on numb feet through the rest of the haunted house, led by the arm that guided her.

What had just happened? Had Max suffered a psychotic break? Had she really just killed him to save another life?

With dry mouth and heavy feet, she plodded through room after room, the vignettes a blur now.

How could this happen? Her chest ached from the impact of the knife handle. Did he really believe they were ghouls? Even when he'd worked in this very same haunted house last year? Her mind could simply not grasp the situation. Shock began to set in.

And then she saw the sweatshirt. It was on the body of a bloody torso in the second to last room. It read "San Francisco State University" in large green letters. Next to it lay a severed head with short, attractive brown hair. The petite woman she'd seen earlier.

Her feet stopped, and she stared down. The arm on her shoulder felt heavier suddenly, and she shrugged it off. Hands tried to grab her as she bent to feel the torso. It was still warm. Blood spilled out of the chewed and severed arteries. The woman's eyes had not yet glassed over. Meg could see teeth marks where her neck had been chewed clean through. A slurping sound in the corner caught her attention and she whipped her head up to see a little girl, face white and skin sagging, eyes yellow and gleaming with preternatural light. She smacked and chewed, eating something. Meg forced herself to concentrate on the bundle of dripping meat in the girl's hands. It was a man's forearm, emblazoned with the tattoo of a bulldog.

Slowly Meg stood. The hands returned, swarming over her, and she tried to spin around, but they held her fast. More and more people emerged from cracks and secret passageways. She felt something bite her calf and shrieked, jerking away from the pain. Then teeth on her shoulder, then in her back.

She swung her fists, slamming into faces and shoving people aside. She kicked and screamed for help, ripping out hair and smashing noses.

But the bodies swarmed over her, crawling on her, forcing her into a corner. She reached her hand out searchingly, trying to find something she could use as a weapon. Teeth dug into her thigh. She thrust her knee out and kicked violently, then her searching hand closed around cold metal. The handle of a knife! Hope bloomed within her and she tightened her grip on it. She yanked it free, propelling a body with it. It slammed into her.

Max.

He stared down at her with gleaming yellow eyes.

"They were so right, Meg," he said. "The power is unimaginable!"

She tried to back away, but the sea of writhing bodies blocked her way.

"They told me about it last year, how amazing it is. I tried to lure you down here, but you wouldn't come. But now you're here, and I thank you." He stepped forward, grinning down at her with teeth gone sharp. "You see, to cross over, I had to be killed by someone who loved me."

And they bore her down, biting and ripping. She thrust her hands out, slick with blood, and prayed she would not end up like Max. But she knew she wouldn't.

None of these people loved her, and she was dying alone.

ANNE OF THE ONE GABLE

Jean Rabe

Jean Rabe is the author of eighteen fantasy novels and more than three dozen short stories. An avid but truly lousy gardener, she tends lots of tomato plants so her dogs can graze in the late summer months. In her spare time (which she seems to have less of each week), she enjoys role-playing, board, and war games; visiting museums; and riding in the convertible with the top down and the stereo cranked up. Visit her web site at www.jeanrabe.com

A gentleman, he arrived on time, carrying a bouquet of day lilies and baby chrysanthemums that smelled musky and sweet and sent Anne's senses pleasantly reeling. With his free hand he took hers and raised it to his lips, bending slightly, kissing her fingers so softly she nearly swooned.

The coolness of his lips was electric.

Anne tipped her head back—her date was taller than she'd expected—stared into his watery eyes, and grimaced.

"You're not Clark."

The gentleman looked offended. "Why, no, ma'am, I surely am not."

She sighed.

It was all this fog—the ephemeral mist that twisted romantically and seductively around them! If it hadn't

190

been for the fog, she would have noticed right away that he was the wrong one.

"Look," she began. "I'm sorry. I—"

"You invited me here ma'am." He smiled warmly, little "happy lines" forming at the corners of his eyes and mouth. "We spoke briefly last night, and you—"

"Yes, I guess I did set this up. But I thought you were someone else." She offered him a smile in return, but hers was not wholly genuine, and it did not reach her eyes. "Yes, I guess I did contact you. And yes, I set up this date, but I thought you were Clark. I'm terribly sorry."

"I never said I was Clark, ma'am. But then you never asked my name."

"I just assumed."

"My name's James, ma'am. But I prefer Jimmy."

Jimmy! Of course! Anne berated herself for not recognizing him instantly. But he looked so young, and was without makeup, was dressed in an old-fashioned suit—like one he'd wore in . . .

"*The Philadelphia Story.*"

"Yes, ma'am. I won an Oscar for that picture back in . . . hmm, back in—"

"Nineteen forty."

"Yes, ma'am, you're right on the year. I wore this very suit in several scenes. Pulled it out of the closet just for you and this special occasion."

She settled against him, the coolness of his lean body cutting the warmth of the early fall. He put his arms around her, holding the bouquet against her back, the chrysanthemum petals tickling her neck.

"Well, you did bring me flowers, Jimmy."

"Not easy to find here, ma'am."

"And I did, I guess, ask you out."

"Yes ma'am, I guess you did."

You were supposed to be Clark. She wrapped her arms around his waist, returning the gentle embrace. *Well, I've nothing else planned tonight, and he is rather good-looking. My term paper's finished. Might as well give you a whirl.*

"So, Jimmy, what do you have planned?"

"I thought we might take in a movie . . . if that's all right with you."

"I love movies." She truly did. "What's playing in this neighborhood?"

"*Harvey*, ma'am. The original. Not the made-for-TV version."

"It's a date, then." Anne drew in a deep breath, accepted the flowers, linked arms with Jimmy, and strolled off through the fog.

Sarah'd had her hair done. Probably at one of those budget salons that clung to the fringes of the campus, Anne guessed, a place she'd never be caught dead in herself. But then Anne usually did her own hair.

Sarah's blond tresses fell in soft curling-iron ringlets to the middle of her back, one side higher because there was a decorative comb in it—very 1950s silver screen. She wore dress slacks, chocolate that complemented an ivory blouse, the top button of which was undone so her gold cross necklace showed. She looked good tonight, for someone thirty or so pounds on the plump side—her girth probably keeping her from getting decent dates. Her earrings were small and tasteful—pearl studs—and she'd draped a jacket over her arm.

Not a wrinkle. Anne could tell Sarah had ironed everything. And she'd applied makeup too, a little blush, mascara, sparkly tan eye shadow and dark brown eyeliner—nothing overdone. The casual, professional look. Oh, and a hint of coral colored lipstick. Anne politely sniffed.

"White Linen, by Estee Lauder. Nice, Sarah, very nice," Anne said. "And on a drama student's expense account. I'm impressed."

Sarah stared at her.

Anne was dressed in blue jeans that were bleached in places and had a hole at the right knee. This was topped with a faded Aerosmith T-shirt, two sizes too big and gathered at the hip with a satin scrunchie; red hoop earrings that bounced against her shoulders; and hot-pink flip-flops that had seen better days on the beach. Her hair was in spongy rollers, and there wasn't a touch of makeup anywhere.

"But I-I-I thought we were going out. Double-blind. I-I-I thought. Oh my. I got the date wrong. Next Wednesday?"

Anne gave her a loopy grin. "Nah, you got the day right, babe. We are doubling tonight, just like I promised."

Anne had met Sarah in junior-year drama class early in the spring semester, and they immediately hit it off because of their love of old movies. Despite being a senior now, Sarah was a dormie, and had never been to a sorority house. But Anne had said they'd meet here before joining the gents on a blind date.

"But I-I-I thought—" Sarah pointed to Anne's T-shirt, then brushed a hand against her own blouse. "I thought we were all going out to a movie."

"Yeah, babe, you're overdressed. But that's my fault. I should've told you to come casual. C'mon up to my room."

"Room? I-I-I—" Sarah squared her shoulders. "I thought you said we were going out."

"Kill the speech impediment, babe. We're not going *out to a movie*. We're going *out with movie stars*. C'mon up." Anne whirled and tromped up the stairs. Her room was on the top floor—the third—of the Alpha Sigma Alpha sorority house on Greek Row, just off the campus of Northern Illinois University in Dekalb.

Sarah waited a moment before following.

Anne's room was clean, if far from tidy. Obscure movie posters covered the walls: *The Misfits*, *Band of Angels*, *Key to the City*, *Comrade X*, *Love on the Run*, *Manhattan Melodrama*, *Forsaking All Others*, *China Seas*, and more. The bookshelf was crammed with the works of William Shakespeare and Oliver Stone video tapes and DVDs. An autographed picture of Mae West, which Anne had bragged about snaring for a ridiculously low price on eBay, hung above a cluttered desk.

"Are you teasing me, Anne, saying we're going out tonight? With movie stars?"

"I'd never tease you, Sarah." Anne locked the door, then dropped to her knees and reached under the bed, moving aside two pairs of spiked heels and bringing out a battered cardboard box with so much masking tape holding it together that any printed words were illegible.

"A game? You are teasing."

Anne made a tsk-tsking sound and took the lid off.

"Ouija board?" Sarah's eyes widened. "What's this about, Anne?" Her face drooped, and her eyes definitely said she thought Anne was playing a horrible trick.

Anne set the board on a thick green rug and reached across it to pat the floor on the other side. "Sit. Sit. Sit, Sarah. You do want to double-date with me, don't you?"

Sarah numbly nodded and looked for a place to put her jacket. She settled for draping it across the back of the desk chair. She sniffed at the incense burning in the lap of a ceramic Buddha—cinnamon and orange. Then she sat cross-legged across from Anne, shoulders slumped. "Don't be making fun of me, Anne. I *can* get a date, you know."

"But not with a movie star, eh?"

Anne wriggled her fingers then laced them together and extended her arms, cracking her knuckles. "Only things is . . . you have to promise not to tell anybody about this date. Swear to it."

Sarah raised an eyebrow.

"If my sisters here knew what I was doing . . . heck, if the campus caught wind of it . . . my reputation, such as it is, would take a major beating. No one would believe me. They'd call me a dozen kinds of nuts. And seeing as how I'm not the type who likes to be made a proverbial laughing stock of . . . well, you gotta promise."

Sarah's face drooped more. "I promise." She made a Boy Scout sign.

"I date dead people."

"What?"

"Shhh. I said, Sarah . . . I date dead people. Or, to be more precise, dead movie stars."

Sarah's mouth fell open.

"Oh, I used to date some of the guys on Greek Row.

Live ones," Anne continued, oblivious to her friend's incredulous stare. "Even went steady for a couple of months with this Italian dude from Sigma Pi. But they were all for groping and such, all squeeze and no substance. I even tried dating some of the guys from the drama department—they're not all gay, you know. But, truth be told, none of 'em are great actors, and none of 'em were great in bed. They don't have, oh, I don't know . . . a presence. None of them float my boat, know what I mean? So I hit upon the notion, about a year or so back, of dating dead men."

Sarah's mouth hung open wider. She hadn't taken a breath since Anne's revelation.

"I always had some talent with this Ouija board . . . my grandmum gave me this when I was a kid. Been toying with it ever since. I just had never used it to get dates before . . . well, before I gave up on breathing men. Sarah . . . breathe, Sarah."

Sarah sucked in a lungful. "You're serious."

"Dead serious."

"Omigod. Look, Anne, thanks for thinking of me and all. But I really do get dates. Once in a while, and—"

"But nothing special, I bet. No one lights your fire." Anne knew she had Sarah there. She suspected the dormie hadn't been out in months.

"No, nothing special," Sarah admitted. She dropped her gaze to the Ouija board.

"Then why not double with me? It'll be an otherworldly experience. I guarantee it."

Sarah visibly shuddered.

"I've been on dozens and dozens of these dates, Sarah. I go out two or three times a week. Well . . . go out while staying right here. And I never have to dress up. In the . . . uhm, otherworld . . . I just picture myself wearing whatever I want. Three nights ago, right after I finished a term paper for my religious history class on the Taiwanese Ghost Month observance . . . that starts on the first day of the seventh lunar month. They call it 'Open Day,' when the underworld gates are opened and the spirits cross into the living world. Eastern religions are just more pragmatic about spirits and such. Anyway, after the paper I went out on a date with Jimmy Stewart, and I wore this black sequined formal, strapless."

"J-J-Jimmy Stewart? *The* Jimmy Stewart?"

Anne shook her head. "Yeah, I know, who'd wanna date Jimmy Stewart? Well, I have to admit I had a pretty good time. But that wasn't who I wanted to go out with—or who I thought I set the date up with."

Sarah looked up from the board.

"I wanted to go . . . *want to go out* . . . with Clark Gable." Anne's expression turned wistful. "I've been trying to channel him for better than a year."

"Clark Gable." Sarah's voice turned dreamy. She looked at the posters again, they were all Gable movies. "I love Clark Gable."

"That's why we get along so well, you and me. But I haven't reached him yet."

"But you reached Jimmy Stewart?"

"Yeah." Anne poked out her bottom lip and let out a breath. It teased a lone strand of hair that had escaped one of the curlers. "I haven't found him yet, Clark. But in the process, I found Spencer Tracy."

"Won an Oscar for *Captains Courageous* in thirty-seven," Sarah supplied. "And in thirty-eight for *Boys Town.*"

"Humphrey Bogart, twice."

"Best Actor in fifty-one for *The African Queen.*"

"Yul Brynner."

"*The King and I* in fifty-six."

"Jack Lemmon."

"*Save The Tiger* in seventy-three."

Anne smiled slyly. "Gary Cooper."

"*Sergeant York,* forty-one."

"Laurence Olivier."

"Wow. *Hamlet,* forty-eight." Sarah drew her shoulders back. "They're all Best Actor winners."

"Well, those are the memorable dates." Anne sighed. "I've been on some less than stellar ones. Uhm, I've never been out with anyone who wasn't famous. Then

there were the Cs . . . 'cause I concentrated on 'Clark'
so much I think. Montgomery Clift, Ray Charles, Kurt
Cobain, Sam Cooke, Bob Crane, and Bing Crosby. I
spent a day at this ghostly ball park with Joe DiMaggio,
watching all these dead guys play a 'Heavenly Series,' he
called it. Then there was Walt Disney . . . lord, all he
wanted to watch were cartoons. Buster Keaton, DeForest
Kelley, Gene Kelly, Fred Gwynne. Oh my, then there
was Moe and Shemp Howard . . . certainly not a fun
date."

Anne touched her fingers to the Ouija piece. "Bela
Lugosi, Fred MacMurray, Peter Lawford, Timothy
Leary—now he was a real trip. Buddy Holly, James
Dean. I think those were my two favorite evenings, Holly
and Dean."

"But never Clark Gable?" Sarah tentatively reached
her fingers forward to touch the Ouija piece. "I played
with one of these when I was a kid." Still the disbelief
hung in her eyes, and there was the faintest quaver in
her voice. "You sure . . . you swear you ain't teasing
me, Anne?"

"Never, Sarah."

"So what do we do . . . to find these movie stars to
date? Use the Ouija board?"

"Sort of." Anne poked out her bottom lip again and
let out another deep breath. "Homemade versions of the
Ouija board date to the eighteen eighties, my grandmum
told me. This thing we have our fingers on? Call it a
planchette. People used to put a pencil or pen or chalk
in the middle. The planchette rested on casters and sat
on a piece of paper. The users asked a question, closed
their eyes, and then touched the planchette. Spirits from
the other side would nudge the planchette and write out
an answer or message. But these modern Ouija boards,
grandmum said Parker Brothers started making them in
the sixties, have the letters and numbers on them. You
just let the planchette float around at the spirit's discretion and spell something out. They usually spell out the
time that the movie star is willing to date you. Then you

come back to the board at that specified time, touch the planchette again, and suddenly you're drifting in the place where spirits go."

"And if the date sucks?"

Did Anne detect a hint that Sarah was finally buying all of this?

"Then you just call it off, and . . . poof . . . you're back in my room."

"So we're just gonna set up the date tonight?"

"Well, if we get two handsome takers, we'll jump in right now. They usually just want to go to the movies . . . figures, since I've been channeling movie stars."

"But not Clark Gable."

"Not yet," Anne said. "But I won't give up on him. He's out there."

Sarah looked up at the poster of *It Happened One Night* hanging above Anne's bed. Clark Gable won Best Actor for that in thirty-four. In his acceptance speech he said: "It's a grand and glorious feeling, but I'll be wearing the same size hat tomorrow."

"So we concentrate on him, huh? On Clark?"

"Yeah, Sarah, we concentrate on him. We find him, he's mine. We'll ask him if Gary Cooper is around for you. No offence, you understand, but I've been trying to find Clark for months and months and months." The wistful look appeared again. "I know everything about him, Sarah. Absolutely everything. He was born in Cadiz, Ohio, in the winter of oh-one, and his mother died later that same year. He was sent to live with an aunt and uncle in Pennsylvania for two years. Then his dad took him back to Cadiz."

Sarah did not seem impressed, but then Anne figured an old movie buff probably already knew all of that. Still, she continued:

"He dropped out of high school when he turned sixteen, then he did some odd jobs until he caught on with a traveling theater company. He was twenty-three when he married Josephine Dillon, who'd been his acting coach. She was more than a dozen years older than him, and it lasted only a half-dozen years. And then he married Maria Langham, who was also more than a few years older than him.''

"His first real part, a small one, was in *Painted Desert*,'' Sarah cut in, smiling that she'd provided some trivia. "And he was nominated three times for an Oscar—the others being *Mutiny on the Bounty*, and *Gone With the Wind*, which he should have walked away with.''

Anne nudged Sarah's fingers. "It was all roses and champagne after that first film, then the year after he got the Oscar he starred with Loretta Young in *The Call of the Wild*.''

"He had an affair with her, Loretta Young, and they had a daughter.''

Anne narrowed her eyes, not pleased Sarah seemed to know such minutia about Clark. She decided to one-up her friend: "He divorced Langham in thirty-nine, starred in *Gone With The Wind* that year, and also married Carole Lombard. She died three years later, a plane crash.'' Anne brightened. "I did have a brush with Carole about four months back, but she didn't know . . . and didn't care . . . where Clark was. See, he married Silvia Ashley, who was the widow of Douglas Fairbanks, in forty-nine.''

"Lasted three years,'' Sarah added.

"And in fifty-five he married Kathleen Williams Spreckles and sort of adopted her two kids. But that didn't last either . . . because he suffered a heart attack in November of sixty and died shortly thereafter.'' Anne shook off that sad fact. "I know more about Clark Gable than anyone in the drama department, professors included.''

Anne detailed Clark's salaries: $7.50 a day for *Forbidden Paradise* in 1924; $650 a week for *Sporting Blood* in 1931; $2,000 a week for *Hold Your Man* in 1933; *Gone with the Wind*, $120,000; *Any Number Can Play* in 1949, $241,250; *Soldier of Fortune* in 1955, $100,000; and $750,000, plus $58,000 a week of overtime in 1960, for *The Misfits*.

"So . . . let's find him,'' Sarah said. "Let's make this Ouija board work and find Clark Gable.''

Anne closed her eyes and started humming, rocking from

one hip to the other. "This is all for effect, you know," she whispered. "Just puts me in the mood." Her fingers twitched on the planchette, and the piece started wobbling.

Sarah closed her eyes too and felt the piece move. "Maybe we should watch what letters and numbers it goes to," she said, her voice a husky hush.

"Don't need to," Sarah answered. "It all gets spelled out in your mind. 'Sides we're looking for dates tonight . . . not just setting something up."

The piece moved faster, floating across the board from side to side, a tingling racing up the women's fingers.

"Calling Clark Gable," Anne crooned. "Channeling Clark Gable."

Perhaps there was magic in the old Ouija board, or in Anne herself. Or maybe her room in the sorority house sat at the junction of spiritual planes. No matter the explanation, the women felt a chill pass simultaneously through them, then felt a mist rise from the rug and wrap around them, hanging just below their shoulders the way the fog often hung above the ground in the cornfields that surrounded the campus.

"Calling Clark Gable," Anne repeated, her voice sounding dreamy now.

Images appeared in the fog, ghostly shapes of people, some seeming to have hats, others carrying pipes and coats, one walking a dog on a short leash. A man drifted toward them, the mist making it difficult to see him clearly. But he had Clark's build and short hair, a mustache—they could tell as he came closer, and a twinkling gaze. But there were two moles on his face, and his grin was too sly and wide.

"It has lifeless eyes," he told them. A snake appeared at his feet and wrapped around his legs. The fog thinned, showing it to be a length of film from a movie canister. "It has black eyes." The frames shimmered and winked out. "The ocean turns red all around it."

"Ugh," Anne pronounced. "Sarah, meet Robert Shaw. He's misquoting some of his lines from *Jaws*. Time to move on."

The apparition appeared disappointed, but it made no move to stop the women from leaving.

Sarah and Anne glided through the otherworld, seeing images of buildings from the 1920s, a WWII bunker, a stretch of jungle complete with a tree house, a log cabin in a field, the Bates Motel, and a bus stop. Sarah explained they were all movie sets, kept in reasonable condition by the memories of this plane's inhabitants. Ghosts drifted among the sets, solidifying and flying closer to the women, then moving along.

"Look," Sarah gushed. "I-I-I think that's—"

"Yep, pardner, that's John Wayne. Won an Oscar for *True Grit* in sixty-nine. I went out with him two or three months back. It was okay."

"I could go out with John Wayne," Sarah said, trying to keep her voice down so the floating spirits would not hear. "I liked him in *Green Berets* and *High Noon*."

"*High Noon*, that was Gary Cooper," Anne tsk-tsked. "See, I said maybe we should set you up with Gary."

Sarah nodded, still trying to take everything in.

"Look over there," Anne gestured with an arm that looked diaphanous, then turned solid.

Sarah noticed that Anne was wearing a shimmering red dress that hit between her knees and ankles, red satin high heels, and a black suede belt. Her hair flared back from her face.

"You look beautiful," Sarah said.

"I said, look at those two fellas."

Sarah did, then gasped and threw her hands over her mouth.

"Yeah, Bing Crosby . . . *Going My Way* in forty-four, and Frank Sinatra . . . *From Here to Eternity* in fifty-three."

"We could double date them," the hope thick in Sarah's voice.

"Calling Clark Gable," Anne repeated.

"There's Burl Ives," Sarah tittered. "Best Actor in fifty-eight for *The Big Country*."

"You'd need a big country for him."

"And Peter Ustinov, Best Actor in sixty and sixty-four, *Spartacus* and *Topkapi*."

"Didn't see *Topkapi*," Anne admitted. "But it's on my list of 'things to rent.' Seen every single one of Clark's movies, though." As they moved through the fog, Anne rattled off seventy-nine of them—from *White Man* in 1924, where he played Lady Andrea's brother, to *The Misfits*, released in 1961, his last picture, where he played Gay Langland. "I don't have a favorite," she said. "I love them all."

"I love Clark Gable," Sarah said.

"But not as much as I love him. I'm sort of singular in my obsession. Call me Anne of the One Gable." Anne led them through phantom back lots and by one trailer after the next, through sound stages and screening rooms and even into a producer's office.

The women were unaware how much time had passed, and they wondered aloud if time passed differently in the spirit world than on the NIU campus. They were mentally exhausted by the time they circled around again to the WWII bunker.

"I suppose we could call it a night," Anne said glumly. "Try again in a day or two. To get home all we have to do is concentrate, picture the Ouija board, and . . . wait a minute. There's a tall drink o' water. Calling Clark Gable. Oh, calling Clark." She moved away from Sarah, nearing a specter with wavy hair and a mustache. "Clark?"

He solidified only a few feet away. Brown hair, sparkling eyes, athletic build . . . but not Clark.

"Errol," Anne pronounced.

A green felt hat with a pheasant feather stuck in it appeared on his head. He doffed it in an exaggerated bow.

"Milady . . . you are looking for male companionship this fine night." His eyes sparkled brighter.

Anne looked over her shoulder at Sarah and gave her a thin smile. *"He'll do,"* Anne mouthed. "Sarah, go back to your dorm or wander around here a bit more. I'm . . . ah . . . gonna go out with Errol for a little while."

"Have fun." Sarah waggled her fingers and watched

as Errol, now wearing his green tights and tunic, bow and quiver slung across his back, disappeared with Anne into the mist.

Sarah waited for several minutes, making sure Anne hadn't changed her mind. Then she cleared her head and spread her arms out to her sides, pictured herself in a violet ball gown decorated with rhinestones and seed pearls. A dainty string of diamonds circled her neck, and more diamonds hung from her ears. She was thirty or so pounds lighter, in this image she'd crafted for herself.

"Calling William Gable," she said. "Anne only thought she knew everything about him. She apparently didn't know Clark was just his middle name." Louder: "Calling William Gable. Calling William Clark Gable."

Suddenly she swooned in his strong arms and looked up into his mysterious, dark eyes. He was wearing his newly pressed suit from *Gone With the Wind*, hair slicked just like in the movie.

"I could not find any flowers, dear heart," he apologized.

"I don't need any," Sarah answered.

"The blooms would pale beside you anyway," he said. He straightened and held Sarah gingerly against him, then backed away just far enough so he could look her up and down. "Beautiful lady, if you've no plans for the evening—"

"Oh, I most certainly do have plans, William." She allowed herself to be bent backward in a long and passionate kiss. "I have plans for this night and the next and the next and the . . ."

MOTIVATIONAL SPEAKER

Scott William Carter

Scott William Carter's short stories have appeared or will shortly appear across a wide range of publications and genres, including *Analog*, *Weird Tales*, *Crimewave*, and *Cicada*, among others. He lives in Oregon's lush Willamette Valley with his wife, daughter, and an assortment of critters. Find out more about his work at his website: www.scottwilliamcarter.com.

The overhead fluorescent lights flashed, signaling that Mart-Co would be closing in five minutes. Craig had spent the better part of an hour scrutinizing the fine print specs on the back of the Tek-King universal remote, and yet he still hadn't decided whether to buy it or not. He was leaning toward buying it, maybe eighty-five percent there, close to ninety percent, really, but he still wasn't sure it was the right one for him.

He could always come back another day. Or just live without a remote, as he had done for the past three years. With a sigh, he hung it in its clear plastic packaging on the metal rod and turned to go. His tennis shoes, wet from the afternoon rain, squeaked on the tiles.

"Oh, just buy the damn thing, already," a woman said.

Craig jumped. The voice had come from right behind him. But when he whirled around, there was no one in the aisle but him.

"Hello?" he said.

"You heard me."

The voice seemed to be coming from the stereo system on the shelf right next to the remotes. It was a vaguely familiar voice, though he couldn't say where he'd heard it before. There was also a very faint beeping noise in the background. *Beep . . . Beep . . . Beep.*

"Okay, very funny," he said. "Somebody's piping in through a microphone. Ha Ha."

"Don't be a flipping idiot, Craig. Just buy the remote and go home. What more do you need, a sign from God? I've never known anyone as wishy-washy as you."

Craig frowned. They knew his name, meaning this was something they had been planning. "Okay," he said, "whoever you are, you can come out now. The fun's over."

A clerk in a green apron poked his head around the corner. His buzz of blond was an unnatural color of yellow, like polished gold. He had a diamond stud earring on his nose. "Need help, dude?" he said.

Craig pointed at the stereo. "You think this is funny?"

"You lost me, man."

"I don't think he can hear me," the woman said.

"There! See there!" Craig cried. "You hear that?"

"Hear what?" the clerk said.

Craig crossed his arms and stared at the clerk. "You mean you didn't just hear all of that?"

The clerk shook his head. "Dude, I don't know what you're going on about, but we're closing in about two minutes."

"All right, fine," Craig said tersely, "I've had enough of this. Great practical joke. Ha, ha! I'm really laughing!"

Feeling a rush of blood to his face, Craig started down the aisle, accidentally knocking off a package of batteries along the way. Being the butt of a joke brought back fresh memories from high school, even though it had been five years since his graduation.

"Wait," the woman said.

She said the word with such a pleading tone that Craig stopped.

"Please," the woman begged. "Don't go."

She sounded more like a lonely little girl now than the confident young woman he had made her out to be. Either that or she was a very good actress. He looked at the clerk again, who just shook his head and walked away.

Craig made his way back to the stereo system. It was just a cheap boom box—black and silver plastic, with two tape decks and a single-disc CD player. It was maybe a foot tall and two feet wide, the speakers detachable. A yellow clearance sticker listed a price of just under twenty dollars, marked down from twenty-five.

Then he noticed that the power was turned off. Not only that, but the stereo wasn't plugged into an outlet. He turned it over, popped open the battery compartment, and saw that it was empty as well.

He felt a cold chill.

"Who are you?" he said quietly.

The woman didn't answer. The beeping continued.

"Game over?" he said.

"No," she said softly. "I just . . . don't remember."

"Okay," Craig said, "let me get this straight. You're somebody talking to me through this stereo who . . . has amnesia?"

She was silent a moment. "I don't know. I guess I *am* the stereo. Or at least I'm trapped inside it. I don't know . . . I can't remember anything before today."

"What do you want from me?" he said.

"What does any woman want?"

"Huh?"

"Humor, Craig. *Gallows* humor, specifically. Helps me deal with the reality of being a disembodied voice trapped inside a bit of plastic and wires."

"How do you even know you're in a radio? You don't have eyes."

"I don't know how I can see things. I just do. I mean, I don't have a brain either, but it's obvious I can think, right?"

"Hmm . . ."

"Buy me, Craig. Take me home. I don't know how things will go beyond that, but it's a start. Come on, come on, what do you say? We're talking twenty bucks here. Geez, you can always return me if things don't work out."

She had a point. Mart-Co had a very liberal return policy.

"Okay," he said, surprising himself.

"Great," she said. "Just one thing. I'm not listening to any country music."

An evening breeze rattled the leaves of the giant oak that took up most of the yard of the ten-unit complex. The light was fading, and the lamplights mounted on black poles glowed a faint yellow.

He set her up on the carpet in the corner of his living room, away from the sunlight and the heating vent, both of which might damage her. Since she didn't actually require any power, he wasn't sure if she *could* be damaged, but he figured it was better to play it safe.

Craig realized there was a practical matter he needed to resolve right away. "What should I call you?" he asked.

"What do you mean?"

"I mean, do you know your name?"

"Hmm . . . How about Lucky? Call me Lucky. I'm sure I'll bring good luck for you."

While he was making dinner—macaroni and cheese, what he made for himself every Tuesday—Lucky asked him a few questions, and gradually he relaxed and talked a little more freely. Had he been married? No. Engaged? No, just dated a little bit, the longest was a woman named Anne whom he saw for four months. What were his parents like? His mother, who died of breast cancer ten years back, had been a stay-at-home mom and something of a zealous Catholic. His father, a silent man, had worked as a CPA for the government. These days, he saw his dad once a year, at Christmas, but neither of them had much to say.

Craig was never very comfortable talking about himself with a real person, but somehow it was easier when it was just a voice inside a stereo system.

The next few days, they settled into a routine, talking during the meals and watching television together in the evenings. Craig hadn't lived with anyone since he left his parents' home—and he wasn't even sure if this qualified—but he was beginning to enjoy having her around. He even opened up to her about his problems making decisions.

"It's just so hard," he said, while he was spooning up some spaghetti, Thursday night's meal. "It's like I just freeze up. Even about the smallest things."

He looked at her across the table, where he now placed her anytime he was having a meal. He wished there was some way to read her reactions.

"Yeah, you really have a problem with that," she said. "Has it always been that way?"

He paused midbite, the steam rising off the noodles, smelling of garlic and cooked tomatoes. "Well . . . no. I was never much of a go-getter, I guess, but I didn't have this problem."

"When did it start?"

He thought about it. "When I was in college, I think."

"Uh huh. And when did your Mom die?"

"Right before college." He laughed sharply. "What, are you going to do a Freud routine and tell me my problem has to do with my mother?"

"Well?"

He dropped his fork, which clattered against the porcelain plate. "Oh, for Christ's sake . . ."

"Okay, okay," she said. "You don't have to talk about it. Hey, let's do something, huh? Let's go for a drive."

He frowned. "Where?"

"Anywhere! Cruise the town. Roll down the windows and whoop. Anything. Just get out of this condo."

"But where?"

She sighed. "Just get your keys."

At first, he clenched the steering wheel so hard his knuckles turned white, but by the end of the drive he was whistling the *Chips* theme song along with Lucky. And that night, when he lay in bed staring at the white ceiling and walls, he thought she might have been right about his mother.

But over the next few days, Lucky's suggestions began to wear on him. She wanted to know what his goals were, and when he said he didn't have any, she kept pressing him until he admitted that he had always dreamed of doing computer programming for a gaming company. Then she kept giving him suggestions on how he could make his dream a reality—taking classes, looking for jobs more closely related to what he wanted. She kept pressing him to try new things—go scuba diving, take a dancing class, fly a kite at the coast—and he always put her off.

"I'm just trying to shake you out of your doldrums," she explained.

He sprinkled the chopped green pepper into the sizzling frying pan. He was making an omelet—on a Saturday, something he had only previously done on Thursdays—as his way of showing her he could do new things.

"Maybe I'm happy in my doldrums."

"Nobody's happy that way. You just need somebody to show you a way out."

He knew she was right, that he wasn't happy, but the more she pushed him, the more uneasy he became. He couldn't sleep. His appetite disappeared. He still loved spending the evenings talking to her, but he was beginning to depend on her, and he didn't like that. What pushed him over the edge, though, was when she asked him to take her out to dinner.

"What?" he said.

He was on his knees in the living room, eating sushi on a TV tray and watching a Bruce Lee movie—none of which he had done before. Well, except for getting on his knees. He had done that plenty of times when he used to attend Mass.

Lucky was perched on a matching TV tray—one that pictured Elvis in his white suit and tinted glasses. Craig had picked them up while "antiquing" the previous Saturday, an activity Lucky had encouraged him to do when he said that going with his mother to antique shops had been something he had enjoyed as a child.

"I'd just like to be treated to a night out once in a while," Lucky said. "I think I deserve that."

He laughed.

"What?" she said.

"Well," he began, trying to find the most tactful way to put it, "you're . . . a stereo."

"So?"

"Don't you think it would look a little odd, me having dinner with a cheap piece of plastic made in China?"

"There's no reason to be cruel."

"But you get my point, right?"

"No. I don't see why you can't treat me like a lady once in a while."

"You're not a lady!"

She started making sniffling sounds, punctuated by bursts of static, which made him feel both useless and awful. He felt awful because he knew he had made her feel this way, and he felt useless because he didn't know how to comfort her. It didn't matter that she was a stereo system, either, because he felt equally helpless around flesh and blood women when they cried.

Back when his mom was alive, he remembered hearing her cry sometimes. She cried a lot, and she could never give any reason. His father never said a word when she cried. He just sat in the corner and read his paper. When he got older, he learned that his mother was bipolar, and that she got that way when she was off her medication.

That's when he realized how much Lucky's crying reminded him of his mother. And then something occurred to him, something that seemed obvious but had eluded him until now. There was a distinct possibility that all of this was in his mind. There *was* mental illness in his family. It all added up.

He knew, then, what he had to do.

Since they often went for drives in the evening, she had no reason to suspect anything was unusual about their drive until he pulled into the Mart-Co parking lot.

She fell silent. Then, softly, she said, "What are we doing here?"

He parked in the same spot he always did when it was available, the one right between the cart rack and the island with the maple tree. It was almost ten o'clock. Fog hung in the air, and the parking lot lights formed golden halos through which he saw tiny streaks of rain.

"Craig?" she said.

He got out of the car, walked around to the other side, the air wetting his face, and got her out of the car. He held her with both arms, so neither of the speakers would fall off.

"Craig, please answer me," she said.

"I'm sorry," he said, starting for the door.

"You're taking me back."

"Yes."

She started crying. "Why?"

"I can't do this any more."

"I thought things were going well. I . . . I thought we were good together."

He shook his head. A young couple holding hands passed him, giving him a curious glance, but he didn't care. He could be crazy one more night.

"You're not real," he said.

"What?!" The word was barely audible, lost in fury of static. Don't be a flipping idiot! I'm real, Craig! I'm a real person in here! I don't know why I'm in here, but I'm not imaginary!"

"You're a voice that no one else but me can hear, Lucky. I think it's safe to say you're not real."

She kept pleading with him, but he didn't answer. His mother had often given in to her madness, but he wouldn't. He took Lucky inside and returned her at the Customer Service desk, having a hard time hearing the clerk over Lucky's stream of profanity.

With Lucky still yelling at him, he turned and walked toward the door, a crisp twenty now gracing his wallet.

He couldn't sleep that night, and the entire next day at work he was miserable. It took him four hours to

install a new sound card in someone's computer, a job
that usually took him twenty minutes. He didn't eat, but
he still managed to throw up three times. The last time,
he didn't even make it to the bathroom, throwing up in
the secretary's waste basket. His boss witnessed the inci-
dent and sent him home for the day.

When he got home, all he could think about was
Lucky.

It was a little after five o'clock when he reached Mart-
Co. The store was bustling with the after-work crowd.
He had hoped that she would still be at the Customer
Service counter, but they told them that the stereo system had been reshelved. He went straight to the place
in Electronics where he had originally found her. The
same yellow discounted price tag hung from the metal
shelf, but the stereo itself was gone. He felt light-headed,
and steadied himself with a hand on the shelf.

"Help you, man?"

It was the same clerk from before, the kid with the
buzz of blond hair and the stud nose ring. When Craig
looked at him, the kid's eyes widened with recognition.

Craig pointed. "The stereo that was here . . . you
sold it?"

"Oh. Yeah! Just a few minutes ago."

Craig felt a new surge of hope. "Do you know what
the person looked like?"

"Uh . . ."

"Please. It's very important that I see that stereo
again." He fumbled for his wallet. "I can make it worth
your while."

"Aw, man, that's all right. He was Asian, short, with
thick black glasses. Maybe sixty."

Craig shook the kid's hand. "Thank you!"

"Yeah, no problem. Too bad Lucy's not here, or she
might even tell you the guy's name."

Craig was already a half dozen steps down the aisle
when what the kid said lassoed him to a stop. He turned
and looked at him. "Who?"

"Lucy. Lucy Redding. She used to work here until

about a month ago. She really liked talking to the customers. Knew a lot of them by name."

Craig felt a tremor of excitement. Lucy. *Lucky.* It couldn't have been a coincidence. He had a vague memory of her, a tall, thin girl with blond hair and a quick smile. And the voice. That might have been why he thought Lucky sounded familiar when he first heard her.

"What happened to her?" he asked.

The kid shook his head. "Motorcycle accident."

"Did she die?"

"No, worse, man. She's in a coma."

Craig took off at a run toward the front of the store. In a coma. Of course. He thought about the beeping noise, and that made sense. It must have been a heart monitor.

He scanned the checkout registers, didn't see anyone who looked as the kid described, then burst through the double doors into the parking lot. The sky was gray, and a fine mist hung in the air. He ran from one row in the parking lot to the next, not seeing anyone who looked remotely Asian, and felt the heavy weight of despair settling over him. He headed back to the store, shoulders slumped.

He was nearly there when an older Asian man in a purple turtleneck emerged through the automatic doors pushing a cart.

Craig froze. He was short and somewhat round, his skin pale, his hair thinning and gray. His turtleneck was too tight for him and pinched at his rather bulky neck, as well as pulled taught around his belly. His dark-rimmed glasses fogged up, and he paused to wipe them on his shirt.

There were two items in the shopping cart: the stereo, and a large box of diapers.

"Lucky?" Craig said, his heart beating so hard he was afraid he might pass out. "Lucky, is that you?"

The stereo didn't make a sound, but the man looked at him, his eyebrows arching.

"Sorry?" He had a slight Japanese accent.

"The stereo," Craig said. "I'd like to buy it."

The man looked confused, then smiled. "Ah, I see. A joke. Excuse me, I must go."

He hurried away, his cart rattling over the black asphalt. Craig followed.

"I'd really like to buy it off of you," he said.

The man wouldn't look at him now, and he doubled his pace. "Bought it for my granddaughter. Very nice. I don't want to sell. Sorry."

Craig pulled out his wallet, leafing through the bills. "A hundred and twenty-seven dollars," he said.

The man stopped, staring at him with a perplexed expression.

"I really want that stereo," Craig explained.

Craig closed the door of his car and looked over at her on his passenger seat. She hadn't said a word yet, but the beeping noise continued.

"You still in there?" he said.

There was no reply.

"Come on, I know you're mad, but I did come back for you."

There was nothing for a moment, and finally she spoke softly. "I hate you."

"You have ever reason to be mad," he said.

"You're a bastard."

"Yes."

"A jerk."

"Definitely. But I think I know who you are and maybe how to get you back."

"You're the worst sort of scum—what'd you say?"

"I know who you are."

"Really?"

"Yes."

"Oh, god, I love you." And then, after a pause. "You're still a bastard, though."

While he headed for the hospital, he told her what he had learned. The gray sky was going dark, and droplets of water beaded on the front window. There was a part of him that was desperately afraid that if she managed to get back into her own body, a girl like her, she would never want to be with him. But he couldn't withhold the information. More than anything, he wanted her to be happy.

"Lucy Redding," she said, trying out the name.

He looked at her, the gray and black plastic in the passenger seat, encircled by a seat belt. "Anything come back to you?" he asked.

"No, but I get a weird sort of electric charge when I say it."

They drove in silence. The hospital was only a few minutes away.

He cleared his throat. "Listen, I'm sorry about leaving you. I think . . . I think I was scared."

He hoped for some encouragement, but she said nothing.

"And—and I think you're not going to want to have anything to do with me when you're back in your body."

"Don't be ridiculous."

"Why would you? A guy like me?"

She snorted. "You ever think that maybe a guy like you is exactly what a girl like me needs? Huh?"

Despite the edge in her voice, he felt encouraged. Pretending to be a cousin, he managed to cajole Lucy Redding's room number out of the reception clerk, and then he rode up the elevator with the stereo Lucy cradled under his arm. He stepped off onto polished gray tiles, the place smelling of antiseptic. The room wasn't far away, and the name written on the sign next to the door confirmed it was her. He pushed open the door.

The room was lit only by the crack of light coming from the partially open bathroom door. Still, he saw her at once, lying on the bed, her forehead bandaged, her body hooked up to various machines. A feeding tube hung from the corner of her mouth. He heard the same beeping noise, only louder, that he had been hearing from the stereo.

"Who the hell are you?"

Craig didn't see the man until he spoke. He sat in the

corner, a grizzled middle-aged man with a bald head and a stubble of gray beard, dressed in a rumpled blue uniform that was stained with grease.

"It's Dad," Lucy said. "I . . . remember him."

"I'm a friend of Lucy's," Craig said. "I—I brought her something." He lifted the stereo.

Craig expected more resistance, but the man just nodded, eyes glassy and dead. Craig took the stereo and placed it on the table next to her, carefully making room for it next to the bouquet of yellow roses in the glass vase. Craig looked down at her face, and though it was marred by bruises and cuts, one of the eyes badly swollen, he thought her stunningly beautiful.

"Gonna play something for her?" her dad said.

In truth, he hadn't planned to do any such thing, but it seemed the right thing to do. He plugged in the stereo. He found a modern rock station, something he thought she might like. He kept waiting for something to happen, for her to open her eyes and look up at him, but she went on sleeping.

"I'm still in this box," Lucy said, sounding irritated. "But I remember. I remember everything, Craig."

"That's great," Craig said.

"Huh?" her dad said.

"Oh, this song," Craig said. "I think she liked this one a lot."

"Oh."

They listened to the rest of the song without saying a word.

"Still here," Lucy said.

"Damn, something's gotta work," Craig said.

"What are you talking about?" her dad said.

"Oh, I just . . . something's got to wake her up, you know. She can't go on like this forever."

The man's eyes turned watery, and when he spoke, the words were strangled. "Something," he said, nodding. "You know, I told her that damn motorcycle would get her killed unless she slowed down. It's the way she did everything—too fast, all the time."

"He was always a worrier," Lucy said. She was silent

a moment. "He was right, though. I think . . . I think I know why I ended up in the stereo. It was the pain. There was just so much pain. I had to get out—but I didn't want to leave. Not completely."

"Wait!" Craig said excitedly, remembering something Lucy had said to him when he first brought her home. "I need to find a country western station."

"But I hate country!" Lucy said.

"But she hates country," her dad said.

Craig turned the dial, searching. "Exactly! It's just the kind of thing that might force her back into her body."

"What in the hell are you talking about?" her dad said. Blotchy read spots appeared on his cheeks. "Just who the hell are you again?"

Craig found a station that was currently playing a Garth Brooks song and cranked up the volume. Her Dad covered his ears with his hands and bolted to his feet. Lucy shrieked—a long, high-pitched noise that started in the stereo and then, suddenly, was coming from the real Lucy on the bed. Her eyes popped open, and her own hands flew to her ears.

Craig clicked off the stereo.

"What in the hell—" her dad began, and then stopped short when he saw Lucy's eyes. He moved to her bedside.

"Daddy?" she said, her gaze darting back and forth. Her voice was garbled by the feeding tube in her mouth, and she coughed a few times. She pulled the cord out of her mouth, gagging. Finally, she saw her father, and she began to cry. "Daddy, where am I?"

Her father put his hand on her forehead. "In the hospital, sweetheart."

"It hurts, Daddy."

Now the father was crying, too. Craig felt embarrassed, intruding on a private family moment. Lucy looked over at him, and his heart skipped.

"Who are you?" she asked.

"I'm—I'm Craig."

She blinked a few times. "Do I know you?"

Of all the reactions she could have had, he hadn't expected her not to remember him. It was devastating. He was nothing more than a stranger to her—worse than a stranger, a stranger who had intruded upon her life at the worst possible time. He had feared that the real Lucy, this beautiful girl who lay broken in bed, would have no reason ever to fall in love with him. His only hope had been that she had already gotten to know him, and that might count for something, but now that hope was gone too.

"Oh," he said, back away toward the door, "I was one of your customers . . . just somebody who, um . . ."

Her eyes began to dim. He couldn't go out like this, full of indecision and doubt. She may have forgotten him, but there was something positive in that, too: She had also forgotten how he had abandoned her. If he got the chance, he could prove himself more worthy of her. He could really be there for her when she needed him.

He cleared his throat. "I want . . . I want to ask you out."

Her eyebrows raised. Her father frowned.

"Let me get this straight," she said. "You came here to ask me out when I'm all beat up, tubes sticking out of me, wasting away in a hospital bed?"

Craig fought the impulse to apologize. It was time to be bold. "Yes," he said. "That's exactly right."

She looked at him for a long moment, and then she smiled. Despite her condition, it was the most beautiful smile he had ever seen, the way it lit up her whole face. He wanted to make her smile again. He wanted the chance.

"Wow," she said.

Craig smiled back. He didn't know if that was a yes, but for the first time in his life, he was sure about something: She *definitely* hadn't said no.

It was a place to begin, and that was all he needed.

THE LOVE PRINCE

Terry Hayman

Terry Hayman is a lawyer who gave up the law
for the joys of writing, and has sold stories to
*Woman's World, Boys' Life, Grain, On Spec, Al-
tair, Stitches*, and many other publications.

*S*ure, sure. You want a story for this coronation? I'll
show *you* a story. Took place in this very same bar
right here, way back when it was still all mechanized. You
know. That metal-robot-automatic-monitoring stuff under
Thad-the-Bad.

Dee-pressing.

*But it did give us a good record of a critical Chai turn-
ing point, okay? Real history. If I can just find . . . kept a
copy when they took the original . . . never know when . . .
somewhere in all this garbage. Ah, yes. Here we go.*

*Potential hostilities. Jumper Saloon, Eye #RCK242
recording . . .*

"What is story?" asked the Faralank, swiveling on his
bar stool. Then he rolled out his prehensile tongue with
a gulping sound as if eager to swallow whatever was
offered.

The human being addressed did not respond. He was
in his early twenties, light skin, soft features, no muscle
to speak of, with a recessed thatch of curly blond hair

starting far back on his forehead. He leaned over his steaming ale with glazed eyes. Behind him, the crowded tables of space crews jostled and burst in to bouts of raucous laughter. Before him, the saloon intelligence hissed another thin sheet of sour-gas across the bar top to disinfect the scratched metal and crystalize spilled liquids.

The young man didn't budge.

So the Faralank poked a claw sharply into his shoulder and asked again. "What is story?"

"Leave off," said the tall figure suddenly on the young man's right. The newcomer's back was straight and his skin dark. He wore the long cloak of a traveling priest.

"Want *story*," the Faralank gulped back.

He turned on his stool and indicated the drunken crowd at the dim tables behind them, most of them caught up now in trying to remember all the words to "The Blackest Hole."

"They stink," the Faralank gulped. "But here . . ." He turned back to the young man. "Chai-Koos. Rich. No guard. Ask about certain *woman*. What story?"

It poked the young man harder, almost rocking him off his stool. Faralanks weren't exceptionally bright, but they were one of the stronger species of the Chai system, quick and deadly. Their scales gave them natural body armor.

Grabbing the bar top, the young man righted himself and finally glared at his inquisitor. "Y'don' deserve it."

"True," said the priest. "The Koos only lie to the best."

"And you," slurred the young man, turning to him. "You're following me. I saw—" He blinked. "Chai-Hona?" He blinked again, clearly fighting to clear his head. "You know her, don't you? You know—"

The priest held up a hand as he cast a glance at the bar cam. "If I do?"

"Take me to her!" The young man almost slipped off his seat as he reached for the other but the priest stepped back, out of reach.

"Why would I do that?

"Because . . . Because . . ."

"Story, lying Koos!" gulped the Faralank. "Tell!"

"Not for you!" the young man roared back, swinging around with his face red.

But the priest stopped him with a quick hand on his shoulder. "Perhaps for me, then. Spin a good yarn."

The young man gasped, grabbed at the round edge of the bar, then for his steaming mug. He drained it. Ordered another. "Then you'll take me," he muttered.

"Perhaps."

"Well then." The youth quavered, then sank his head forward between his shoulders as the battered bar-bot slid along its rail, stopped before him, retrieved his mug, and refilled it.

"Started just over seven months ago. My naming day."

The day you turn twenty-two on Koos West, you get your adult name given to you. But when you're a member of the royal family, Prince Inheritor, seed of the tri-God, turning twenty-two is a Really Big Deal.

Theoretically, now that I'm twenty-two, my uncle Thadeus could drop dead or get assassinated and I'd be the ruler of Koos West, which, you pathetic little peons know, makes me virtual ruler of the whole pinwheeled Chai system. You, you, most of the people in here.

Wowee.

Shut up. No snorts or gulps.

So.

Where . . . ?

Right. My naming day. I went from being called Tuck, short for Tucker, to William Ambrosian Tucker Chai-Ker, Royal Prince of Koos, 18th Glaum of Ker, Royal Seed of Leighton-Bird-Longduke, Inheritor of the Alabaster Throne.

Tickler alert activated. Name twig. Searching feeders. Searching. . . .

Fun thing, right? All that pomp and circum-such.

If you're a drone.

Or maybe a big goopy lizard, hunh?

Me, my feet ached, my back hurt, my neck itched from the tight collar I had to wear, and the Duke of Lansoad to my right was so old that he forgot to bathe regularly. He smelled foul. I was sure I was going to either keel over in a faint or break out in hysterical spasms. It went on for four love-your-mother hours!

Then, just when I thought it was done, when all the extended family had groveled and left and all I wanted to do was run off and scream, my father and mother— they drag me downstairs in the palace to this hall where Thad usually brings emissaries from the other planets when he wants to scare the excrement out of them.

The place is dimly lit, dank and fishy-smelling like it seeps in from the ocean nearby, and the walls are made to look unfinished and marred like . . . what? It's a place for shooting dissidents and rebels? I hate it. My mother used to threaten to lock me in there when I didn't want to study.

Now I'm twenty-two, and it's the first place they take me.

We marched in with the two of them positively beaming, me being just named prince and all, and I see there are a bunch of folks there already. I recognize a few of Uncle Thad's advisors but not the group of young women herded together inside an energy ring in the center of the floor. They're like a bunch of ranchos inside a spinning lasso. All different races, human and non. All Chai, though, I think. Clothing optional.

Oh, stop. I didn't arrange it, didn't ask for it. It's this royal name-day thing. A welcoming into manhood-type, as if anyone past puberty stays a virgin in the palace.

"Choose, Tucky," said my mother.

She was eager. Excited. Tugging at the tight pull of hair around her surgically clipped ears. What was *that* all about?

I looked at my father, and he nodded too. He had this knowing grin. I figured he wished he were me right then.

So, red faced, I walked over to the group of women. I did say young, right? The oldest was maybe twenty-five. A few looked barely sixteen, all sweaty and scared. And you know I also said I didn't recognize any of them? Well, I didn't, but . . . it was like maybe I should have. Something familiar with some of them. The shape of their cheeks or brows or something. It unnerved me.

The ring manager snapped at them to keep their eyes down, not look at me. Which made me blush more. I started to turn back to my parents, tell them I didn't want this, when the ring manager swore and buzz-shocked one of the women in the ring.

She grunted, and I caught her eyes—not looking down, not looking away. She was smooth skinned and brown. Beautiful, of course—they all were—but almost crazed. Like she was panicking inside, desperate to cry out, but fighting it. I could see her swallow. The Adam's apple in her long neck bobbed.

"Look away!" the ring manager repeated and was about to shock her again, but I held up my hand.

"Her," I said.

"She was Chai-Hona," said the priest to the young man's right.

"What?" The young man shakily took his still-steaming ale, drained the clear mug, then motioned to the bar-bot for another.

"That would have been illegal—holding her like a slave. We are a nomadic people. Even more than the Enols who fight you now, even more than the Draigs, the Hona cannot stand confinement."

"Really," said the young man, fixing his eyes straight ahead until his new drink arrived.

"I don't like this story, Chai-Koos."

The young man grunted and drank.

The Faralank to his left poked him. "Say louder," it gulped.

"William Ambrosian Tucker Chai-Ker" found. High priority identification request.
Adjusting resolution. Track to match.
Tracking . . .

* * *

They released her from the ring, and I half-expected her to run, not that she'd have gotten anywhere. But she didn't. She walked straight to me, with that on-the-edge look in her eye, took my hand, and knelt in front of me.

How do I describe this? She was one of the clothed ones—a simple tunic cinched at the waist, with undergarments so nothing was revealed. But when she took my hand, I felt a tingle go through me that rippled from my toes to my scalp. My skin tightened. My heart squeezed, then seemed to go so hard I could hardly breathe. My mouth went all dry.

"My lord," said the woman.

She was about my age and height, her hair wiry black curls, her build athletic, her hands rough, as if they knew how to handle weapons, her voice low and almost throbbing. On top of all the other sensations she'd sent through me, I now felt fear as well.

I'm not an athlete. I'm not gen-modded like our soldiers. Up until the age of seventeen, I was raised to be a spoiled duke, cousin to the future king. Then Thad's son dies in a stupid knife fight with some goon sporting illegal mods, and I'm suddenly next in line. I'm suddenly on a forced diet of history, laws, theories of government, manipulation, commerce—everything but how to fight. Because my Mama doesn't *want* that. They'll just crack down on everyone else instead. Outlaw non-Koos mods. Disarm the other planets.

Which meant that now all it would take to kill me would be one strong, trained, warrior woman who managed to get me alone long enough to—

I laughed suddenly, in both relief and bitterness. Because of course I would never be left alone with her, would I? Now that I was the prince, I'd probably never be left alone again.

"Take her upstairs, Tucky."

Mother again. Her eyes shone. Her tongue touched her lips.

I gestured for my choice to rise, and I led her from that awful smell of fish and oppression.

And maybe it was the docile way she followed me out, her hand trembling a little in mine, that did it. But when we reached my room in the upper west wing, I kept the guards out and locked the door. Then I looked deep into my prisoner's grateful eyes and went positively stupid. I ran to my bed. I knelt and powered up the privacy shield and cancelers I'd just installed that week but had been too scared to use.

She shook her head in disbelief. "You think now they won't see and hear us?"

"For awhile," I said, more sure than I felt. "So . . . you don't have to . . ." I waved my hands about. "You change into a robe. I'll say it was great."

She laughed roughly. "Very amusing." But it seemed to touch her nonetheless. Something I didn't recognize flashed over her face, then she strode toward me and caught me before I could step back. "Stay," she said.

With one quick motion, she unwrapped and removed her tunic.

"Go on," she said fiercely.

It took me almost ten seconds to remove my more elaborate costume.

What followed was an act I thought I had learned well with the help of women servants, cousins, and assorted female visitors to our palace. But, as practiced by this Hona woman who'd been enslaved for my name-day pleasure, the act of lovemaking became at once more terrifying and thrilling than anything to that point in my life. The passion seemed to make her limbs ripple, almost, become so unnaturally *strong* that she could . . .

Anyway.

And yet *tender*. Something inside her, beyond the awfulness of her lot, her enslavement, seemed to reach out to me. Like one person recognizing himself in another, flesh to flesh, heart to . . .

She . . . touched me right here with her fingers and stroked me in a way that made me cry like a child. Right there, on her naked breasts. My tears. I licked them up. She kissed them from my face.

Kissed me.

Sorry.

When we were done, she was different in my eyes.
She'd become a part of me. From the look in her eyes,
I could tell that I'd become part of her too. We filled
each other the way the smell of our lovemaking filled
my room. All from this simple act of sex. It was not the
sex my father had longed for, nor my mother, I was sure.
Not anything I'd learned of from any of my readings or
teachers or friends.

An alien thing, then, I decided. Something to do with
her being Chai-Hona.

Is it?

The Hona priest to whom the young man had addressed this question to did not turn his face from the
back wall of the bar where he gazed so fiercely.

"Rarely. Never with a Koos."

"But it happened."

"Not possible."

The Faralank banged the top of the bar. "Not kill
story! More!"

"It happened," said the young man.

Maximum enhancement. Identification confirmed.
Sending report . . .
Sent.
Monitoring . . .

They gave us twenty minutes to just lie on our damp
bedsheets and stare at each other. I think she was as
stunned as I was. Then the palace detail burst through
the door. Naked, my companion drove a foot into the
lead guard's face that sent him spinning back to the wall.
She knocked down two others just as easily before they
managed to drag her out.

If the lovemaking hadn't clued me in, that should have.
I knew the sort of bio-mods the palace guys had. No
simple unarmed woman anywhere should have been able
to best them.

All I could think, though, was that I had to straighten things out. I had to call my uncle.

But when I finally got through to him on the com, he turned me down. "She fooled the scans. She's barren. She's nothing. Forget her." He said it almost in boredom. Then he reconsidered and spent almost fifteen minutes haranguing me for choosing a Hona woman when the Chai-Hona had been growing a quiet resistance to our rule for years now. Didn't I recognize the political leverage the Hona would have had if the girl had actually been fertile? His voice was hard and grating. It was the first time he'd ever attacked me directly.

All of which should have made me drop the entire matter.

It didn't.

Instead, my blood boiled. How dare Thadeus treat me as though I were still one of the palace flunkies who served him? He'd been at my name-day ceremony mere hours before. He knew I was now his heir.

Or was that precisely the problem? Was he now threatened by me, worried he couldn't control me as if he had his brawling, stupid son?

I didn't care. Something in what had happened had jumbled me up inside, and all I knew was that I didn't want to lose this nameless Hona woman who'd come out of nowhere and changed everything about my world.

So I got devious. The lying Koos, right? Trained to deceive. I first made a calculated gamble that whatever Thadeus was playing at was a solo game, or at least a kingly one; my parents, lowly duke and duchess that they were, probably knew nothing about it. Yet they still had power. They'd been around. And they were so cravenly obvious in their ambitions for me.

I went to my mother first. It was almost midnight when I entered her rooms in the middle wing. My father was, of course, not there. He'd set up separate sleeping quarters years ago, far enough away that he could entertain the occasional nighttime guest with discretion. It's a Koos royal tradition.

My mother was sleeping alone when I entered, beautiful in her slippery sheets. In the dim light I saw one of her long white arms dangled off the edge of her bed, stretching her nightgown taut across her breasts, almost exposing a nipple. And charged as I was from my earlier encounter, I felt a rush of love for her that I couldn't remember having felt since I was a little boy. I saw her as a woman now—beautiful, alone, abandoned. It made me want to fall by her bedside and weep.

She woke. "Tuck?"

"Yes."

"What's wrong?"

I didn't have to hide my face as I knelt beside her bedside and blurted, "The woman, Mother. I . . . she's . . . like no one I've met before. I need her. When I begin my tour tomorrow, I need her *with* me."

Even in the half-light of her massive bedchamber, I could see my mother smile and pull herself to sitting, taking my hands in both of hers and pulling them up onto her inner thighs, soft and warm through the fabric of her gown. It was as if she wanted to pull me back inside her, or maybe share an unnameable need only she understood.

"You shall have her, darling. I just need her name."

"I don't . . ." My heart clenched tightly inside me.

"Anything."

"She is Chai-Hona and . . ." I stopped and my eyes went wide as I suddenly remembered vividly the woman's lips by my ear, breathing hard as I moved inside her, breathing her first name to me like a secret, over and over.

"Yes?"

"Her name," I whispered with a feeling of dread, "is Alina."

Alina. Name twig. High priority.
Searching feeders . . .

"That is not a Hona name," said the priest. His eyes glared at the young man.

The young man nursed his drink and didn't look up. "She told me it came from her great-great-gazillion greats grandmother from before the system was even settled. It means 'beautiful.'"

"Yes. Good," gulped the Faralank, his tongue snaking out. "Goo-o-o-od."

"And with only this information you gave her, this foolish first name, your 'mother' was able to locate where the king had taken her?"

The young man's head wove back and forth over the vapors of his drinking mug. "The name was enough. She'd helped pick her for the name-day group in the first place, remember."

The priest's face was almost white. "For the group of breeders. She helped you find this Alina again so that she'd have another chance to carry your seed."

The young man raised his head finally and smiled foolishly at the priest. "You don't get it. Of course my mother wanted that. It was my time. It was now allowed for me. But any of the other name-day women could have done it just as well. My mother helped me find Alina because she saw I was in love."

"Yes!" The Faralank bounced recklessly off its bar stool now, its heavy-grav-born limbs too much for the .9-Koos gravity of this outpost. "Tell, lying Chai-Koos! Tell!"

The young man's smile grew wider.

So my mother found Alina, and we secreted her aboard my ship with my retinue—loyal to me, not my uncle—for my name-year tour of the Chai system.

We went to Enol, Faralank (I had gravity sickness the whole two days we were there), Malás (if you've never been there, don't bother—it's so far from Chai that it never rises even to freezing and everyone stays underground), and Draig.

We were supposed to then circle back through Wato,

and finally Hona, Alina's homeworld. I'd left Hona to last because something told me I would lose her there. Not because she wanted to leave me but because she'd have to.

I was wrong. I lost her long before that.

Identification: Alina O'ka'alliphal. Fugitive notice. Extreme danger alert. High priority apprehension tag.
Preparing report . . .
Report sent.
Record all contiguous data.
Recording . . .

It happened on Draig, our fourth planet.

For the first three, we'd been subdued. Alina was tired, worn out by her ordeal with my uncle. Faralank's gravity didn't help. But by the time we reached Draig, Alina's energy was back, and my retinue had accepted her as a royal fact. They therefore turned a blind eye when I snuck her out alone one afternoon to borrow a Draig fly-cloud, much like one of our own skimmers but capable of high-altitude glides.

We soared high enough that the Draig fields were patches and the horizon curved, put it into autopilot, and could then make love higher than the birds.

But the experience must have gone to our heads. Our lovemaking grew too energetic. We knocked something we weren't supposed to. Suddenly the stern of the fly-cloud dipped, we slid sickeningly to the right, the bow plunged, and we were in an accelerating spin. The blue horizon whipped by the upper viewport. The ground spun by, brown and green, the horizon, the sky, the ground . . . I was going to puke.

Not Alina.

"Stay there," she said and began tearing through the cabin. She found an evac suit—*one* evac suit. She threw it at me. "Put it on!"

I was too dizzy to reach it. She leaped to me and strapped it on me like a baby.

"Cover your face," she said.

She'd pulled on a top, pants, and boots and now kicked open the front viewport in a crunch of poly, bodily picked me up like I weighed nothing, and threw me out.

"Alina!"

She hit me from behind, driving the wind out of me and wrapping her arms around me at the same time. Then she activated the suit's floatsheet.

When I could breathe again, when I could see and feel, I gripped her back tightly and thought, that's my girl. Stronger than ten men. And my fingers tried to ignore the feeling of the spine scales jutting through her clothing, the roughness of her cheek.

On the ground, in a farmer's fallow field, she wouldn't talk to me. She ran off and hid before my long-suffering retinue could track us down. For two days I wondered if she was gone for good, but I wouldn't let us leave the planet Draig. Just like I wouldn't let my guards search for her.

She was either with me, part of me, or . . . not.

Then, the evening of the third day on Draig, she somehow slipped past all my guards in our royal compound and into my bed. I woke as her warm smoothness slide down against me.

"Alina . . ."

"My Lord."

"No. Just Tucker. Tuck."

She cried then. In an echo of our first night, her tears washed *my* chest, and she licked them away while I kissed her hair, the tight curls smelling of Draig's clover fields. There was no roughness to her skin, no deformation of spine or muscles. Everything of her was the opposite of deformed. I wanted to drink her musk with my eyes, my fingers, my nose and mouth. Her legs slid warm under mine, her hips, the curve of her waist and ribs . . .

"Genetic modifications," she whispered into my neck. "Interspecies. Mutable Faralank sequences. They're stress-activated."

My whole body chilled. "I don't believe you."

"You don't want to."

True, but . . . "You couldn't have been selected as a woman for my name-day. It would have shown up on the physical scans."

"They can be faked."

Even my uncle had said so. "How?"

"How did you manage to get me aboard this tour with you when your uncle king wanted me locked away to 'study?' He suspected me, you know. They started tests on me the same night they took me from your room."

She shivered long and hard against me, but I had no warmth to give. My skin was crawling. My arms were wrapped around what I now thought was some kind of monster.

"Why?" I said.

"Why do you think? I was sent to kill you like my brother killed your cousin."

"Treason." I was finding it hard to breathe.

"Rebellion. War. We fight with the only weapons the Hona can use against the Koos—your pride, your foolish monarchy."

"You came to kill me?" It began to sink in, and I let go of her to scuffle back across my tangled sheets.

But her eyes when they looked at me now weren't those of an assassin. "Until our first time together. Until we *knew* each other. Then I understood you were not Koos."

"I *am* Koos," I said and rolled from my bed, yanking at my hair and stumbling about the oval-shaped Draig room.

"Not in your heart."

"In my heart! In my head! I'm not modified with anyone or anything else. It's just Koos from the time I was conceived. Your enemy! The one you perverted your body for!"

"What we did was not—"

"I'm not talking about that! I'm talking about YOU!"

I sprang across the bed at her, but she whirled out of reach with a fast breath and an odd move of her mouth. I sprawled in resigned horror as the muscles of her arms and legs bulged and rippled. Her skin roughened. Her bare breasts and stomach puckered.

"No," she moaned. "No!"

She tore her gaze off from herself and dropped to her knees, pressed her face to the floor. Her shoulders shrank back to normal as they started to shake.

And I, inside, came apart even more than before. All the neat threads of my life, held up proudly on my name day to the entire Kes, to the continent of Koos West, fluttered loose and twisted inside me. I knew who I was supposed to be. I sensed who Alina wanted me to be. I had no idea who I was.

Still, I dropped to the floor beside her, naked with her, and drew her up to me. And though I was the weaker of us two, I lifted her up onto my borrowed bed. We slept wrapped together.

In the morning she was gone.

"Yes!" gulped the Faralank. It slammed his claws on the bar top.

The young man grabbed his mug of steaming ale before it toppled and finished it with a long swallow.

"Many months, yes? You look and look! No find!"

"Seven Chai months and twenty-seven days," the young man said.

"Good story! Good lie! Yes! Prince In-heh-ree-tor."

The young man wiped his mouth sloppily and turned to the Hona priest. "What do *you* think? Good enough tale?"

For a long minute the priest did not answer but regarded the young man with a frown. "As the 'prince' of the story," he said at last, "you claimed you did not know who you truly were. Yet you ultimately abandoned your retinue to go from planet to planet and every spaceport in between, seeking this 'Alina.' Why?"

The young man shook his head. "I never said I abandoned them." His words still slurred but his eyes became watchful. "They're . . . watching over me."

The priest's mouth twisted. "Outside the bar. Six of them. And, of course, your uncle."

"Hunh?"

The priest gestured with his chin to the bar-cam.

"Your search has been tracked on the feeders for at least two months, accessible to those who know the royal Koos codes or how to break them. Your uncle—watching, yet not coming to collect you. Why does he do that, do you suppose?"

"Because I'm . . . important, but not important. I'm not needed at court for a full year. This is my name-year. This is . . ."

"A time for visiting spacer bars, seeking a woman with illegal bio-mods who managed to turn your head."

"That kind of thing's *expected*. Almost tradition. It's my name year. My uncle probably loves that I'm as dumb as his son was. And he said Alina was nothing. Barren. She's—"

"Due to bear you a son soon," said the priest.

The young man gaped.

"You didn't actually believe your uncle told you the truth about her, did you?"

Meme twig—Hona heir—activated. High priority. Analyzing . . .

The Faralank goggled as its long tongue danced out happily. "You also lie!" it complimented the priest. "Yes! Join in story! Hona lies!"

The priest stepped around the young man, grabbed the Faralank by his drab pilot's uniform, and delivered a chop to the creature's throat. Despite the throat's heavy scaling, the Faralank slumped quietly face-down on the bar.

Then the priest turned to the young man, who was wiping back his blond hair with shaky strokes.

"You haven't answered my question," said the Hona man. "Why are you looking for Alina? Who are you now?"

"She . . . knows I'm looking? I—You *were* following me. She sent you to find me."

"Time is short. Who are you now?"

The young man slid off his bar stool and found his bearings on the sticky floor. He looked at his feet, at the roomful of space jocks and outpost mechs who carried on carousing despite what was happening almost in their faces, then at the priest. With great effort, he pulled himself up straight.

"I'm William Ambrosian Tucker, Prince Inheritor of the Alabaster Throne of Koos. If I survive until my uncle Thadeus dies, I will be king. And I swear by the tri-God I will negotiate a new freedom amongst the planets of Chai. I'd like to do it with a Hona queen by my side. And my son."

For the first time since the young man had met the Hona man, whom he now doubted was a priest at all, that taller man smiled.

"Dangerous words," he said.

"The truth can be," the young man replied.

"So my sister tells me."

"Your sister."

"There is a way out of here that will leave your retinue and anyone following you behind us."

"To go where?"

"A safe place."

"Tell me."

"Better, I'll show you. But first . . ."

Hona subject priority identification. Match to murder suspect Matjasz O'ka'alliphal.
Full bioscan and pattern requested.

With an odd mouth movement, the Hona man drew back the sleeve from his scaly right arm and flicked something metallic at the bar-cam.

Starting biosca—*

And that's how our little show ends. Jumpin', hunh? The first ever meeting of Prince William Ambrosian Tucker Chai-Ker and his future Minister of Peace, Matjasz O'ka'alliphal.

Nope, we don't know how, exactly, the prince and O'ka'alliphal eluded the Chai royal guards, but . . .

*Yeah. Yeah. Sure. Sure. You can stop crying in your
SweetSqueeze. You want to know how the prince got together with his future queen, Alina O'ka'alliphal, so they
could produce Prince Alesasz.*

*Here! Gonna read it to you, scoffed out of a feeder
bootleg of the king's own diaries.*

Matjasz led me up a long, winding trail to her tent. It
was set well apart from the others on her own insistence,
high on a grassy field overlooking Hona's great Valley
of Solstice. I could smell its pungent wet grass as a wind
rushed up the valley to almost blow me over. The canvas
of Alina's dwelling flapped and snapped before me.

Here, eight months pregnant, she was so exposed.

Yet I understood. Alina could not huddle beside rock
or in a more permanent shelter. Her memories of captiv-
ity were still too fresh.

And her memories of me?

I turned to ask Matjasz if he had told her I was coming
but found the tall man had slipped away. Nor were there
other Hona anywhere to be seen. I gathered from Matjasz on our hurried flight here that he and his sister were
from a respected bloodline. The other Hona respected
her isolation.

For just a moment I hesitated. A memory of her stress-
induced scales and strength washed through me and I
wondered what her pregnancy would do to her. What
her modifications would do to our unborn son.

Then I swallowed, dry-mouthed with both eagerness
and fear, and pulled back the tent flap to walk in.

She sat cross-legged on a thick fur watching me as I
entered. She wore no clothes. Whether this was by Hona
pregnancy custom or her private need to show me all
she was, I did not know then.

But the sight of her smooth, tanned skin, and her swollen breasts protruding over an enormous rounded belly
undid me. I fell to my knees before her.

She smiled. "It's your name-year, Prince. The time
when you may at last spread your seed. Have you spread
it far and wide?"

Still my mouth seemed glued shut, but I shook my head.

"Only here, then?"

"Only here," I managed.

And though her brother or other spies must have surely told her this, hearing it from me made her breathe faster. Her dark eyes started to fill.

"Because?" she said.

So, still on my knees, I told her what I had told her brother and with each passing second became more certain of. That she was my heart and my future, and the future of us all.

When I was done, the tears were flowing freely down her face. A sudden flurry of bumps appeared on the bare skin of her belly, drawing down her eyes, and she laughed.

"Tuck, would you like to feel your son?"

I nodded, walked forward on my hands and knees, brushed the dirt from my palms, reached out, and, with awe and reverence, touched our future.

The truth, so help me, gods. And raise a glass with me now to that future. May he reign as well as his father, King Tuck.

Huzzah!

WITH ADMIRATION

Gail Selinger

Gail Selinger is a writer, college lecturer, and teacher of pirate lore. Active in the Port Royal Privateer Re-Enactment Workshops, she has written *The Complete Idiots Guide to Pirates*, several pirate-themed romance novels, as well as serious articles for publications for pirate enthusiasts.

"**W**here's Dad? I've looked everywhere." He rushed into her bedroom, breathless from the exertion.

His sister glanced up from her book. "Father left already."

He slumped onto the burgundy satin cushion next to her. "He didn't waste a second."

"When does he?"

"I hope he's this prompt returning."

"When is he?"

"If only he'll stick to the agreement." Her brother always worried about that.

"Has he ever?" she said.

"I pity the girl."

"When don't you?" she answered, and returned to her reading.

"Ahhh," Phoebe kicked off her spike-heeled navy slingbacks and wiggled her red painted toes in sheer ecstasy.

Sinking deep into the hotel suite's plush gold brocade sofa, she rummaged through her matching purse—it was almost large enough to qualify as luggage—and pulled out the walkie-talkie.

"Charles, are all the conference tracks still running on schedule? Good. I'll meet you in the banquet hall as soon as I change shoes."

"Hang on. Charles, go on without her for now. Phoebe, I need you for five minutes." Rachael, Phoebe's codirector for the conference, pour iced mint tea into two hand-cut crystal glasses—the hotel provided a set in each suite—and handed her one.

"I thought it was my turn to serve?"

"It is, but you look too comfortable to move right now. Besides, you've been working off your well-toned rump since you lost the bet and gave Simone's lectures piggybacked onto your own. I figure I'd be magnanimous. Take a break. Enjoy it. It won't last."

"Gee, thanks."

"Seriously, I just received a few politically problematic last minute confirmations and some no shows. We need to go over the fixes."

After raking her fingers through her long dark auburn hair to see if she could dislodge the headache Rachael's words induced, Phoebe shook her head. "I don't think I'll survive this conference to have a vacation."

"You always survive. You're just one step beyond exhaustion right now. The conference is almost over. Keep thinking Greece in spring time."

Phoebe took a long slow sip of tea, and inhaled deeply. "So who's in a snit now? Make this fast. I only have an hour to rearrange a banquet hall for 4,000."

The warring cloud of perfumes and aftershaves wafting from the crush of people milling about the reception area added to Phoebe's headache. It seemed that every person in the space had decided to try a different fragrance. The effect of all the scents together was probably not what their designers had in mind. It was more like chemical warfare than perfume. The subtle taste of the champagne she sipped was overcome by the intermingling scents assaulting her taste buds.

It was early yet, and her head felt as though it were swelling. Her nose was already itching. She hated her allergies!

Glancing at her watch, she hoped the niggling throb across the left side of her temple, first signs of an incipient migraine, would not escalate to the light sensitivity stage. If only the headache held off for another hour, she could escape to her room, take an additional dose of sinus medicines and her emergency migraine pill, lie down, and pray the current pain didn't turn into a full-blown ordeal.

Damn it! She had to be well enough to be packed and checked out by noon. As much as she would love to spend her four days of vacation here at the Alsos, the hotel's convention rates ended at midnight. She couldn't afford the price of one of their broom closets, if it was available for occupancy. But there were plenty of other options here in the Greek Islands, and she'd made arrangements to enjoy them. If she survived tonight.

Phoebe defiantly sipped more champagne, knowing the alcohol wouldn't help her one iota. It would in all likelihood make her headache worse.

"A great success all round I would say, Miss Velicia."

"Why, thank you." Phoebe turned and was rewarded with an overbearing whiff of Paco Rabonne aftershave, with undertones of sweat. She tried not to sway after the sensory assault. She took two small steps backward, hoping Professor Charvey wouldn't notice the movement, or perhaps that he would but would put it down to personal space issues.

"Most interesting and lively conference I've been to in ages. Ages," he laughed and slapped her on the forearm. "Get it?" he chortled, nodding toward the bright purple and white nylon banner announcing 'Gerontology—Aging is International.' It was the theme of the gathering, which attracted people of all ages, despite its topic. These days, aging was such a growth industry it even attracted the young. "The whole experience has been a pleasure. You've been quite clever, my girl. Good work."

"Thank you, Professor. Oh, look, the band is here. I must make sure they have everything they need. If you'll excuse me, duty calls." Phoebe plastered on her most professional smile and began to elbow her way through the packed crowd toward the bandstand.

"Expertly done." A deep baritone whispered above her head.

Phoebe turned and stared up into a pair of mischievous twinkling blue eyes. The eyes were the main attraction in a nicely chiseled face. *The rest of him isn't bad either*, she thought. "Thank you. I've learned through the years that I shouldn't offend the guest speaker. Even when it's his aftershave I object to, rather than him."

"Still, a nice evasion," he said. He towered over her, in the nicest possible way. "Especially since you look unwell."

Phoebe was taken aback. Men, in her experience, noticed babes, food, and sports, generally in that order. They might notice someone was hurting if that someone was on fire or missing body parts. Over the years she had learned through necessity to hide the excruciating episodes of her headaches. These days, she was so adapt at it only Rachael recognized the subtle signs. This man, even though he didn't know her, had recognized her problem at a glance.

"Migraine."

"Ah," he straightened to his full height. "My condolences. Don't let me keep you then."

He had a lovely baritone, full and rich. Her whole body was affected by it as she felt his words vibrate through her. *Yummmm*, she thought. If she weren't in charge of pulling off this banquet, and felt even an iota better right now, she'd snag this one and pursue. Why did she have to meet the most interesting man she'd seen in years when she couldn't do a thing about it?

Her timing was terrible. But duty called.

"Well, nice meeting you." She nodded at him and continued toward the bandstand.

She wondered if she'd see him again. She hadn't even managed to get his name.

He watched her zigzag through the crowd until she reached the band. Only then did he raise his arm waist height and snap his fingers. Immediately a waiter appeared by his side.

"Yes, Mr. Demandrous?"

Silently he pointed to Phoebe.

"Yes, sir, Mr. Demandrous."

The soft rapping sounded to Phoebe like a jackhammer. The soft morning light assaulted her closed eyes, despite the hotel's blackout drapes.

But she felt almost human.

Her luck had held. She had downed a double dose of her medicine and this morning merely felt like she'd been run over by a truck, as opposed to DOA.

"You stay where you are. I'll get the door, Phoebe." Phoebe heard Rachael dragging herself out of the bedroom on the other side of the suite and turned over to return to her slumber.

She snuggled deeper under the down quilt, not caring who was trying to disturb her precious hours of rest. Rachael could deal with it.

But her friend's low whistle piqued her interest. "Phoebe, get in here. You have got to see this."

She struggled free of the covers, fumbled into her robe, and shuffled to the living room archway. Rachael was grinning like the proverbial cat about to swallow the canary, and by the looks of the huge two-tier serving cart in front of her, Phoebe could see why. There was a lone perfect silver rose in the center, but the rest of the cart overflowed with chafing dishes.

"Rachael, you didn't decide to embezzle from the conference treasury to feed us, did you??"

"Nope." Rachael systematically uncovered the dishes. "Did you?

"No. Then who . . . ?" Drawn by the aromas and the mystery, Phoebe walked over to the array of food.

Even through her post-headache funk, it smelled fabulous.

"It's for you. This came with it." Rachael handed her an envelope made of a heavy silver-gray paper.

Pheobe's full name was boldly handwritten in blue ink.

"Well," Rachael said, "come on. Open it. I'm dying here."

Phoebe ripped open the envelope and read the letter aloud.

Ms. Velicia,
I hope your migraine has subsided sufficiently for you to enjoy this feast. Please accept this meal and enjoy your lodging here for the remainder of your visit in my country as my guest.

Sincerely,
T. Demandrous

"Holy hamsters, when did you meet the owner?"

"Huh?"

Rachael whipped the note from her friend's hand and waved it in front of her face. "When did you meet the man who owns this hotel?"

"What's he look like?"

"Tall, blond, handsome. The man's a walking romantic cliché."

"Oh. Then, last night, I guess."

"You guess?"

"I spoke to a good-looking stranger in a room full of people before the band started up. We weren't formally introduced. I was kicking myself about that, but I was too busy to stop and talk."

"It looks like he took matters into his own hands. And it looks like he's got good taste. Why can't I ever score?" Rachael stuffed a jelly-covered croissant in her mouth.

"It wasn't anything like that," Phoebe protested. "We spoke for three minutes tops. I had no idea who he was until now."

"Yeah, sure." Rachael said. "Hey, enjoy is what I say. He's rich, you're on holiday, he's a foreigner . . ."

"Rachael, this is Greece. We're the foreigners."

"Same difference. Do you want that chocolate cannoli?"

Phoebe followed the tall, stately redhead. By now she was not at all surprised that Mr. Demandrous' office manager was not only gorgeous but smart as a whip. It also didn't surprise Phoebe that she was expected. She'd spent some time doing research on the internet. The efficient and successful Mr. Demandrous was apparently famous for his attention to detail. He might not spend much time at each of the business he owned, but he made sure that they ran like clockwork. He was equally famous for his insistence on the best. In fact, his business associates found his abilities to root out the best to be somewhat uncanny.

Phoebe was discovering that for herself. When they reached the intricately carved mahogany door, the assistant, Ione, which she insisted Phoebe call her, tapped, and gestured her to enter.

The man from last night sat behind a glorious antique desk, but he immediately got to his feet and came around it to welcome her.

"Please, sit down," he said. "You must be exhausted after you exertions at the conference topped by your illness last night. Are you feeling better?"

"Thank you, yes." She sat in the chair he pulled up for her. The plush upholstery threatened to swallow her.

"Was breakfast to your liking?"

"How could it not be? Thank you for it. As for the rest, Mr. Demandrous, I'm honored by your gracious offer. However, I simply must refuse. It's not . . ."

"Please, my close associates call me 'Tee'."

She gave him a slight nod of acknowledgement. "Call me Phoebe. Now, seriously . . ."

"I have an aunt named Phoebe. It's a lovely name."

"Mr. Demandrous! I can't accept your offer."

"As I said before, call me Tee, and you most certainly can."

Phoebe mustered her infamous business persona. When she went all official, corporate CEO's took notice, opened their wallets, and generously donated to her gerontology research programs. "Why, Mr. Demandrous?"

He peered down at her upturned face, her black eyes flashing in challenge. He liked a good challenge.

"Why not?" he asked.

"I can't afford it. I've already made arrangements to move to someplace more suitable. And I insist on paying my own way. I can't even imagine what this place would cost me."

"Let's see. Hmmm . . . suntan lotion, souvenirs, depends what type of shopper you are. Difficult to determine the way the U.S. dollar is fluctuating in today's market."

He flashed a mischievous smile at her.

That smile, and damn, those dimples did her in. She couldn't resist. Phoebe threw up her hands in mock defeat.

Of course he had to have dimples! She was a sucker for dimples. His platinum blonde hair, though tied back now, fell below his shoulder blades. Phoebe wondered, if she succumbed to her baser instincts, how long she could resist setting his hair free. On top of all that, he was gorgeous. He made Michelangelo's David look like a poor cousin. Of course, the statue was naked. This man had been dressed by top-flight tailors. Phoebe squashed the urge to discover how much of what she saw was tailor's art and how much was nature's. She'd just met the man. She shouldn't be stripping him with her eyes.

"Couldn't we take this a step at a time?" he said. "How about lunch? I'd love to show you the best of my country, and my staff tells me that you only plan to spend four more days here. If lunch isn't to your liking, we'll renegotiate." He smiled again. More dimples. She caved in without the slighted struggle.

"Lunch, then," she agreed.

"And a bit of sightseeing. You may have half an hour to get ready."

After the frantic bustle that had been a constant during the conference in the suite that her organization had booked, now an eerie stillness hastened her preparations. Rachael had headed out to make new plans since they weren't relocating. Slipping on a comfortable pair of Capri pants, a loose shirt and her well-worn hiking boots, Phoebe stuffed everything she thought she'd need into one of the leftover convention totes that boldly announced in purple lettering, "Aging: It Isn't For Cowards."

She figured that she'd pulled herself together as well as she could in the given time limit. Curious to see what the fascinating man she'd agreed to meet had in store for her, she headed downstairs.

"Phoebe?"

Mr. Demandrous' baritone made the hairs on her arms tingle. She turned. He stood so close she almost bumped into his chest.

"Let's see what the day has to offer us, shall we?"

Overcome by attraction, Phoebe threw caution to the winds. "Let's."

Like a scene from a Hollywood musical, a doorman opened the glass doors. They stepped out into sunshine and heat. Phoebe had expected Demandrous to impress her by chauffeuring her around in a fancy limousine, but he surprised her. Two valets approached, each carrying matching gold motorcycle helmets. A third wheeled a big gold motorcycle to the curb.

"That thing," Phoebe said, "looks like it's ready for the NHRA."

He shrugged. "The roads in old Athens are narrow. It is practical. And I like speed. Are you up for the challenge?"

"Why not?" Strapping on a helmet, Phoebe tucked in behind him on the double leather seat and wrapped her arms tightly around him. She felt his muscles shift and bunch as he revved the engine and prepared to take off. Apparently, her comparison to the David statue was apt—this man was astonishingly fit.

"Are you settled?" he asked.

"Absolutely," she shouted over the roar of the engine.

They took off for a whirlwind tour of the city that took Phoebe's breath away. He took her to all the usual sites, leaving the Acropolis for last. The view of the city from the path to the Parthenon was breathtaking. She could see why Pericles had taken over the hill when he had decided to rebuild Athens into new greatness. Even all these thousands of years later, it still cast every other thing in Athens into the shade of its greatness. Phoebe stopped every few feet, as she had at every other place they had visited.

"Mr. Demandrous, this is beyond spectacular!"

"I'm happy you are pleased. It is even more beautiful when you get to the top."

Phoebe was glad he stopped insisting she call him Tee. Somehow, he seemed larger than life, and using his first name didn't feel right, at least not yet. She wasn't quite ready to cross that line.

When they reached the top, Phoebe walked between a set of marble columns into the center of the Parthenon. She stopped in dazed amazement. As she slowly circled the interior of Athens' tribute to Athena, the grandeur and beauty of the carved temple ruins poured over her.

"Do you think, I mean, if there really were gods like the ancient Greeks believed, that Zeus would have been jealous that his daughter had a city and all these gorgeous temples dedicated to her? Don't you think he'd want something here for himself?"

He moved so close that she felt the warmth of his body against her back. He rested his hands atop her shoulders and leaned in closer.

"I think Zeus would be proud of his daughter," he replied.

They stayed on the Acropolis long enough to watch the sun set. But their day together was far from over.

"Now for the real heart of Athens," he said.

He kicked up the motorcycle stand and waited for
Phoebe to mount. True to his word, they drove to the
local hangouts, shops, and cafes.

Afterward, they agreed to meet for a late dinner.
Phoebe allowed herself a hot bubble bath in the suite's
glorious bathtub. She'd been eyeing that tub the entire
convention, but she'd been too busy to indulge. She'd
barely had enough time to shower and dress. Now she
luxuriated in the warm water, speculating how the evening would end.

She knew how she wanted it to end.

She dressed accordingly.

When Phoebe opened the door, all her preparations
were instantly justified by the appreciative look on his
face.

Phoebe stared right back.

He wore a white dinner jacket over a dark teal shirt,
white tie, and black tuxedo trousers. He looked as if he
stepped out of a glossy magazine ad. "Are you ready?"

"I'll get my wrap."

Dinner at his restaurant, *Ambrosia* stood up to its
world-class reputation. Their private dining room was se-
cluded enough from prying eyes, yet open enough to
hear the pianist located in the front room. Dish after
dish was brought to the table, each a new and amazing
culinary experience. After their first round of appetizers
Phoebe lost count of the number of courses and of the
amount of wine they'd consumed. The champagne that
accompanied the last course had been her undoing. She
knew she was far from sober, though she didn't feel
drunk.

"Good thing I'm not driving," she said under her
breath.

"I beg your pardon?"

"Did I say that out loud?" Phoebe giggled. "I think
I'm a bit tipsy."

"Yes, I believe you are." Demandrous said. "I believe
we'll switch to coffee. Do you care for dessert? The
cheesecake here is exceptional."

Phoebe leaned over the table toward him, as if to share a great secret. "I *love* cheesecake. But only if it's plain. I think all that fruit stuff on top just ruins the whole thing."

He gestured, and a new course magically appeared.

"This is heavenly," Phoebe purred, as she ate. The coffee was more than welcome. She wanted a clear head so she could properly appreciate this night, what was left of it.

"Did you know," Demandrous said, watching her eat, "that cheesecake was first served to the athletes that attended the original Olympics in 776 B.C."

"Really? I read a lot of history, but I've never read that.

"And," he added, leaning across the table toward her, "the rumor around Athens it that this is the original recipe."

"Really?"

He poured them both another cup of coffee, then leaned back against his chair. "It's possible."

Phoebe wasn't sure how they ended up in her room, but there they both were in front of the brocade sofa kissing like teenagers.

He pulled away the slightest distance possible, just enough to look into her black eyes, shining in the night like obsidian. "It's your choice, my sweet." His husky voice would have been the deciding clincher right then and there if Phoebe hadn't made up her mind hours before.

"I never invite a man to my bed until I know his first name. His full first name." She waited.

"Theros. Theros Demandrous, at your service."

"Pleased to meet you, Theros. Care for a night cap?"

"I believe I do, starting with you." He shrugged out of his dinner jacket.

Much, much later, Theros pulled away long enough to order a snack.

"Champagne, chocolate, and strawberries," he said, running a hand along her shoulder after the treat arrived.

The warm smell of molten chocolate from a small fountain filled the room. He dipped a bright berry into the streaming liquid and then offered it to her. "For renewed energy."

Before she could say anything, the room shook with the force of an earthquake. Phoebe grabbed the headboard for support, then rolled off the bed to her feet.

"Theros! Earthquake!" she said, grabbing a robe. "We need to get out of here."

He jumped to his feet, landed in a defensive stance next to her, and steadied her. "Stay calm, my sweet. I think this is no mere movement of the earth, though it would be safer if it were."

"What? You're not making any sense!" She tried to run for the doorway—she'd heard standing in a doorway was what people were supposed to do in an earthquake.

Theros grabbed her hand before she could get far. The room shook again, and a blazing flash of light lit the space.

Phoebe's knees went weak, but not because of the light or the quake. The eight-foot woman now standing before them was what sent her nearly into hysterics.

But the woman only had eyes for Theros.

"Trickster!" she shrieked. "You have broken the pledge."

"Don't dare call me trickster, Hera. You lie! I broke no pledge."

"Hera?" Phoebe said. "Hera!"

Phoebe turned to Theros, but his attention was still on the eight-foot apparition. Hera extended her arm, palm upward. An hourglass appeared in her upturned hand. The few grains of sand remaining in its upper portion continued to trickle downward.

"You have bedded her. But your time is running out, Zeus."

"Zeus?" Phoebe said. "*ZEUS!* I *knew* I drank too much."

Hera looked down at Phoebe and cackled. "I see you are still choosing them witless."

"Now, wait a minute!" Phoebe said, wagging her index finger at her nemesis. "I'm not taking that insult even if you are a drunken hallucination after a night of debauchery."

Theros stepped between Phoebe and Hera. "She's real, Phoebe," he said in a low serious tone.

"Nope. I don't buy it," she said. "Earthquake, concussion, hangover—maybe they're real. Her? Nope, not real. *Not real*, Theros."

"Husband, are there not enough of our own kind for you to seduce?" the giant woman screamed.

"Keep it down," Phoebe said to the woman. "Don't wake the neighbors. He may own the place, but he runs a tight ship."

Hera turned her full attention to Phoebe. "Witless child, he does more than own the place. Theros means Zeus! The sands of his time for dalliance have run out, and according to the pledge, she must be dealt with."

Phoebe watched as the man she had toured Athens with all day and then made love to all night grew to the height of his accuser. She hadn't had nightmares like this since she was in college. She closed her eyes and swore to avoid champagne for the rest of her life.

She opened them again, and both of the godlike giants were still there.

Theros gazed intently at the narrow channel of the hourglass in Hera's hands.

When he looked up, his face was red with rage.

"Wife, there are still a dozen grains of sand to fall. My time is not up, and she will be left unharmed. You know the rules. Once a month, for a glassful of hours, I may do as I please. Afterward, I must return betimes, or you may do as you please. By acting too early, you have forfeited this round. Go!"

"Not alone, I will not, husband!"

Thunder and a kaleidoscope of colors filled the room. When all went quiet, Phoebe opened her eyes and crawled out from under the table, where she'd retreated for safety's sake. Unsteadily, she pulled herself up onto the nearest chair.

She was alone in the suite. Her rapid heartbeat and ragged breathing were the only sounds in the room.

"Okay," she said aloud to the empty room. "I'm having an alcohol-based hallucination. The place is empty. He left hours ago. I have overindulged. And I'll never drink another drop of champagne again."

Dizzy, Phoebe moved to sit in front of the chocolate fountain and reached for a strawberry. Apparently her nightmares were well catered. A glint of light caught her attention. She reached between the fountain and bowl to retrieve a necklace she hadn't noticed before.

It felt heavy in her hand. The chain was made from hammered red gold in the shape of oak leaves on a branch. An eight-inch pendant suspended from the chain appeared to be made of platinum, set with the shape of a thunderbolt in diamonds. The whole thing was warm, as if it had just come from the jeweler's forge. Gingerly she turned the piece over.

She almost dropped it in shock.

There was no mistaking the inscription. In block lettering it read:

> IT WAS A WONDERFUL ADVENTURE.
> WITH ADMIRATION FOR YOUR BRAVERY
> ZEUS

Phoebe set the necklace down and reached for the unopened bottle of champagne. Never mind all her vows. She needed it.

"If you're interested, Father's home." Artemis leaned against the pink marble archway into her brother's quarters.

"Did he make it in time?" he asked, looking up from his project.

"Yes."

"What was Mother's reaction when he returned?"

"She went down to retrieve him."

"No!"

"Yes. Apparently Father had quite the vacation this

time. Relax, Hermes," Artemis said. She walked over to survey his worktable, just to be irritating. "Nothing of consequence occurred. Mum was a dozen grains too early."

"Lucky woman."

"Yes, this one was. Unfortunately, there's always next month."

Artemis turned and left Hermes to his task.

THE URBANE FOX

Jacey Bedford

Jacey Bedford lives in Birdsedge, a tiny village
high on the edge of the Yorkshire Pennines, in
the north of England. She's been a librarian and
a postmistress, but now she's an unashamed
folk singer—performing all over the world with
vocal harmony trio Artisan, (www.artisan-
harmony.com.) When she's not on the road—
and even when she is—she's hardwired to her
laptop keyboard, writing science fiction and fantasy. This is her fourth story for a DAW anthology and she's currently working on a fantasy
novel for young adults, based on the Tam Lin
ballad.

It all started normally enough, with an e-mail that arrived late on Friday afternoon:

To: mail@orphansofthestorm.uk
Subject: Special Order
From: john@urbanefox.elf
Date: 3 June 2005 14:17:29
*Dear Ms Argent, Do you undertake special costume
commissions? It's urgent. Delivery by 19 June. I can sup-
ply the fabric, design, measurements, etc. Sincerely, John
Reynard*

Izzy responded with a price list and thought no more
about it. She and her partners at Orphans of the Storm

made clothes for a living; not everyday clothes but doublets, robes, cloaks and gowns. Their customers were re-enactors, small theater companies, upmarket fancy dress shops and weirdos. Rich weirdos.

On Monday morning Izzy heard the shop doorbell tinkle. A few minutes later Alice, the sales assistant, called her through from the workroom.

It was the Urbane Fox himself, without a doubt. Six-one or maybe six-two, slim-hipped, powerful shoulders without being muscle-bound—and that was a fact because it was all on display, courtesy of a sleeveless vest-top worn casually over denims that were more John Paul Gaultier than Levi Strauss. His hair, deep red-brown, hung casually below his shoulders looking as though it had been designer-mussed, though driving here in the classic MG open-topped sports car parked by the shop window might have had something to do with the engagingly not-quite-sleek look. He had a short, dense beard, slightly darker than his hair but no less red, and one red-gold earring.

"John Reynard, I presume. I see where you get your e-mail address from, Mr. Fox." Oops, that might be a little too familiar for starters. She hoped he had a sense of humor.

"Ah, you spotted the bushy tail and the gray goose dangling down-o." He grinned and held out his hand. "Yes, indeed. John Reynard, and you're Isobelle. I claim my five pounds."

She laughed and held out her hand, which he took and with all seriousness touched his lips to her fingers.

"I'm more used to Izzy." She looked into his eyes, brown and glittering with more than a hint of animal magnetism, and couldn't look away. It was only Alice's protracted and very much staged throat clearing that kept her from making a complete fool of herself.

When she finally closed the shop door behind him and carried the box of fabric and design drawings into the workroom, she had the dizzying feeling that their brief meeting had gone well, despite the fact that she couldn't actually remember a word of their conversation. She was suddenly acutely aware that her pulse was racing, and she felt slightly breathless and wanted to giggle. And, dammit, she'd promised delivery in two weeks. She must be mad! She'd have to use every spare moment of her time, cancel her cinema trip tomorrow, and maybe even give up her early morning runs.

She took a deep, calming breath, opened the wide cardboard box and lifted out a bolt of black cloth, obviously a dense-weave silk. In the bottom of the box there were two hanks of copper embroidery thread and a pack of best quality needles for embroidering the emblem, a detailed fox mask set in beech leaves, on the breast of the tabard.

By the end of the first week Izzy had completed the shirt and trousers and had begun the tabard, which was simple to make but painstaking to embroider. She spent every evening from Monday to Friday in her favorite chair by the window. The glorious view across open fields enriched her soul, even though she barely had time to raise her eyes from neatly stitching.

Using the new pack of needles, she began with a smooth, even satin stitch for the fox, then Cretan stitch, stem stitch and woven picots for the leaves. Through the evenings the rhythm of the stitching hypnotized her into serene daydreams of a wily red fox in the deep woods.

By late Friday it was almost finished. With the natural light fading fast, she turned the work to fasten the final thread on the back, but as she did so the needle slipped and stabbed into the side of her ring finger. She jerked her hand away and a drop of bright blood dripped on to the fabric.

"Oh, hell!"

She sucked her finger, jumped up and found a paper hanky, but the thirsty cloth had swallowed the blood as if it had never been. Even when she got a fresh tea towel from the kitchen and dabbed the place with clean cold water, she couldn't sponge any blood out of the fabric. Luckily, when she turned it back to the right side, there wasn't a mark. *A narrow escape, girl,* she thought, *least said, soonest mended.* There wasn't enough fabric or enough thread to remake the tabard even if she'd had time. She finished the last stitch and put it away, falling into bed, deeply tired, to dream of dark earthen burrows lined with leafmold and rabbit fur.

She'd been hoping not to have to work on the order over the weekend, but there was still a bit of finishing to do on the tabard itself. Finally, on Sunday evening, it was ready.

Bleary eyed, she e-mailed Mr Fox, as she'd started to think of him. By now his e-mail address was firmly in her mind, john@urbanefox.elf.

Dear John, It's finished. Come and collect it anytime Monday. I need a week off to recuperate. I hope you like it. I'm very pleased with the way it turned out—Izzy.

Within ten minutes there was a reply in her inbox.

Dear Izzy, Thanks for your e-mail. I'll be there in the morning. Looking forward to seeing the suit and especially looking forward to seeing you again. Since we spoke I've been thinking . . . and I have a favor to ask you—John.

Conscious of the fact that she'd spent the last week in a trance communing with needles and thread, Izzy went to bed early on Sunday and woke at six-thirty on Monday morning looking forward to going for a run. She'd let her morning running routine go to hell while she'd been absorbed in making the suit for the urbane fox man, so she donned singlet and shorts, tied up her hair, let herself out of the back shop door, and ran and ran until the sweat trickled down between her shoulder blades. By the time she got home, the blood sang in her veins and she felt so *alive* as she dropped her sweaty togs in the washing basket and stood under the shower to sluice off.

She always dressed for comfort at work—the shop was no place for tight shoes and the sort of clothes you didn't want covered in loose threads and tailor's chalk—but today, though she wore her usual jeans, she chose a silver-blue silk camisole that brought out the blue in her eyes. Maybe she took a little more care in twisting her hair and pinning it up, and maybe she went to the bother of applying the faintest trace of mascara to her eyelashes, but it wasn't in anticipation of meeting the Urbane Fox again. Of course it wasn't.

He arrived midmorning. She heard Alice's call, smoothed her top and checked to make sure that there was no loose cotton trailing from her fringe and went into the shop. She'd remembered him as being gorgeous, but that was an understatement. He was built like a minor Greek god, and when he smiled at her she felt as though someone had just turned the sun on in her universe.

"I hope you like it. I've been working through the evenings, cursing this thing all week, trying to get it finished in time."

His smile disappeared. "Not truly cursing it, I hope."

"Not as such, no." She grinned. "Though I did have to tell it off for bad manners when it kept slipping and sliding in the sewing machine. Oddly enough it seemed to behave itself after that. It needed a firm but fair hand."

He smiled. "Then you have the knack of it, and I think you've earned your fee by your exceptional workmanship." He wrote a check and signed it with a flourish. "My friend Galinda suggested I should come here, and she was right."

"Galinda the witch?" She was one of Izzy's regular customers who fell into the interesting weirdo category and with whom she'd had several fascinating conversations about the reality behind legends and folklore.

He nodded. "You made her robes."

"I only half believed she was a witch, but she certainly knows her stuff about English traditions and legends."

"Oh, she's the genuine article all right. A good woman to have on your side." That almost translated as *and not one to make an enemy of.*

"Do you want to try the suit? See if it fits?"

"It will fit. I can tell just from looking at it."

"I'd have liked to have seen you wear it. I poured two weeks of my time and my art into it, and it's not finished until someone wears it."

"You'll see it." He smiled. "Tomorrow night if you'll come out with me."

"What?"

"Tomorrow. You and me. A date. Would that be acceptable? I said I had a favor to ask. Forgive me if I misread . . ."

Izzy's heart felt as though it had turned a somersault.

"You didn't misread. That would be lovely. Thanks."

"I'll pick you up at nine."

"Where are we going . . . er . . . should I wear anything special?"

"The where of it is a secret. Even I don't know until tomorrow, but it's a midsummer ball. It's why I needed my suit so quickly. One never presumes that one will be called, but . . ." He smiled. "Don't worry about a box, I'll just take these on the hangers." He picked up the suit. "Tomorrow at nine."

Izzy was ready half an hour ahead of time, wearing a silvery white silk dress with a long handkerchief hem. She checked her image in the mirror, then changed her mind about her hair and let all the carefully pinned black coils fall. She brushed it again and settled for a very simple style with the sides taken back and braided together into a single slim plait over a waterfall of loose hair. It looked almost medieval with the shot-silk dress.

She heard John's car on the road and reached up to turn off the light switch. Damn—her hand was shaking like a schoolgirl. Was she excited or apprehensive? A little bit of both, she decided. There was something about John that was not entirely ordinary. Not entirely *safe* on a hormonal level.

She ran lightly down the stairs and unlocked the shop door just as John reached it and raised his hand to knock.

"Isobelle, you look so lovely." He half bowed.

"Why thank you Mr. Reynard, sir. You are too kind." She hid behind mock formality and stepped back a pace to let him into the shop. The fox head embroidery on the tabard glinted and looked almost real. Damn, she'd done a fine job. Lucky the bloodstain hadn't come

through to the front. Her finger itched where the needle
point had stabbed it.

"I have something for you, a small gift. Please wear it
for me tonight." He handed her a plain box. Inside was
a pendant, an elegant silver fox head, Art Nouveau in
design with two sparkling diamond-cut stones for eyes.
They looked real, but she didn't like to ask, and she
didn't know enough about expensive jewels to be able
to tell. She certainly hoped they weren't real. She'd feel
uncomfortable accepting expensive gifts. It was only a
first date after all.

She hesitated.

"Let me . . ." He held out the two open ends of the
chain, and she turned and stepped between his hands,
feeling his breath on the back of her neck and the
warmth from standing so close. He fastened the clasp
and let it drop onto her neck, but his hands never
touched her skin. She was almost disappointed. The
chain was short, and the elegant pendant hung just below
the hollow at the base of her throat.

"Perfect," he said.

"Where are we going? You said it was a big secret."

"It is. It's a masque. I only found out the location
this morning."

"Mystery on mystery. It must be a very elite party."

"Oh, it is." He almost breathed the words.

Once outside, with the shop safely locked for the night,
Reynard opened the door of his elderly two-seater and
handed her a gauzy scarf to wrap round her hair against
the buffeting winds.

He reached into the space behind her seat and presented her with a velvet bag. "I hope you don't mind, I
took the liberty of making this for you since I hadn't
warned you about the masque."

Nestled between its folds was a half-face fox mask,
delicate in its detail, made from, Izzy thought, layers of
papier maché, lined with silk and covered with silver fox
fur, dark round the eye holes and graded to white at
the edges.

Izzy held it up to her face and it seemed to fit perfectly from the tip of her nose to the top of her forehead.

"Keep it on. We don't want anyone to see us unmasked on the way there." He took out his own mask, red fox fur to match his hair and beard. Save for the length of the snout, it looked like a full face mask. He grinned, and she almost imagined slightly elongated canines.

They drove along country lanes, the elderly MG stately as a carriage, and as the last light was fading from the sky, they finally turned through an impressive gateway, beneath a stone arch.

"I've driven down this road hundreds of times and never noticed this gateway before." Izzy said.

"I understand it was hidden behind undergrowth until fairly recently."

"But I thought this was the Elphinstone Estate. Wasn't the old house pulled down years ago?"

"I'm new to this area. I don't know, but the cour . . . the party is held somewhere different each summer. I've been hoping for an invitation for years and finally . . ."

He stopped the car on the driveway behind a BMW. "But you made it all possible. Our hostess wouldn't let me in without a suitable partner."

"Oh, you must have had girls queuing up for the job."

He shook his head, brief but emphatic. "I'm a very . . . private person. I have my reasons."

Oh, I hope he's not gay. Izzy let him come around to her side of the car and open the door. *That would be such a waste.*

He grinned sideways at her. "It's not what you're thinking."

"What was I thinking?"

"You were wondering if I was gay and I'd only brought you here as window dressing."

"I was not!"

He laughed. "Are you cold?"

"No."

"It's past eleven. Even in June you'll need something

to keep you warm in the dead of night. Did I tell you the masque was outside?"

"No, you didn't. Is there anything else you haven't told me?"

"Maybe." He smiled and opened the boot of the car and took out a bundle. Even in the gloom, Izzy could see that it was white. He shook it, and a waterfall of white fur resolved itself into a cape. He draped it over her shoulders, and she felt its softness and stiffened. "This is real animal fur."

"Silver fox." He took out a second cloak, red fox, for himself.

"I'm sorry I don't wear real fur. I don't believe in—"

"And I respect your beliefs, but these are not from any earthly fox. . . . Besides, does it not feel so very natural next to your skin? And tonight we may both need the cunning of the fox."

"We might?"

"Oh, you know how these social occasions can be—traps for the unwary."

"And here's me thinking we were just going somewhere for a quiet romantic evening for two."

He took her hand, his grip firm, his fingers warm next to hers. "You're shivering. That settles it. Fox fur tonight and we'll argue about ethics later. Come on, it's this way. I can hear music."

They walked along a narrow path between trees that were only dark shapes and rustling leaves in the midsummer night. Gradually the sounds of music and chatter grew loud enough to fill the air, and turning past a bank of dense cypresses they emerged into an ocean of light. Lanterns hung round the grove in swathes, and in the background the windows of Elphinstone Hall, clearly not demolished, glowed yellow with hundreds of lamps.

A crowd of people, beautifully dressed in elegant outfits and elaborate bird and animal masks, stood and talked in groups or paraded about the grove. Eight masked musicians played ethereal music on pipes and drums, harps and flutes. John offered her his arm, and she slipped her hand through his crooked elbow, feeling him guide her subtly. Izzy felt her footsteps fall into the rhythm of the music until walking almost became a dance.

"Reynard, is that you?" An apparition in a black crow mask descended on them—almost literally—and stopped their progress across the grove. Izzy could have sworn she heard the flapping of strong wings, and when she turned, there was the Crow Lady.

John dipped his head deferentially. "Have a care when you speak my name. There are plenty of folk here who would deny me my chance, but the Lady summoned me, at last, and here I am."

"And with a partner, too. That's new for you. You've been alone since . . ."

"A man can change."

"A *man* can, yes."

Izzy heard but barely understood; however, she recognized the dress the Crow Lady was wearing. "Galinda? I recognize your dress, I made it for you."

The Crow Lady turned and looked hard at Izzy. "Isobelle Argent?"

Izzy nodded, expecting a warm greeting, but even beneath the crow mask she could see Galinda's mouth set in a tight line as she rounded on John.

"Are you mad?"

John laughed—a strange, hollow sound. "Mad. I guess that's what I must be, Galinda. You told me about Miss Isobelle Argent. Talented, you said. Sweet, you said. Smart as a coat of new paint, you said. Lithe and fit, you said. You didn't tell me she was beautiful as well . . . a perfect silver fox."

"Would you mind not talking *about* me and start talking *to* me, please."

John looked as though he was going to say something, but Galinda grabbed Izzy's elbow and swept her to one side. "What has he told you?"

"What do you mean?"

"About tonight."

"Nothing. A masked ball." Galinda's questions were so fierce, her attitude so intense that Izzy was having a severe attack of the weirds. "What's the matter? What's wrong?"

"I'll tell her." John Reynard grasped her other elbow. "This isn't just any masque, Izzy, it's special. Tonight the Faerie Court meets, and the Queen herself attends."

She blinked and stared at him. He said it so seriously that she almost thought he believed it for a moment. Then she laughed . . . but he didn't . . . and neither did Galinda.

"I'm not joking," John said.

She felt her insides contract, and her blood seemed to run colder in her veins. She'd walked into something strange here, and she wanted out. Out. Out. Out.

Faeries or not—and she didn't believe in such things— the people here were obviously into the kind of weird she didn't want to be part of. Galinda was a self-confessed witch for goodness sake, and . . . oh how stupid could she be, it was the midsummer solstice in . . . she looked at her watch . . . about eighty minutes. All the unsavory jumbled ideas that she'd ever heard about witches and sabbats and covens passed through her mind.

"I think I'd like to go home now."

How was she going to get home? This place was miles from anywhere. She'd stupidly left her bag and phone in the car, which was . . . she looked around . . . which way had they come in from the driveway?

"Izzy, please . . ." Reynard took her hand, and she yanked it away. Funny how real that fox mask looked in the lantern light, how sharp his canine teeth.

"Izzy, I'm sorry. I mean you no harm."

Galinda hurrumphed in the background and drew Izzy's attention.

"Okay, Galinda, what do you know that you're not telling me? Is this some hijinks your pagan friends organized?"

"I know it's hard to take in, but it's real. We've talked about this before. The reality behind the folklore. Faer-ies, magic, the Lady—she who can never be named—all exist. And this one . . ." she nodded toward Reynard . . . "the Urbane Fox himself, earned her displeasure many years ago. She banished him to the Outer Realms, that's what we call your world, and at last she has invited him to plead his case for readmittance to her court."

"If I please the Lady tonight, Izzy, I can go home. Do you know what it's like to lose your home?"

Izzy, for whom Orphans of the Storm had been more than just a snappy business name, *did* know. She'd been at boarding school in England when her parents' house had been washed into the Indian Ocean.

"But what I can't understand," Galinda cut off any reply from Izzy, "is why you brought a partner tonight—not just a partner but a mortal—when you've been alone for so many years? How could you expose an innocent to all this?" She spread her arms to take in the company.

"The Lady bade me bring a silver vixen. She commands and we all obey."

"I don't like it, Reynard."

Izzy had had enough. "*You* don't like it! What about me?"

John took her hand. "I truly believe the Lady would not harm an innocent, not on my account. My crime . . . if *my* crime it was . . . was to lose my wife to the hunt. Elin was always reckless and never biddable, but she was one of the Lady's favorites, and the Lady charged me with being careless of her life . . . banished me until I could show a better regard for all living things."

"The Lady was grief stricken, Reynard. You must not blame her for harsh judgement." Galinda rested her hand on his shoulder, but he shrugged it off.

"And I wasn't?" He closed his eyes for a moment, then turned to Izzy. "I have spent these last few hundred years saving what lives I could. I was a surgeon in Nelson's navy, a ward orderly in Miss Nightingale's hospital in the Crimea. I drove a field ambulance on the Somme and worked with the underground in occupied France during the Second World War. Later there was Korea, Viet Nam, and the Peace Corps in Africa. Whatever the Lady thought of me then, or now, I have always had a regard for life. Perhaps I have proved it at last."

"And now you will prove it one more time, my fox, with the help of your vixen."

At those words the three of them turned to face a presence that Izzy could only think of as both beautiful and terrible, real and unreal. It was as though the Lady burned brighter than the sun and all the stars together, yet her light was known rather than seen. Her presence took Izzy's breath away. All the questions about the hunt and the length of time John Reynard claimed to have lived and . . . everything . . . died halfway between her brain and her lips. She could only fall to one knee and bow her head in the presence of such a wonder, just like Galinda and John Reynard, kneeling on either side of her. She no longer questioned the reality of the Faerie Court and the Lady who ruled over it.

"Isobelle Argent, please stand."

One command, and Izzy obeyed without thinking, standing under the Lady's scrutiny for what seemed like an eternity, not daring to meet those young-old eyes.

"Isobelle, walk with me." She turned, and Izzy followed. "I think you have some regard for my red fox, do you not?"

Izzy nodded, then realized that the Lady was barely glancing back at her. "I do like him, or at least, I think I do. This is our first . . ." Date seemed like such an odd word in this context, and Izzy stumbled over meanings.

"There is much honor in him, but he still has to prove himself to me. Will you stand as his witness?"

"I . . . If I can."

"What I ask is not beyond your capabilities, though it may test your limits. And to you, who likes to run with the wind, I will give a great gift, though you may not thank me for it until later."

Izzy was still thinking about that when the Lady stopped and turned to her. She put her hands on either side of Izzy's head and looked deep into her eyes. Izzy felt as though her whole soul had been turned inside out for inspection, but at length the Lady nodded. "Good. It is settled." She turned and paced back to the others.

The Lady beckoned Reynard and Galinda to rise, and she put Izzy's hand in Reynard's.

"Reynard, my fox, I have watched your progress through the Outer Realms. You have done well, and Galinda, my crow, you have watched him for me and have testified many times on his behalf. Now there's one more test, Reynard. If you can keep your silver vixen safe until morning, you may come home."

Izzy felt Reynard stiffen as somewhere outside the grove they heard the sound of a distant hunting horn and the yip of hounds.

"The hunt, Reynard. Do you understand what will happen if they catch you both on this night?"

"I understand, all too well. My Lady, and I beg you . . . Please, let Isobelle go free. Even to gain your pleasure I would not risk her life."

"The decision is not yours. Isobelle has agreed . . ."

Izzy began to shake. Was this what the Lady meant? Surely she couldn't be sending the hunt after them. A pack of foxhounds could easily outrun two humans . . . *if Reynard was human* . . . Besides, hunting with dogs was illegal . . .

"Isobelle!" The Lady's voice brought her to attention. "Yes."

"I think there are many things you do not understand, but you will. You should know that I do not set anyone a task that is impossible to fulfil. Reynard has chosen his vixen well. If he wins through, you may come to my court with him."

There was a crack like thunder, and Izzy felt herself falling down to her hands and knees, and then her world twisted and dimmed. The Lady's feet grew larger in her vision, and beside her a perfect red fox was picking himself up off the grass and shaking himself. She backed away and found instead of hands and knees, she was perfectly balanced on four feet, pads and claws almost sensing the ground beneath her.

A glossy black crow flapped its wings and launched upward with a loud caw and the red fox tilted back his head and watched it fly. Then he looked at Izzy and seemed to say, *Follow me if you value your life.*

I'm a fox . . . This can't be happening . . . I'm a fox . . . I must be dreaming . . . I'm a fox . . . I'm really a fox!

Cold terror was driven from her body by a plague of sensations. There was terror in that, too, but also wonder and a heady excitement. Magic tasted like metal on her tongue and made her an instant believer.

A hunting horn sounded to Izzy's right, and instinct kicked in. Heart pounding, she streaked across the grass and into the trees, running shoulder to shoulder with Reynard, feeling the land beneath her feet and finding her nose swamped with information yielded by damp earth, summer grass, the scent of small creatures going about their business. She stretched out low to the ground and ran as if she had been made to run. Four legs instead of two. This was *real* running! It was exhilarating!

Reynard, appearing not at all disturbed by his transformation, took the lead by a head and she bounded after him—over pasture and plough, hill and dale, through thicket and copse, over hedges and ditches, running until her muscles burned and her breath came in short gasps.

Then the wind eddied, and the rank stench of hounds on their trail assailed her senses. She tasted their hunger, excitement, and eagerness for the kill. She heard the occasional yip and the snap of the huntsman's whip and knew what horrors were barely a misstep away.

The lead hound gave tongue and was joined by his fellows. Izzy dare not turn her head to see how far behind they were. She concentrated on keeping four legs pounding and four feet placed just so for the next leap. Animal instinct replaced human thought. What little reason she had left still said, *this can't be happening.* But she wasn't going to stop running and put the impossibility of events to the test.

She smelled fear and knew it was her own.

The fox in her wanted to run and run and never stop, but the human thought ahead. How long could she keep going?

There! Reynard nudged her down a slope and into a

stream where the fast-flowing water soaked her fur and came as a welcome relief to sore paws and dry mouth. She would have stopped, but Reynard nudged her up along the stream bed, leaped across slippery rocks, and disappeared into the mouth of a burrow. She followed and sank down exhausted onto a bed of decaying leaves, sneezing at the bewildering array of scents.

She heard the hunt, pounding hooves and jangling bridles, gallop past, and then the voices of the hounds stilled as they lost the scent.

Reynard nuzzled her ear and licked her snout. Every line in his face said, *I'm sorry . . . I didn't know*. Too tired to even snap at him, though surely he deserved it, Izzy let him creep close and snuggle next to her. She took comfort in his red furred body between her and the burrow's entrance.

The sound outside changed. The hounds were questing now, coming back downstream to see if they could find the broken trail. Reynard raised himself on his forepaws and his ears pricked, all attention. She tensed, ready to spring forward, but he pushed her down and back with his head, an obvious, *stay here*. She didn't want to stay, she wanted to run, but she remembered his wife, *always reckless and never biddable*. There was a line between reckless and stupid. She sank back.

In a flash of fur he was up and out of the burrow and leading the pack away from where she hid. And then all was quiet. Izzy let her nose rest on her paws again and waited, lying somewhere between waking and sleeping, gathering her energy, trying not to think. It was only then that she realized the silver fox pendant was tangled in the fur of her ruff.

As the first light of dawn softened the night and filtered across the mouth of the burrow, she heard a small movement outside and a whimper. Cautiously she emerged and found Reynard, limp, exhausted, and covered in blood from an ugly gash on his flank. She rushed to him, but fox paws were no match for human hands when it came to staunching blood. Frantic, she licked his ears and snout and pushed him toward the shallow edge of the fast-flowing stream, where he lay while the water washed his wound clean.

Enough now. She nudged him out of the water and up on to the bank, trying to get him to the burrow in case the hunt returned. He shook his head, a curiously human gesture, and staggered to his feet, setting his course to return to the Faerie masque with more determination than energy.

When he could no longer walk alone, Izzy let him lean his weight against her side, willing him to take one more step and then another until, as the sun came up, they staggered into the grove, empty now of courtiers, and both fell at the feet of the Lady, utterly spent.

Izzy's world changed once more and she found herself in human form, naked beneath the silver fox fur, with Reynard, a man again, by her side. She struggled to sit up and drew Reynard's head on to her lap. He was all but unconscious, maybe dying.

"John." She smoothed tangled red hair back from his pale face and put her head close to his, stifling the urge to lick his ears.

"John, what can I do?"

With trembling hands she pulled back the red fox fur. Blood soaked his side from ribs to thigh. Too much blood. Izzy's tears burned hot down her cheeks.

She looked up at the Lady's face, not sure what she read in her expression. "Do something."

"You command me?"

"I beg you. He saved my life. Please don't let him die."

A flurry of glossy black wings resolved into Galinda. "My Lady, he led your hounds away from Isobelle's hiding place at the cost of his own wounds."

Izzy watched the Lady's face, hardly daring to breathe.

"So he's given his blood for you, Isobelle Argent, but would you give yours for him?"

Reynard stirred in Izzy's lap, rolled to a sitting position and struggled to his feet with Izzy's and Galinda's help. "My Lady, I respectfully remind you that this test is mine, not Izzy's."

"But I must know if the one you saved is as worthy as the one you lost all those years ago."

"She needs no test. She has already given her blood for me."

The embroidered fox mask hung like a medallion round Reynard's neck. He snatched it off and handed it to the Lady. "Her blood bound this to me, Lady. Blood given in the following of her art. And know also that in return she wears the symbol of my own house."

Izzy's hand went to her throat. The pendant was still there.

"My protection. Forgive me my deception, Isobelle. I needed your help, and I doubted you would believe without seeing."

Forgive him? The jumble of the night's happenings crowded in on her, and she realized that she was still standing and—amazingly—she was uninjured.

The Lady nodded and raised her voice. "The test is passed. Reynard may return to my court if it pleases him, and so may the Lady Isobelle."

Another crack like thunder and Izzy felt Reynard take his own weight. There was no sign of blood or dirt on either of them. She wore her dress again beneath the fox fur, and her shoes were back on her feet. Reynard's suit was whole, and the fox embroidery was once more a part of the tabard.

"My Lady." Reynard bowed low, and Izzy heard him wince and saw his hand move to his side. "You leave me with something to remember this night by."

The Lady laughed. "Only a small reminder, Reynard. It is healing, and the scars will fade in time. Will you return with us now?"

"I'll see Izzy home safe, My Lady."

"A wise decision. I believe the Lady Isobelle may have much to say to you after this night, and none of it undeserved." She laughed. "You have passed my test; now I think you must pass hers." With another thunderclap she vanished, and so did the lanterns. Elphinstone House once more stood as a ruin in the June sunrise.

A big black crow cawed as it took off and flew above the trees.

"I told you Galinda was a good person to have on your side."

"But there were a lot of things you didn't tell me. The Lady's right about that—I do have a lot to say, and you're not going to like all of it."

He put his arm round her and began to walk her back toward his car. She found she didn't object to his touch.

"I deserve all you have to say to me, and I promise I'll tell you everything if you'll give me the opportunity. But it's a long story, a story that may need more than one evening to complete."

"Are you suggesting a second date?"

"And more if you wish it."

She hesitated. There was something inside her that had responded to that frantic dash across country with Reynard by her side, something that still responded to the warmth and the smell of him. Her heightened senses had still not settled back down to human level. Maybe she didn't want them to. The memory of running with the wind still sang in her blood. Maybe she would take the Lady up on the offer of a visit.

"As long as you warn me next time you want to go running by night." She smiled to herself and felt her canines just a little sharper than before.

DESSERT

Rita Haag

Rita Haag was working in business and technical communications when a personal genealogy
search revealed an ancestor's role in the German
Revolution of 1848. The discovery piqued her
imagination and led to her first short story. A
novel followed and soon she realized that while
writing was her strength, fiction was her passion.
Several novels, short stories, publishing credits,
and awards later, including two of the prestigious
Pushcart Prize, she's fortunate to be doing what
she loves with the support and encouragement
of her family, friends, and fellow writers.

She pulled her collar tighter, waiting while Ted, her
date, dug in his pocket. Her nerves jangled like his
keys, her mind flipping from one thought to the next.
She didn't know him that well, yet she'd always been a
good judge of character. He was appealing, yet not movie
star handsome. The restaurant had not been too extrava-
gant nor too cheap, with a nice variety on the menu. He
had insisted on paying for dinner but allowed her to
open her own doors. That was a toss up—she might have
preferred splitting the bill and having him open doors,
but he seemed like the kind who'd be willing to discuss
it. The fact that they were entering his apartment on the
first date made her feel vulnerable, but she had her cell-

phone. She peeked into her purse and saw the reassuring glow. Just in case.

He pushed the door open and flipped on a light. The place looked clean. The afghan on the couch gave it a homey feel. Probably knit by an aunt who thought the dark blues and purples looked masculine. The room was a little too crowded for her taste. One too many chairs and the extra didn't even look that comfortable. From the kitchen, she guessed. A captain's chair. The set looked older. He'd probably gotten most of this furniture from his mother. Or some relative. Another good sign.

She should quit reading those slasher stories. It was fun to be frightened in her safe little apartment, but now she was envisioning the scene where Barry nonchalantly opens the refrigerator and instead of the angel food cake he's told Alexis about, there's a head on a plate, and then Alexis sees a bloody saw lying on the table.

She imagines that head now, with blood pooling on the plate. Actually, she can't get a good fix on the head because it's the red puddle that draws her attention. Could you ever use a plate like that again?

"Oh, yes, thanks. Uuuh . . . I'll take the Merlot." Maybe she shouldn't have chosen the red. But . . . really, she was being silly. Ted was the friend of a friend. He'd come well-recommended with good credentials, including an administrative position with a local hospital. Not to mention that she'd had more fun with him than with either of the last two guys she'd dated. Definitely more fun than she'd ever had with Bryce. Which was a shame because he was a good kisser, but so boring. No wonder she'd been reading slasher novels.

Ted entered the room and handed her the wine, then sat beside her and asked if she'd ever solved that problem she'd been having at work.

"Oh. That." She nodded and laughed. "I told her if she didn't want to give my ideas a fair chance, I was going to ask to be transferred to another group." The new account exec whined about a lack of creativity and then snickered through most of their brainstorming sessions. "I can't understand how she even got hired. Well . . . she looks like Sharon Stone. Maybe that helps."

Ted thought most men were too narrow minded when it came to beauty. Even women whose features weren't as attractive as hers could be beautiful. It wasn't just about looks.

She appreciated the way he managed a compliment without sounding like a chauvinist pig. Then he said he really didn't have a type. He went out with all kinds of women. She noted the present tense, suggesting that he dated regularly and hadn't been judged as creepy or weird. And it had been a really pleasant evening. Dinner, movie, back here for dessert. Unless by dessert he'd meant . . . but probably not. He'd kept a decent amount of space between them when he'd sat on the couch. She thought of the new novel she'd just picked up: *Our Second Date Was a Scream*. Maybe she'd toss that one aside for awhile.

He was telling her about this real estate deal a friend of his wanted him to go in on. A nice fourplex in a better part of town. He said he'd always intended to move as soon as he could afford it, but when the chance came, he decided to stay put because he realized he was in such a great location. Then, practically overnight, the crime rate had soared. Burglaries, muggings. In one of them, after the guy gave up all his money—a couple hundred or so—the robber still stabbed him. So . . . anyway, he'd been thinking about moving to a more stable neighborhood.

She wished he hadn't added that part about the stabbing. He could have made his point without it.

"Your neighborhood looks pretty nice," he said. "You like it there?"

"It's great. I like that it's a mix of apartments and houses. It's older—well, you saw when you picked me up. But they've been well taken care of. The landlord lives a few blocks away, and anytime I have a problem, he's right there."

He told her that was one of the things that scared him. He really wasn't that good with his hands.

"They look pretty capable." They *were* rather large and muscular, and she noticed that his tanned skin set off blond hairs and his veins rose like tiny blue snakes and—

Barry! No wonder that description had come to her so easily. Her mind had repeated it practically word for word from that ridiculous novel. When she realized she'd been staring at Ted's hands, she laughed to cover her self-consciousness.

Fortunately he'd taken her comment in stride and was now explaining he'd been a good athlete in high school and college. He said he'd kept up with the weight lifting and running and stuff, but his strength was pretty much wasted on practical things. She briefly entertained the possibilities of impractical uses, landing on strangulation about the time he insisted he wasn't real handy with a hammer or a saw.

Her mind took over, grabbed that saw and ran to his refrigerator, but before her imagination pulled the door open, she distracted it with rearranging her body on the sofa, moving a few inches away from him, and patting her purse to locate the lump that was her cellphone. He went on about how his friend said there was a third guy who might be interested, a guy who knew about plumbing and all that other maintenance stuff.

She nodded to show her interest, but she was back to thinking about that saw and hammer he mentioned. Then she realized he probably didn't even own a saw. This was an apartment. The kitchen was obviously on the other side of that wall, and the bedroom was over there. No room for tools here. Her breath came easier, and she told him about her experience in high school. "We all had to take shop and cooking. Mostly it was just to show us that whatever you make, you just have to have the right tools and know how to use them." She felt more comfortable having said that, because that's what hammers and saws were, after all. They were tools, not weapons, and this was reality, not a slasher novel, and an overactive, wine-fed imagination was no excuse for going batty on this poor guy.

Then he told her he'd actually rented out an extra bay

in the apartment complex's garage and had a whole shop full of tools, a lot of them hand-me-downs from his dad. He said one of these days he intended to build something, then admitted that while his dad could work miracles with them, he himself barely knew what most of them were called. But he hadn't given up yet. He still liked the wicked sensation of smacking a hammer against the palm of his hand.

Her heart gave a little jolt, but she kept her cool and asked if he'd seen this fourplex his friend had told him about.

He shook his head and said the whole thing was still in the concept stage. The idea was that he would live in one, his friend in the other, and they'd rent out the other two.

"What about the guy who's going to do the maintenance?"

Tim's already got a place, he told her. They'd supply the capital and Tim would supply the labor. "Well," he said, "I promised you dessert. More wine?"

"Oh, no. I've had plenty." She felt a need to keep her wits about her, not get so hammered she couldn't think. When the word hammered came to mind, she had another thought. "Maybe I should be going, it's . . oh, look. Ten o'clock already."

"No, you're not getting away from me that easy," he said, and when he winked, she felt a knot in her throat and swallowed hard.

"Oh. Okay," she squeaked and he asked if he could at least bring her a glass of ice water with her dessert and she nodded. "Do you need help?" she asked.

"Nope," he answered. "I can handle a kitchen knife with the best of them. The secret is to keep it razor sharp," he explained, and when he emphasized razor, she froze and recalled the scene where Alexis begged for her life and cried out *don't hurt me*, and the deranged Barry smiled, and his brows rose causing his eyes to open even further, revealing their bloodshot intensity, and he said to her: "Hurt you? Oh . . . my dear . . . *this* knife is so sharp, you won't *feel* a thing."

By the time he brought back the ice water, her hands were so sweaty she grabbed it with both of them so she wouldn't drop it. He disappeared around the corner into the kitchen where the knife awaited, and she opened her purse and pulled out her cellphone and dialed 911 so all she had to do was hit the send button.

She heard a clattering in the kitchen, then an "oops" followed by muttering about a dark red stain on a white floor, and she pictured the plate slipping and the blood splashing to the floor. What was he slicing? And which part was she going to get?

She came to on the couch and immediately realized that the two hands coming at her with a cloth meant he wouldn't carve her up until he'd smothered her. She made a move to bat his hands away when she noticed a policeman standing over them holding a plate. He put a forkful of a bloody mass in his mouth, and she wondered if she'd gotten stuck in a nightmare.

"Good pie," the policeman said. "This one of Aunt Ruby's?"

"Yeah," her date said, still looking at her. "Mixed berry."

A mixed berry pie! She pushed herself up and nodded when her date asked if she was all right. He explained that when he came back into the room, she was lying on the floor, and a few minutes later, his brother showed up. He figured she must have dialed 911, then passed out. He introduced his brother, Bob, a cop in the precinct.

She stared at the two men and realized that the phone must have fallen on the send button. Or she'd fallen on it. It was kind of a relief the way it happened. At least they didn't think she was loony.

"You've got something on your . . ." she pointed to the side of her mouth, and when the policeman's tongue came out and licked the blood-red spot, she grabbed the cold cloth and pulled it to her forehead.

Policeman Bob advised her to take a deep breath and relax if she felt dizzy again. He'd checked her vital signs, and she was fine—apparently had just fainted. He asked if she was going to be okay, and she nodded. Then he turned to her date, thanked him for the pie, and headed for the door.

Well, I guess if your date's brother is a policeman, he must be alright, she told herself. The only problem here was those novels! She thanked Bob, and he patted her on the head, then wished her good luck in a brotherly sort of way. She turned the now-warm cloth to the other, cooler, side and took another deep, relaxing breath.

Bob put an arm around Ted's shoulders and gave him a half hug. "So long, little brother," he said. They walked to the door, and she turned in time to see Bob nudge him with his elbow and barely heard him whisper: "See if you can keep this one alive."

ME AND BEANS AND GREAT BIG MELONS

Dean Wesley Smith

Dean Wesley Smith is the bestselling author of
over eighty novels under various names. He has
published over a hundred short stories and been
nominated for just about every award in science
fiction and fantasy and horror, and even won a
few of them. He is the former editor and pub-
lisher of Pulphouse Publishing. His most recent
novel in science fiction is *All Eve's Hallows*. He
is currently writing thrillers under another name.

I have never thought, wondered, or even pondered the
idea of having a supermarket love affair. If I had, I
certainly wouldn't have thought it would start and end
in front of the green beans. I'm the kind of guy who
really doesn't eat green beans, red beans, black beans,
or any other color bean. I'm not prejudiced in my bean
selection. I pretty much just hate them all equally.

And I flat don't understand how anyone could even
eat the things.

I met my supermarket lover as I tried to figure out
which Hamburger Helper would work for the night. I
was an expert in Hamburger Helpers and all the different
incarnations of the stuff. I could almost make it without
looking at the box. Almost.

"Excuse me," a soft, husky voice said.

I jerked around, realizing that my cart and my body had made an effective road block in the aisle. And I hadn't even set up any detour signs.

A woman stood there with one of those yellow baskets for small amounts of stuff. Just like me, she was wearing jeans and a blue tee-shirt, but unlike me she also had a brown purse over her shoulder.

The purse, oddly enough, accented the wonderful color of her hair. I wondered if she had bought the purse because of that or changed the color of her hair to match the purse. It was a question I would never think to ask any woman, even a woman I didn't know.

But yet, for some reason, she had made me think of it. I made a note to myself mentally to write down the weird supermarket moment. I hoped to be a writer in the future, when I could find the time, and often made notes about things that might come in handy in a story some day.

I found myself attracted to this woman wanting to get past me, and I did an instant inventory of her appearance.

Before I was laid off down at Sears, I had done lots of inventories of the warehouse and had become known as "Innes, the Inventory King." I had decided one day to practice the same craft on women I met, and grocery stores were great places, full of inventory.

Using my skills, I instantly looked her over while moving my cart out of her way. She wore a loose blue tee shirt with nothing written on it, tight jeans, and expensive tennis shoes. Total inventory cost of two hundred bucks. She had on no jewelry at all, not even an earring. She was an easy inventory subject.

Miss Brown-Hair-Yellow-Basket: two hundred bucks.

"Sorry," I said, as I finished my inventory and cart moving at the same time, leaving the cart in front of the green beans, never thinking that she might actually be trying to get to that area. If I didn't eat green beans, no one else did I was sure.

My first wife had called that self-centered-universe attitude my defining characteristic. I had considered that a
compliment and still do.

"No problem," the brown-haired, two-hundred-dollar-
woman said, giving me a wonderful, bright smile as she
moved past me. The aroma of fresh soap caught me, and
I stared at her from behind for a moment, first watching
her long hair move against her matching purse, then her
ass under her tight jeans.

I had always been an ass man, staring at woman's asses
before any other body part if the chance arose. This
woman had a stareable ass, of that there was no doubt.
Really tight.

A stareable tight ass wasn't worth anything on my inventory list, but it should be.

She walked a few steps and stopped, looking at the
canned vegetables.

I went back to trying to decide which Hamburger
Helper to pick to eat while the football game was on
tonight. Packers against the Rams. Could be a real
shouter.

"Sorry to bother you again," she said from behind me.

I turned around to look into the deepest green eyes I
had seen in a long time. If all women had eyes like her,
I would shift to being an eye-man instead of an ass-man.

She pointed at the bean section that my cart was
blocking.

"Oh, sorry," I said, moving to pull the cart out of
her way for the second time. "I didn't think anyone ate
that stuff."

She laughed. "Usually I like my beans fresh. But when
I can't get them fresh, I make do with canned."

Usually I'm not real honest with the women I meet,
but this woman ate beans and had annoyed me by making me move my cart twice in the middle of my Hamburger Helper shopping. So I said the first thing that
came to mind.

"I'm that way with women," I said. "When I can't find
the fresh stuff, I resort to the canned as well."

She stared at me for a moment.

I returned her stare.

The faint store music went away; the sounds of the other shoppers went away. It was a movie moment.

Of course, I had no doubt this movie moment was going to end with the woman walking off in a huff. At least then I could watch her ass and get back to my shopping.

But she surprised me.

Suddenly her smile returned, followed by the richest, deepest laugh I had heard in a long time. It echoed off the cans of corn and surrounded me, pushing me back against the shelf of Hamburger Helper.

"Now that's an opening line I've never heard before," she said after she caught a breath from the laughter.

"Opening for what?" I asked.

She smiled. "My legs."

I looked her right in the eye. "Now tell me why I would want to get between the legs of a woman who eats beans?"

Again I was serious, and again she stared at me, stunned into a second movie moment right there on aisle four.

Then she damned near lost a lung laughing that wonderful laugh of hers. I guess to her I was a real laugh-a-minute kind of guy.

She finally caught her breath and stared at me, her bright smile lighting up everything.

"Well?" I asked. "I'm waiting for my reason."

"Because," she said, "beans go well with franks at a picnic."

She stepped forward and grabbed my crotch, never letting her green-eyed gaze drop from mine.

She rubbed me through my jeans a few times as again we were having a movie moment, only this time it was a sex scene right there in front of the Hamburger Helper. I doubted I was ever going to be able to eat Hamburger Helper without a hard-on again.

"I assume little Frank here wouldn't mind a picnic in the park."

"His name is Ben," I said as she kept rubbing. "Big Ben. And he likes melons on his picnics."

"I think that could be arranged," she said, rubbing one small, tight breast against my arm. Whatever she had thought, that wasn't a melon. More like an apple.

"Any other menu items?" she asked.

Any man with a woman rubbing his crotch on aisle four of a grocery store might have trouble answering a question like that. I didn't. "A television to watch the game while I eat."

Her hand came away from my crotch like Big Ben had lit a match and burnt her. She stared at me, then said, "My ex-husband would have rather watched television than make love to me."

"Did he like Hamburger Helper?" I asked, adjusting Ben a little to ease the tension of tight underwear.

"Yeah," she said, clearly upset at my request for a television at her picnic.

"Figures," I said.

Now she was starting to get angry. A moment ago she was offering me a picnic, basket, apples, and all. Now she was mad. I had never had a woman mad at me on aisle four in a grocery store before. Two things new in one day, both on the same aisle. I would really have to write this down for the story I would do some day.

"And why does it *figure*?" she demanded, as if I owed her an answer just because she had given Big Ben a quick rubbing.

I shrugged. "You eat beans."

She made a choking sound, grabbed two cans of green beans, held them up for me to see like she was giving me the finger, put them in her little yellow basket, and walked off.

I watched her ass until she turned the corner and disappeared toward aisle five. Because her ass was so nice and tight, and her hand had felt so good on Big Ben, I thought for a moment about following her. But I knew there was nothing I could say to her to calm her down.

Besides, she ate beans. I hated beans, and no amount of Big Ben rubbing was going to erase that difference.

Also, if I spent time dealing with her over on aisle five, it might carry on to aisle six, and then even into the frozen food section on aisle eight, and if that happened I might miss the opening kickoff.

No bean-eating woman with a nice ass was worth missing the kickoff to a Packers-Rams game. Even if she had offered Ben an offer he had trouble refusing.

It seemed that my supermarket love affair had started and ended on aisle four.

I went back to trying to figure out which Hamburger Helper to get, finally picked up just the standard, and headed for aisle two, where the Pabst Blue-Ribbon Beer lived and breathed and waited for me. No Hamburger Helper football game dinner was complete without Pabst.

I turned the corner onto the aisle. There was a short woman with a nice ass and short red hair parked right in front of the Pabst. She was studying the beer on the other side of the aisle as if reading labels would make the stuff any better.

I knew right off she was an alien, off one of them big ships from some other planet that had landed a year or so ago. All the alien women that I had seen on Fox News had short, bright-red hair and great bodies.

There had been hundreds of thousands of them, and all the countries of the world welcomed them to live. After a while, they weren't even headlines anymore unless one of them got drunk and punched a cop or something.

The aliens had said they had come in friendship and just wanted to learn about us, but I had read stuff, and I knew better. More than likely they were going to kidnap us all and take us away and make dinner out of us.

But still, alien or not, she was standing in front of the Pabst and I had a game to watch.

"Excuse me," I said.

She turned to look at me, a puzzled look on her very human but very alien face.

Her dark eyes were like magnets, swirling pink and orange and brown. They held me with some unseen force. She was dressed in jeans and a blue tee-shirt, just like I was. Just like Miss Brown Hair had been. Only instead of apples in the tee-shirt orchard, she sprouted the biggest melons I had ever seen, especially for an alien as short as she was.

I did a quick inventory. Same as Miss-Brown-Purse. Two hundred bucks. It seemed it was two-hundred-dollar-woman-day in the supermarket.

"Yes?" she asked. "Can I help you?"

Very formal, like the secretary at my doc's office. But oh, Miss-Alien-With-Melons' voice could melt grease in a cold frying pan.

I pointed to the beer. "Hamburger Helper and a hand job are never complete without Pabst."

For some reason it was my day to be honest with women. And aliens it seemed. Maybe someone had put something in the grocery store air to make me do it. Or maybe it was the excitement of a good football game that was causing it. I would have to think about it later, after the game, if I could stay awake long enough to do so.

She kept staring at me, then slowly smiled as she moved aside. "Aren't you forgetting one thing?" she asked.

"What's that?" I asked, figuring an insult to be next out of her mouth. Something about the rudeness of humans in social situations and that we all needed alien training or something. I grabbed my half case of beer and placed it next to the Hamburger Helper.

"A good Packers-Rams game."

Now it was my turn to stare at her like she was a winning lotto ticket. I didn't know alien women watched American football. Fox News had never mentioned anything like that. Maybe there was hope for all of us after all.

So, with that encouragement, I went ahead and asked the all-important question.

"Do you eat beans?"

She made a face. "Are you kidding? No human or alien should eat those things."

"Good," I said. "How's your ass?"

She turned around to show me, then said, "Engineered to be as tight as they make them. How's your big fella?"

"Big," I said.

She smiled, and I smiled back.

I loved those alien eyes.

Then, after my third or fourth movie moment of the shopping trip, this time right there in front of the beer, I stuck out my hand. "I'm Innis. I count things and hope to write stories."

She took my hand, her smooth skin sending wonderful warm sensations through my body right there in the cold beer section.

"Here on your planet, in your language, I'm called Melody," she said. "I'm not from around here. I rub things and hope to paint things. And if we don't hurry we're going to miss the kickoff. How big is your screen?"

Her eyes seemed to swirl, and she smiled with that question.

"Sixty inches," I said, proud of the moment I could say that to an alien woman.

She smiled even wider and then reached down and touched Big Ben through my jeans. "Sixty inches, huh? Mind if I join you? I'll buy the hamburger."

"Deal," I said, enjoying the fact that Ben was getting a workout right there in the supermarket.

She put a second half-case of Pabst in my cart, left her empty cart in front of the other beer, and helped me push mine to the meat section, letting one of her wonderful large melons rub firmly against my hand.

It pleased me that she hadn't intended to share my Pabst. I really had to know a woman, or an alien for that matter, before I let that happen. Even if she was sharing her melons.

On the way past aisle six, we passed Miss Brown-Hair-and-Matching-Purse, who gave me a very, very long and angry look.

"Wow, what is her problem?" Melody asked, turning with me to watch the angry woman walk away. "Besides the fact that she has a tight ass."

"Very tight," I said, agreeing. "But she hates football and eats beans."

"Oh, that explains it," Melody said, shaking her head.

"One of my people's biggest puzzles about your planet is how anyone could eats beans. They are poison to us. It may be a mystery we will never solve."

I was starting to really like these aliens.

"Let me know if you do," I said.

"The moment we figure it out," she said, laughing a high laugh that sounded very off-worldish. With that, me and my first alien supermarket lover headed for the checkout counter and a Hamburger Helper football game.

SNAP-A-TRAP, INC.

Louisa M. Swann

After experimenting with numerous occupations, Louisa Swann, a native Californian (ack! She admits it!) settled on writing as her long-term mental aberration. During her excessively loud oral dissertations (proven integral to her writing process as evidenced by numerous short story sales) her husband and son shake their heads and mutter something about "the muse." In the interest of survival, husband Jim acquired an eighty-acre compound complete with coyotes, frogs, and screech owls to serve as nightly backup band for a raving writer's rants. Now neighbors wave and smile as the Swanns drive by instead of casting sidelong glances that cause hubby to wonder when the Men In White will be showing up. Luckily dog, cat, and horses understand Louisa perfectly; she often goes to them for grooming when the outside world bares its claws.

San Francisco, California. A city that's been shaken more times than a Double-O martini and lived to brag about it.

The city was shaking again today, but it wasn't the Big One everyone was waiting for. Just enough of a shaker to make my current position—head and shoulders wedged under a wrought iron bench—rather uncomfortable.

No need to brace myself. The shake, rattle, and roll faded away like a disappointed sigh, carrying with it the fear of 750,000 residents.

Oh, well. There's always next time.

Right now I had a job to do. The same job I'd been doing for hundreds of years—catch mischievous faeries and send them back over the rainbow where they belong.

I'd survived tsunamis, Mark Twain, and the stock market crash. Quakes were no big deal—except for days like today when I was out on a hunt. Tremors sent my quarry skittering for cover. One breath they were there; the next breath they were gone.

I could swear I heard a giggle as I shoved myself further under the bench. Concrete bruised my knees, and a pebble dug into my palm. Would've been easier to stretch out my legs, but the current flow of skateboards, roller blades, and dog owners jogging down the sidewalk turned a simple leg-stretching into a death wish.

The stench of dead fish and rotting seaweed permeated the still fog. The park I'd chosen as hunting ground this morning was only a hop, skip, and jump from the bay. If I held my breath and listened, I could hear waves lapping against the Fort Mason piers.

The bushes in front of me giggled again.

I ignored the urge to slip an extra hand or two free of their corseted bondage. Ten hands—all mine. A veritable cornucopia of handiness. You'd think folks could appreciate all those hands, especially the guys, but noooo. All the men I'd tried to hook up with over the years had a thing about my appendages. Too many of them.

In this city known for its tolerance, I'm the only one who doesn't fit in.

Go figure.

I inched forward far enough to move the trap baited with ginger—faerie folk couldn't resist the pungent root—into position and started to slide my left hand into the stiff, thorn-laden bush growing wild against the bench.

This was it. The decisive moment. Hunter against hunted. Trapper against trappee . . .

Reggae music burst forth from the jacket tied around my waist, scaring the beejeezus out of both predator and prey.

Cell phones. The curse of humankind.

"Hell's bells!" I shoved my hand deep into the bushes, hoping against hope to find the critter I'd been chasing half the morning frozen into a mound of quivering faerie jelly.

No such luck.

Another round of reggae beat its way through the fog-laden air.

"Phone's ringing."

The phone I could ignore. The breath—pungent as an overripe fruit stall—I could tolerate.

But that voice—that smoke-laced, whiskey-sodden, I'm-dying-tomorrow voice coming only inches from my ear—sent me leaping clean out of my skin. Figuratively speaking of course. There was nothing figurative about the pain bulleting through my skull when flesh and bone impacted against wrought iron.

Definitely the wrong move.

"Ouch!"

I rebounded from the head bump only to discover a hunk of fog-frizzed hair—*my* fog-frizzed hair—had glued itself to a McKinley-sized mound of used gum. From the feel of the wad imprisoning hair to bench, park goers had been making contributions to this particular repository for years . . . decades . . . eons.

The phone blared another round of reggae. Too bad I couldn't reach the darn thing—I'd heave it all the way from here to the bay.

"You want me to get that for you?"

Who was this guy, and was he talking about the phone or my hair?

"I'm fine, thanks." The only thing visible from my rather awkward position were bushes, concrete, and a pair of oversized penny loafers.

Again with the reggae.

Time to go cell phone diving.

Whatever I chose as cell phone transporter—purse, pockets, even a holster on my belt—became this bottomless gorge the minute I dropped my cell phone in. Digging in my left pocket resulted in nothing but fifty more strands of hair being sacrificed to the goddess of used gum.

"I think it's on the other side."

A creepy-crawly insects-on-my-skin feeling wrapped itself cocoon-style from my head to my toes. Who was this guy, anyway? Commuter? Tourist? Street person looking to spread out on my bench?

"Thanks," I said through gritted teeth. Rapidly shifting hands, I checked out my right pocket.

"Maybe I could try to move the bench?"

"A wrought-iron bench bolted to a car-size slab of concrete? I don't think so." If that guy decided to give his plan a try, however, underneath the bench was not the prime place to be. I abandoned the cell phone search, shifted into reverse, and shoved both hands against the concrete. A fist-size tangle parted from my head as my nether parts gained momentum. Then I was sitting on my derriere staring up at the longest pair of legs I think I've ever seen.

The guy actually had the temerity to clap.

I leaped off the sidewalk quicker than a monkey on speed, twisted my ankle, and landed—in a sitting position—on the bench I'd just been imprisoned under. Not a bad move, though totally unintentional.

"For Pete's sake." I tucked an errant finger back inside my freshly torn shirt, dug the phone out of my pocket, and crammed it to my ear.

"This is not a good time," I said, trying to decide whether ankle, head, or bottom end hurt more.

"You're supposed to be home, not out gallivanting around," Fifi said. "He's going to be at your apartment any minute."

Oops.

"I'm running errands," I lied. I didn't want to be home

right now. Being home meant meeting the man my sister thought was 'Mister Right.'

Then again, she thought every man was Mr. Right.

I chewed my lip and scanned the guy standing way too close in front of me. Halfway through the toe-to-head visual review something popped in my neck. This was no ordinary man, no way. This guy was a giant.

Not that I was jaundiced or anything. It's just that tall people, not just sorta tall—really, really tall—have always intimidated me and not just because I can barely see myself in the bathroom mirror. I grew up around small. Small is good. Small is beautiful.

I tried to scoot away, but the bench held me prisoner. Ignoring the guy didn't work. Every time I looked away, my eyes looked back.

He smelled of fruit salad and fog, not a bad combination. Even with damp, tousled hair and a day-old beard, the guy was more than good-looking. He was . . . elegant.

Not a word I thought I'd use to describe any member of the human race. But there was something about the guy in front of me that lent itself to the description. Dark hair. Long, but not horsey, jawline. High cheekbones. Deep-set hazel eyes more green than brown.

And a smile as broad and innocent as a kid's.

My heart kicked into overdrive about the same time something sucked my lungs dry. Talk about tunnel vision. For a long—make that very long—moment no one else existed.

Then Hunk-a-chunk broke the spell.

He climbed *onto* the bench and started pulling gum from my hair. The fog horn sounded a melancholy note as spearmint-enriched bubblegum added a special tang to the dead fish and gingerfied air.

"Look." I reached up with my free hand. Tried to grab the persistently plucking hand. "I prefer picking at my own hair."

"Excuse me?" my sister said.

"Nothing," I said, juggling the phone while glaring over my shoulder. The guy kept grinning and picking.

"Quit!"

"Who are you talking to? You're out hunting again, aren't you?"

Oops twice.

"No," I said, way too fast. "I told you. I'm . . . running . . . errands."

I slapped the guy's hand. He drew back, a puzzled look on his too-handsome face.

Time to make like a banana and split. I tried to stand up and failed miserably. Something about a giant hanging onto my hair.

"Don't worry," I said to the phone. "I'm just a few blocks from the apartment."

"You can't fool me. I'm your sister. You're out on a hunt," Fifi said. "You mess up this dating thing again and we'll be sent packing. Illegal aliens are not in vogue right now. They're looking for any excuse to get rid of us . . ."

"Enough already, Sis-O-Mine. I won't mess up. Not this time. I promise." Didn't matter that we'd been in this country for years—hell, we'd been here before there was a country—Fifi and I were aliens, born and raised just the other side of the rainbow. With new immigration laws being bounced around government halls, Fifi was convinced that if I didn't get married to a local citizen soon, we'd be headed back home.

Thing is—neither one of us could remember anyplace but the bay. San Francisco was home. We couldn't get deported.

Neither one of us would survive.

But staying meant marrying a human. The very thought made me shudder. Fifi had no problems snuggling with humans. She would've jumped into the marriage bed with all four paws. And that was the problem. My big sister was a dog—literally. At least in this world. The city was tolerant of religion, politics, and sexual preferences, but we both had a feeling the good citizens would draw the line at human/dog relations.

That left the marrying part up to me. I'd been around

humans too long to want to marry one of them, especially with their extra-hand-a-phobia, but at least I looked human. Sort of.

What felt like another hundred strands of hair twanged from my skull. I whirled around and found myself staring into a pair of emerald-flecked eyes. Hunk-a-chunk tipped his head sideways and gave me a quizzical look.

"Gotta go." I flipped the phone closed and forced a smile, dragging my hair from its fleshy prison.

"Nice meeting you," I said to the tall man. "We'll have to do this again sometime."

I raced into my apartment at ten o'clock straight up. I'd made it on time. But was I ready?

A quick check of the apartment made sure everything was in order. I tried to see the place through the eyes of a stranger and decided my particular decorating style was eclectic: a little bit of a lot of stuff. Everything else— carpet, wall paper, linoleum—was pure seventies.

Just the way I liked it.

Fifi had made the dating arrangements via Internet. She'd even done a background check on my date. I hadn't seen his file, but she'd sworn on her favorite bone he was "the man of my dreams." I wasn't so sure. I'd put off the big event for a month to take Internet self-defense classes.

I took a deep breath.

No more delaying tactics. Fifi was right. If we were going to stay in the city and not get shipped out with all the human illegals, it was time to rock and roll.

I glanced down at the fingers waving through my torn shirt. Holey shirt, dirt stained jeans . . . On second thought, maybe I should call the guy and cancel. Make up some story about being mugged in the park.

The doorbell rang. Twice.

Trapped.

No way could I let my date see me like this—too much of the wrong parts of me showed, a repair that was going to take more than simply changing my shirt.

"Just a minute," I hollered as I made my way down the hall to the bathroom. Maybe this guy would give up and go away while I made myself presentable.

I hopped up on the step stool, took one look at the wreck in the mirror, and groaned. Must've been my lucky day. The mirror didn't crack.

The doorbell rang again.

Quickly I grabbed a bottle of foundation and went to work. The right makeup can do wonders for a girl.

All it takes is a little time.

When I finally opened the front door, there was no one standing outside. Relief hit hard and fast, so fast I almost had to sit down. Along with that relief, however, was a twinge of disappointment so small I refused to acknowledge it.

A quick glance up the hall, just to make sure I was giving a proper report to Fifi—I'm sorry, dear, but the man must've been sick or something—then another glance down the hall . . .

Oops. One too many glances.

Sitting *in* the window box overlooking California Street was the guy from the park.

Before I recovered my senses and ducked back inside, he turned and saw me.

"Hi." He hopped off the window box, swung a knapsack onto his shoulder, and strode down the hall, long legs eating up the distance between us like it never existed.

Suddenly he was close.

Too close.

"How did you . . . ?"

The truth slammed home like a lightning bolt—he'd followed me home.

I was being stalked.

A quick scan of the musty, orange-carpeted hall showed no neighbors sticking their noses into my business for a change. There wasn't even a sign of my delinquent date. Of all times for this place to go silent.

"Sorry. Wrong apartment." I slipped inside and tried

to slam the door. Not easy with a six-foot-five-inch stop between door and jamb. Talk about intimidation factor.

"Sorry," I said to the guy stuck in my door. "You're going to have to leave. Someone's coming . . ."

"Company?" the guy asked. He wedged the door open another inch. "I like company."

The only weapon at hand was the cell phone I'd clipped to my belt. I glanced around the living room. Might be able to whap him with a gooseneck lamp and damage his knee cap or something . . .

Some people chew their nails when they get nervous. Some fiddle. Others talk too much. Me? I sweat bullets. We're not talking damp armpits here. In less than five minutes I look like I just stepped out of the shower.

And I was more than a little nervous. I was on the flip side of panic mode. As a result, the fresh blouse I'd exchanged for the torn t-shirt was starting its river run.

Normally this embarrassed the heck out of me. In this particular instant—embarrassment became idea.

"Excuse me. I think I need some air." I backed away from Stalkerman, dashed through the livingroom and into the kitchen. Unfortunately, the window refused to cooperate with my impromptu escape plan.

The sound of feet whispering on seventies linoleum drew my attention away from the window and back to my intruder. He was standing in the kitchen doorway, a curious look on his face.

"Come on," I muttered to the window. I grunted and hissed and otherwise made a complete ass of myself, but the window wouldn't budge.

Then he was behind me. My pulse skidded and came to a complete stop.

This was it. I was dead meat.

I could feel myself uncurling from the inside out. I couldn't beat the guy to death with the cell phone, and the knife drawers were at least five feet away. But I could always resort to the weapon of last choice—I could throttle him with my bare hands.

All ten of them.

I spun around as the stalker put his arms around me.

Now was my chance, but he was so close there was no way to free hands from corset. He bent low. Exhaled fruity breath in my face. Pressed hard against me. And grunted.

I closed my eyes.

"There." Stalkerman stepped back and grinned.

Cool air pooled against my back, spilling down my legs to the floor. I sagged back—out the now open window.

"Uh, thanks." Without hesitation I climbed onto the fire escape, spun around, slammed the window closed. Then I slumped against the railing and fanned myself with fog.

Nice fog. Gorgeous fog. The kind that oozed across the window as it kinked my hair into a thousand curls.

Ah.

I unclipped my phone and flipped it open. Time to bring in the troops. But before I could press the 911 speed dial, the traitorous bit of technology spouted another round of reggae.

Fifi.

Talking to a live sister was better than sitting on hold waiting for emergency services to pick up so I answered.

"There's a stranger in my apartment!" I glanced inside at the stalker. He'd gone over to the kitchen counter and was rifling through the drawers. One by one he held my cutting knives to the light, carefully examined their blades, and laid them on the counter in a neat line of gleaming death.

"Terrific!" Fifi sounded more excited than I'd heard her in years. "How's it going?"

"I don't think you get it." I tried to stanch the nervous sweat tickling my sides. "There's a strange man in my kitchen."

"Relax. You're just nervous. You know how you get when you're nervous."

"I'm not nervous . . . Well, I *am* nervous . . . but not for the reason you think. There's this guy . . ."

"Just take a deep breath . . ."

A scrape caught my attention. I turned around and felt my eyes go wide as the stalker climbed through the window. Hadn't taken him long to figure out the lock only worked on the inside.

"He's coming out," I whispered to Fifi. Talk about panic. Trapped on a fire escape. An iron rail around an iron grate with iron ladders. Great place to come face to face with a stalker.

There were only two ways I could get away from this man—up or down—and neither seemed particularly inviting. Especially in this fog.

"Hi," I said to Stalkerman. I pointed at the phone. "I'll be done here in a minute."

He looked at me without saying a word. A row of goose bumps climbed up my spine, the kind of chill that had nothing to do with the damp air.

Suddenly I was acutely aware of just how high five stories was. Last night five stories meant an incredible view of the bay. This morning five stories was a long, long way to fall.

Going splat! on the streets of San Francisco was not my idea of a glorious demise.

Stalkerman moved over to the edge of the fire escape. Looked up. Looked down. Stroked the railing.

My oozing heart seized tight. "Fifi? You still there? Don't you dare hang up on me."

Any minute now, I thought. He's going to grab me by the waist and fling me over the railing. "If you hear a sudden scream, call the cops . . . No, forget the cops. Call the funeral home."

I inched my way away from the rail. There was only one way I was going off that fire escape—back through the kitchen window.

Something down on the street caught Stalkerman's attention. I clambered back over the windowsill, set the phone on the table, whirled around and slammed the window shut. A flip of the wrist almost wrenched my hand off, but the lock reluctantly clicked into place.

Then I fell to my knees and kissed that wonderful seventies linoleum—cockroaches and all.

*   *   *

Stalkerman came over to the window and peered inside, a puzzled look on his way-too-handsome face. He pressed his nose flat against the pane, then twisted his head to one side, like a puppy trying to figure out what he'd done wrong.

I snatched up the phone and stalked over to the counter. One by one I dropped the knives back into the drawer. Except the smaller paring knife. That one I tucked into my handy bosom. I didn't think he'd try to break through the window, but it didn't hurt to be prepared.

"I've got to go, Fifi. He's trapped on the fire escape. I'll let you know as soon as the cops get here . . ."

"What do you mean, cops?"

I jerked the phone away from my ear. No turning down the volume on that screech.

"I told you—he's a stalker. Now if you don't mind . . ."

"What does he look like?"

"Excuse me?"

"I said—what does he look like?"

"He's tall. Really tall. All right? I'm hanging up now."

"Wait!"

"I'll let you know when it's all over."

I didn't bother opening the video file Fifi sent until after the cops arrived. Surprisingly enough, the stalker didn't give them any trouble. His eyes grew wide and sad when they put on the handcuffs, but he didn't try to struggle.

I bit my lip to keep from blurting out something inane like don't hurt him. He'd been stalking me, for Pete's sake. Probably with the intent of doing me bodily harm, or worse.

So why this sudden feeling of remorse?

When I caved in and finally bought a cell, it had to have one option—internet access with video capabilities. I hadn't used the internet video options too many times, but I used it now. The video provided a distraction while the cops did their thing.

It also proved that my stalker was actually my date. Milton B. Flannigan III.

"Oops." I flipped the phone closed and held up a hand to stop the cops. They looked like twins in their blue-on-blue uniforms. Both of them rested their fists on overloaded utility belts and frowned.

"Sorry," I said. "Looks like I may have the wrong guy."

The cop on the left shrugged. "You sure? Maybe we should take him downtown. Make sure he checks out."

"I'm not going to press charges," I said, more to my used-to-be-stalker than to the cop. I held up the cell phone so the cop could get the picture. "See? Says right here. Milton B. Flannigan III. The guy's a Wall Street wiz. It also says this guy's dad is some kind of big wig judge."

That got the cop's attention.

"Judge Flannigan?" He looked Stalkerman over as if seeing him for the first time. "No way. I've known the judge for over ten years. Never saw this guy before."

"I suppose you're close to the judge," I said with a shrug. "With all the dinners and birthdays and such you've attended together, I'm sure you would've met his son."

Out of the corner of my eye I could see the cop stretch his neck as if his collar had suddenly shrank a size or two.

Milton B. Flannigan III, bless his heart, hadn't said a word during the entire exchange. He just stood there, looking confused and innocent.

I gave him a wink. Good boy.

The cop pulled a set of keys off his belt, unlocked the handcuffs, and shook Flannigan's hand. "Nice to meet you, son. Tell your dad I said hi."

Stalkerman nodded. "Nice to meet you."

The cop headed out the door without another word, missing the next little piece of action.

Milton B. Flannigan III—son of a judge and Wall Street wiz—stuck out his not-so-elegant tongue.

*   *   *

As soon as we were alone, I took my date's hand and led him out to the kitchen. I walked as nonchalantly as possible to the sink, filled a glass with water, and swallowed it like a shot of whiskey.

Fortified by chlorine I braced myself against the counter and turned, coming face to button with Milty's chest. I looked up, up, up. "What do you say we start over? My name's Zola."

"Pleased to meet you. My name is Chip. How about a kiss?"

The speech sounded too canned to be offensive.

"No kissing on the first date," I said. Maybe his being so tall wasn't bad. He'd closed his eyes to deliver the kiss and ended up smacking the air overhead.

Looked like my date was loosening up.

The cell phone sang its reggae beat.

Fifi. Again.

The woman's timing was impeccable.

"I really think you're gonna like this guy. He's just your type."

Yeah, right.

"Fifi," I said between gritted teeth. "He's tall."

"So? He's got money."

I could almost see my sister's chin get all pointy and stubborn.

"Yeah, he's got money," I said, "but that doesn't get him positive points in my book. He's likely to be stretched tighter than your collar at Christmas."

"You're just being a prude. He checks out just fine," Fifi said. "I got a file on the guy. Remember?"

How could I forget?

"And he's not that tall—only six-six," Fifi said, with an accusing note that made my hair stand on end. "Come on. You promised."

I really wasn't that convinced this was going to be a match made in heaven. I wasn't even sure this was going to be a match made in Frisco . . . uh, the city.

Fifi started to go on, but suddenly I wasn't paying attention.

Milton had discovered the water faucet. His fascination

with flowing water almost matched my fascination with his fascination.

"Zola? Are you listening to me?"

I tore my gaze from the gorgeous hunk at the sink and turned to look out the window.

That's when I saw her.

The same blasted faerie who'd escaped my trap earlier. She flipped her lavender wings. Then she turned and wiggled her tiny faerie butt.

Nobody, especially a faerie, can wiggle their butt at me and get away with it.

"Gotta go, Fifi." I shut the cell phone, stuffed it in my pocket, and grabbed Milton's arm.

"Come on," I said as I pried open the window. "You and me are going on a date."

"Zoo."

Chip swung his to-drool-over body back inside the cable car and plopped down beside me on the wooden bench. I'd given up hanging off the side of the trolley like a tourist years ago, but monkeyman couldn't get enough. He settled the knapsack—he'd insisted on going back for the ratty thing—between us, then stared at me.

"The zoo is that way." I pointed southwest. Then I pointed east. "We're headed that way."

"I want to see my mom," Chip said. I took a deep breath, glanced up the hill to make sure the faerie was still on her original course. The little witch was taunting me. No other explanation for her cruising so blatantly up the hill.

No matter. I'd go where she led. Then I'd snap her tiny bedonkadonk into one of my traps.

"Look, Milton . . ."

He shook his head. "Chip."

"Okay—Chip. How about we save the mom thing for later? After we get to know each other better."

Maybe this guy was a half pint short of full, but he was definitely easy on the eyes. If you ignored the height thing, that is. His face brightened like a kid who's been handed an ice cream.

"How about a kiss?"

Gads, did the guy have one thing on his mind or what?

No time to ponder the kissability issue. The faerie had evidently reached her stop.

Unfortunately, said faerie didn't believe in waiting for the cable car. The car lurched forward as I grabbed Chip's hand, gave him a grin, and jumped.

Landing on pavement was a little tough on the ankle I'd wrenched that morning, but I managed to stay upright.

So did Chip.

"Good job." I decided against trying to reach his shoulder and patted his elbow instead. "Let's go."

The faerie darted on ahead, weaving around corners and dodging down alleys. We ignored blaring horns and cursing drivers, keeping up without much problem until she paused just long enough for me to realize where we were headed.

Coit Tower.

The rounded edifice loomed above landscaped apartments. Unfortunately we were on the east side of Telegraph Hill.

Where no roads dared to go.

A tiny giggle drifted through the air, punctuated by the sound of barking sea lions drifting up through the fog.

Then the faerie, wings fluttering merrily, headed straight uphill.

By the time we made it to the top, Chip looked as though he'd just strolled around the block, but I was a wreck. He'd practically carried me the last hundred feet or so. My short legs weren't meant for climbing that many stairs.

"Thanks," I gasped, almost choking on the scent of übersweet honeysuckle blooming at my right elbow. "Not much of a date, huh?"

Chip shrugged. "It's fun."

Darned if the guy wasn't growing on me. Not only did he have killer looks, he didn't mind chasing faeries all over town. Maybe I could overlook the tallness factor.

A gray-haired man with an equally gray-haired woman stepped up onto the landing. They hadn't even broken a sweat.

I forced a grin and tried not too look soggy.

"Morning," the man said.

"Morning," the woman echoed. Her polite smile turned to a startled frown as she passed by. I glanced down at the finger poking out of my cleavage and quickly shoved the offending bit of flesh back where it belonged. I glanced at Chip, hoping he hadn't noticed.

No such luck.

"Sorry," I said to the woman. She huffed and turned away.

No use asking if she'd seen a faerie flitting about.

I thought about confessing all to Chip right then and there, but a funny sensation took hold in my chest. I couldn't face his rejection.

Not now.

"Let's go."

The puzzled look disappeared from Chip's face as I plodded on. We circled Coit Tower twice. Didn't find a trace of the little imp who'd led us on this wild faerie chase.

Chip seemed inclined to go wherever I led, curiously studying each residence, bush, and tree as we passed by.

Except for one place—Stairway to Heaven.

Looked like a clinic of some sort. His eyes got all big and round and sad again when he saw the place. It was the only time he insisted on going another direction.

The next time we reached the landing, I stopped. Somewhere far below in the fog a car door slammed. I shook my head, reluctant to admit the bratty little faerie had escaped once again. "We've covered every inch of this hill and we're still going in circles."

Chip pointed at a bush about ten feet away. The dark green foliage was covered with lavender blooms.

"Time to run," he said as I tried to figure out what he was pointing at.

One of the blooms giggled and took off downhill—the same way we'd come up.

*   *   *

After a hop, skip, and a bus ride we ended up on a small beach—rocks and sand giving way to grass and big, leafy trees. A walkway fronted part of the bay. Posts strung with heavy rope attempted to keep children and adults back from the water's edge on the steeper side. Everyone seemed to ignore the posts, scrambling under and between the ropes to scamper over the riprap, flicking fishing poles high to send baited hook as far out as possible or exploring the nooks and crannies to see what goodies other fishermen or the sea had left behind.

The salt-laden air helped ease the headache I'd picked up during our long trek uphill. Down here at the beach I was almost back to normal.

Almost.

That's when I saw her. A tiny faerie no bigger than my thumb standing on the back of a nearby bench.

"Ssshhhh!" I took hold of Chip's arm and motioned for him to duck down behind a scrawny bush. My traps were all back at the apartment, but that was okay. I'd caught these little buggers barehanded before.

Fifi was right about one thing—I lived for the hunt.

Time lost all meaning when I was hot on a trail. My heart rate picked up. Breathing quickened. Everything outside my peripheral vision blurred into frozen slush.

I made my move, darting a hand in front of the faerie. She leaped backward as I predicted. My other hand was already in place. Her wings flapped furiously as she tried to get airborne, but I was too fast for her.

Left, right, up, down. The faerie tried every which way except the way that would guarantee her freedom.

Straight at me.

Instead she bolted downward, probably thinking she could duck under my grasp.

Wrong move. I snaked out a few extra hands and snatched the little imp right out of the air.

"Wow!" Chip clapped.

I jumped so hard I almost lost my hard-won prize. The faerie shivered in my hands. I reached around behind me. Snatched Chip by the collar and pulled him around where I could see him.

"You didn't see this," I said, waving my unoccupied hands in the air. Kids' screams of delight echoed down from above. Another family headed for the beach.

I held out the faerie. "Here. Take her. And don't let her go. That's my next month's rent you're holding."

Chip cradled the faerie tenderly in his big hands while I shoved my extra flesh back into place.

Careless of me to forget myself like that.

Reggae time. I studied Chip's expression as I yanked the cell phone from my belt.

"Yeah?"

"There's been a mixup. Your date, Milton Flannigan III, you see, he's not really good old Milty . . . well, he is, but he isn't . . ."

"Calm down, Fifi. I know he doesn't like to be called Milton . . ."

"That's just it. He's not Milton. At least not mentally."

Okay, this was definitely weird. I'd never heard my sister so upset.

"That stay in the hospital? Well, he lost his mind. Literally."

Great. No wonder he was such a loon.

"So, who am I running around town with?"

"His name is Chip. He's the resident anthropologist's chimpanzee. The chimp was in the process of kicking the bucket when Milton's mind went kaput. Guess who the anthro's girlfriend is? Milton's psychiatrist. Baddabing!"

"But . . . he talks." Duh.

"Seems Chip's been taking English as a second language, stuff like that. He graduated last weekend and hasn't been seen since. The psychiatrist finally called, wondering if he'd shown up for his date. Guess they thought dating was the next step in Chip's adjusting to his new humanity. They've been looking everywhere for the guy . . . uh . . . chimp."

Okay.

"Thanks, Sis." I snapped the cell phone closed and

turned back to Chip. A light breeze drifted off the bay, lifting a strand of dark hair from his face. He looked at me with those big hazel eyes . . .

Then he opened his hands and let the faerie go.

Men have died for less.

But Chip wasn't a man.

Looked like there was gonna be some adjusting to do. I took Chip's hand, climbed up on the bench, and looked him in the eye.

"It's okay this time that you let her go. I didn't have a place to put her anyway. But it's how we make our living, capiche? It's what we do. If you're gonna stick around, you'd better get used to it."

Chip turned away and fumbled around in his knapsack.

"A chimp," I muttered, watching the muscles ripple under his shirt. "Who'd've thought?"

Time to test the mating waters. A quick glance up and down the beach showed the intruding family occupied down at the water's edge. I slipped a third hand out of my shirt. Reached across and stroked Chip's arm.

The man/chimp glanced at my hand. "Cool," he said. Then he held out a banana—freshly peeled. Why did I get the feeling that accepting a peeled banana from a chimp was like accepting an engagement ring?

Maybe it was time, I decided, staring out at the Golden Gate. The fog had thinned enough that I could see most of the way across the bay. A patch of blue sky opened overhead, revealing the bridge in all its glory.

There were three reasons I'd stayed in San Francisco all these years.

The view—Oh, how I loved that Golden Gate.

The faeries. A girl's got to make a living somehow.

I slid an arm around Chip's waist. Took the banana from his hand and . . .

. . . took a big bite.

Delicious.

Reason number three for staying in San Francisco?

The food.

Of course.

Kristen Britain

The **GREEN RIDER** series

"Wonderfully captivating...a truly
enjoyable read." —Terry Goodkind

"A fresh, well-organized fantasy debut,
with a spirited heroine and a reliable
supporting cast." —*Kirkus*

"The author's skill at world building and her feel
for dramatic storytelling make this first-rate
fantasy a good choice." —*Library Journal*

"Britain keeps the excitement high from beginning to end, balancing epic magical battles with
the humor and camaraderie of Karigan and her
fellow Riders." —*Publishers Weekly*

GREEN RIDER   0-88677-858-1
FIRST RIDER'S CALL   0-7564-0209-3
and now available in hardcover:
THE HIGH KING'S TOMB 0-7564-0209-3

Tanya Huff's
Blood Books

Private eye, vampire, and cop: supernatural crime solvers—and the most unusual love triangle in town.
Now a Lifetime original series.

"Smashing entertainment for a wide audience"
—*Romantic Times*

BLOOD PRICE
978-0-7564-0501-4
BLOOD TRAIL
978-0-7564-0502-1
BLOOD LINES
978-0-7564-0503-8
BLOOD PACT
978-0-7564-0504-5
BLOOD DEBT
978-0-7564-0505-2

To Order Call: 1-800-788-6262

Tanya Huff
The *Smoke* Series

Featuring Henry Fitzroy, Vampire

"Fans of *Buffy* and *The X-Files* will cheer the latest
exploits of Tony Foster, wizard-in-training.... This
spin-off from Huff's popular Blood series stands
alone as an entertaining supernatural adventure with
plenty of sex, violence, and sarcastic humor."
—*Publishers Weekly*

SMOKE AND SHADOWS
0-7564-0263-8
978-0-7564-0263-1

SMOKE AND MIRRORS
0-7564-0348-0
978-0-7564-0348-5

SMOKE AND ASHES
978-0-7564-0415-4

To Order Call: 1-800-788-6262
www.dawbooks.com

MERCEDES LACKEY

Reserved for the Cat

The *Elemental Masters* Series

In 1910, in an alternate Paris, Ninette Dupond, a penni-
less young dancer, recently dismissed from the Paris
Opera, thinks she has gone mad when she finds herself in
a conversation with a skinny tomcat. However, Ninette
is desperate—and hungry—enough to try anything. She
follows the cat's advice and travels to Blackpool,
England, where she is to impersonate a famous Russian
ballerina and dance, not in the opera, but in the finest of
Blackpool's music halls. With her natural talent for
dancing, and her magic for enthralling an audience, it
looks as if Ninette will gain the fame and fortune the cat
has promised. But the real Nina Tchereslavsky is not as
far away as St. Petersburg...and she's not as human as she
appears...

978-0-7564-0362-1

And don't miss the first four books of
The Elemental Masters:

To Order Call: 1-800-788-6262
www.dawbooks.com